PRAISE FOR K. A. DOORE'S
CHRONICLES OF GHADID

THE PERFECT ASSASSIN

"It's queer AF, well-paced and fascinating and political, and grapples with the morality of assassination in a thoughtful and considered way."
—Sam Hawke, Aurealis Award–winning author of *City of Lies*

"Full of rooftop fights, frightening magic, and nonstop excitement and mystery, I absolutely loved it!"
—Sarah Beth Durst, award-winning author of
The Queens of Renthia series

"A thrilling and poignant tale on the costs of loyalty—part murder mystery, part family saga, part coming-of-age chronicle."
—Tochi Onyebuchi, author of *Riot Baby*

"In a high-flung desert city, a reluctant assassin's choices threaten his family's way of life, those he loves, and, worst of all, the spirits of the dead. . . . The ensuing intrigue forms the core of a highly exciting adventure."
—Fran Wilde, Hugo and Nebula finalist, and
Andre Norton Award–winning author

"Set in a world of believable richness, *The Perfect Assassin* combines a suspenseful plot with a memorable cast of characters, and an assassin protagonist who is compelled to make hard choices."
—Ilana C. Myer, author of *The Poet King*

"Fascinating world-building with all the mystery and appeal of the One Thousand and One Nights."

—Duncan M. Hamilton, author of the Wolf of the North series

"[An] outstanding fantasy debut . . . Doore is a force to be reckoned with, blending a stirring plot, elegant world-building, effortless style, and diverse, empathetic characters. Her debut is sure to be a hit with fans of Sarah J. Maas and George R. R. Martin."

—*Publishers Weekly* (starred review)

"Doore's thrilling fantasy debut is a suspenseful murder mystery wrapped around a coming-of-age story, sprinkled with family intrigue, vengeful ghosts, and a gentle but bittersweet m/m romance. . . . This author is one to watch."

—*Booklist*

THE IMPOSSIBLE CONTRACT

"What a phenomenal book filled with sublime world-building and memorable characters! Seriously, I cannot praise it enough. Doore never flinches from telling a story that is fast-paced, brutal, and fantastic in every sense of the word."

—Jenn Lyons, author of *The Ruin of Kings*

"Doore's second novel continues the lush world-building and inclusive characters of the first, while establishing exciting action—and emotion-filled sequences that will keep readers engaged."

—*Library Journal* (starred review)

THE UNCONQUERED CITY

K. A. DOORE

TOR A TOM DOHERTY ASSOCIATES BOOK
NEW YORK

THE UNCONQUERED CITY

Copyright © 2020 by K. A. Doore

All rights reserved.

A Tor Book
Published by Tom Doherty Associates
120 Broadway
New York, NY 10271

www.tor-forge.com

Tor® is a registered trademark of Macmillan Publishing Group, LLC.

The Library of Congress Cataloging-in-Publication Data is available upon request.

ISBN 978-0-7653-9859-8 (trade paperback)
ISBN 978-0-7653-9860-4 (ebook)

Our books may be purchased in bulk for promotional, educational, or business use. Please contact your local bookseller or the Macmillan Corporate and Premium Sales Department at 1-800-221-7945, extension 5442, or by email at MacmillanSpecialMarkets@macmillan.com.

First Edition: 2020

Printed in the United States of America

0 9 8 7 6 5 4 3 2 1

For Sarah—for your patience,
kindness, love, and ability to
suffer through the worst doore jokes.

THE UNCONQUERED CITY

1

The wind cut like broken glass across Illi's cheeks, cold and biting and sharp. The carriage thrummed beneath her feet as she and her cousins soared down and away from the bright warmth of the platforms toward the shifting and treacherous sands below. Her eyes watered with the speed. She blinked away the useless tears; she needed to see what was coming.

This time over a dozen guul had emerged from the Wastes. The drums had cut through Illi's dreams and raced her through the streets, across bridges and platforms, to meet up with her other cousins still bleary with sleep, but strapping on their belts, their swords, their knives. Or, in Dihya's case, her machete.

Illi leaned against the carriage railing and picked out the guul below, little more than dark blemishes on the sand. Beside her, Zarrat grunted, a stray curl of dark hair escaping from his tagel.

"They always look so small." He held up a hand and brought his forefinger and thumb together. "Like I could just squish 'em."

Yaluz leaned next to Zarrat, but still managed to tower above everyone else in the carriage. Once, Yaluz had been the smallest and the fastest of Illi's cousins. But after the healers had balanced out his blood, he'd grown long and angular. "If only it were that easy."

Zarrat glanced at Yaluz. "What—I thought you enjoyed this."

"I do," said Yaluz. "But I'd enjoy it more if the guul'd had the decency to wait until I'd woke up properly and had my tea."

"You could've stayed back with Hamma," said Illi. "Four of us is more than enough."

"What, and miss out on all the fun?" Yaluz's eyes crinkled in a grin above his tagel. "Yeah but no. It's just the *decency* of the situation I take issue with. Besides, Hamma always stays back."

"*Decency.*" Dihya snorted. "Just be glad the call wasn't at midnight."

"Oh, I would've been awake at midnight."

"What in all the sands were you doing awake *then*?" Azhar sounded faintly horrified.

"Now *what* isn't quite the right question—"

But before Yaluz could finish, the carriage hit the pole with a resounding *clank* and shuddered to a stop. Illi tightened her grip on the railing to keep her balance, then swung open the carriage gate and dropped the foot or so to the sands. Her cousins followed, a series of soft thumps right behind her as they landed on the ground. Before the carriage stopped swaying, Dihya hit the cable three times with the flat of her machete. A moment later, the ropes on the sides of the carriage went taut and it zipped back upward.

Illi rubbed her hands together, trying to bring feeling back to her cold-numbed fingers. It was only the beginning of winter, but this close to dawn the cold was at its sharpest. She wiped her nose on her sleeve, which was already stiff with snot.

Dihya's way of keeping warm was to toss her machete from one hand to the other. "Watchmen said thirteen guul, right?"

Illi nodded. "Two for each of you and five for me."

"Hey, you can't keep all the fun to yourself," whined Zarrat.

Illi shot him a grin full of teeth. "Then you'd better keep up."

"Yeah, we'll see about that." Zarrat fidgeted with his sword, glancing back up the cable. "First one who takes out a guuli gets a round from the rest of us."

"Thanks," said Illi.

"For what?"

"For the round."

Zarrat groaned and Dihya slapped him on the back with a laugh. "You walked right into that one, Zar."

Azhar chewed her bottom lip, her already pale features somehow paler. She'd pulled her fine dark hair back into a tight bun, but she kept running her fingers through it and now strands of hair floated free, softening her otherwise sharp features. "Is no one else worried that there's so many this time?"

Silence was her answer. Illi peered up the cable as her cousins shifted uncomfortably. Thirteen was a lot. Thirteen was three more than they'd ever fought at one time. But Illi wasn't worried about that; she and her cousins were more than enough against the guul.

The bellow of an unhappy camel cut the silence. A heartbeat later, the cable thrummed as it caught the weight and motion of the carriage once more. It was both mere moments and yet hours before the carriage returned, now bearing their mounts.

Then all worries were lost in a flurry of motion; there was no more time left to waste. Illi was the first to help her camel off the carriage. She checked its lead, tucked her soft leather charm beneath her wrap—even with all the guul about, they still had to worry about something as banal as wild jaan—then swung up. Zarrat started to call to her, but she'd already given her camel a hard kick and now leaned forward over its neck as it surged into motion.

Her braids beat a rhythm against her back in time with the

camel's loping stride. She tightened her grip on her sword hilt. Ahead, the dim, morning gray of the sands gave way and she could finally see her marks: a spread of dark blotches that soon resolved into erratic, unnatural monsters. Behind, her cousins fell in and caught up. All around, camel feet thudded like so many drumbeats.

Illi didn't have to pick her mark. One veered away from its pack and charged on a course to meet her. The guuli was a mess of collected parts it had scavenged from corpses. Sun-bleached bones stuck out from its back like spines. Feathers and scales patterned its body as a vulture's beak screamed angry recriminations at her. But worse than any of those was the human skull it wore like a mask. Eyes like coals burned in the deep sockets, slicing her bravery into ribbons.

She'd been hunting guul for years now, but they never ceased to send a thrill of fear down her spine. Fear—and resolve. The guul would have to get through her and her cousins if they wanted Ghadid.

Illi squeezed her knees tight and leaned forward as far as she dared. She yanked her camel to the side at the last moment. The guuli's talons flickered and caught only air. Illi's sword caught its neck. The human skull flew free, hit the sand. Its too-bright eyes flared like twin lanterns, but they didn't go out. Illi could feel the guuli's hate-filled glare as she yanked her camel around and into the path of the next monster.

But before she could reach the guuli, another camel cut her off. Yaluz swung his curved sword and the guuli's head went flying, its body collapsing to the sand. Yaluz pulled his camel parallel to Illi's so they were charging alongside each other.

"That one was mine!" shouted Illi.

Yaluz's only answer was a victorious smile.

To the right, Dihya cut down another guuli with her machete. To the left, Azhar chased down a guuli that was fleeing back west. Ahead, Zarrat let out a loud whoop as he circled his camel around a corpse. Illi was falling behind.

Illi flicked her lead and she and Yaluz broke off and curved back toward the city and the remaining guul. Ghadid loomed ahead, its metal pylons splitting the sky like stalks of grain in a glasshouse, straight and tall and strong. But unlike grain, each of these pylons was topped by a circular platform, which in turn held the stones and life that made up the city. Up there were all the people she was protecting, all the people that relied on her and her cousins to keep them safe. From guul, from bandits— and from themselves.

The sun flickered through those stalks, having just peeked above the horizon. The light dazzled her eyes and made it harder to pick out the hunched, loping forms of the remaining guul, made it more difficult to judge the distance between her and her next mark.

Then the guuli was all but under her camel's feet. It gargled a cry and swiped claws short but sharp as razors. Her camel roared. Bucked. Illi's knees lost their grip and she flew. She hit the ground with an *oof.* Grains of sand flew up her nose and into her open mouth. The wind blew more sand into her ears and eyes. Illi tightened her grip on her sword, but her fingers only closed on air. The sword was no longer in her hand.

A growl. Illi pushed herself up. Her camel was galloping back to Ghadid and safety, but it hadn't gotten too far. She might still catch it. That was, if it weren't for the guuli between them. This one had a shattered hip bone in lieu of shoulders and dry, tattered skin still stuck to it in patches. Its head had been taken from a gazelle. Horns as long as Illi's arms twisted out of the skull.

A glint of metal was the only sign of her sword, a full camel's length behind the guuli and half buried under the sand. The guuli lowered its head, too-long horns pointed at Illi's chest. Illi checked her belt but all she had was a small dagger. The guuli charged.

Illi jumped to the side, slashing at the guuli with her dagger, but she might as well have spit at the monster. The guuli continued past, its momentum carrying it a few more feet before it could turn. Illi glanced at her sword, still out of reach. She'd have to chance it, though. Even if she could hurt the guuli with her dagger, only the sword could bind it.

She lunged. The guuli charged again. She heard the clack of its bones and the thin growl in its chest as it came for her. Her feet slipped through sand. The sword was still impossibly far. She wasn't going to reach her weapon in time.

And then—a flash of green. A grunt. A wet sound. Of flesh. Of blood.

The guuli never reached Illi.

She picked up her sword and turned but it was too late. Yaluz was between Illi and the guuli. His own sword dropped from limp fingers as a dark stain spread across the back of his wrap. A piece of white stuck out of the stain's center: the guuli's horn. Yaluz groaned and folded forward as his knees gave out from under him. The wind swept the coppery tang of blood to Illi.

Somebody screamed. Illi wasn't sure if it was her or Yaluz. Her ears rang and her vision narrowed. It was happening again, it was happening *again*. She'd watched her cousin Ziri die the same way, gutted by a dead man with a spear. And now she was going to lose Yaluz.

But no—no, she wasn't. Illi forced herself to focus. The horn hadn't gone through Yaluz's middle, but his side. He could live. He *would* live.

The guuli's horn was stuck. The monster tugged, jerking Yaluz back with it. The guuli's hands came up, covering Yaluz's head as if in an embrace, but Illi knew it meant to snap his neck. She wasn't about to let that happen.

She freed a dagger from her belt with shaking fingers and sighted along the blade's edge. Two steps back and a half turn. She breathed out. Threw. The dagger caught the guuli's upper arm. With a shriek, the guuli let go of Yaluz's head, but he was still stuck to its horn. Yaluz let out a low moan. He was still alive. As long as Illi could get to him and stabilize him, he'd survive. First, she had to remove the guuli.

The sand sucked at Illi's feet, but she fought to cross the distance between her and the guuli, trailing curses behind her. The monster pulled the dagger from its arm and tossed it away. Illi slid the last few feet and raised her sword. She brought it down hard on its neck. The blade bit through bone and flesh and something else, something sticky and resistant. The words carved into the blade's metal flared with darkness, and cold bit into her fingers, deeper than winter. Illi held tight and then the blade was through and the guuli's body fell away.

Unsupported, Yaluz sank to his knees. His fingers scrabbled at the horn piercing his side, but they slipped through blood, unable to gain purchase. His breathing was ragged and uneven and his wrap was torn. Illi kicked the guuli's body out of her way and grabbed its severed head by the base of its skull. She pulled.

Yaluz screamed. The horn came out by a few inches, then all at once. Illi fell back, hitting the sand with the skull held in front of her. Its bright eyes met her gaze, unblinking. Disgusted, Illi tossed the skull away. She scrambled across the sand to Yaluz, trying and failing and trying again to unhook the water skin from her belt.

Yaluz's wrap was soaked with blood, turning it from a vibrant green to a sickly brown. His breathing was shallow and strained, but Illi didn't mark any gurgle or sounds of wetness. So his lungs hadn't been pierced. But other organs might have been, which was secondary to the amount of blood Yaluz was currently pumping onto the sand. Already his soil-dark skin had an unhealthy gray sheen.

Illi dropped her sword and undid the knot of her water skin with trembling fingers. *Dust*, there was so much blood. She'd watched people bleed out from wounds both shallow and deep, and yet the amount of blood a body could hold always surprised her. She used a dagger to tear a long, wide strip from her wrap and pulled Yaluz's wrap back. The fabric was already growing stiff with dried blood, but more blood just kept pumping out. She peeled the fabric away layer by layer until she reached skin. She wadded up one of the pieces of fabric into a ball and applied pressure to the wound.

It wouldn't be enough. Yaluz's eyes fluttered, now open and watching, now closed. He was fighting to stay conscious and losing. Time was hissing past and if Illi didn't do something, *now*, Yaluz wouldn't make it to the carriage, let alone to a real healer. He had to live, he *had* to, if only so Illi could berate him later for trying to save her.

Illi poured water into her palm, but she was shaking so badly that she spilled half of it. Yaluz sighed and closed his eyes. His breath rasped and hitched and his fingers twitched and—

Smoke stuck in Illi's nose, burning through the stench of death. The stones were warm beneath her hands. Distantly, she heard yells, cries, and screams. Illi bent over another body, this one already dead. Illi hadn't been fast enough and now those open eyes stared at her, an unblinking accusation. Illi closed those eyes. Stood.

Or at least, tried to stand.

The body spasmed. The fingers twitched, closed around her wrist. The eyes opened, but they were lifeless and glazed. The corpse dragged itself upright, a hiss gurgling in its throat. It wrapped its fingers around her neck.

Illi screamed. She kept screaming even as she remembered where she was—on the sands, far from that night of horror, safe, safe, *safe*—

An arm wrapped around her chest and pulled her close. "Shh. It's okay. You're okay. Breathe, Illi. Breathe. Be *here*."

The scream fizzled and died. Illi gasped for breath. She wanted to turn and bury her head in her savior's chest, to let the fabric of their wrap muffle the world for a few precious seconds. But she didn't have a few seconds. Yaluz *needed* her. Illi couldn't let her cousin die because he'd been stupid enough to try and save her. She pushed the arm away.

"I have to—"

She looked up into honey-warm eyes and a broad face: Dihya. Her features had softened, but the grim severity would always be there, etched into the lines of her face by that same night seven years ago that was etched into Illi's mind. Dihya had lost everything, too. Yet here she was, not falling apart. Why couldn't Illi be that strong?

Deep breath. Focus. Yaluz needed her. Illi poured water into her palm and this time it didn't spill. She breathed out and with the ease of years of practice, pushed all her thoughts away. It was just her, the water, and Yaluz. She closed her eyes and, with more than just her hands, reached out.

She felt the wound in Yaluz's side like a gap in a weave. Natural-born and more experienced healers would have been able to close that gap, but Illi's healing was as clumsy as a novice's, even after years of practice. All she could do was stop the bleeding. That would have to be enough.

She opened her eyes. The water in her palm was gone. A blue haze still lingered on her arms and across Yaluz's chest, but that vanished in another heartbeat. She met Dihya's gaze.

Dihya stooped and picked Yaluz up, cradling him like a baby. "I'll take him back," she said. "Take my camel and get those last guul."

She didn't wait for Illi's response. Dihya turned, found the nearest cable, and started running, feet sinking deep into the sand with each step. Illi always envied Dihya's strength and speed, but now she was also jealous of her cousin's ability to keep it together. Not once in their years fighting the guul had Illi ever seen Dihya lose her composure. Not like Illi just had.

Illi took a deep breath, willing the shaking in her hands to cease. She stood and picked out the remaining guul. She wasn't finished yet. She'd never be finished, not until every last guuli had been quieted. And the Wastes were yet full of them.

So until then—

Illi pulled herself onto Dihya's camel and marked the nearest guuli. It never saw her coming.

2

"The way you got that first guuli, Illi—*wham*." Zarrat mimicked the motion with his mug, spilling date wine on the floor. "That was pure beauty."

Illi smiled, but her lips felt numb, her face stiff. "If you actually come to train with us, I can teach you how."

Zarrat waved his fingers dismissively, pale eyes twinkling over the top of his brown tagel. More curls were loose now, but this time they were strategic. He'd never seemed to fully get the point of wearing a tagel. "Why mess with a good thing? I got the pattern down. It's not like the guul are going to suddenly learn how to parry or block. How many were there this time, anyway? I always lose count."

Azhar wove her fingers around her mug. "Thirteen. I think that's a new record."

"You're not wrong," said Dihya, leaning into Zarrat. "The number of guul has increased over the last few months. We should consider training more cousins."

"That's a problem for another day," declared Zarrat. "Right now, we're celebrating. Did you hear? There's a caravan, finally. They're setting up the market now. It'll be up this afternoon. Are you going? I'll be there tonight, at least. . . ."

Illi only half listened to Zarrat as she turned her mug around and around, still as full as it'd been when the server had set it down. She wouldn't have asked for date wine, but someone from the crowd thronging them had already paid for it. Someone always did. In another moment, there'd be real food, too, more than just the plain rolls that sat untouched in the middle of their table. Just the thought of a bowl of hot porridge filled her with longing. In all the excitement of the morning, it'd been easy to forget to eat. But now that the nerves were a memory, her hunger reminded her she hadn't had anything since last night.

She picked at a roll while scanning the crowd for a server. But a flash of bright yellow tagel on a tall figure caught her off guard. She shook her head to clear the confusion. It wasn't Yaluz. He was with the healers.

"Has anybody checked on Yaluz?" she asked.

The mood at the table immediately grew somber and Zarrat's chatter stumbled and died.

"He's sleeping," said Dihya. "He'll be all right."

Dihya patted Illi's arm comfortingly, but Illi didn't feel comforted. She'd lost herself down there on the sands, completely forgotten where and when she was. She stared at the grain of the table's veneer, tracing her finger along one tight whorl. She swallowed, but she couldn't get rid of the lump lodged in her throat. It'd been her fault after all. She'd messed up and Yaluz had helped her and that help had nearly got him killed. Illi pressed her finger hard against the center of the whorl, shaped not unlike the eye of a guuli.

A woman approached from the crowd to thank them. Dihya edged away, eyes downcast, but Zarrat welcomed the attention. He was a former slave, and even though he'd been part of a drum chief's household and trained in all the right decorum, he occasionally acted like an iluk fresh off the sands. But he'd fought alongside everyone else during the Siege, and when the surviving drum chiefs had formally freed any remaining slaves, he'd chosen to join their makeshift militia of cousins and volunteers.

Thana called all of the newcomers cousins, but Illi couldn't. Not yet. Not when they hadn't bloodied their hands. Maybe not ever.

"Thirteen guul," repeated Azhar. She was an iluk, an Azali whose tribe had helped the refugees survive until they could reclaim their city. She had helped rebuild, had fallen for a marabi, and decided to stay. She was proficient with the sword, so when the guul began to arrive from the west, she'd been one of the first to volunteer. "On top of the ten from last week and the eight before that—where are they all coming from?"

"You know where," said Dihya darkly. "The Wastes must be full of corpses."

"Yes, but *why*?" said Azhar. "Why do they keep coming here? And more and more each time? What will we do if there're twenty? Thirty? Fifty of them?"

"We'll stop them all," said Illi.

"Really? Us against fifty?" pressed Azhar. "We'll die."

"Then we'll die protecting Ghadid." Illi stood, the bread like dust in her mouth. She pocketed a second roll for later. "I'll see you at training tonight."

Zarrat broke away from his growing circle of admirers. "But we take the night off on hunt days."

"*You* might," said Illi.

"There's a *market*," whined Zarrat.

"I'm not stopping you," said Illi. "Enjoy your night off."

She left the table and her still-full mug of date wine. Zarrat would drink it.

Dihya caught up to her just outside. "Hey—are you okay?"

She put her hand on Illi's shoulder. "I know Zarrat can be . . . dense. But you've got to give him some slack. He's not like us."

Illi bit her tongue. Zarrat wasn't just not like them, he *wasn't* them. He wasn't a cousin, he hadn't been there when they'd lost Ziri, when the Serpent had given her life, when Dihya had put an ax through her best friend's neck. He'd never understand and he never could. But Dihya knew all that just as well as Illi did; after all, it was exactly that innocence that had drawn Dihya to him.

"It's not that." Illi forced a smile. "I'm okay."

Dihya's frown only deepened, her eyes searching Illi's. "In case you forgot, I was there, too."

Illi didn't know which Dihya meant: that she'd been on the sands when Illi broke down or that she'd been beside Illi during the Siege. It didn't matter.

"It's okay not to be okay," said Dihya. "You don't have to be strong all the time, Illi. No one is, trust me."

"I'm *okay*," repeated Illi. "I just—panicked. But that's in the past. Everything's in the past. We have to be prepared for the future."

But Dihya still wasn't leaving her alone. "You're not yourself. Really, if you want to talk about it—"

"I'm *fine*," snapped Illi. She took a deep breath and let it out. Smiled. "Really. I've gotta get those skulls to Heru before he gets cranky, okay? I'll see you tonight."

"We're taking tonight off," said Dihya. "We all need the break. You should, too. You're not invincible, you know."

"We'll see about that."

Illi didn't stay for any further protests. How could any of them think about rest or celebration? Yaluz had nearly died. And it had been Illi's fault. She needed to be faster. More resilient. She needed to train harder.

She had to be prepared in case the Siege happened again.

The sack over her shoulder clattered with each step, like a bag full of awkwardly shaped, overly large dice. Inside were the skulls of the guul they'd felled today. Illi had to keep shifting her grip. The sack was more awkward than heavy; empty skulls didn't weigh much, even thirteen of them. But she'd already brought them all the way up from the sands and now she had to carry them across the city and even the light weight began to drag on her.

Around her, a market was being set up and the crowd was already dense. Offers to help with the sack were flung at her almost as frequently as offers of food, but Illi shrugged them all off, kept her sight on the ground, and walked faster. Somebody patted her arm and praised G-d for her bravery on the sands. Illi muttered something that she hoped sounded like *thanks* but didn't look up.

Zarrat might drink in the praise and adoration, but Illi couldn't stand it. They were cousins. This was just a part of who they were.

The city withdrew and empty echoes replaced the cries from the market as Illi crossed more bridges and pressed farther west, into its heart. Or what used to be its heart. The Siege had taken more than half Ghadid's population and even with the freed slaves and the influx of iluk it would be many generations before they could breathe life into these platforms. The drum chiefs had unanimously decided to focus their rebuilding efforts on just those platforms they needed. That focus had meant abandoning the western half of Ghadid. That it was also the side closest to the Wastes and the guul invasions probably had leant weight to that choice.

But just because they'd been abandoned didn't mean they were empty. Those who needed space, those who needed solitude, and those who had simply lost too much cultivated their existence in the burned-out shells of buildings and homes here. Illi knew many of them because she'd lived here, too, at first. After the Siege, it'd been the only place she'd felt safe. But she'd grown tired of the silence and the cold and eventually accepted Thana and Mo's standing invitation to share their home.

The wind blew through open doorways and across vacant streets. Even though she'd once made her home here, the emptiness now sent a shiver up her spine. She touched the soft leather of her charm, but it remained only as warm as her skin. On the sands, the emptiness and quiet were natural, expected. But up here, the hollow echoes were a vivid reminder of all that had been—and all that had been lost.

Yet even in this desolate place, Illi still found hope. The abandoned platforms were more than the homes of the broken and the lost—they were also the perfect place for a reclusive and cantankerous en-marabi to set up his lab.

Heru Sametket. He'd traveled to Ghadid to broker their surrender to his Empire. Instead, he'd helped Thana tackle a sajaami and kill his Empress. It should have been enough to earn their trust, but Heru's insistence on continuing to study and practice the en-marabi art of jaan binding meant that the rest of Ghadid shunned him. Even in changed times, outright blasphemy wasn't acceptable.

So here he was. Far from the heart of the city. Alone. Forgotten, until Ghadid needed him again.

Illi could understand that.

The difference between Heru's platform and the others was subtle at first. Elsewhere in Ghadid, and even more so in the abandoned half, unswept sand slipped beneath her sandals, but as she crossed this platform the grains disappeared and the stones were smooth.

Once she reached the center, the difference became far less subtle. Before Heru had moved in, this platform had been like all the others in Ghadid's abandoned half: coated with old blood, gray with ash, and smeared with dust. The stones had blended together into one gray and black blur. But now, each stone was scrubbed clean, their mottled browns and faded reds laid bare to the sky.

Around the circle, all of the doorways were empty, the fabric that used to cover them long burned or repurposed. All—except one. In the center of a row of doorways, a length of white cloth covered one entrance. The cloth was free of dust or stains or dirt, an impossible white that blazed in the morning sun, unavoidable and unmistakable: a signal or a warning, but never an invitation.

Illi reached the white fabric, but didn't go in. She paused and knocked on the wall next to it. Then she counted under her breath, listening.

Something bubbled and clanged inside, but no one appeared at the door. Upon reaching the count of ten, Illi drew the cloth aside. When no reprimand was flung her way, she entered. She let go of the cloth and it fell back into place, weighted on the bottom to keep the wind out.

Even though she'd been here many times, her first breath of

Heru's lab was overwhelming. Equipment choked the room, but every piece had its place. Glass bowls and glass beakers and glass vials lined shelves along the walls and benches in the center of the room. Every surface was free of fingerprints or smudges, the stone floor swept clear of any specks of sand, and even the air held a slightly sweet, slightly bitter medicinal edge. A fire ran hot in the hearth, its heat kept at bay by a thick pane of glass.

And at the center of it all hung the orb, snug in a corona of light.

As it did every time, the orb drew her gaze. As Illi came farther into the room, the glass flask floating in the orb's center slowly filled with a thick, warm glow. Thin, dark, looping script smothered the flask and flavored its light. Water separated the flask from the orb and kept them both safe. The orb itself hung by a metal chain from the high ceiling, twisting and turning even in the absence of a breeze.

The light built to a blaze that cut shadows sharp and firm. Across the room, hunched over a bench, his hands occupied with two bowls, Heru looked up. One eye focused first on the flask, then across at Illi. His other eye didn't move; it was glass. Heru hadn't bothered trying to match the glass eye to his original, so instead of a mild brown, its iris was a circle of gold with black lines radiating out from the pupil like a miniature sun. His white wrap hung off of him like it might a skeleton, the pale mourning color doing little to improve his already wan complexion. His white tagel barely covered his mouth, an affectation more than an attempt at modesty.

"You're late."

Heru had specified at the beginning of their association that she get the skulls to him within a half day; longer than that risked failure of the simple binding that kept the guul from escaping and finding new bodies. It was still midafternoon and therefore well within that time frame. But she didn't correct him. She'd only made that mistake once.

Heru finished what he was doing, then wiped his hands off on a cloth and walked around his bench. "Bring them here, girl. How many guul were subdued today?"

Illi heaved the bag onto the bench, the skulls clattering within. "Thirteen."

Heru nodded to himself. "As I thought."

"You knew?"

Heru narrowed his eye. "Of course. The number has been increasing, even if at an uneven rate. It appears to jump every few months. The last jump was predicted by the formula I'd devised and now it has been confirmed."

"So Azhar is right, the attacks really are increasing." Illi rested her hands on top of the bench. "Why?"

"The increase was subtle enough at first to be missed by anyone less meticulous, but yes." Heru reached into the bag and gingerly extracted a skull. He set it with overt care on the bench, as if it were made out of flawed glass instead of bone. "While we might have started out with just one or two errant guul in the beginning, this last year has proven that we should no longer consider that our baseline. All recent, available data indicates we are on a path of exponential growth, which means these skulls are becoming more and more indispensable."

Heru laid out each of the thirteen skulls on the metal bench. Blazing eyes tracked Heru as he moved, and when he was done, he basked in their collective, hateful gazes. Illi stood to one side, out of the guul's immediate line of sight. Still, the hair on the back of her neck rose. Although she'd seen the skulls like this over a dozen times, it never failed to unnerve her. Taking the head off a body should be deadly. Yet the Siege had broken even that rule.

Thankfully, Heru's magic—which he called "science" or "research"—sealed these guul within the bodies they'd stolen. He'd done it ostensibly to keep Ghadid safe, but Illi understood him well enough now to know that he never did something unless it benefited him, too. That didn't matter to her, so long as the end result was the same.

The first time the guul had attacked, her cousins had met them and met them well. But when they'd separated head from body, a buzzing darkness had rushed out: the guul itself. After all, guul were only jaan that had realized they could build bodies instead of destroying them. They still wanted form, a body to protect them from the elements.

And there had been so many bodies nearby.

No one had died or been permanently driven mad that day, but they'd come too close. Heru had been able to extract the guul from the possessed cousins before they'd burned up from within, although his concern had been for the maddened spirits instead of their hosts. Then he'd disappeared for two weeks before reappearing with a solution: the words engraved on their swords.

Now, instead of spilling into the air, the guul became stuck in their pillaged bodies. Usually the head, but occasionally the odd body part. Illi had once collected a very angry femur. She was the only one who'd been willing to bring back the skulls for Heru. No one else dared venture so deep into the abandoned platforms, or so close to an en-marabi, no matter the good he did.

But Illi had lived in the emptiness and she knew Heru for what he was: eccentric, driven, but mostly harmless. Out of all the people in Ghadid, she'd never once worried about him. Heru

Sametket had always known exactly what he was doing, and even the wounds he sustained were intentional. Like every other en-marabi, he strove for immortality, a way to tie the jaani to the body and sustain them both indefinitely. His goal might be blasphemous, but he wasn't dangerous. At least, no more so than what Illi had already been through.

Heru's lab was the only place in Ghadid where Illi felt safe, where she could relax and stop worrying, if only for a moment, that the Siege could happen again. As long as Heru was here, as long as Heru was working, it never would. The more respectable marab who stuck to quieting jaan and performing funerals couldn't promise her that.

Heru broke his reverent silence with a sudden breath. Before he could bark his order, Illi had already brought him a knife, a metal bowl, and a folded cloth. Beside the cloth, she set a bread roll she'd grabbed from the inn, now cold; Heru often forgot to eat. He gave her an appreciative nod, then pulled a tray from beneath the bench. Neatly arrayed clay bowls and a rack of stoppered vials filled the tray.

Each bowl was about the size of Illi's palm and held finely ground powders. Some Illi had figured out—they were dried herbs or spices, colorful salts, and sand as fine as dust. Some still eluded her and some worried her—the dark red powder that smelled like sweet copper, for one. Heru rarely explained what he was doing, but that didn't stop Illi from watching closely. She'd learned a lot that way.

Heru took the metal bowl and splashed water into it from the skin at his hip. Then he took a pinch of this and a scoop of that and swirled it into the water until it had dispersed or dissolved. Finally, he took the knife, rolled back his sleeve, and cut his forearm.

The slice brimmed red with blood, which he let drip, counting under his breath, into the bowl. Once he had seven drops, he tied a clean white cloth around his arm, tightening its knot with his teeth. The cut would heal, becoming another scar to add to his collection. He shook his arm and his sleeve fell back into place, hiding the pale scar tissue that covered his skin like spiderwebs.

The liquid in the bowl had assumed an unhealthy sheen. He unstopped a vial and scooped some of the liquid into it. Then he covered the vial with his thumb and shook it. The liquid shimmered, gray and oily.

"Give me a hand," he ordered. Then his gaze flicked to Illi and the very corner of his mouth, just visible above his tagel, twitched with what might be amusement. "Or perhaps I should say: Give me a skull. Because, see, you might otherwise attempt to give me an actual hand, which would be less than ideal."

As with every time Heru attempted a joke, Illi wasn't sure if she should laugh or not, so she didn't. Instead she grabbed the skull by its short, curved horns and held it in front of her as Heru pried apart its teeth and spilled the liquid into its mouth. There was nothing stopping the liquid from sloshing through the skull's gaping neck hole onto Illi's sandals, yet her feet remained dry. Instead, the skull vibrated in her hands and let out a whining shriek so high-pitched it made her teeth itch.

Heru worked smoothly and efficiently, his movements perfected through the hundreds of times he'd performed this same act. He replaced the empty vial in the rack, then pulled a clear glass sphere from his pocket. The sphere was hardly bigger than his remaining eye. He set it between the skull's jaws and muttered unintelligible words.

The skull shook harder, but Illi had expected that. She held on. Then all at once, darkness swarmed around the skull, buzzing and thick like a swarm of locusts. It pulsed outward, once, twice, before being sucked into the glass sphere. Then the darkness was gone and the skull felt oddly empty and light in a way that had little to do with weight.

The sphere, on the other hand, glowed almost as bright as the flask above them. The glow faded until the glass held nothing but a murky red smear.

Heru set the sphere in its own bowl. His eye roamed over the remaining skulls as he grabbed the next vial. Illi set the empty skull on the table and picked up the next. Together, in practiced silence, they repeated the procedure on the other twelve skulls.

Thirteen guul became thirteen empty skulls and in turn thirteen murky red spheres. Heru placed the spheres into a woven basket and tied a scrap of leather over the top. Then he unlocked a chest at the back of the room, spilling a bloody red glow across the floor. He set the basket inside and closed the lid before Illi could get a better look, but she knew what was in there: seven years' worth of guul attacks and over a hundred more spheres.

The lid clicked as Heru locked it. He hesitated, his palms on the top of the trunk. When he stood, it was as if he were a vulture unfolding from its kill. His eye found Illi and he frowned, as if he'd forgotten she was there. Then the eye tracked upward, squinting against the light from the flask. His eyebrows came together in a thoughtful expression.

"I should go," said Illi, already backing toward the doorway.

"Yes," said Heru, not quite listening. "Yes, of course."

By the time Illi reached the curtain, Heru had turned back to his table. He'd grabbed a roll of parchment and was leaning over it, scritch-scritching with a pen. He'd already forgotten her.

3

Blue—pale as glass, thin as smoke—pulsed between Illi's fingers. But as quickly as the blue had appeared, it evaporated. Illi peered through her fingers at the empty bowl beneath that had contained water only a few heartbeats ago. She felt nothing. Frustrated, she poured more water into the shallow bowl and tried again.

It was hard to focus. Her back prickled with heat from the hearth and she shifted again and again on her cushions, trying to get comfortable despite the weary ache of her limbs. Across the room, Thana was sharpening knives. The rhythmic *shnk-shnk-shnk* of blade across stone was unusually irritating. And every time Illi managed to clear her thoughts and began to feel the water, she was back down on the sands, Yaluz bleeding out beneath her hands.

But if her healing, weak as it was, would ever be useful, she'd need to be able to focus at any time. Especially when she was uncomfortable.

She breathed deep, feeling for the water despite the distractions. It slipped cool over her consciousness, like the breath of early winter. The faintest blue tickled her fingers.

Then the door opened. The blue vanished.

Illi ground her teeth in frustration and looked up. Mo was

already halfway across the room, her faded blue wrap stained with dust and sweat. Her gaze landed on Illi and she slowed, the weariness on her round face tightening to concern.

"You should be resting."

"That's what I told her," said Thana, the *shnk-shnk-shnk* never wavering.

Illi dropped her gaze back to the bowl in her hands. "I can rest later. I need to practice now. More guul could attack tomorrow."

Mo's footsteps were little louder than a breath as she approached. "There won't be any guul tomorrow, nor will there be any next week. And if there are, you'll still be ready. No guuli will ever take you by surprise."

Illi's fingers tightened on the bowl. "One did. And I—I almost *couldn't*. I let myself be overwhelmed and Yaluz could have died. That's why I need to practice. Please, Mo."

Mo sucked in a breath, then crouched and put her hands over Illi's. "The Circle was very clear about water usage in the coming weeks. We need to preserve enough for the rite. That means no wasteful healing."

"It's not wasteful if it will save a life."

Mo sought Illi's gaze and held it. "Are you saving a life right now?"

"No, but—"

Without breaking eye contact, Mo slid the bowl from between Illi's hands. "Then no." She stood and set the bowl at the end of the pile of cushions, out of reach. "If it's practice you want, we can work on your breathing techniques later."

Illi sat back into the cushions, letting out all of her breath in a sigh. "We shouldn't even need water for this rite. It's not like there are any bodies. We burned them all, remember."

A click sounded from the other side of the room as Thana

set down the dagger she'd been sharpening. "It's still possible that performing the rite will help their jaan. The marab believe there's a chance, anyway, and I'm more than willing to waste some water on a chance." She picked up another dagger and began dragging the whetstone across it.

"The marab are wrong," said Illi. "Those jaan are all wild. There's no helping wild jaan. And with this drought we barely have enough water just for the living. Why waste it on the dead?"

"I wouldn't discount the marab so easily. They've had seven years to perfect a new rite," said Thana.

"And seven years for this drought to worsen. I still don't see the point. They're gone. They're in the Wastes. Heru thinks—" Illi cut herself off, but it was too late.

Thana set the dagger she'd been sharpening down and turned her full attention on Illi. "You know what I think about you spending so much time near him."

"*Somebody* has to understand what he does," said Illi. "He's the only one who can stop the guul. What if something happens to him?"

"He's been helping," said Thana with a nod. "But so have the marab. His way may be faster, but it's not the only way. Everything he does goes against G-d."

Illi bit her tongue. She wasn't going to get into this fight again. She didn't understand how Thana and the others could still believe there was a G-d after the dead had crawled out of their own crypts during the Siege.

Thana came around the table, palms up and out in a gesture of peace. "You have your training with Mo. Isn't learning how to heal enough?"

Illi glanced at the healer, whose muted blue wrap was warmed by the firelight. Her long braids were only sparsely populated by salas, the colorful bits of string and cloth she'd been given by the lives she'd saved. Mo was one of only a few healers who had survived the Siege; she'd been halfway across the Wastes at the time. She'd removed all of her salas when she'd returned to Ghadid and now only accepted them rarely. Mo blamed herself for what happened almost as much as Illi did.

"I'll never be good enough," said Illi. "I'm not a natural healer. There's just no overcoming that."

"No, you'll never be as good as a natural healer," admitted Mo. "But you can improve. We need every healer we can train, even those not born to it. There's more to healing than the use of water."

"Bandages and poultices won't save someone from the guul."

Mo let out a long sigh. "You have to stop treating healing like a weapon. You *also* have to heal yourself. Rest. Your actions reflect your healing and your healing reflects your actions."

"I can't rest," said Illi. "I'm too wound up. Better I do something useful than lie in the dark with my eyes open."

Mo pursed her lips. "You don't have to sleep to rest. Go out— be with your cousins and friends. Isn't there a market tonight?"

Illi nodded slowly. Zarrat had mentioned the market, but it had been almost too easy to forget. Caravans were few and far between since the Siege. Most of the other cities in the Crescent had been completely emptied and it simply wasn't worth the Azal's time to make the trek. But some did, those willing to take the risk of walking the Wastes for salt, those who had family members who had settled in Ghadid, and those who knew how useful Ghadid glass could be, how powerful the charms made by Ghadid's marab. Those who didn't heed the warnings.

"Sounds like fun," she said, and it wasn't a lie. Caravans brought new faces and new stories, new weapons and new methods of fighting. Over the years, she'd learned a few things from the hired guards that accompanied caravans across the desert. Maybe she'd learn something new tonight, something useful.

"Then listen to Mo and go," said Thana. "You're released from all household duties tonight as long as you don't come back until second bell after sunset. Just bring me one of those buns with the minced dates in the middle. No—bring me *two*." She cut a glance toward Mo. "And maybe one for Mo if she wants."

Mo laughed and swatted Thana playfully. A smile finally broke Thana's features and her harshness melted away. In one quick motion, Thana wrapped an arm around the shorter woman and drew her in close. Thana pecked Mo on the cheek, then the nose, then finally on the lips.

Illi sighed. "*Guys*. I'm still *here*."

"Exactly," said Thana, although it came out distorted, smooshed as she was against Mo's lips. "Go away."

Illi rolled her eyes, but left. The air outside was still warm, but evening's chill was already on the wind. Waning sunlight painted the stones in the walls and across the ground a warm golden brown. She paused to get her bearings just outside the faded red door of her adopted home. Inside, knives clattered as they hit the floor and someone giggled. Well, now she definitely couldn't return for a few hours.

Illi closed her eyes, ignoring the people brushing past. A greater commotion came from the south, and the air was already laced with the smell of roasting meat, honeyed almonds, and cinnamon-laden tea.

"I thought I'd find you here," said a familiar voice.

Illi opened her eyes. Dihya stood only feet away, her wrap a fresh purple that brought out the warmer undertones in her skin. A faint smile twisted her lips, which seemed redder than usual.

"Did you paint your lips?" asked Illi.

Dihya lifted her chin, daring Illi to say anything. There was also a brush of black kohl around her eyes, accentuating the specks of copper in her irises. Dihya looked strong and beautiful and amazing.

"You look . . . nice," said Illi lamely.

Dihya smiled and somehow managed to look even more amazing. "The others decided to check out the market. Want to join us?"

Illi took a deep breath. She'd prefer to be alone, wandering unnoticed and anonymous through the crowd. But Mo's words drifted back to her: *you also have to heal yourself.* Maybe this would be good for her.

"Yeah."

Dihya started walking, slow enough that Illi could keep pace. Her cousin was nearly a full head taller and built like a wall. If Dihya wore a tagel, she could have been mistaken for a man. Her arms were thick with muscle that Illi envied. No matter how hard she trained, Illi would never have that kind of mass.

Their cousins were only a platform away, as was the beginning of the market. Most of the stalls were still being set up and stocked, but a few were already in business, trading colorful eastern fabrics and bags of southern spices and expensive northern wood for Ghadid's glass and stringwork and leather. Zarrat was gnawing on a stick of roast meat, its hot juices darkening the bottom of his tagel. Azhar was browsing a stall with leatherworks, turning a sandal this way and that.

Between them should've been Yaluz, teasing Zarrat or helping

Azhar find the right sandal. His absence hit Illi like a blow and she was once again reminded of her failure. She should've been quicker, faster, *more*—

"It's not your fault," said Dihya. "You can't protect everyone."

Illi started. She hadn't realized she'd stopped. She rubbed her arms self-consciously. Nodded. "You're right. He was stupid. He should have been more prepared."

Dihya sighed. "That's not what I meant."

But Illi had a smile on and was already approaching her cousins. They greeted her with equal warmth. Zarrat offered to share his snack and Azhar asked Illi her opinion on the sandal's leather stitching and for a little while, everything was all right. Almost like it had been.

As they drifted through the marketplace, Dihya took Zarrat's hand and she laughed as he commented on some of the stranger wares. Illi couldn't help but smile at the two of them; while she didn't care for Zarrat, she could appreciate that Dihya did. And if Zarrat ever broke Dihya's heart, then Illi would have a good excuse to remove his. Illi grinned at the thought.

"I'm glad you're feeling better," said Azhar softly.

Illi coughed, glad Azhar couldn't read her mind. "Yeah . . . it helps knowing a caravan will still come all the way out here, even during this drought."

"Things are pretty good, aren't they?" said Azhar. "I mean, despite so much. We're doing okay. Everything we were so afraid of—none of it came to pass. The caravans came back. The dead didn't. I can hardly believe that it's been seven years . . . in another month, we'll finally put those who died to rest. We all thought the world ended that night, but it didn't. It only changed. We're still alive. Still here."

Illi swallowed. "Aren't you ever afraid it'll happen again?"

"No," said Azhar, but she sounded puzzled. "No, I don't. It was such a bizarre event. I can't imagine anything like it happening again. Can you?"

"Once something like that happens, how *can't* you expect it to happen again?"

Azhar gave a half shrug. "I guess . . . I mean, the Empress is dead. There's no one else like her out there. No one is going to conquer this city anytime soon." She laughed, but the sound was hollow. "I mean, why would they? So we've got that going for us."

"It won't be the same thing," said Illi. "It'll be something else entirely. Something completely unexpected. No one could have imagined what the Empress did. No one will be able to imagine the next terrible thing that happens."

"Why does something have to happen?" asked Azhar. "Why can't the Siege just have been a once-in-a-thousand-lifetimes event?"

"I just . . . I want to be prepared."

"Illi—you can't be prepared for everything."

"That's where we disagree."

Azhar shrugged. "I'm just saying—life is going to surprise you no matter what, for bad, but also for good."

Illi started to answer, but she caught the flash of gray cloth approaching them before Azhar did and let her argument dissolve on her tongue. Menna stepped in their way, stopping them both. She was a whole head shorter than Illi, her skin as smooth and pale as milky tea, her features soft, and her braids short. A black stripe along the edges of her wrap marked her rank as an elder marabi.

Azhar broke into a wide smile and threw her arms around Menna. "So you decided to join us after all."

Menna glanced at Illi. "As long as I'm not interrupting any-thing."

"Nothing." Illi waved her hand. "We were just arguing."

"Good," said Menna. "Well, continue. Azhar could use the practice."

"Hey."

Menna held up her hands. "What—it's true. You could stand to be meaner. And more combative."

"I'm plenty combative," protested Azhar.

"Like a bunny," said Menna, half grinning. "Just lookit your claws."

"I'll show you claws." Azhar curled her fingers like she was going to scratch Menna. Then she paused and peered at her nails. "But I just cut them . . ."

Menna barked a laugh and then slipped between Azhar's arms and up against her neck, nuzzling her like the animal she'd just been disparaging. They kept walking, but Illi fell behind, watch-ing them with a mixture of longing and regret. Dihya and Zar-rat, Mo and Thana, Menna and Azhar—all of them had moved on. All of them had dared to love, to live. Even Dihya, who had beheaded her cousin Azulay herself. Even Thana, who had lost her mother. Even Menna, who had broken her oaths, committed blasphemy, and burned her city.

Only Illi was still caught in the past, unable to move forward. Not for the first time, she wondered if she was broken, if a piece of her would always be stuck in that night, unable to escape.

She let Azhar and Menna drift ahead, scanning the nearby stalls for anything useful. She stopped next to one that carried all sorts of dried plants—for healing, for cooking, and for the marab—but the owner waved her on.

"Sorry, ma, but you should come back later," he said. "Got someone scheduled for his pickup and you'd rather not be here when he comes by."

Illi hardly registered his words, a thorny twist of branches catching at her attention. Certain thorns were supposed to help with healing if you chewed them raw. "I'm sure I won't be a bother, sa."

But the merchant grabbed her wrist as she reached, a warning in his eyes. "No, ma. He's a dangerous sort. I've heard dreadful things about what he does on that platform of his. I shudder to think what he might do if you displease him."

That caught Illi's attention, as well as her anger. All at once she knew exactly who the merchant meant. It was the hour Heru typically ran his errands, after all: right after the market set up, but before it really got started, so he could dart in and buy everything he needed without any unnecessary conversations.

Illi jerked her wrist from the merchant's grip but didn't leave. Plenty of people knew only enough about Heru to fear him, but Illi couldn't help herself. "If you're so afraid of this man, why do you do business with him?"

"Better than letting him hoard baats and water," said the merchant darkly. "I'd rather not do business with him at all—who knows what foul, dark things he really does, but he can't do any of that with *my* herbs. G-d would never allow it."

Illi glanced around at the merchant's stall again, recognizing several different twists of herbs and roots that she knew Heru used for binding. She bit her lip, gaze drawn back to the thorns, torn between her anger and her curiosity.

"Why the drum chiefs don't do anything about him is a mystery, sure is," continued the merchant.

"Maybe because he's the only one who's known how to stop the guul," snapped Illi, her anger burning through any remaining curiosity.

"Our own people stop the guul," said the merchant with a smugness that only gave fuel to Illi's flame. "We don't need some jaani-stealing iluk to save us. And what has he really done to help? The guul still come. More and more of them. Maybe *he's* the one bringing them. Wouldn't surprise me. Wouldn't be the worst of his blasphemies, either."

"He's the only reason Ghadid still stands," said Illi, fighting to keep her voice even.

"Seems to me he's not done anything the marab can't."

"Seems to me you don't know anything about marab."

The merchant crossed his arms. "My brother's a marabi, ma. Besides, there're lots who agree with me. Won't matter what the drum chiefs think if he ever shows his true colors. Ghadid will protect itself."

"Because we sure did a fine job of that last time, huh?" If Illi closed her eyes, she'd see the flames, smell the smoke. So she kept her eyes open and fixed on the merchant.

But the merchant only nodded, held her gaze. "We did."

Illi's hands tightened to fists and she had to fight her anger just to take a deep breath. Then she shook her head and turned and left, not trusting herself with another word.

She knew when someone didn't want to hear and it wasn't like this was the first time she'd run into someone so blindingly ignorant about Heru. As much as she wanted to pick a fight with this man, it'd be just as bad as picking a fight with a wall. Even though it'd make her feel better, she couldn't change the merchant's opinion and she'd be the one carrying the bruises. If anything, it'd only make him like Heru less. And Heru had enough of an image problem already with the rest of Ghadid.

It wasn't her place to make them understand.

She walked without any real direction, blind to the stalls around her, trying only to calm her anger. Then her gaze caught and snagged on a table displaying iluk knives, and her hand immediately went to her baat pouch. The weight of coins told her she had more than enough.

She weaved through the crowd toward the table. When she got closer, she noticed throwing knives in the mix. Perfect: something to distract her from her anger. The woman behind the table was still laying them out, her loose trousers and wide belt marking her as an iluk from the far east. Another person was already there, perusing the blades.

As Illi approached, she assessed the person browsing. They wore a tagel that was thick and long like the Azal, the people who controlled and ran the caravans, but this tagel was the color of dried blood instead of the more common shades of blue and they wore too many weapons at their belt to be just another iluk merchant. Not an Azali, but still an iluk—maybe one of the caravan's hired guards?

Learning something new from a guard would be a far better use of her time than arguing with an ignorant merchant. Illi sidled up to the table, nerves replacing her lingering anger. She had to walk a narrow railing to convince this guard to teach her. She couldn't be too competent or eager, but she also couldn't let them think she was just a know-nothing wannabe.

The guard glanced at her as Illi examined the knives. She looked to the merchant for permission, then picked up one of the smaller blades. It was barely the length of her finger, but it had a heft to it that made Illi want to throw it right then and there. Being so small, it wouldn't do much damage, but it'd feel nice.

The guard cleared their throat. "Do you compete?"

Their voice was a soft, medium timber and Illi couldn't decide if they were a man or a woman. Even up here and away from the sands, all the Azal and many iluk wore tagels, not just the men, so that wasn't enough to go by. It didn't matter; Illi could learn from anyone.

Pinching the blade lightly between her fingers, she spun it. "No, sa."

"Then you should know: any weapon you throw is a weapon that's no longer in your hand," said the guard. "These are perfect for a show, but if you're looking for something to actually defend yourself with, you should find Hatham. He has a wide range of axes and machetes."

"Do you compete, sa?" asked Illi.

"No," said the guard.

Illi turned, still spinning the knife between her fingers. "Then you should know it's always good to be prepared."

She moved, quick as a snake. One second the knife was spinning between her fingers, the next it was at the guard's throat. Or, it would have been, if the guard hadn't deflected her attack with their own, arm driving the blade off course while their fingers came at her eye. Illi blocked just in time. But the guard only slapped her hand out of the way and continued driving their own at her.

The merchant gasped. Illi jerked back. The guard's fingers grazed her eye and pain bloomed, bright and distracting. She blinked, trying to refocus as the guard came at her again. She slashed the air in front of her to keep them back, but they grabbed her wrist, twisting until she dropped the knife. It clattered to the stones.

That was all right. Illi had more. With her other hand, she freed another dagger and slashed at the guard. This time they didn't block, but jerked away. Illi moved into their space, feinted with the knife, and planted her foot against the guard's stomach. She kicked. The guard stumbled back. They regarded each other warily, the guard with their fists up, Illi with her knife out.

Then the guard laughed. They relaxed by a degree, but Illi waited another heartbeat before lowering her knife. She nodded at them, still blinking away tears from her smarting eye.

"You're quick," said the guard.

"So are you, sa," admitted Illi. "And either brave or foolish, to take me on without any weapons. Can you teach me how to block like that?"

"You won't always have time to get a weapon," said the guard.

"Is that a yes?" pressed Illi.

The guard regarded her for another long moment. Then they smiled. "Only if, in return, you show me some of what you did."

Illi slid the knife back into its sheath and held out her open hand. "It's a deal."

The guard took her hand, shook. Illi picked the throwing knife up from the ground and returned it to the table. The merchant was regarding them both with a mixture of amusement and wariness, as if she still wasn't sure whether she should call the watchmen. Some of Illi's exhaustion had been wiped away by the fight and now her body thrummed with energy.

"What's your name, sa?" she asked.

"Canthem." They bowed deep, touching a closed fist to their forehead while their other hand extended behind them, fingers splayed wide. It was an absurd gesture, like a bird flaring its tail. Illi laughed once, a soft *heh*.

When Canthem straightened again their eyes danced with amusement. "I pray you're not laughing at my name."

"No, sa." Illi quickly shook her head. Then, to cover up any awkwardness, she announced, "Illi Basbowen. Uh . . . just Illi."

"From the way you fight, I don't think there's any 'just' about you."

Illi's cheeks warmed. She cleared her throat. "Did the caravan hire you?"

Canthem shook their head, a sharp motion. "I'm part of the general's guard. We accompany any caravans that go through Hathage. It's our mission to see them safely through the Wastes. You might not be aware, but this area is rife with guul."

Illi snorted. "Sa, I behead guul on a regular basis."

"Do you?" asked Canthem, eyebrows raised. "Then perhaps you'll have more to show me than a few moves."

Illi smiled and this time it was genuine. "You have no idea."

Canthem glanced up and down the growing market. "The market will still be here in another hour. A little introduction won't take much longer than that. Do you know a place we can practice?"

Illi's smile widened. "I do."

Illi kicked off her sandals, savoring the warmth of the stones on her bare feet. Across from her, Canthem was busy shedding their weapons, setting them each on top of a compost barrel. So far Illi had counted two swords, one short dagger, a set of brass knuckles, and a leather bag. They pulled another knife from their boot and dropped it on top with a final clatter of metal.

The wind curled lazily across the rooftop. Past Canthem, the market bloomed and spread, adding light and voices to its tangle of colors and motion with every passing minute. She wasn't missing anything, though; the market would be there when they were done. Besides, the market couldn't sell her anything more useful—or more interesting—than what this guard had to offer.

The way they'd parried her attacks, as if a blade hadn't been a hair's breadth from their face. As if her attacks were just *nothing*.

Canthem finished tightening the knots of their tagel. Illi sighed her disappointment. She'd hoped they'd take it off for the fight. She was becoming increasingly curious about whether or not they were a man. On the one hand, they wore a tagel. But on the other hand, Canthem moved with the fluidity and grace of a woman. And on the *third* hand—

"You can ask."

Illi started, then her cheeks grew warm. She'd been staring and Canthem had caught her. She unclipped her own weapons and dropped them one by one on the stones, their leather sheaths muffling the clatter.

"I don't know what you mean, sa," she bluffed.

"You want to know if I'm a man or a woman."

Illi set her collection of small knives down with care before straightening. "That's none of my business."

"You're right," said Canthem. "But you're going to keep wondering anyway. And you keep using 'sa.'"

Illi winced. "I was trying to be respectful—"

"It's all right. You can drop the 'sa.' And the answer is: neither. I'm not a man. I'm not a woman."

"Then what are you?"

"Me."

They struck, fingers jabbing at Illi's eyes. She jerked back before she realized it'd been a feint. Canthem caught her leg with a kick that turned and caught and swept her off her feet. Illi hit the ground hard. Canthem held out their hand.

Illi jumped up on her own, a smile warming her lips. "Do that again."

Canthem did. When Illi fell this time, she immediately sprang up and tried the maneuver on them. Canthem knocked her down with ease, but then showed Illi what they were doing, moving with her through the motions step by step.

So they progressed, round after round. Canthem slowed enough so Illi could copy their movements, and then they traded jabs and feints. Illi laughed every time she messed up and Canthem got the better of her. It'd been too long since she'd had a real challenge.

Sweat dripped down her back and into her eyes. Her arms burned from the repeated motions. Illi lost track of time. She realized night had fallen with a sudden jolt.

"Once more." Illi stepped back and put her empty hands up as Canthem had shown her. "It's growing too dark. I'll have to put off my turn to teach until tomorrow."

Canthem nodded. "Let's make it count."

They lunged. Illi blocked. They traded blows, circling around each other on the rooftop as Illi tried and tried again to get close enough to Canthem to drop them. It was much harder without a weapon to force distance. They kept Illi back with aggravating ease. Already exhausted from fighting guul earlier and collecting skulls and then a full hour of training, Illi knew she didn't have much left in her. So she circled and then pressed her attack, opening herself up to Canthem's fists in a desperate effort to drive them back.

Back—and into the glasshouse. When their back hit the glass, Canthem hesitated for the briefest of moments, but it was enough. Illi got close, then swept their legs out from under them.

They fell and hit the stones with a noise that was half grunt, half laugh. Illi fell with them, driving her knee into their stomach. Then she slipped into a grapple, pressing her body against Canthem's so that their arms were locked and they couldn't get up.

She grinned at them, her face only inches from theirs. Through their wrap, she could feel Canthem's taut muscles relax.

"You win," they said.

But Illi didn't let them up. Canthem smelled like honey and cinnamon, and their hot breath brushed her cheeks. Their warm, dark eyes watched her carefully, hungrily. Suddenly, Illi was very aware of how alone they were on this rooftop. Of how long it'd been since the last caravan had stopped by.

She really didn't want to let Canthem go.

Beneath her, she felt Canthem move but didn't do anything to stop them. Their arm slid up and between Illi's and with a single push, broke her hold. Then the world was spinning and the air was pushed from her lungs, her back connecting hard with the stones as Canthem switched their positions, their arm pressed into her throat, their body against hers. Illi's heart beat harder, but not from exertion.

Canthem's other hand brushed up her leg. They clicked their tongue as their fingers found one of Illi's knives.

"Not playing fair after all."

"I didn't use it," said Illi.

"How many other knives do you have?"

"Why don't you find out?"

Canthem met her gaze again and Illi held her breath. It was hard to measure Canthem beneath that tagel, but she enjoyed the challenge, enjoyed the uncertainty. What was the worst that could happen? Rejection? Canthem would be leaving in a few days anyway.

And if Canthem didn't reject her, they'd still be leaving in a few days. She couldn't learn too much about them and they couldn't learn too much about her and—most importantly—she couldn't fall in love. Either way, Illi won.

"Are you always so forward?" asked Canthem. They hadn't moved off of Illi, but their hand was still trailing up her thigh, fingers as light as feathers.

"Life is short," said Illi. "I don't see the point in playing coy."

Their hand found her hip, where it rested for a heartbeat before moving inward. Illi sucked in a breath, but didn't dare break eye contact.

Canthem removed their hand from her leg and their arm from her throat and sat up, straddling Illi. Looking down at her, they reached up and began slowly, methodically, undoing the knots of their tagel. Then Canthem pulled it off.

Skin tingling and heart pounding, Illi drank in Canthem's features. They weren't what she'd expected, not by a long shot, and yet clearly they belonged to Canthem. Illi noticed their hair first, impossibly straight and black and—released from the tagel—cascading over their shoulders like rainwater. Their hair contrasted neatly with their skin, which in the darkness seemed to glow on its own. Then there was their sharp nose and apple-round cheeks and—

Canthem bent and pressed warm lips to Illi's and any other thoughts vanished like water on stone.

4

Illi stirred and stirred and stirred her porridge, lost in memories of the night before. She kept trying to replay her lesson with Canthem, the specific way they'd blocked her attacks and taken her down, how they'd feinted and how they'd moved quick and liquid as water, but all she could think about was her lesson *after*, when Canthem had taught her new ways to use fingers, knees, and tongue.

Mo had been right; taking a break *did* make her feel better.

A yawn from across the room broke Illi's thoughts. Mo had stopped at the foot of the stairs to stretch. She smiled at Illi. "I take it you had fun at the market?"

Illi took a bite of porridge as her cheeks warmed. She nodded, not quite trusting her voice.

"Good." Mo crossed to the table and began making herself a bowl of porridge. "Then as your healer, I prescribe you two more days of market."

"Yes, ma."

Mo swatted playfully at Illi, and Illi dodged with a grin, her mouth full of warm, sweet porridge. For the moment, her breakdown on the sands felt as unreal and distant as a dream. She should visit Yaluz later, see how he was doing. Bring him something from the market.

The door opened.

Mo paused, her bowl in her hands, as Drum Chief Amastan entered the room. He wore a muted red wrap, simple black embroidery around his sleeves and hem. His tagel was a dusty brown and today he wore it high so that only his eyes were visible. He had a sword at his hip that Illi knew for a fact wasn't ceremonial, despite the engraved hilt, and his fingers glittered with rings. Some of them for show, some of them for his position, and some of them filled with poison.

Only Amastan's cousins knew about that last bit.

"Amastan—" started Mo.

But she stopped when a woman entered after Amastan. The dust darkening the edges of her clothes immediately marked her as iluk, and that was before taking her shoes, her hair, and her skin into account. She wore a fitted dress the color of gold, cinched at the waist and flowing all the way to her feet to drag along the ground. Sleeves cascaded down her arms, but didn't obscure her hands, which were free of any adornment.

Her skin was the color of sugar-dusted porridge, a brown as pale as sandstone. Her hair was a mass of tightly wound honey-brown curls, held back from her face by a ribbon as gold as her dress. She wore sandals that covered her toes in pale leather, ornamented with brightly colored baubles. Whether they were glass or stone, it was too lavish for something you wore on your feet.

But the strangest thing about her were her too-pale eyes. Her black pupils stood out like pinpricks, widening within a circle of green as they caught on Mo and Illi at the table. Those eyes were like tinted glass, too impossible a color to exist naturally. Like Heru's glass eye, but these eyes moved and focused, taking in the small, now crowded, room—these eyes were real.

When she spoke, her voice was throaty with dust. "Thana Basbowen—I've heard so much about you."

Mo glanced around, then raised a hand to her chest. "Oh, I'm not Thana, ma. She's still upstairs. I can go get her—?"

"No need," said a voice from the stairs, still thick with sleep. Thana stifled a yawn and gestured at the woman. "Who's this, 'Stan?"

"She arrived with the caravan," said Amastan. "She came to the Circle and specifically requested an audience with your, ah, friend."

Thana ran a hand across her hair. "Heru. His name is Heru. Speaking it won't summon him, you know." She sighed. "Why did you bring her here? I'm not his keeper."

Amastan shifted uncomfortably. "She refused to tell me anything else. I thought you might have a better handle on what's going on. And you know how Heru can be." His gaze met hers and held it until Thana nodded.

The woman cleared her throat. "My name is Merrabel Barca," she announced with a flourish of her hands and a bend of her knees. "I have come on behalf of the crown. I must speak with Sametket immediately. It's a matter of utmost urgency."

Thana's eyebrows raised. "Crown? The Empress is dead, ma."

Amusement flashed across Merrabel's face, there and gone in an instant. "No crown as crude and illegitimate as hers. You've heard of the kingdom of Hathage, of course."

Thana pressed her lips together while Illi tried to remember the maps she'd seen, but it was Amastan who answered, "It lies to the north. Hathage was a province of the Empire. I take it that's no longer the case?"

"Hathage hasn't been a province since the Empire fell," said Merrabel. "Its puppet governor didn't last long without his precious Empress." Her lips curled into a smile. "We're a free country now and we look after our own interests. Which is why King Thamilcar sent me to find and speak with Sametket. So unless you're willing to insult His Majesty, you should escort me to Sametket immediately."

Thana crossed her arms. "Ghadid's a free city. We don't take kindly to empires *or* kingdoms trying to throw their weight around here. Heru is a busy man—if he wants to see you, he will."

"I only ask for the opportunity. And directions."

Thana exchanged a glance with Amastan that held the weight of a thousand unsaid words. Illi shifted uneasily. Heru had a past with the Empire, had done terrible things for his Empress, and there were many still alive who yet blamed him for her crimes— some even in Ghadid. But that was just that: past. Heru had redeemed himself a hundred times over during and since the Siege. Whoever this woman was, Illi didn't trust her. She set her spoon down and stood.

"All right," conceded Thana. "I'll take you to him. But it's up to him if he wants to speak with you."

Merrabel's smile softened. "Oh, let me assure you—he'll be very interested in what I have to say."

"Heru—someone's here to see you."

Thana drew back Heru's curtain without waiting for an answer. Merrabel followed at her heels, gazing around at Heru's lab with open curiosity. Illi came last, lips pressed tight and a hand on the sword at her waist.

The orb twisted in its invisible breeze and brightened in greeting. Merrabel tilted her head back and studied the orb. Then she turned her gaze on the back of the room, where Heru hunched over his bench, elbows on the metal surface, his brows creased in concentration as he tilted one of his beakers over a wide bowl. A roll sat half-eaten at his elbow.

Merrabel cleared her throat and then, in a voice that echoed through the room, said, "Heru Sametket, second advisory marabi of the late Empress Zara ha Khatet."

Heru didn't look up. A drop gathered and fell from the edge of his beaker. A wisp of steam curled from the bowl and dissipated. Heru stirred the liquid with a wooden spoon, then dipped a vial into the bowl, scooped up some of the milky white liquid, and capped it. He set it in a rack along with a row of other glass vials, equally full.

Merrabel coughed into her hand, then tried again. "Heru Sametket, second—"

"You are interrupting a very important experiment." Heru laid his palms flat on the table and looked up, dark eye flashing with annoyance. "Technically, I'm now the first advisory marabi, but I know my own name. I don't care to know yours. So unless you are here to hold a flask or otherwise offer your assistance, please leave."

Illi started forward, memory and habit enough for her to know that Heru needed a specific reagent for what he was doing—one on the second shelf of his cabinet, a clear liquid in a clear jar—but she stopped abruptly when Thana clapped her hands together.

"Okay, you heard him—"

But Merrabel's smile only broadened. "Ah, now I know it's truly you. What are you doing here, Sametket? Why are you hiding in a village in the Wastes?"

Heru turned away and grabbed a towel from another bench. Wiping his hands clean, he said, "The Mehewret Empire no longer has the stability I require for my work."

"The Empire has fallen."

Heru paused. "Fallen?"

"Sametket," said Merrabel, "you told me yourself."

Heru frowned. "I am certain I did not, seeing as how I have only just learned of the possibility."

"The possibility is reality. And you told me in that letter of yours." Merrabel made a show of pulling a piece of folded vellum from a pouch at her belt and opening it with a flick of her wrist. She held it up as if she needed more light, pursed her lips, and scanned the lines with one long fingernail. Then she read. "*I am conducting a thorough survey of this region's remaining en-marab. As you are no doubt aware of by now, the Empress Zara ha Khatet— long may she live—is deceased. So it is therefore of the utmost importance . . .*" Merrabel let her voice trail off and snapped the vellum shut again. "And then there's some nonsense about surveys and statistics."

"But that letter was in regard to the Empress, not the Empire."

"Correct." Merrabel dropped the vellum on a nearby table and folded her hands in front of her. "And your Empress set up no formal line of succession. When she didn't return from the Wastes, Na Tay Khet tore itself apart. Most of the provinces seized their opportunity for freedom. Thanks to your timely information, Hathage led the way. I doubt you would be welcome in your home any longer, but Hathage could have a place for you—one at its heart, instead of cast aside and forgotten, as you have been here. No one told you what happened to your Empire? *Truly?* The news must have made it all the way out here." Merrabel glanced at Thana, eyebrows raised, but Thana met her gaze with even silence.

Heru took a moment to assimilate the information, then shrugged. "I am quite comfortable here, in this small backwards town. They do not bother me and I have all of the subjects I could wish for, fresh from the sands."

Merrabel approached one of the benches, trailing her fingernails along the metal. "You could have more. Full labs, Sametket. Willing assistants."

"More people to get in my way." He narrowed his eyes. "I still do not know who you are. I sent that exact letter to over a dozen colleagues."

Merrabel put a hand to her chest. "You don't remember me? I'm shocked, Sametket. We once studied under the same roof. But of course, that was back when you went by 'he Fet' instead of 'Sametket.'" Without taking her gaze off of Heru, she pulled up the hem of her dress and curtsied. "Merrabel Barca, His Royal Highness's official emissary from the kingdom of Hathage."

Heru tilted his head to one side. "Barca? But I thought you were dead."

Merrabel lilted a laugh. "Just because I never answered your letter doesn't mean that I'm dead."

Heru frowned. "I specifically asked the recipients of my correspondence to respond so that I could count who survived the Empress's purge. It was essential that all respond, otherwise my survey would not be accurate. You did not respond, ergo, you were dead. Now you wish to inform me otherwise? You've thrown all of the results of my survey into question. This is why . . ."

Heru trailed off as it became clear that Merrabel was ignoring him. She ambled across the room, fingers trailing along the long metal bench. She glanced once at the orb overhead, which brightened as she passed beneath. Illi kept a few feet behind, but she might as well have been another bowl for all Merrabel noticed. Thana stayed at the door, one hand on the hilt of her dagger, watching and wary.

Heru cleared his throat. "Why have you journeyed all this way when you couldn't be bothered to answer my letter?"

Merrabel paused at the first guuli skull in the line. She traced the contour of its forehead with a finger, the scrape of nail across bone setting Illi's teeth on edge. Then she tapped between the empty eye sockets and listened to the hollow thud. She nodded to herself before continuing on to the next skull.

"Why—" began Heru, louder this time.

"Because I've been looking for the source of the disruption." Scrape, tap, nod. She looked up. "These are all empty. Are you starting a skull collection, Sametket?"

"They contained guul. I have siphoned the guul out and stored them safely elsewhere."

"Where?" Merrabel looked around, her gaze skipping over Illi as if she weren't there.

"It is not important."

"No." Scrape, tap. "I suppose it's not." Merrabel tapped the third skull thoughtfully and considered its gaping nasal cavity and spiraling gazelle horns. One of them was still crusted with blood: Yazul's.

Merrabel glanced toward Thana. "I'm not sure Heru will want an audience for this. This is a matter of scientific discussion and merits privacy."

"Heru and I have an understanding, ma," said Thana, her hand tapping the hilt of her sword. "I'll stay."

Merrabel rolled her head toward Heru. "Are you certain you wish to discuss potentially sensitive matters in front of one of the locals?"

"That particular local has earned my trust," said Heru.

"If you insist," said Merrabel. Then her gaze caught on Illi and those too-pale eyes finally saw her. "And what about this one?"

"She's my assistant," said Heru.

Illi felt a surge of warmth. He'd so rarely acknowledged her assistance, only assumed and expected she'd be there to help, like a particularly useful piece of equipment. To be fair, he always treated his equipment with great care.

"Rumor has it that your assistants don't last long," said Merrabel, more to Illi than to Heru.

Illi met Merrabel's gaze and narrowed her eyes, thinking of a particular merchant. "Rumor can be wrong." When Merrabel's gaze didn't lighten, Illi asked, "What did you mean earlier, about a disruption? Does it have something to do with the guul?"

"Do you let your assistants speak so freely?"

"I find it helpful if they can voice their concerns aloud, especially when those concerns might involve broken glass or errant jaan. The girl has the right question." Heru pushed himself back from the table. "Answer it."

"I'd've thought such an intelligent man as yourself would've noticed it by now."

Heru crossed his arms, but his expression relaxed. "There have been many disruptions, some to the Wastes, some affecting the guul, some the sajaam. You must be more specific."

"From my own research: all of the above." Merrabel sniffed the air, twisting her fingers through nothing. "A balance has shifted. It rains where it shouldn't and it doesn't rain where it should. Guul have stepped out of myth and become a frequent danger. Bindings are less effective. Our caravans have been attacked, sometimes outright destroyed. Our trade is threatened. Even the bandits have become desperate. Something has changed, and every point of data indicates that change originated here or nearby."

"A sajaami was released from its bindings some years ago,"

said Heru. "I imagine the release of a being of such power could cause some changes to the local environment, but I cannot speak to the changes you describe without further examination of your data, which I assume you have brought with you."

"Oh, don't fear, Sametket: you'll have a chance to take a look yourself. But humor me for a moment—" Merrabel rolled her head back, her gaze landing on the orb. "—and tell me: what's this strange bauble you have hanging in your lab?"

The light had grown as bright as ever and now shone steady throughout the room, turning shadows crisp and dark. Despite its brightness, Illi couldn't help but follow Merrabel's gaze. It had never occurred to her to ask Heru what the orb contained. When she'd first entered his lab, everything had been a mystery, and many things still were. The orb had just remained one secret among many. It had hung in the lab's center since Heru emerged sans one eye from the Wastes with Thana and Mo and three dead camels seven years ago.

Now Heru hesitated. His gaze flicked to Thana; she shook her head once, the message clear. *Don't.*

Illi's interest was piqued. So was Merrabel's. A smile spread across her lips.

"That's it, isn't it?" she breathed, her face awash in the orb's light. "That's the sajaami."

Illi started. She looked again at the orb. Sajaam were dangerous, violent creatures, more powerful than jaan, more willful than guul. If the stories were true, they'd all been sealed away because they'd been foolish enough to believe they could be gods. They'd destroyed countless civilizations and created the Wastes. Over a dozen tribes had come together to stop them.

Heru couldn't have a sajaami here, in the city itself. That would be dangerous. Madness. Surely Thana would never have let him—

Merrabel glanced at Heru out of the corner of her eye, her smile twisting. "Oh, don't be modest, Sametket. Only the most powerful marabi could have trapped a sajaami. If that really is a sajaami in there, then that means you're the best of all of us. Or are you only mediocre?"

Heru puffed up. "Of course I'm the best."

Illi rolled her eyes as Merrabel asked, sweet as sun-dried dates, "Then that's the sajaami?"

"Yes," said Heru with no small amount of pride.

Illi's stomach lurched, as if she'd stepped off the edge of a platform without a rope or a plan. Thana breathed out a long sigh. Merrabel smiled in triumph. Illi took a step back, two. The sajaami's light still bathed her in its cold glow. Or maybe that was only the glow of the water, holding its destructive power at bay.

"Where did you find it?" asked Merrabel, her words thrumming with barely suppressed excitement. She reached up with one hand, fingers stretching as she rolled to her tiptoes, as if she could simply will away the distance between her and the orb. She stretched upward for a moment, two, then curled her fingers back and dropped her hand.

Heru turned his gaze on the orb with a mixture of lust and wonder. "Through copious and thorough research, I discovered the location of the sajaam sealed centuries past deep within the Wastes. The Empress Zara ha Khatet foolishly released one of them, believing she could harness its power by binding it to her body. She briefly became immortal." He smirked. "It did not last."

His gaze dropped from the orb to Merrabel and his expression turned solemn. "I had been preparing for that eventuality ever since I learned that the sajaam still existed in our world. That flask you see is the result of weeks' worth of work and decades of learning. The Empress couldn't contain the sajaami because she was impatient. I, however, have been able to contain the sajaami for seven years to no ill effect."

Merrabel's eyes widened briefly, but she smothered her surprise with a snort. "No ill effect? Sametket, I'm only *here* because of its ill effect."

Heru frowned. "What do you mean?"

Merrabel pointed in triumph. "*That's* the disruption. That's what has been causing the Wastes to expand and the guul to attack—your city as well as my own and others all along the coast. Sametket, you have to get rid of this sajaami. Before it destroys your city and my kingdom."

5

"The sajaami has been contained," said Heru dismissively. "It is perfectly safe while I continue with my experiments."

"No, it's not." Merrabel jabbed her finger at the orb. "If it were contained, it wouldn't react to our presence like that."

"Like what?"

"Sametket—it's glowing."

Heru glanced at Illi, then crossed his arms. "The sajaami has never done anything else. It does not affect its environment. It cannot. You seek causation but you have only proven correlation. The guul attacks have been increasing, the drought worsening, yes, but the cause of both—if there is even a single, coherent cause—isn't here, Barca. It's unfortunate that your long journey was for naught, but you are confused. Still, you may feel free to leave your notes with me. I am certain a more careful eye will see the nuance that you missed."

"I'm not confused." Merrabel put her hands on her hips. "Do the people of this city know you're harboring a sajaami?"

"I do not see what that has to do with—"

"I'll take that to mean no." Merrabel smirked. "You know—I couldn't help but notice you're on your own back here, all alone on an abandoned platform. They let you live in their city as long as they can forget about you, don't they?"

Heru bristled. "I require ample space and quiet for my work. It is best if they do not disturb me."

"It's best if you don't disturb *them*, I bet," continued Merrabel. "What would they do if they knew what you get up to in here? What would your drum chiefs say if they found out you keep a sajaami?"

Thana moved slowly, almost imperceptibly, a knife already in her hand. Illi stood frozen, mouth dry as sand, still stuck on the fact that she had shared a room with a sajaami for all these years. But her first reaction wasn't fear: it was rage.

How could he?

Heru considered Merrabel as if she were just one in a line of guul skulls. "They would not understand. They are simple creatures that don't grasp the fine distinctions of en-marabi research and the potential it has for them."

"So they might be a little . . . upset?"

Thana was halfway across the room now, silent as a snake. Thana didn't need to get any closer to strike; Illi had seen her hit a charging guuli with a knife from the back of a camel. But if Merrabel was anything like Heru, then Thana would only have one chance.

Why? The question pinged through Illi's head, unanswerable. Why had Thana let Heru keep a sajaami all this time? Why would Heru risk it? Risk his life, risk his position in Ghadid, risk *Ghadid*?

Heru was the only one able to quiet the guul. Illi needed him. They *all* needed him.

Merrabel raised her voice and announced to the room, "If you kill me, you'll only make this worse for yourselves."

Thana froze. Merrabel turned and smiled at her, but Thana didn't put her knife away.

"Even if you could kill me," continued Merrabel, her voice lower, "the rest of your city will notice. They'll remember the beautiful foreigner who went to visit their hermit en-marabi and never returned. I asked around when I first arrived and no one had anything nice to say about your friend. In fact, they were all quite eager to share the most terrible and unlikely rumors. If they don't see me leave with the caravan, smiling and alive, they will wonder. They will talk. They will come to their own nasty conclusions. And then they will turn on him. It probably wouldn't even take that much."

Thana lowered her knife. Heru stayed still as stone, considering. Finally, he nodded. Thana lowered her knife, but didn't move away. She kept guard, arms crossed, an unspoken threat.

"Good," said Merrabel. "I'm glad we agree. Now, to the matter at hand—the sajaami." She gestured at the orb. "It can't stay here. This close to the Wastes, it's only destabilizing them. And that's a danger for everyone who lives on this continent. If the Wastes destabilize, then they will expand to take the rest of us. And while you may have adapted to live in a waterless, sand-strewn wasteland, the rest of us haven't. It would be a disaster akin to the last climate shift, centuries ago. Do you want that on your conscience?"

"I disagree," said Heru. "Until we can prove beyond a doubt that the sajaami is linked to this 'disruption,' the sajaami is safest here, with me. It has been quieted and contained and that has sufficed for the last seven years. We shouldn't act before we understand the whole of this potential issue you have brought before me."

"We're talking in circles and I don't think you recognize the immediacy of the problem." Merrabel's voice sharpened. "I've generally admired your persistence, but right now you're just being stubborn. That's fine; I know how to work with stubborn." Her smile sharpened as well. "What do you think would happen if the people here found out you were secretly keeping a sajaami?"

"They won't."

Merrabel shook her head. "Do you understand nuance? Maybe if I state it plainly, you will: the sajaami cannot stay here. Either it leaves with me or I go to your leaders and tell them what you've been doing behind their backs and they will throw you and the sajaami out. Which do you choose?"

Heru glanced from Thana to Merrabel, clearly wishing he could just make this annoyance disappear. "I reject both of the options you have presented. Neither of them are optimal."

"Optimal would be a nice bath and a slave rubbing the calluses from my feet," said Merrabel, sounding tired. "Reality is this." She pointed at the orb. "Make your choice, Sametket."

Illi opened her hands placatingly. "Give him time, ma. You claim to know Heru—then you know you can't just walk in here and make demands. Share your research with him and let him think it over. He'll come around to your point of view if this danger really is as threatening as you claim."

Merrabel stared at Illi, those pale eyes disconcertingly sharp. Her face remained as blank as a tagel as she mulled over Illi's words. At least this time she didn't dismiss them out of hand. Finally, a smile broke through.

"I do know Sametket," said Merrabel. "I know he won't change his mind. But the caravan won't be returning to Hathage for a few days. I will give you that much time to try to convince him to hand over the sajaami. And please do— its danger is greater than you can possibly imagine. Besides,

I don't want to share a caravan with him when he's inevitably forced out."

"We kill her."

Thana leaned over the table, both of her hands splayed on it to take her weight. Mo slid the teapot in front of her and its thick steam drove Thana back. She waved her hand in her face and scowled at Mo, but her wife had already turned to retrieve a few cups. Instead, her scowl found Illi, who stood like a piece carved from stone near the hearth.

"You can't kill her," chided Mo. "She's right. It'll be conspicuous if the rich iluk who visited our Heru turns up with a knife in her chest."

"Doesn't have to be a knife," said Thana. "I was actually thinking poison. I have this one I bought off the last caravan that I haven't had a chance to try out yet—"

"You will not kill her."

Illi started; she'd forgotten Drum Chief Amastan was there. He'd been silent the entire time Thana had recounted what had happened in Heru's lab. Thana had summoned him as soon as they'd returned. Now he wore a simple beige wrap, his tagel low, the mark of his station tucked away. At the moment, he wasn't a drum chief; he was merely a cousin.

"*Amastan*," whined Thana. "Be reasonable."

"We don't do contracts anymore," said Amastan firmly. "And we're not murderers."

"If it's replacing Kaseem you're after—"

"Did you know?" interrupted Illi.

All heads turned toward her. She hadn't meant to interrupt,

but the words had been clattering in her head since the revelation in Heru's lab, repeating over and over and over again, and she'd had to get them out.

"No," said Amastan immediately, but Thana hesitated and Mo kept her back to them all.

"You knew."

The words were a rock, thrown at Thana. She flinched.

"How could you?" asked Illi, voice low.

"It was contained—" started Thana.

"What else have you lied about?"

"*Illi*," warned Mo.

But Thana held up a hand. "I never lied to you. The secret was Heru's to keep and he decided not to share. Maybe it wasn't the best decision, letting him keep the sajaami, but we'd survived so much. And it was contained. The years passed and nothing happened and G-d knows we had enough to worry about. So you'll forgive me for forgetting to mention something that wasn't a problem."

"*Wasn't*," spat Illi. "Now it is."

"How do we even know it *is* a problem?" asked Amastan. "We only have Merrabel's word. Her research was inconclusive, yes? Perhaps she has another motive."

Thana crossed her arms. "I didn't think I'd ever hear *you* defend Heru, 'Stan."

Amastan spread his hands. "I'm not defending him. I'm pointing out that we know little to nothing about this foreigner and that perhaps her ravings about doom and destruction may be less based in reality than we've assumed. Better to trust the devil we know until we have proof otherwise."

Illi let out a breath, but she didn't relax. "She's not entirely wrong. The guul attacks have been increasing. Heru has been mapping them. And the drought . . ."

"We've had droughts before," said Amastan, frowning. "Most of our records burned in the Siege, but droughts were well-recorded. The longest lasted a decade. I see no reason to believe this one won't end soon."

"Does it matter whether or not that woman is right?" asked Thana. "She threatened to tell the Circle. You know what will happen if the other drum chiefs hear about the sajaami."

Amastan's sigh was his only answer.

"But she can't have it," continued Thana. "So that leaves one option: we silence her before she can spread rumors."

"No murder," said Amastan sternly.

"Why can't she have the sajaami?" asked Illi.

"It's too dangerous," said Thana. "I've seen this one up close and it was scary enough contained. If it was released, the damage it could do . . ." She trailed off and shook her head.

"They want to be G-d," said Mo softly. "They tried to destroy all of mankind once. I doubt being imprisoned for millennia will have tempered that impulse at all."

"Then all the better that this iluk takes the sajaami far and away from here," pressed Illi. "She came looking for it; she must be prepared to handle it."

"No. Heru knows what he's doing. We don't know if Merrabel can handle the sajaami safely. We'll have to find a way to persuade her to leave it alone."

"Or for Heru to go with her," said Amastan.

Illi shook her head, but none of them even looked her way. They were going about this all wrong. Heru needed to stay, *had* to stay, at all costs. He was their defense against the guul, the only one who could stop another uprising. He couldn't leave. Which meant the sajaami had to go. It was simple, really.

They were still arguing when Illi slipped out.

6

The sun was bright and the streets were full of life; a rare combination. But winter often twisted everyday life into unrecognizable shapes, like a storm reshaping the sands. And so most of Ghadid was out, enjoying the sunlight instead of hiding from it. The sun's warmth was a tepid touch against Illi's bare skin; she'd rolled back her sleeves to take in its heat.

The market was in full swing, a press of bodies and a swirl of colors and a crowd of sounds in a too-small space. On one side, someone argued at the top of their lungs with a merchant over the quality of their leather. On the other, a group laughed even louder. Illi breathed in the scents of cinnamon and anise, roasting meat and hot cheese, salt and sweat. She sidled sideways through a particularly thick clump of people and stepped on someone's foot. The yelp trailed her, followed by a sharp patter of foreign words, but no one tried to grab or stop her. A lot of feet would be trodden upon in the coming days.

The market usually made her uncomfortable. There were too many variables, too many sights, too many sounds, too much to possibly be aware of every danger. But the same things that normally disconcerted her were exactly the things Illi needed right now. The market made it difficult to breathe, so she let it smother her.

She'd tried to hammer a plan into place on her own, but she'd gotten nowhere. So she'd sought out her cousins—not to ask them for help, but to let their presence take her mind off the matter. Sometimes, not thinking about a problem was the best way to solve it.

Dihya had been all too willing to spend a few hours at the market. Thankfully, Zarrat was busy with the carriages. Azhar had come, too, although she kept lingering to talk to the Azal she knew. Eventually, Dihya and Illi had stopped waiting for her; she always found them again.

The crowd bore them along at its own pace and Illi took in stall after stall, one display of vibrant blues from the Azal and pungent purples from Hathage blending into the next. She passed a half baat across for a skewer of grilled goat and ripped off chunks with her teeth as she walked. She traded another baat for a small jar of southern honey that she tucked into a pocket; Yaluz loved honey, but he'd be holed up at the healer's until well after the market was torn down and the caravan had moved on. A third baat got her a length of red ribbon: a salas for the healer who'd saved Yaluz's life.

As Illi tucked the ribbon into a pouch at her belt, Dihya said, "He's awake, you know."

Illi didn't have to ask who Dihya meant. "You visited him?"

Dihya nodded. "You should, too. He asked after you. He knows you saved his life."

Illi smiled vacantly. "Sure." Then she pointed. "Oh look, a glassmaker."

Dihya sighed. "You've got to stop avoiding what happened. I think going and seeing Yaluz will help you feel better."

"I will." Illi approached the glassmaker's stall, not looking at Dihya. "I just . . . I've got other things to worry about right now."

"Like what?" asked Dihya.

Like an iluk woman meddling in things she shouldn't. Like a sajaami being kept in the city. Like the threat of Heru being kicked out, exiled—or worse.

"Nothing much."

"We can't help you if you don't let us."

Illi bit meat off the skewer so her mouth was too full to answer. She took in the stall, trying to find the smaller glass baubles she was looking for, the ones that could be used to make charms. They'd need stronger charms than the leather ones they usually wore if the guul attacks kept increasing. Glass glinted, glared, and threw sun into her eyes. Bright baubles spun in tight circles on pieces of string and leather cords. Panes of glass hung in a line behind the glassmaker, clear and green and bubbled and yellow. The glassmaker held a large blue sphere up to the light for an interested customer to inspect.

The sun hit the glass and it glowed the exact shade of blue of Heru's orb. The calm Illi had cultivated while browsing was gone in that instant. Every minute that the sajaami remained in Ghadid, it was a danger. All those years it'd been hanging there, in the middle of everything, while Illi was ignorantly unaware. How was she going to convince the world's most stubborn man to give it up?

"Just Illi?"

Illi spun at the familiar voice, raising her skewered meat like a weapon. Canthem plucked the skewer from her hand. The sight of them was like a strike to her sternum: suddenly she was off balance, pulse pounding, mouth dry. All thought of the sajaami was wiped away.

"Thanks." Canthem's warm eyes twinkled. "I was just getting hungry."

They slid a piece off the skewer and under their tagel, never breaking eye contact. Illi swallowed, remembering what the face looked like under that tagel, those lips, that tongue. She realized her hand was still up in defense and her face flushed hot. But before she could drop her arm, Canthem put the skewer back into her hand, curling her fingers around the metal.

"Hi," Illi finally managed.

"'Hi'? That's it? That's all I get?"

"You'd rather I ask you if you're sane?"

Canthem immediately straightened. "I am. Praise be to G-d."

Illi laughed. "I was joking. We're not on the sands."

"As am I. How can I claim sanity around such an entrancing person?"

Illi tried to answer with something pithy, but nothing would come. Beside her, Dihya coughed and Illi almost jumped out of her skin. *Shards,* how could she have forgotten about Dihya?

"Who's this?" asked Dihya.

"Just . . . someone I met," mumbled Illi.

But Canthem's eyes lit up as they danced across Dihya. They bowed in that extravagant way of theirs, fingers splayed behind them. "Canthem, ma, part of the Guul Guard."

"*Guul Guard?*" echoed Dihya, eyebrows raised.

"Not the official name, ma," said Canthem. "We're a segment of the King's Guard that has been trained by the general herself to defend caravans from guul. I hope I'm not keeping you from anything."

"A fitting name, then." Dihya's gaze flicked to Illi, and the smile that curled her lips was equal parts bemused and devious. "Oh yes, I just remembered—I've got a meeting. With—ah—Azhar. On the next platform. Why don't you go on without me and I'll see you later?"

Illi frowned. "Azhar's just—"

"*Waiting impatiently for me,*" hissed Dihya.

Before Illi could protest, Dihya waved and stepped backward into the flow of people. The crowd swallowed her up, leaving Illi alone with Canthem. Somehow, her heart started beating even faster.

Canthem stepped close, their wrap brushing hers. They brought their head down, near her ear. When they spoke, their breath was hot and it sent a thrill down to her core.

"You owe me a lesson, Just Illi."

Illi flushed with memories from the night before. Had that only been yesterday? Now she had so much more to worry about than being unable to keep Yaluz safe. But she'd come to the market for distraction, and Canthem would definitely provide one.

"Then let me pay my debt." She grabbed Canthem's wrist and began pulling them along. "Come on."

Canthem resisted, surprise pushing their eyebrows higher. "Now?" They glanced around at the market. "But it's midday."

"And? We'll have plenty of light to practice by. Why?" Illi stopped so abruptly that Canthem all but ran into her. She met their gaze as unabashedly as they'd met hers earlier. "It's not like we're doing anything illicit."

Canthem leaned into her, eyes glinting with mischief. "That's a shame. I'd rather hoped we would."

"I *was* going to take you somewhere a little more private," said Illi. "Now I'm not so sure I should. You might take advantage of me."

"Me?" Canthem feigned shock. "Never. Now *you* on the other hand, I'm fairly certain you took advantage of *me* last night."

"And *I'm* fairly certain, you were the one on top, unfairly pinning a girl down."

"Only because you let me."

"I think I like you," said Illi, before turning and continuing down the street.

"I've heard it's hard not to."

Illi snorted and tightened her grip on Canthem's wrist. They let her draw them through the crowd. The market fell away almost as soon as Illi stepped onto the westernmost bridge. Then they were surrounded by the normal pulse of everyday life in Ghadid. A dancer performed to the beat of a drum at the center of this platform, his gauzy fabric swirling around him like a dust twister, glass jangling at his wrists, ankles, and ears. When Canthem slowed to watch, Illi tugged them along.

Another bridge, another platform, another center. This one was quieter. Just a handful of people talking in doorways as they knit and mended and shelled. As Illi passed, they called out greetings, which Canthem heartily returned.

But after the next bridge, the city fell away completely. This platform was quiet, mostly deserted. Illi knew that at least one of the faded, crumbling buildings was inhabited, but no one called a greeting and Illi picked up her step.

On the next platform Canthem finally asked, "Why is this area deserted? What happened?"

Illi slowed, scanning the open doorways for a familiar sign. There: a mark of red paint, faded to pink from the sun. A crack cut through the front wall and all of its windows had long since been stolen or broken, but otherwise this building was stable. Unlike some of the others, it hadn't yet fallen to a storm or time, and likely wouldn't for a few more years.

She also knew no one had claimed this place for themselves. At least, not since she'd last been through here. That mark was her own, a warning to anyone who might have been looking for a place to live. There were enough empty buildings that competition wasn't a problem. Illi had just wanted to be left alone.

She'd gotten her wish. She'd been left alone until she'd grown sick of it. The silence hadn't quieted her memories of the night of the Siege. If anything, the silence had made them louder.

She led Canthem inside. Scuffs in the accumulated sand and dust on the floor indicated someone else had been here recently, but the pans and bowls she'd scavenged sat untouched next to the empty hearth. Everything potentially valuable she'd taken with her.

The walls were still clean, at least. She'd scrubbed the scorch marks and repainted with scrounged paint when she'd moved in. The smell of smoke and ash was long gone and now all Illi could smell was dust and the cinnamon that seemed to whirl around Canthem like a cloak.

"Why—?" Canthem started to ask again.

"We lost more than half of our population to a plague," said Illi. It was the truth, in a way. The curse that had forced the dead awake again had spread like a plague, through their pumps and their water. She didn't have the words to explain the Siege at that moment, not when she was trying so hard to forget the possibility of another. She held up a finger. "Wait here."

She took the stairs two at a time, trusting Canthem to stay below. The crack in the wall outside was wider up here and sunlight spilled in through holes in the roof. She moved on quick feet, wary of lingering too long. The second floor was unstable. It was also where she'd hidden her things in case she ever needed to return.

Stringwork still dangled beside a broken window, the jagged pieces of glass at odds with the delicate designs. A badly thrown clay pot accumulated dust on the floor next to a number of other useless trinkets. Useless to anyone else, that was. These were the few things Illi had scavenged from her home after the Siege. Her mother's shears, bright orange with rust. Her father's spice jars, melted and deformed by fire, whatever spices they'd once contained now little more than ash and dust. A simple, silver ring, which had once fit but was now too small. Half a clay figure that was supposed to have looked like her mother. The only things that remained of her family.

She hadn't been strong enough to take them with her when she'd left the abandoned platforms. But she also hadn't been strong enough to destroy them. Now she passed them over without a second glance, knowing that if she looked, she'd linger. If she lingered, she'd stay. If she stayed, she'd become overwhelmed. And then nothing would get done.

She focused instead on a poorly patched leather sandbag, a target drawn in kohl on one side. She hefted the target over her shoulder and brought it back downstairs, where she dropped it in front of the hearth.

"That's our target?" asked Canthem with a pinch of incredulity.

Illi sighted along a knife. "I can make a smaller one," she offered.

She stood on the opposite side of the room. Breathed out. As the last of the air left her lungs, she stepped and turned and threw. *Thunk*. The center of the target had sprouted a hilt. Canthem clapped.

"Fine for a show. But I still don't understand how that can help in a real fight."

Illi yanked the knife out. Sand dribbled from the wound she'd made in the target. As she walked across the room, she held the knife up as if to inspect it. But when she was halfway across, she stopped, turned, and threw. Canthem jerked back as the knife just missed their shoulder. They twisted around to see where it had gone.

When they turned back to Illi, she was already in their face. She threw the series of jabs that Canthem had taught her, pressing them backward even as they easily blocked each one. Then their back hit the wall and their next block was off just enough that Illi could slide underneath. Illi pressed her forearm against their throat, another knife pricking their side.

"That's how," said Illi.

"All right," wheezed Canthem. "You can let go now."

Illi lingered another moment, then pushed herself back. Annoyed, she said, "Don't let me win again."

"What?" asked Canthem innocently. "You think I went easy on you?"

"Yes." Illi let the knife dangle between them.

"Well, maybe I was hoping for a kiss."

Illi pointed the knife at their chest. "If you don't give this your all, I'll give you a kiss. Just not the kind you want."

Canthem held up their hands. "All right. Business, then."

Illi picked up her other knife. "Throwing a knife will probably never win a fight for you," she said. "But it's a tool just like the things you taught me. And it can be a useful distraction."

Canthem raised an eyebrow and pushed themself away from the wall. "How did you learn all of this?"

Illi grinned, showing all of her teeth. "I was trained."

"But for what purpose?" Canthem straightened their wrap, but their gaze never left Illi's. "I mean no offense, but fighting guul doesn't require anything beyond knowing which end of a sword to hold. But you—you fight like you were born to it. You already have training that takes years, the kind that I received when I joined the guard. But this city doesn't seem like it needs or can even sustain its own army."

"Not an army, no."

Illi hesitated, not sure how to handle their curiosity. Most of the guards she'd trained with before had seemed content to share just that experience with her and nothing more about themselves—or her. Illi didn't want, or need, anything beyond that.

Even though it'd been years since the last contract had been given out and even longer since Drum Chief Amastan had all but forbidden them, speaking the truth of their family and profession wasn't exactly encouraged. No one needed to know that she and her cousins were trained assassins. Such knowledge could only cause anger and resentment, even panic, in the city, even if those same assassins had saved Ghadid.

But what did it matter if Canthem knew the truth? They'd be leaving in a few days anyway and she'd never see them again.

"I was trained to kill."

Canthem shrugged. "So was I."

Illi stared. That wasn't the reaction she'd been expecting. Then she realized her error. "No—I mean, I'm an assassin. Or, well, was. My cousins, all of us—we were trained since we could walk. We keep this city safe. The drum chiefs and watchmen could only ever do so much—we did the rest. At least, we did until the Siege."

Canthem waited, expectant. They were good at that. But patience wouldn't get them anything this time.

"But we've moved on from being assassins," said Illi brightly. "Now we're the only thing protecting Ghadid from guul and any other horrors the world might throw at us."

"That's pessimistic," said Canthem.

"That's life."

Canthem raised both eyebrows incredulously, then shook their head. "But none of that explains why you're throwing away perfectly good weapons. Surely you didn't go around tossing knives at people as an assassin."

"No," admitted Illi. She twirled the knife by its handle. "It was more an exercise in precision and control than it was practical. But that precision has helped me with other aspects of my fighting. It takes a cool heart and steady hand to throw well. That's also useful when you're surrounded by guul."

Now Canthem leaned forward, eyes bright. "That's what I'd like to hear about. My company in the guard deals almost exclusively with the guul. Anything you can teach me that will work against them . . . well, I'd like to know it."

Illi stopped twirling her knife and held it out to Canthem, hilt first. "Then let's stop wasting time."

Canthem took the knife, fingers wrapping around its hilt in a fist. Illi clicked her tongue and adjusted their grip.

"You want your thumb *here*," she said. "This gives you the cleanest release. Otherwise you're going to get wobble and it's not going to go as far or as fast. Okay." She stepped back, nodded at the target. "Try it."

Canthem breathed, then threw. The knife clattered off the wall. Canthem grunted, but Illi was already pressing another knife into their hand.

"Here, you gotta be in line with your target. And also you've just . . . got it all wrong."

She pulled Canthem over a few inches, then guided their arm through the motion of throwing, pointing out the finer details as she nudged over their foot and leaned into them to shift their weight. This time when Canthem threw, the knife smacked the target before clattering on the ground.

Illi adjusted a few more things—back a few inches, turn the hand *here*, quicker release—keenly aware of the knife and the target, but also of Canthem's sturdy physicality, their muscles as they stood still for her, tense but pliable. They were so strong—stronger, even, than Illi. Yet at the moment, they were like dough beneath her hands. She could get used to that.

On Canthem's third throw, the knife found the target, if a bit high. Canthem let out a low whoop, but Illi was already pressing another knife into their hand.

"How many of these do you have?" asked Canthem, incredulous.

"Let's just say I'm never without a weapon."

Illi kept adjusting Canthem's form with each attempt until, finally, the knife bloomed from the target's center. Then she left them to stretch their shoulder as she retrieved her knives. She set the blades in a line on the ground and pressed the first into Canthem's other hand. They stared at her.

All Illi said was, "Again."

It was another hour before Illi was satisfied. The target was bleeding sand from the many holes, but Illi already had a length of thread and needle and started mending the tears while Canthem collected her knives. They gathered them on the floor nearby, counted them, and shook their head.

"You go everywhere with these?"

Illi shrugged. "Don't you?"

Canthem laughed. "Even in the Wastes, I just have my sword and a dagger or two. That's more than enough against guul. But you don't expect guul to attack you all the way up here, do you?"

Illi stabbed the target with her needle, her mouth suddenly dry for a different reason. "They have before."

"What? Really?"

But Illi wasn't ready for that conversation, so she didn't answer. She tied off the thread and stood, leaving the target next to the hearth. Canthem turned at the sound of her footsteps, expression inscrutable beneath that sands-cursed tagel.

It'd been so good to train again, as she once had with her cousins. Back when being a cousin was more complicated than merely separating a guuli's head from its body. Back when being a cousin required years of practice and refined skills. Back when it could easily take a few months to complete a contract.

Illi had never had a chance at a contract; she'd still been several years shy of her test when the Siege happened. She could only imagine what it would have been like, surveilling a mark. Learning everything about them, their schedule, their habits, their predilections. Slipping into their home or their life undetected. Stealing what was most important to them: their life.

Of course, a life wasn't always the most important thing. Heru seemed to be particularly, dangerously keen on the sajaami.

Illi stretched her fingers, feeling the soreness in her muscles and watching Canthem watch her. But at the same time, she was also in Heru's lab, standing beneath the glowing orb. What affixed it to the ceiling? What kept it there?

And could she take it?

Illi set her feet as Canthem had taught her and spread her hands to show she was unarmed. "Your turn."

Canthem glanced from the knives to Illi. "How do I know you're not hiding any more blades somewhere?"

Illi smirked. "Why don't you find out?"

When Canthem attacked, Illi let her muscle memory take

over so she could split her concentration teasing apart the problem of the sajaami. It was almost too simple. Remove the sajaami, remove the problem. All she had to do was get the orb to Merrabel, and in another day, both would be gone.

No one would need to know that Heru had been hiding something so dangerous in the city. He could stay and continue his research. He'd be safe. They'd all be safe. And one day, he'd find a way to stop the guul forever.

Illi was a cousin. She'd never had a contract, but she still knew how to pull one off: observe the mark, wait for an opportunity, and then act. She had the observation down; she'd been working alongside Heru and the orb for almost five years. She—

Illi's back hit the wall. She'd let her attention slip and Canthem had trapped her. That was all right. She knew exactly what to do when trapped.

She came at Canthem hard and fast, heedless of their strikes. Pain blossomed along her arms, but they were afterthoughts. They'd be bruises later, but later didn't matter. What mattered was *now*.

And *now* she was tired of being backed into a corner. *Now* she was tired of thinking. *Now* she wasn't about to go down without a fight.

"You know, you can slow down a little," said Canthem.

Illi blocked their next attack, slid in, and swept their feet. They hit the ground with a thud and a laugh. They started to get up, but Illi had a knee in their stomach and a need in her chest.

She leaned down so that her lips brushed across Canthem's ear and whispered, "Never."

7

The hardest part wasn't waiting for a time when Heru wouldn't be in his lab. No, Heru was nothing if not predictable. While he occasionally demanded Illi bring him this or that, he preferred to acquire the bulk of his supplies himself. Allegedly to assure quality, but sometimes Illi suspected even Heru got lonely.

The hardest part wasn't sneaking into his lab. No, a weighted curtain might keep out a breeze, but not a cousin. Heru had wards in place to alert him if anyone crossed his threshold, but half of those he'd taught Illi how to put down herself, and the other half Illi had watched him place. It was a simple thing to disconnect a string here and step over a line of salt there.

The hardest part wasn't even gathering the courage to act. If Heru caught her, she had a hundred excuses at the ready. She also had a tranquilizer that would put even the fussiest mule to sleep. But despite all of Thana's dire warnings over the years, Illi knew Heru wouldn't hurt her. She was a dependable piece of lab equipment and if anything he'd be too confused that she acted at all to touch her.

No, the hardest part was getting *to* the orb.

The orb hung over twenty feet in the air, far from any walls. The building Heru had built his lab in had once been two stories, but half of the second had collapsed under the stress of the fires spread during the Siege and a number of squatters had picked away at the other half until it was a single, tall room. Heru must've secured the orb first before filling the lab with all of his tables and equipment. Illi could see how, in an empty room, one might reach the ceiling, how one might secure that thick chain, how one might fix those wide bolts.

But now there were long tables in her way, now there were countless perfectly lined and perfectly stacked jars and flasks and bowls and vials. If she'd had a few days, she could move it all and stack a few tables and have the orb between her hands and then put it all back where it belonged. But she only had the drip of minutes while Heru was doing his rounds.

So she'd found another way up.

A rope dangled through the hole in the ceiling where one of the orb's thick bolts had been. Three more kept it firmly in place, but not for much longer. It'd taken her most of the afternoon to first find the bolts on the roof, then pry one loose. They'd been hidden by more than just dust and sand. Someone—Thana, probably—had been smart enough to nestle them beneath a perfectly fitted roof tile. And then they'd tightened each bolt until it would never move again.

Heru clearly had very little intention of ever removing the sajaami.

But with enough cursing and sweat and strategically applied oil, the bolt had loosened. Then it'd come free and fallen the twenty or so feet to the cushion she'd "forgotten" on the floor below. She'd closed her eyes as it hit with a soft *plop*, and held her breath as she waited for Heru—across the room, back turned, head down over his notes—to notice. But he hadn't looked up, let alone moved.

She'd secured a rope and left it on the roof. Then she'd gone below and brought Heru his bowl and his knife and his towel and another roll and she'd palmed the bolt. When Heru departed at his usual time, she'd returned to the roof and dropped the rope through the hole where the bolt had been. Now she tugged that rope, confident that the hardest part was over. All she had to do was climb.

She still wasn't completely certain how she was going to get the sajaami *down*, but she'd figure it out once she was up there. After all, Heru had attached the orb somehow, and while he was proficient at his particular work, he wasn't exactly an engineering genius.

Illi tucked the rope between her feet and began to climb. Hand over hand over hand until her head brushed the ceiling and the orb hung before instead of above her. Then she held the rope between her feet, letting it take most of her weight as she examined the chain holding the glass orb in place.

Each link was as thick as a finger and they coiled tightly around each other. It'd be a challenge to break, but Illi had come ready for a challenge. From her belt, she freed the extra-thick glass cutter she'd bought at the market earlier, the one the merchant had assured her could also cut through metal, looped the rope around her arm, and reached for the orb.

As soon as her fingers brushed the glass, every single hair on her body stood on end. Even her scalp itched as the hair there fought against her tight braids. It was like the static that preceded a sandstorm. Every grain of her screamed *danger.*

But something else whispered, *Who are you?*

Illi yanked her hand back. The orb had been glowing since she'd entered the lab, but now it seemed to pulse brighter. At the same time, the thin lines scrawled across the flask seemed to darken and thicken—but that had to be a trick of the light.

She could feel the water inside, but she knew if she reached as if she were healing, she wouldn't be able to use it. That water was already locked in to another use.

Illi swallowed and pushed down her rising fear. That sensation, that voice—that had to have been one of Heru's wards. One that would frighten her away. She wasn't frightened, though; she knew exactly what Heru could do. Or, at least she thought she did. He'd never gone out of his way to actually teach her.

But she had to do this. The sajaami had to go, for the city's sake, if not Heru's own.

She examined the orb from all sides, her legs starting to tire from keeping her up. But there were no lines of chalk, of salt, of ink. No wards aside from those scrawled on the flask inside the orb. Nothing to explain that peculiar prickling sensation and certainly nothing that might alert Heru.

She reached again and this time when her fingers brushed the orb, a warmth spread across them as if she were catching a breath in her hand. Her mouth filled with the taste of summer heat, and something seemed to catch her and push back.

Easy as breaking glass.

That's all it would take. She didn't need to deal with the chains. All she had to do was crack the orb. But as soon as the thought came to her, she yanked her hand back and eyed the orb warily. That was definitely *not* what she needed to do. She might not know much about sajaam, but she doubted taking away a layer of the protection that kept it here would be wise.

Instead, she loosened her wrap, unknotting it here and there until she had enough give that she could cradle a large glass orb in the fabric without having to touch it. Maybe she should have brought gloves, too. She touched the leather charm at her neck and was unsurprised to find that it was warmer than usual. This would've been a good time for the added protection glass charms would give, but the leather ones would have to do.

Without touching the orb this time, she brought the glass cutter up to the first chain. The blades bit into the metal just as the white curtain over the doorway parted with a *swish*.

Illi was already halfway down the rope before Heru had stepped fully into his lab. She let go still a few feet up and landed with a soft thump. She was straightening just as Heru's eye found her. Then his gaze slid past her to the rope and his eye narrowed to a thin slit.

"What in all the seven hells do you think you're doing?"

"Cleaning." Illi gestured toward the ceiling with one hand as she slid the glass cutter back into her belt with the other. "You've got so many cobwebs up there, I thought I'd clear some out."

Heru's eye flicked up, toward the orb, and Illi realized too late she shouldn't have pointed it out. The orb was glowing even brighter than usual. Heru's mood darkened further.

"I know exactly how many cobwebs are up there," snapped Heru. "And that number is: *zero*. I've warned you before not to go anywhere near that orb."

No point in denying it. Illi crossed her arms. "It can't stay. You know it can't. The drum chiefs know about the sajaami now. They won't let it stay in Ghadid—and if you don't give it to Merrabel, they'll throw you out with it."

Heru went to his work bench, where he began uncovering bowls he'd left out and retrieving tools from underneath. As he moved, he said, "Allow me to count the many ways you're mistaken. One, the drum chiefs do *not* know about the sajaami; only Amastan does. Two, he's beholden to Thana, who has proven her loyalty to me and I don't foresee her betrayal except under the direst of circumstances. Three, Merrabel is insufficiently educated about the subject of sajaam and therefore is unacceptable as its keeper. Four, I cannot simply *remove* the sajaami from its confinement." He paused, one hand still outstretched for a vial, to glare at Illi. "Anything less than the most careful preparations could see the sajaami freed. *Including* mishandling by a foolish girl who has just proven how very little she's learned despite spending so much time in such prestigious and genius company."

Illi didn't rise to Heru's bait. From him, that was practically a compliment. Instead, she approached his bench, leaving the rope to hang alone in the center of the room. "All right. Then how do we start those preparations?"

"There's no point," said Heru. "They'll take days. The caravan won't wait that long for us. Therefore, the sajaami stays."

Illi shook her head. "Why didn't you say earlier? Surely Merrabel will understand. She doesn't want the sajaami free."

"I do, in fact, recall her from our academic days together in collegium," said Heru. "Unless she has changed greatly, she's too stubborn to listen. If I had explained the situation, she'd only have found a way to wrest the sajaami from my control sooner. This way she'll be forced to leave with empty hands."

"There's nothing stopping her from staying, either."

Heru shrugged. "Then she may stay. The important thing is that the sajaami doesn't leave."

"But the sajaami *can't* stay," said Illi, exasperated. "If Merrabel is right—"

"I refuse to work under duress," interrupted Heru. "With sufficient time, we will arrive at a solution."

Illi's stomach sank. "You have no plan at all for the sajaami."

"I always have a plan." But he spoke a little too quickly and his gaze stayed trained on the bowls in front of him. He coughed and added, "I don't see why you're so upset. This doesn't concern you."

"Doesn't concern me?" echoed Illi, incredulous. "*Doesn't concern me?*"

"Repeating my words back to me does little to clarify—"

"I lost everything once," said Illi. "I'm not going to stand by and lose it again because you refuse to see reason."

"You know nothing of which you speak." Heru turned away as he measured out powder from one of the bowls into a vial. "Leave the matter to those who are experienced in it."

"You never gave me a *chance* to become experienced."

"You do not know what you ask, girl," said Heru, more to the vial he was holding up to the light than Illi. He placed the vial gently in a rack, then brushed off his hands. "What does that have to do with our current situation?"

Illi sucked in another breath. She was getting too wound up. Heru would only listen to reason. Except—he *wasn't* listening to reason. That was the problem. The sajaami was a blind spot for him. Every other problem he'd attacked head-on, chipping away at the what-ifs until he had a solid plan. Finding a solution for the guul had only taken a few weeks. Figuring out a way to purify their entire water supply had only taken a few days.

So why was the sajaami taking him almost a decade?

The curtain swished. Illi spun, hand going to her belt. Merrabel paused in the doorway, her gaze skipping across Illi to Heru before finally rising up to the orb. A ghost of a smile twitched at her lips, there and gone in the span of a heartbeat. She crossed the room, gloved hands clasped before her.

"I've come for the sajaami."

Heru ignored her as he finished pouring a thin yellow liquid into another vial. Without looking up, he said, "Then you'll leave disappointed."

Merrabel peered into one of his bowls. "Really, Sametket? I thought we'd come to an understanding. Were the notes I dropped off for you yesterday not convincing?"

"They were convincing, yes," said Heru. "They convinced me that the frequency of guul attacks has increased and continues to increase not only in our vicinity but all along the edges of the Wastes. They convinced me that the area we define as the Wastes is expanding. They convinced me that there has been a measurable atmospheric imbalance, leading to a sudden and extreme disparity in precipitation both inland and along the coast. They were thoroughly convincing in regards to the possibility of a disruption in our local ecosystem."

"Wonderful." Merrabel clapped her hands and smiled. "Then you comprehend the severity of the problem."

"The severity, yes." Heru set his last vial in the rack along with the others and finally lifted his gaze. "But not the cause. You jump to conclusions with no basis in reality, no grounding in true research. *Something* is happening, yes, but I see no evidence that this something is linked to the sajaami, let alone caused by it."

Merrabel's smile became a rictus grin. "Sametket—you said yourself that the sajaami's release caused changes in the Wastes—"

"I *hypothesized* that a release of that magnitude *could* affect its immediate environment," said Heru. "Until you can present data that confirms your *hypothesis*, the orb will stay with me and, until my research is complete, I will stay in this city." Heru abruptly turned away and picked up another bowl. "May your trip back to Hathage be uneventful."

Merrabel let out a sigh, but it held no disappointment, only regret. "Then you force my hand, Sametket. I wonder what your drum chiefs will have to say about this."

"They will see reason."

"*Heru*," hissed Illi. "Tell her the sajaami can't just be removed."

"Oh, *that*," said Merrabel. "Sametket is overly cautious. I'm certain your drum chiefs will help convince him that swiftness is a virtue." Merrabel pushed herself away from Heru's bench. "Last chance, Sametket."

Heru only grunted in response.

Merrabel headed for the door. Illi slipped in front of her, hands up. "Please. Why don't you just stay in Ghadid and work with him? There will be another caravan."

"Not necessarily," said Merrabel. "Not with the way this disruption is progressing. The guul attacks are increasing—it won't be long before the caravans are no longer willing to take such a risk for salt and glass. Besides, Sametket has made his choice. He knows the consequences."

She stepped around Illi as neatly as if she were avoiding a mangy cat. Illi turned to Heru, but he was bent over his bench once more. Merrabel reached the door unimpeded. She paused as if expecting further objections, then pushed through the curtain and was gone.

Illi watched the curtain settle. Merrabel took her dissonance with her and, for a few moments, the lab was as it always had been. But that safety was only an illusion.

"You're just going to let her tell the drum chiefs about the sajaami?" asked Illi without turning. When the only reply was the slosh of water, she continued. "If she does, Amastan won't be able to protect you. Neither will I."

A bowl clinked as it was set down. The sloshing stopped. "I

saved this miserable city from a plague that would've bound all of your jaan and turned you into mindless slaves to the Empire. You're indebted to me."

"That debt doesn't give you license to do whatever you want," said Illi. "You know what the people think of you. You know they've only put up with you because you stay out of sight and out of mind. Because you're not a threat." Illi gestured at the orb. "But that? *That's* a threat."

"For the thousandth time, it is *contained*—"

"I know!" said Illi. Then, quieter, "I know. But they don't."

"That's not my problem."

"It should be."

Illi turned and found Heru drying glass with a towel. *Maybe he's the one bringing them,* the merchant had said. Her gaze flicked to the orb, still glowing steadily. Heru wasn't drawing the guul, but if Merrabel was right it wouldn't matter who or what in this room was truly at fault. They'd all be turned out.

Ghadid will protect itself.

Well, Illi was a part of Ghadid.

"You understand what she's going to do, don't you?"

"She's going to bring her complaint before the Circle."

"No." Illi took a deep breath. "She's going to present her hypothesis as fact and misrepresent your work."

Heru stiffened. He lifted his eye to stare directly at her. "Don't try to manipulate me, girl."

"If you stay here and hide, you won't be able to correct her. She'll convince the drum chiefs that the sajaami *is* causing whatever this disruption is. They can't possibly understand the intricacies of your research if you're not there to discuss them. She'll gloss over important details. She'll jump to conclusions."

"She doesn't comprehend my research," said Heru, voice cold.

"Yet you're okay letting her explain it to the drum chiefs by herself."

"No. I'm not." Heru put the bowl on its shelf and folded the towel on the table. "If they must learn about my research, then they'll learn it from me. Only I can give an accurate representation of my methods and my results, heretofore."

"You'd better hurry," goaded Illi. "She's got a pretty good head start."

She shouldn't have bothered; Heru was already halfway to the door. He pushed through the curtain without bothering to see if she was following.

Heru paused in the bright light of midafternoon and seemed briefly disoriented, as if he couldn't remember which way was civilization. Then he found east and started down that direction, Illi trailing by a solid dozen feet. As they passed over bridges and crossed empty platform after empty platform, the distant sound of wind became a distinct rumble which in turn became the grumble of a crowd.

The clumps of people Illi had walked by earlier on her way to steal the sajaami had paused their shelling, their mending, and their knitting to exchange hushed words or had disappeared entirely, their doors shut and their windows drawn. Curtains twitched as they passed, curiosity getting the better of some. Silence trailed Heru as the people still outside, still around, abruptly stopped their whispers to turn, stare, and even some—bravely, stupidly—to point.

While Heru ignored them as he always did, Illi no longer could and her fear wrapped tight around her throat.

They met the crowd on the next platform, spilling like sand

between the buildings, at first a few grains here and there and then so dense Heru had to shove his way through. But it only took one touch for the awareness of his presence to spread like cracks through glass, the crowd shattering before him, only to re-form immediately behind, leaving Heru a bubble of space to move through, unimpeded.

She kept close now, sliding into the spaces he'd opened before they could narrow and disappear. Conversations spun all around her, disorienting and dissonant, but she caught enough to know that the crowd was curious, confused, and concerned, but not angry. Whatever Merrabel had planned, she hadn't done it yet. Illi could still stop her.

But as Heru passed through, the conversations slowly changed. Concern deepened, and more than one person wondered what *he* was doing here. By the time they'd reached the center of the platform and the crowd's attention, the whispers had turned to mutters and Illi knew she'd made a mistake thinking Heru could change anybody's mind.

But it was too late for regret and perhaps it was time for Ghadid to see Heru for who he was—an earnest if arrogant person, and not the monster they so wished him to be.

The crowd gave way at the dais, revealing a figure all alone at its center, still as stone. Merrabel shone in the morning sun like a star herself, her arms behind her back and her chin up, waiting. It took Heru two attempts to climb onto the dais. Merrabel ignored him.

"Barca." Heru's voice carried easily above the crowd. "You are being rash. I would expect a scientist of your standing to understand the importance of thoroughly collating and curating your research before presenting your findings to the unwashed masses.

They must be properly calibrated to avoid undue associations or panic, and that assuming your conclusions are not incorrect—which, by the way, they are."

Merrabel started to tap her foot, but she didn't answer or even turn to Heru. Illi's fingers brushed across one of the knives at her hip, but the hundreds of pairs of eyes on Merrabel were better protection than any armor.

"They won't understand you," continued Heru. "Come down from here—"

"Someone called for a drum chief?"

On the other side of the dais: a raised hand, fingers glittering with rings. The onlookers around them gave way, revealing a figure wearing a green so violent it could've been cut from a gem. Intricate black embroidery spilled down the front and across the sleeves in geometric tangles that seemed to move on their own. Gold hung around their neck and from their ears. Illi recognized the colors as those belonging to Drum Chief Basil.

Merrabel loosened at her voice, finally looking around. "I did. I have something I must discuss with the Circle. It's of the utmost importance for the security and safety of your city."

"Then come down from there, ma," said Drum Chief Basil. "And we'll assemble the Circle. There's no need to cause a scene. We have protocols for this sort of thing, you know, and rules for when someone can use a dais."

"That's what *I* was saying," groused Heru.

"What's going on?" asked another voice.

Hope fluttered in Illi's chest as she turned with the crowd and saw Amastan pushing his way through. He'd be able to handle this. He was quick and clever and—

"Ah, two drum chiefs," said Merrabel. "That will suffice. It's time we discuss the sajaami this man has been hiding in your city."

The roar in Illi's ears was so loud she didn't at first realize the crowd had fallen dead silent. All the breath had left her lungs, otherwise she'd be screaming. Drum Chief Basil stared dumbly at Merrabel, her lips forming an unvoiced, *what?* But Amastan had climbed onto the platform and positioned himself in front of Merrabel and Heru, hands raised.

"The Circle will convene immediately to discuss this accusation," he called as the crowd began to mutter and simmer. "In the meantime, it's only that—an accusation. No judgment has been made. You will disperse."

The murmurings roiled anew, this time tinged with fear, panic—and anger.

"—should never have let him—"

"—*blasphemy*—"

"—but sajaam are a myth—"

"En-marab!"

The last one was hurled like an insult and behind it came more: "Monster!" "Demon!" "Leave!" Merrabel basked in the simmering resentment while Heru glowered. Something hit the dais at Heru's feet: a rock. The crowd began to boil as people shoved their way forward, brandishing fists and shouts. More objects were thrown at the dais: an empty skewer, another rock, a metal bowl. The last connected with Heru's leg.

Amastan wilted under the onslaught. He tried to shout above the crowd's anger, but his voice was drowned out. Drum Chief Basil joined Amastan on the dais and lifted her arms high.

"*Disperse,*" she boomed.

A few people jumped. But the crowd only grew more agitated. A second rock hit the dais and a third smacked Basil's upraised arm. People shouted and pushed against each other, trying to get to the center and to Heru. Illi was shoved into another body, who growled at her and swung a fist. Illi ducked and turned to the side, but somebody grabbed one of her braids. She retaliated with a jab to the neck. They gurgled and let go.

Too close, glass shattered. A hush blew across the riot, sobering as a winter wind. Thrown objects and fights were one thing, but breaking glass was unlucky, verging on blasphemy.

Drum Chief Basil took advantage of the lull. "I said, *disperse!*"

The watchmen finally arrived, diving into the crowd from all sides and forcing people apart with their elbows when possible and their swords when necessary. The anger still simmered, but the rage had broken, and now the crowd began to split. A few people hurried down the streets and they were soon followed by larger clumps and groups. The watchmen only harried them until they'd left the platform's center, then they pulled back toward the dais. Their swords remained drawn, but Illi slipped past them before they could stop her.

Basil waited until the center contained only a few persistent dregs, then jumped down from the dais. Her gaze swept the area, lingering on a pane of shattered glass, before landing on Illi and narrowing. But Heru slid over the edge of the dais and confronted Basil before she could speak.

"I demand the opportunity to make my case," said Heru. "Barca is misrepresenting the facts of the situation in a most dangerous manner."

"We'll convene the Circle immediately," said Basil. "But it appears the damage has already been done. At this point, facts no longer matter."

"Facts *always* matter," said Heru.

Merrabel joined them at her leisure, a soft smile warming her face. Illi caught Amastan's glare before the drum chief could smooth it away, but Merrabel didn't appear to notice or care.

"I'm ready whenever the Circle is," Merrabel announced to no one in particular.

"Right." Amastan sighed. "Then come with us."

Illi started to follow them, but before she could get a few feet, Amastan stopped and put a hand on her shoulder. The others continued without them.

"Go home, Illi," said Amastan. "This is between us and the foreigner."

"But—you know Heru," protested Illi. "He needs someone to translate for him. He doesn't know how to talk to people, especially drum chiefs. The Circle won't be fair."

"Your presence won't help him," said Amastan. "Not this time. If anything, it'll look even worse if he's seen associating with a cousin. They'll think he's corrupted you. I'm sorry, Illi. Take this time and prepare for the worst."

"No," said Illi, shaking her head. "No. You're wrong. This is wrong. Heru has only ever helped us. We can't do this to him. We *need* him."

Amastan looked exhausted. "I'll do what I can. And so should you—go home, Illi."

8

Thunk.

The knife hit the center of the target, its repaired seams already leaking fresh sand. Four other knives stuck out of the target in a perfect semicircle. Illi had already freed a sixth knife from the strap across her chest and was sighting down its blade.

Thunk.

"Murdering that piece of leather isn't going to make the Circle decide any faster," said Mo.

She sat at the hearth, repairing an old wrap, white for mourning. A pile of them waited for her at the table, another reminder of the seven-year rite that Illi didn't want to think about. "You know they like to take their time on these things. Go outside, get some air. If Amastan comes by while you're gone, I'll make him wait."

"Thanks, but I'm going to stay." Illi approached the target and removed her knives. The cuts in the leather bled sand, spilling the fine grains all over the floor. If she didn't remember to sweep it up later, Thana would have her skin. "If Heru is thrown out, then I'll need to be ready. I'll be the only one who can stop the guul."

Mo paused her stitching and pursed her lips. "That's not true.

You have your cousins. You have Thana. All of us are working together to stop the guul."

"Maybe." Illi returned to her spot on the floor a fair distance from the target. She took two steps back and reset her stance. "You're all very effective at defense. But they're not stopping. There's more of them all the time. At this rate, we'll be overwhelmed one day, and that day will be sooner than we can prepare for. Heru was the only one trying to find the reason the guul keep coming. And I'm the only one who knows anything about his research. So. It's up to me."

"We'll find other ways to stop the guul permanently, without resorting to blasphemy. The marab will find their own way. I might not have all the answers now, but you're not alone in this, Illi."

Illi sighted. Threw. The knife hit the target dead center. "The marab haven't found a way yet. Only Heru's methods have actually worked."

"And he's the one with a sajaami in his possession," said a familiar voice.

Illi started. Amastan stood in the doorway, the bright light of midday turning him into a featureless silhouette. She hadn't even heard him arrive. Amastan stepped inside and closed the door, cutting off the light and becoming just an older man in a dusty wrap. If possible, he looked even more exhausted than earlier.

"What happened? What did you decide?" demanded Illi.

"Heru can't stay," said Amastan.

"No," said Illi. "*No*—you don't understand. The sajaami can't be removed. I know he doesn't explain things well, I should have been there—"

Amastan held up a hand, stifling her protests. "Nothing Heru—or you—could have said would have changed our decision. The moment that foreigner proclaimed in a platform's center that he was harboring a sajaami, Heru's fate was written. This city is still far too fragile and new to risk allowing him to stay. We would lose the confidence of the people. They would take matters into their own hands and then where would we be? Chaos, confusion, hysteria. You saw only a hint of that when the foreigner spoke. No. Heru must leave."

"He *saved* our city," snapped Illi. "You're only doing this to save your own hide."

"Illi—"

"Where is he?" she interrupted. "Is he already gone?"

"No. We gave him a day to prepare. He'll leave with the caravan first thing tomorrow. Where's Thana? She should know about this."

Illi didn't hear Mo's answer. A day wasn't anywhere near enough time. Her pulse thudded too loud in her ears. She was already halfway to the door before anyone noticed she was leaving.

"Illi, wait—where are you going?" asked Mo.

But Illi ignored her and threw open the door. The roar that had overwhelmed her hearing earlier returned and with it a thickening sense of dread.

It seemed obscene that nothing had changed in the streets outside, on her platform or the next. Surely everyone else would feel the effects of the Circle's decision, would be muttering or rioting in the streets. Yet the sun still shone as bright as ever and her neighbors smiled as she passed. A chicken *ur-ur-ur*ed from its cage and a baker cooled his wares on his steps.

Even Heru's abandoned platform was unchanged. Still as

empty as ever. Still as silent as ever. Only the stones weren't as well-swept as usual, sand gritting beneath her sandals.

Illi pushed aside the white curtain without knocking, expecting to find Heru hard at work packing his things or hard at work pretending nothing had changed. She certainly didn't expect what she found.

Everything had changed. The familiar had been smashed, shattered across the hard stone ground. Glass glittered everywhere, an obscene reflection of the night sky, as if its stars had been bled out across this floor.

Liquid pooled, still drying, in the cracks between the stones. Little had been left untouched. Whoever had done this had even gone to the trouble of overturning one of the metal benches, smashing the glass in front of the hearth, and dousing the fire within. Even the half-eaten roll had been ground to crumbs underfoot. And if their intent hadn't been clear enough through the destruction alone, they'd scribbled in black charcoal all over the walls.

LEAVE

MONSTER

DEMON

In an instant, Illi took it all in. But what caught her attention and made her blood run cold was at the center of the room. The rope was gone. In its place was Heru, white wrap smeared with dust and dirt, hunched over a glass orb. Overhead hung nothing, which was just as startling as the chaos in the room. The glass beakers and flasks had accumulated slowly over the years, shifting their places. But the orb had always been there.

Now it spilled warm light across the glittering mess, returning some life to Heru's pale features. He looked up, both his glass eye and his real one piercing Illi and nailing her to the spot.

Sweat streaked his forehead and turned the edges of his tagel dark blue, sticking it to his face. Effort strained his features as he pressed with both hands on either side of the orb.

The orb pulsed brighter and Illi saw the crack that ran down its center. Blood trickled from beneath one of Heru's hands. All at once, Illi understood. He was keeping the orb together. If he let go . . .

Fear touched her chest with one icy finger, then pressed its full palm against her sternum. Illi's heart sped up and a high-pitched buzzing filled her ears. Despite the orb's—the *sajaami's*—light, the room was dark. She could smell smoke, blood, death. It would happen again. If the sajaami got out, Ghadid would be destroyed. And it was all her fault. If she hadn't left the rope behind, they couldn't have reached the orb. They would've ignored it completely. They—

"Took you long enough," snapped Heru, interrupting Illi's spiraling panic. "Come here. I require your assistance."

There was no time for guilt. Illi went to Heru's side, the light from the orb brightening with each step, and crouched next to him. This close, she could feel that same electric tension she'd felt when she touched the orb earlier today. This close, she could see that Heru was shaking with the effort of holding the orb together. Water seeped from between his fingers, snaking across the floor in a single, thin rivulet.

"What do I do?"

Heru stared at the orb, his silence so long that Illi wasn't sure he'd heard. But just as she was about to ask again, he said, "I can't keep this contained much longer. While I'm tempted to let go and allow the sajaami to find and punish the fools who did this, I'm aware that the sajaami will be indiscriminate in its wrath. Regardless, I'll have to let go eventually, but the flask was compromised in its fall. Even if it wasn't, its long stay within water has damaged the original seal. The flask won't hold long. The sajaami will be free."

"Isn't there any—"

But Heru wasn't done. "There's one option." He looked at Illi now, his single-eyed stare intense. "The sajaami appears to have an affinity for you, although I can't fathom why. Between that affinity and the fact that a human body is a stronger vessel than any glass brings me to the conclusion that I may be able to contain the sajaami in you. But doing so will go much smoother with your consent. So: do you trust me?"

Illi stared. Affinity? Vessel? Her? Did she trust him? No, not even for a second, but—

"I'm running out of time," said Heru through gritted teeth. "An answer. Now. If you will."

It wasn't even a choice. She'd trade her life if it meant Ghadid would be safe. "I'll do it."

"Good." He breathed deep, then let go of the orb, stood, and hurriedly backed away, past Illi. "A warning: this might hurt."

The orb cracked and split, spilling water across the floor. It swirled briefly around Illi's bare feet, warm as a breath, and then it thinned to a shallow puddle. Inside, the flask dropped and sang as glass hit glass. It lay there, unmoving and unthreatening. The cramped, looping script that covered its surface was the only thing differentiating it from the other glass flasks now shattered on Heru's floor.

The flask pulsed with light, drawing her in. She wanted to touch it, to see if it was real. All those years it had hung over her head, its light steady and reassuring. How could such a small container hold such a violent and powerful creature? It shouldn't have been possible.

"Go on," said Heru, his voice low but close. "Pick it up."

Illi didn't need further encouragement. The glass was warm, as if it had been sitting outside in the sunlight. She picked the flask up by its neck. It was lighter than she'd expected, as if it held only air. She shifted her grip to turn it and examine it further. Her thumb smudged one of the lines.

Cra-ack!

The flask exploded, shooting glass across the room. A burning redness burst out of the container, swirling tight and fast like a dust twister. A moment later, Illi felt the pain from the glass sing across her cheek, her arm, her palms. Warmth dribbled down her face and she knew it was blood without checking.

The redness took shape, flinging out arms that spread into wings, a column that split into legs, and a head that split wide with long teeth and roared. The sound shivered down Illi's back, but she stayed soldered to the spot, her bleeding hands held before her.

Then: *click*. A metal bracelet snapped shut around one of her wrists. Illi hadn't even seen Heru move. But then, how could she when the sajaami had filled the center of the room and her sight? Beneath the roar of the sajaami, Heru muttered, quick and fast. He articulated words she'd never heard before with clipped precision, spitting them out fully formed. Too late she realized that this, *this* was what Thana had warned her about.

But Illi didn't have time for regret. Two spots of darkness formed in the sajaami's head, above that horrible mouth. Eyes. They filled with a bright light, the same light the orb had once glowed with. And they found Illi.

"Who has freed Nejm?"

The sajaami's voice boomed as loud as thunder. A small part of Illi noted that now, for certain, Heru would no longer be able to stay in Ghadid. The whole city had to have heard this monster.

"Tell him that you have," hissed Heru in her ear.

Do you trust me? Illi swallowed, her throat dry as dust. "I—I have."

"You did so willingly, mortal? Do you claim ownership or anything so foolish?"

"Willingly . . . ? Yes. And no, I don't claim ownership." She couldn't imagine anyone trying to own this creature that somehow both filled the room and expanded beyond it.

"Then I accept your sacrifice."

"Sacrifice?" echoed Illi. She blinked dry eyes and tried to find Heru, but too late realized she couldn't move, not even her head. Panic spiked through her; she really *was* stuck. "No, I—"

A hand clamped over her mouth, cold and smelling strongly of pungent herbs. The sajaami swirled tighter, losing its shape, becoming a column of bright, violent red. In that moment, all seven years of her time spent in Heru's lab seemed insignificant. Nothing she'd learned could have prepared her for this.

Vessel, Heru had said. *Containment.*

This might hurt.

The fabric of her wrap on her back moved suddenly, as if jerked. Then: pain. Bright and hot and sharp as a knife. She cried out. And that was when the sajaami decided to overcome her.

Nejm broke across her like a storm. It smothered her senses and dulled her world until all she knew was its roar in her sight its redness in her ears its taste of scorching heat and touch of smoke. Pain blossomed fresh down her back, again and again, as if someone were slashing her skin with a knife.

Illi wanted to scream, but her mouth and throat and nose and eyes were clogged with the sajaami.

And then . . . and then . . .

Sand. Heat. Fire. Rage. Illi was vast: a storm, a mountain,

a desert. She could see for miles, the sands spread out below her like a blanket. Cities rose and fell beneath her, but they were insignificant, little more than gnats that buzzed and bit at her ears. She brought the storms the desert needed, the rain and the winds. Beneath her glittered water. A sense of rightness, balance, and calm filled her.

And then the gnats grew and the storms shifted and that balance shattered. The desert that she and her brethren had cultivated and shepherded was spreading beyond their control. The water vanished. The gnats multiplied until they were more than a nuisance: they were a threat.

And they had to be wiped out.

Click.

Illi blinked, disoriented. She was suddenly so small, so impossibly confined. The room was stifling and cramped. She couldn't breathe. Her back was on fire, yet as she shifted her wrap clung to her. A wetness rolled down the back of her leg. But she was still early in her cycle. . . .

Heru stepped away and the full weight of a second metal bracelet pulled Illi's arm down, anchoring her. She breathed. Focused on the pain. Focused on the here.

Her arms trembled as she held them up. On one wrist, a bracelet scorched black. On the other, a bracelet polished silver. All around her, shattered glass.

Thin lines had been inscribed in the metal. Upon closer inspection, Illi could make out letters and words, although they were again in a language she'd never learned. Illi turned her wrists, feeling the weight of the bracelets as they slid across her skin, one cool and one still hot. She breathed. The numbness slipped away. Then—

—*pain*. It flared through Illi as sudden and as hot as flames. A cry brushed the inside of her skull, reached her fingertips, rolled down her back, before withdrawing just as suddenly. But she could feel it now, could trace the sensation back to a point in her chest, small as a pinprick but pulsing with something alien, something that wasn't *her*.

The sajaami.

"How are you feeling?"

Illi blinked again. Heru was in front of her, his eye flicking between hers.

"My back," she managed to choke out, her throat still full of dust.

"Yes, that will hurt for a while. I had to make the necessary marks to contain the sajaami."

"Marks?"

"Runes from an ancient, powerful language that another enmarabi helped to create and I've since refined. Once the cuts heal, you shouldn't feel any pain. At least, not from them."

Cuts. Illi reached behind and ran her fingers over the tattered cloth of her wrap. They came away smeared with blood. She stared at them for a moment, distantly calculating the cost of replacing this wrap, then her legs folded beneath her and she sat down on the warm stone floor with a heavy *thud*.

"What did you do to me?" Her voice sounded so strange, so hollow.

"Only what was necessary." Heru stayed standing, but his gaze followed her down, watching her like an interesting experiment. Which, of course, now she was. "Unfortunately, since I was unable to prepare for this eventuality, my work is a little messier than usual. Ideally, I would've had weeks to compose the proper wording and ease the pain while encouraging the accumulation of scar tissue. What I lacked in time, I made up for through my own ingenuity. And a blunt knife."

Illi winced. Her back thudded along with her heartbeat, the pain blurring into a constant, dull ache. Already the wetness was beginning to dry, which meant the wounds were clotting. A weakness stole through her limbs. She didn't want to think about how much blood she'd lost. Instead, she held up her wrists, the metal bracelets sliding down only half an inch. They could have been made for her. One charred black, the other liquid silver. They contrasted neatly with her skin, a shade of brown between.

She swallowed and this time her throat hurt slightly less. "What are these?"

"Binding rings," said Heru. "I've been working on this model for years. Those are the third prototype. I tested them on the guul in the limited capacities I have available to me, but they have not yet been tested on a living specimen and, obviously, they've never been tested on a sajaami. If they work as I've hypothesized, then they'll not only strengthen the binding on the sajaami, but help you to control it. Don't try to remove them."

Illi ran her fingers along the edge of the burnt bracelet, and some of the char flaked off, revealing tarnished silver beneath. Everything felt as if it were happening to someone else. Her head spun and exhaustion crashed over her. But the exhaustion was beyond anything she'd felt before, a fatigue that hollowed out her chest and her bones, aching to be filled. She ran her tongue over her cracked lips.

"Water," she said, a request and a question and a hope.

Something flashed across Heru's face, there and gone in an instant. If Illi hadn't known better, she would've thought it was worry. But no, Heru didn't worry. He planned, he prepared, he acted, and then he reassessed.

Keeping his eye on her, Heru reached for the water skin at his belt and unclipped it. He held it out to Illi and she took it with shaking fingers. It was all she could do not to rip the leather neck open and drain the skin dry. Instead, she fumbled at the knot until she'd undone it, then took several measured sips. Then several more.

Only when the skin was noticeably emptier did she force herself to re-knot the neck and hand it back. Her throat felt better, but her thirst was far from slaked. She needed something else, something more than water, something that pulsed at the edge of her awareness, just out of reach.

The room wobbled but steadied as she stood. The bracelets slid a half inch the other way, warm against her wrists. She stretched and, distantly, felt a sensation not unlike bubbles popping. She was beginning to feel a little better. A little more normal. Her gaze passed over the wreckage of the room again, a half-formed question at her lips. But she didn't need to ask who'd done this. It was obvious.

Ghadid had. Her city had turned against them, provoked by the words of an iluk, a foreign woman. But it hadn't all been Merrabel's fault. For years, Heru had barely been tolerated. All it had taken was a suggestion to ignite their simmering fear.

"You will come with me," said Heru. It was a statement of fact, not an order.

Illi stared at the bracelets, her world slipping away from her. He was right. She held the sajaami now. She would only be endangering Ghadid if she stayed. A bitter laugh bubbled up her throat but died at her lips, tasting like rancid citrus. Of all the possibilities she'd feared, she hadn't even thought to fear this one. At least they'd bought more time; but at what cost?

"The sajaami—you kept it for seven years, Heru," said Illi. "That's over now. Promise me you'll find a way to destroy it."

Heru had stepped away and was surveying the destruction of his lab. He stayed silent so long Illi thought he hadn't heard. When he finally did answer, she wasn't sure if he was talking to her or his broken lab.

"I promise. None of this will be in vain."

9

Illi slid through the open window and into her room, her sandals touching the floor with a whisper. She kicked them off and under her bed, then shut the window. Her back pounded with fresh pain from the climb, the cloth of her wrap sticking uncomfortably to the dried blood on her back. Fresh cuts itched on her palms from helping Heru clean up all the shattered glass. She hadn't dared look in a mirror yet.

First things first. She grabbed a bowl and opened her water skin. Sitting in the middle of her floor, she poured a fist of water into the bowl, then set the bowl in her lap. Eyes closed, she let her thoughts drift free, felt the pulse of the water as it settled in the bowl, felt the pulse of her wounds as her body tried to fix itself, achingly slow. She pushed on the water to help that process along, but it felt as if she were pushing on a wall.

Relax, Mo would say. *Work* with *the water. Don't force it. We're healers, not en-marab.*

Illi forced herself to breathe: in through clenched teeth, out through loose lips. She became keenly aware of the thud of her heart, the creak of movement downstairs, the murmur of voices in the street outside. But the water refused to move. Her broken skin remained broken.

Illi dropped her hands and stared into the bowl of water. She looked worse than she'd imagined. Her eyes were a raw red and dust mingled with sweat and dried tears on her face, although she couldn't remember crying. She clenched and unclenched her fist, relishing the pain that blossomed anew, the blood that trickled free. Then she took a cloth and began cleaning the blood from her hands, her arms, her face, and what she could reach of her back.

As she worked, she set aside her self-pity and guilt. After all, what she had done was done and what she had to do was simple. She'd leave with Heru and they'd find a way to destroy the sajaami. Meanwhile, she'd learn everything about guul and en-marabi magic she could from him. And when she returned, she'd take up where Heru had left off. *She'd* find a way to stop the guul.

Destroying the sajaami would be like a contract, back when the city could still sustain contracts. Instead of a person, though, her mark was a powerful and immortal sajaami, but that didn't change the rules. She still had to understand her mark, learn its routines, its life, its weaknesses. And Illi wasn't just any cousin; the Serpent herself had trained Illi, before the Siege, before the end of contracts, before the end of everything she'd known.

She wouldn't let everything end this time. She'd destroy the sajaami before anyone got hurt. And if that meant leaving her home . . .

Then so be it.

She finished cleaning the blood and soot from her hands and arms, then turned to her wrap. She undid the knots, holding the fabric in place so it wouldn't pull against her drying wounds. Once the knots were all undone, she took a breath, then peeled the cloth from her back.

It hurt less than she'd expected, but it still hurt. She hissed

through the pain. Then it was done and she stood mostly na-
ked in her room, skin bubbling with goose bumps from the cold,
the tattered remains of her wrap held before her. She might be
able to salvage a few scraps, but most of it was a mess of gaping
slashes and matted blood.

She shoved the wrap beneath her bed to deal with later. Then
she found her spare wrap, a length of fabric the color of stone,
and draped it over her chair. First, though, she needed to clean
her back. The water in the bowl was already a bright red, but
she didn't dare waste any more cleaning her wounds, so soon
the red turned brown, then black. When she squeezed the cloth
out over the bowl, red water dripped from between her fingers.
Disgusted, she draped the cloth over the edge of the bowl and
pushed it away. The worst of the blood was gone, at least. She
could use oil for the rest.

She sat hunched in the middle of her floor for a moment, letting the cool air dry her. She was acutely aware of every cut Heru
had made. She'd traced them as she cleaned and now she traced
them again onto her back in her mind's eye. She recognized most
of them: marks for binding, marks for quieting, and marks for
strength. Some of these same marks adorned her sword.

But the rest were entirely unfamiliar to her. She tried to
fit them into a broader context with the other marks, but her
thoughts stretched and frayed. She was too tired. Besides, she
would have more than enough time to learn and understand
what Heru had done in the days, weeks, months ahead.

Even though all Illi wanted to do was sit here and gradually
succumb to sleep, time was falling. She had to pack if she was
going to leave with the caravan at daybreak. She uncurled from
the floor and pulled her wrap around her shoulders, hissing as its
rough fabric brushed across the cuts. Her fingers moved as slow

as her thoughts as she knotted the clean wrap, careful to wear it high enough to cover all of the wounds. Thana couldn't know. Mo couldn't see.

They might try to stop her. And she couldn't be sure she wouldn't let them.

She cleaned her face last. Then she left her room and took the stairs as silent as a snake. The hearth was alive with the evening fire and Mo stooped over it, stirring a pot. The air reeked of cinnamon and sugar and cloves thickened with camel's milk: sweetened porridge, her favorite meal. Illi's stomach churned and she remembered the last time she'd eaten was at daybreak. Was it only this morning she'd failed to remove the sajaami and Merrabel had stepped into Heru's lab?

It'd been a long day.

Thana sat at the table, a stretch of white cloth before her. Half of it was covered in scrawls of black ink. Thana dipped her pen in the inkpot and began to add more. Illi felt a pang of regret; she should be sitting with Thana, writing her own litany for her parents. Seven years dead, they'd be a part of this rite. And the prayers the survivors wrote would be even more important this time, since so much of the dead had already been lost.

But what did it matter when their jaan were lost as well?

Illi paused on the last step to compose herself. She was fine. Everything was fine. Holding that truth in mind, she drifted across the room, drawn toward the smell of cloves.

Thana looked up from her writing, her fingers stained with ink. "Illi—when did you get home?"

"I've been home for a while."

Thana's eyes narrowed. "Yeah? Then why didn't you come down when I called?"

"I was asleep."

Thana folded the cloth and set it on the table with a sigh. "You should know better than to lie to me."

Illi looked to Mo for help, but although she'd stopped stirring the pot and held the metal spoon by its cloth-covered handle, porridge clumped on one end, she didn't turn around.

"You don't need to sneak through windows unless you want to," said Thana. "If it was a boy, just bring him by sometime. You know we don't mind, as long as you're taking all precautions. Mo can show you which herbs—"

"It's not a boy," said Illi quickly, her face growing hot as she thought of Canthem. She passed Thana, hunger drawing her toward Mo and the porridge. "But I did meet someone at the market."

Mo had finally turned and now flashed Illi a smile, bright as the day. She swung the metal pot off of the fire and began gathering bowls.

"A girl?"

"No—" started Illi.

"Then what's this?"

Quick as a cobra, Thana grabbed Illi's arm as she passed. Thana jerked her arm up and Illi's sleeve fell back, revealing the silver bracelet.

"I didn't know you liked to wear jewelry. Or is this a reminder of the person who gave it to you?"

Thana's lips curled in a mocking grin, but then her gaze tracked down the bracelet to Illi's hands and her grin collapsed into a frown. Too late, Illi yanked her hand back and tried to fix her sleeves so they covered the cuts again.

"What happened to your hands?" asked Thana.

In a heartbeat, Mo stood on Illi's other side, the porridge forgotten. She took Illi's hand between her own and pushed back the sleeve. The cuts were still inflamed from washing, each of them a bright red gash across Illi's skin. There was no point trying to hide them.

"Shards," said Mo, half curse, half assessment. She met Illi's gaze, her eyes dark and wide. "You'll have scars if these aren't healed soon. Thana, bring me—"

"No."

Illi pulled her hand out of Mo's and stepped away. If Mo tried to heal the cuts, she'd sense the wounds on Illi's back, too. Then everything would unravel and Illi would be too busy arguing with them to pack and leave on time.

Mo's expression hardened. "What were you doing? Those look like you stuck your hands in a bowl full of glass."

Illi sucked in a breath and decided a little bit of the truth couldn't hurt. "Someone smashed Heru's lab. I was helping him clean up."

"*What?*" Thana's hand went to the sheath at her waist, but it was empty, her sword safely wrapped away elsewhere. "Amastan needs to know about this. It's bad enough the Circle is forcing Heru out, but to let him be attacked like that—"

"Amastan can wait," said Mo sternly. "Illi needs healing."

"Really, I'm fine. We need to save water for the rite. They're just cuts." Illi held up her hands to show Mo, only realizing her mistake when Mo noticed the cuts on her arms and her eyes widened further. Illi dropped her hands, but the damage was done.

Thana's eyes narrowed. "Those bracelets—where did you get them?" Her voice dropped, became dangerous. "Did Heru give them to you?"

"I got them from the market." Hoping to distract them, she added, "Canthem gave them to me."

But Thana's expression only darkened further. "You forget I

spent a long time with Heru. He was my mark, once, and I had to understand him better than my mother. Those are of his own hand. What has he done?"

Illi stepped back, holding her arms to her chest as if she could protect the bracelets. As if she even wanted to. But she did, didn't she? Because if something happened to the bracelets, the sajaami would be freed.

Thana tried again, this time with more calm. "Illi—we don't keep secrets in this family."

"Then why didn't you say anything about the sajaami?" snapped Illi.

Silence cut through the room like a sword. Mo took a step back, glanced at Thana. But Thana only stared at Illi, surprise, then hurt, then finally anger flashing across her face.

"That wasn't my secret to share."

"Wasn't it?" pressed Illi. "You were there, as you like to say so often. You helped stop the sajaami. It was your secret as soon as you let Heru keep it."

"You know Heru as well as I do," said Thana. "There is no 'let' involved with him. He does what he wants and we continue tolerating him."

"But a sajaami, in our city, all this time?" Illi spread her hands, now deliberately showing off her cuts. Mo winced, but Thana's gaze didn't waver. "Did you think the drum chiefs would never find out? You know they were always looking for a reason to get rid of him."

"I honestly thought they'd never know," said Thana. "The sajaami was contained. What was the chance another en-marabi would cross the desert just to find Heru? If you knew how difficult it'd been to convince the drum chiefs to let Heru stay—"

Something flipped in Illi and any remaining grasp she'd had

on calm slipped away. "It doesn't matter! You should have tried! And now they're forcing him out and there'll be no one to keep the Wastes back, no one to quiet the guul—"

"Illi. Calm down."

"—no one to stop it from happening again!" Illi finished with a shout. She glanced wildly from Thana to Mo, her breaths coming quick and fast as if she'd just been running.

"It won't happen again," said Thana quietly. "It can't. The Empress is dead."

"You don't know, you can't know for sure, you weren't there." Illi's eyes smarted and she blinked furiously. Her skin was crawling with static and her head was ringing again, but at a different pitch. She tried to take a steadying breath, but her chest was too tight.

"I was there. I killed her myself."

"That's not what I mean," said Illi, choking on her words. "You weren't *here*. You didn't see the panic. You didn't see the bodies. You didn't see it happening. You didn't have to burn your home. You didn't see all the people. You didn't have to see your mother—" Finally her voice broke, her words choked off.

Arms found her, enveloped her. Mo held her close as she breathed, too fast, too shallow. Her skin thrummed. She was falling apart, just as she had down on the sands with Yaluz. Why couldn't she handle this? Why couldn't she be strong?

"I didn't see my mother," said Thana, her voice as hollow and light as ash. She shook her head as if trying to rid herself of her own terrible memories. "You're right, I wasn't there. But I was out there"—she jabbed her finger west, toward the Wastes— "and I saw what happened to our people. And I'll do everything to stop it from ever happening again."

"But what can you do?" asked Illi, her voice too high, but she couldn't control it. "You're not an en-marabi. Without Heru, there's nothing stopping it from happening again."

"Heru was part of the reason it happened to begin with." Thana bent so her eyes were at the same level as Illi's. "I know you're scared, Illi, but you're also being irrational. If anything, we'll be safer without Heru or the sajaami. It's time he moved on. You've got over a dozen, very capable cousins and we know what to do. We'll protect you. We'll protect the city."

"You couldn't stop it," repeated Illi. She knew she sounded crazy, but the fear clawed at her throat, the possibility of the past repeating itself too overwhelming.

"Not that time." Thana sounded tired far beyond her years. She took Illi's hands in her own and looked into her eyes. "But I promise, never again. Now come on, have dinner with us. If I'm not mistaken, Mo made your favorite."

You can't make that promise, thought Illi, letting Thana lead her to the table, too tired to resist.

But I can.

Illi wasn't entirely certain the thought had been her own.

Later that night, Thana was waiting in the alley below Illi's window. Illi hadn't seen her at first, but when she dropped the last few feet to the stones, Thana materialized out of the darkness. The older cousin wore a dark green wrap that almost perfectly matched the shadows.

Illi froze, too late to pretend she hadn't just climbed down from her window, too tired to scramble back up. For a moment, she knew Thana was going to stop her from leaving. And, for a moment, Illi wanted Thana to; she was so tired. If Thana stopped her, maybe the sajaami could be somebody else's problem for a little while. Maybe Illi wouldn't have to do this by herself.

Then Thana smiled and even that slim hope vanished.

"I know you're leaving with Heru," she said. When Illi tensed, Thana held up her hands. "I'm not here to stop you. I just wanted you to know that I understand. I might not agree with your decision, but I'll support it. Heru needs a minder, after all. He'd get himself killed if he was left alone."

"Didn't *you* try to kill him?"

Thana waved a hand dismissively. "Yes, well, there were extenuating circumstances." She held out her hands. Illi hesitated, then placed her hands in Thana's. "We'll be here when you return, whether you destroy the sajaami or not. We're your cousins—your family—and once a cousin, always a cousin." She squeezed Illi's hands, then let go. "That's it. I just . . . wanted to make sure you knew that."

Illi's throat had gone all tight. "Aren't you going to insist on coming with me or something?"

"No," said Thana. "You'll feel better if I stay here and keep an eye on things. Besides, Mo would never forgive me if I tried to leave her behind, and *she's* needed here. The only thing I'm going to insist on is that you take this."

Thana pulled a ring off one of her fingers and set it in Illi's waiting palm. The ring was heavier than Illi had expected, a simple bronze loop with a large polished stone that shimmered like oil in the thin light. She closed her fingers around it.

"That was my mother's," said Thana, her voice gone rough. "The Serpent's. Twist the stone and you'll find a little hollow. I left a present in there: a fast-acting, semi-painless poison. Be careful opening it. And only use it on Heru if he's being a *particular* pain."

Although Thana said the last part with a smile, Illi wasn't sure if she was joking. She smiled back, then slid on the ring. It stood out on her bare fingers, heavy and cold.

"You'll want to get a few more to complete the set," said Thana. "They're also a useful weapon in a close fight."

"Thank you." Illi didn't trust her voice to say anything else.

Thana waved away her thanks. "Just come home safely."

10

The cold seeped through the thick fabric of Illi's wrap, finding her skin, finding her bones. She shivered and rubbed her hands together before she remembered the cuts. Too late—her hands stung with fresh pain. She folded them under her armpits instead.

Around her, the caravan creaked and groaned and muttered as Azal and pale-faced iluk readied the camels and checked their wares one last time. The black of night smeared to dark blue across the horizon, a faint precursor to the color that would soon blossom and bloom across the sky. But for now, it was dark. And cold. So cold.

Illi hugged close to her camel, Awalla, soaking up her warmth and thinking of the honey and salas she'd left by Yaluz's bedside before riding the carriage down. He'd be up in another day or two according to the healers.

Awalla peered at Illi from under too-long lashes, her jaw busily working last night's cud. Technically, Awalla didn't belong to her. Legally, the camel belonged to Ghadid, one of the dozen or so that had settled in with the refugees. But no one would notice her missing from the stalls, not until the caravan was already well on its way.

Awalla carried a sack stuffed with dried food, tins of tea, full water skins, an extra wrap, and a dozen small knives. A blanket was draped across Awalla's hump that would hopefully keep Illi warm even on the coldest of nights. She had a metal bowl for water and a thick salve for chapped skin. A tagel hung loose and unknotted around her neck. She was prepared for anything.

Anything—but Canthem.

As the caravan started forward, its camels surging upward in tandem, Illi spotted the guard through the cluster of bodies. They walked on the edge of the caravan, one hand resting on their sword hilt, their gaze—thankfully—outward and west.

Then another guard wearing the same color wrap passed them, pausing for a moment to exchange words. Canthem turned their head and Illi caught the glint of eyes scanning the caravan before she finished yanking her tagel over her mouth and nose.

Her fingers fumbled with the knots. She'd completely forgotten about Canthem. And who could blame her? Usually she spent a few evenings—and nights—with someone from the caravan and then they were gone, out of her life for the next year or two or longer. No strings, no guilt. She could rest easy knowing they'd survive whatever was out on the sands as easily as they'd survived her. And if any had ever returned to Ghadid, none had bothered to seek her out. She never had to worry about lingering emotions or awkward feelings or—worse—falling in love.

She'd certainly never intended to see any of them again. And now she'd be sharing a caravan with Canthem for the foreseeable future. What was the proper etiquette in this situation? Acknowledge their presence, their shared moments, and then try to be friends?

No, better to pretend she hadn't seen Canthem and avoid running into them for the rest of the journey. Shouldn't be a problem.

A gasp broke through her thoughts. Illi had her hand on the hilt of her sword, but it was only one of the Azal. A woman, by the softness of her eyes and the subtle curves beneath her dark blue wrap. Above the fabric of her tagel those eyes were wide now, the warm gold of an eagle's. Illi knew those eyes, knew them very well. They'd met hers from beneath a bush of hair and across a torso shuddering for breath. Lunha: an Azali warrior from whom Illi had learned a thing or two about swords—among other things.

Oh, thought Illi. *Dust.*

"Illi!" Lunha opened her arms wide. "It's been generations!"

Illi fought for a smile—and won. "Lunha. Hi."

She grunted as Lunha wrapped her in a tight hug, body close and that crisp, fig-like smell achingly familiar. Lunha let go and stepped back and gave Illi a once-over. Her eyebrows drew together for a second, but then she nodded and her features brightened again.

"You still look a bit like yesterday," said Lunha. "How's the life?"

"Fine," said Illi carefully.

"What are you *doing* here? I never took you for the traveling sort. But then, if that is your sort, maybe we could arrange a thing . . . ?" Lunha's gaze flicked down, then back up, and her eyes caught a sly glint.

"Not this time," said Illi, and it was an easy thing to say because she meant it. The temptation was there, all right, but it was only that: a temptation.

Simpler to pass on that now than to follow where it led. In such a tight and conveniently intimate space as a caravan, it would be too easy to start with a *thing* and end up talking over tea, sharing space beneath a tent, and exchanging oaths within glass by the time they reached their destination.

And even though Illi envied that connection between Mo and Thana, and between some of her other cousins, she knew if she allowed a feeling that intense to burrow deep, it would break her. Something would inevitably happen to Lunha, to whomever she cared about that deeply, and Illi couldn't lose someone she loved. Not again.

Easier, then, not to love.

Disappointment passed across Lunha's eyes like a midseason cloud, there and gone again in the same instant. "Oh, I can see it. You've got another in your eyes, now."

"No, that's not it."

Lunha's smile sharpened. "You go on stitching up that tale for yourself. But if you need anything, even an ear to fill, you call on me." Her gaze slipped past Illi and that smile turned sly. "Although you might have someone else to call on."

Lunha touched her forehead in a shallow bow and slipped away before Illi could press her on that last, enigmatic observation. Then another voice cut through the air right behind her.

"Just Illi, right?"

Illi bit her tongue. She spun and Canthem was right there. Her cheeks flushed so hot she knew they'd be able to see the heat coming off. She didn't know whether or not to meet Canthem's eyes, so she settled on staring at the hollow of their neck where their tagel didn't quite touch their wrap.

"Oh—hi. I didn't know you'd be here."

Canthem's laugh was just this side of awkward. "Where else would I be? As much as I enjoyed our time together, I'm still a part of the Guul Guard and this caravan needs us. I should be asking what *you're* doing here. Or were you just that desperate to see me?"

Illi was surprised by how much she wanted to reach out and

grab Canthem's wrist, feel their warmth under her fingers. Lunha's presence had been a teasing memory, but Canthem's threatened to overwhelm her. Illi resisted. Whatever they'd had, whatever they'd built together, it was over now. It had to be.

"I'm traveling with Heru," she admitted. "He wanted me to keep an eye on his more sensitive equipment."

Canthem tilted their head ever so slightly. "Heru? Heru Sametket? That Heru?"

Illi breathed deep; maybe she could use Heru's notoriety for once. "Yes. I'm his assistant. You know him?"

Canthem laughed again, but this time it was genuine. "What a world—that's the man our general came to find. I didn't realize he'd be traveling with us, too."

Illi felt like she'd missed something. "Wait—but Merrabel—"

"General Barca?"

Illi stared. "Oh. She's your—*oh*." She started to lift a hand to rub her forehead, then remembered her bracelets. She dropped her hand, shaking her arm so that the sleeve still covered the metal. "But—why does a general know so much about guul?"

"The better to fight them," said Canthem. "The guul are Hathage's primary threat, now that the Empire has crumbled. A general should know her enemy, don't you think? She's studied them like a scholar and it's through her research we were trained. We're just one contingent of her defense; she's also sent trained marab to all the towns and cities on the edge of the Wastes. I'd assumed that was part of why she came here, to begin helping the towns within the Wastes."

Illi frowned. "Ghadid isn't in the Wastes."

Canthem shrugged. "I don't make the maps."

"Maps lie."

They walked together in silence for a few moments. Illi felt the distance growing between her and Ghadid with each step. But she didn't dare look back. She needed to focus on what was ahead of her: keeping Heru alive. Destroying the sajaami. Neither of which included getting to know Canthem.

"So, I was thinking . . . since it'll be a while yet before we reach the Aer Caäs, and we only had time for a few lessons back in the city . . ." Their fingers tapped nervously against the hilt of their sword. "Do you want to pick up where we left off?"

No was what she needed to say, just as she had to Lunha. Cut Canthem off now, before whatever they'd had found its roots and spread.

But when Illi opened her mouth, her lips betrayed her.

"Yes."

"What's your plan?"

Heru didn't look up from what he was writing when Illi slid under his tent and took a seat on his rug. The sun was high overhead, its heat finally substantive, and a rest had been called out down the line of camels, halting the caravan for now. A cup of honey-brown tea sat forgotten at Heru's side, steam still curling from its unbroken surface. Illi's own thirst flared and she reached for the cup before she remembered herself. She dropped her hand, but for a moment it felt as if she were still reaching. Then she felt a gentle *pop* and the sensation was gone. Along with her thirst.

Now Heru glanced up, his pen poised over the paper, his eye narrowed. He seemed to be searching her for something, but when he didn't find it, he went back to his writing. "I have many plans," said Heru. "The foremost of which is focused on surviving this interminable and sand-ridden journey with my sanity fully intact."

Illi shook her head. "We've only been traveling a few hours."

"Hours during which I could have been making headway on my research, instead of exploring the robust and diverse scenery that miles and miles of sand has to offer."

"What about the sajaami?" asked Illi.

Heru put his pen down and looked at her. Or at least, he looked at her wrists; the cloth of her wrap carefully covered her bracelets. "We have much work to do on that, but most of it will have to wait until I have a fully operational lab once more."

"And when will that be?"

"Child, it could be weeks or months," said Heru, annoyed. "In case you haven't noticed, over the course of one day my lab was smashed and I was exiled without any due process or chance to appeal. I, of course, was always prepared for this eventuality, but even with those preparations, rebuilding will take time. First, we must arrive at our destination—which from what I've overheard, appears to be the capital city of Hathage. Then I must find a place for my lab. Then I will have to acquire the components—"

"There must be *something* we can do now," said Illi. "You've had the sajaami for seven years. You must have had some idea of what to do with it or how you might destroy it if it ever got out."

"Of course," said Heru. "I have many theories—and many questions, all of which require methodical testing. I don't think you appreciate the unique opportunity this sajaami presents and we can't risk squandering this chance. It has been thousands of years since a sajaami was free in our world, and our understanding of jaan and binding has continued to grow and expand during all of that time. How much of that knowledge can we apply to the sajaam? That is a question not easily answered."

He will not help.

Illi started, then hid the motion by fidgeting with the hem of her wrap. That thought had not been her own. It also hadn't been wrong.

A shadow fell across the tent, and a moment later, Merrabel was ducking under the fabric. "Mind if I join you?" she asked.

Without waiting for an answer, she settled onto the rug next to Illi. Heru turned his head so that both of his eyes stared at Merrabel, the glass one just as accusing as the real one. Ignoring his glare, Merrabel undid her tagel, letting her curls loose across her shoulders and neck. She swept them back and then held her open palms out to Heru.

"Sametket," she said. "Here we are. To be honest, I didn't expect that we'd *both* be thrown out."

"That was the most logical conclusion," said Heru.

"Perhaps," admitted Merrabel. "I'd planned on you surrendering the sajaami to me. Clearly, I was wrong. But it's not too late. We're both on this journey together, it seems, and there will be plenty of time for you to change your mind." Her smile broadened. "I can be equally persuasive in writing. Your chiefs might listen. Perhaps they would be willing to take you back, once I explain things to them more thoroughly and your people have had a chance to return to a more rational way of thinking."

"You've done enough harm," snapped Heru. "If you were concerned about the sajaami before, you should be doubly—no, *triply*—so now. The sajaami had been contained and stable, within a city that was likewise contained and stable. Now it has been let loose on the sands with only myself and a handful of unskilled guards to keep it safe from guul and other would-be assailants."

Merrabel smiled. "If you're so concerned about the safety of the sajaami, you should give it to me. Unlike you, I was prepared to convey something so dangerous across the Wastes. Besides, Sametket—you've already proven that you can't be trusted with the sajaami. How far have you come in destroying it, let alone understanding it?"

Heru gritted his teeth, but he didn't deny it. Seven years, and in all that time, what had Heru done with the sajaami but let it hang like a pretty bauble in the center of his lab?

Not a bauble—a trophy.

A trophy, it seemed, he'd intended to do nothing about.

"Not very far," continued Merrabel, crossing her arms. "I promised His Majesty that I would find and stop the disruption. And I will, at any cost. Can you make that promise, Sametket?"

Illi laid her hand across her wrist, the metal cool beneath the cloth. She thought she felt the sajaami stirring, curling and un-curling like a fist. But that could have been her own churning gut, her own worries and fears. Merrabel was the one who'd up-ended everything. Her carelessness could have gotten them all killed. And Merrabel had known exactly what she was doing, up there on the dais. Heru might have built his own pyre, but Merrabel had struck the spark.

"Leave," she said, startling herself as much as Heru and Merrabel.

Heru's eye finally seemed to see her instead of her bracelets. Merrabel regarded her for the first time since entering the tent. Then she turned back to Heru.

"Do you always let your servants speak out of turn?"

"She's my assistant, not my servant," corrected Heru. "In this instance, she is not incorrect. You have overstayed your welcome,

Barca. If you are as prepared as you insist, then you will have brought your own tent."

Merrabel nodded. "I appreciate our conversation, Sametket. I'm looking forward to future such conversations with you. After all, we've many days before we reach Hathage. I pray we'll come to an agreement by then."

"I highly doubt it."

Merrabel smiled, stood, and ducked out of the tent. Illi watched her go, resenting the unease she'd left behind. Illi needed to trust Heru. He'd saved Ghadid from tainted water and from the guul. He'd find a way to save them from the sajaami as well.

Do you trust me?

The weight of her bracelets dragged at her. She had no choice.

||

When the sun fell away and the caravan halted for the night, most of the Azal built fires and set up tents. Illi was still in the middle of unburdening her camel when she heard the swish of a light wrap and the soft *shh* of approaching steps. The familiarity of both those sounds shot a thrill through her like a static shock, sending her pulse racing and stealing her breath. Her reaction was all the more reason why she kept her head down and hoped they'd keep on going right past her.

Then she felt a tap on her shoulder and she couldn't ignore the inevitable any longer. When she looked up into warm brown eyes, she remembered how they'd stared into hers so recently as their fingers drew out her gasps. Heat rushed up her neck and inflamed her cheeks, turning her mouth as dry as the sands around her.

"Oh, hi," she said, attempting nonchalance, but her dry throat coughed the words out and made them too loud, too awkward.

"Are you ready for your next lesson?" asked Canthem.

Damn that tagel, thought Illi, because she couldn't tell if Canthem was smiling or smirking. She pushed away her breathlessness. She couldn't let this become anything more than a sparring match. If she could stick with that, then she wouldn't have to worry about the fluttering in her chest and the way she kept thinking about those lips beneath that tagel.

"I have a few minutes," said Illi.

"Let me help with that."

Without waiting for an answer, Canthem stepped close, hefting the heavy blanket from the camel's back. The scent of them washed over Illi: honey and cinnamon. It was all Illi could do not to press herself against Canthem's side, feel their strong body beneath their wrap, weave her fingers behind their neck and bring their face down—

Illi took a sharp breath as Canthem moved away, dropping the blanket next to the rest of Illi's things. They glanced at her, eyebrows pressed together in an unasked question. Illi shook her head. Then she attacked.

Canthem blocked and then they were trading practiced blows. It was easier for Illi to ignore Canthem and whatever this feeling was while sparring. There were just too many details to keep track of—where to place her feet, how to hold her hands, when to block, when to twist, how much to twist, how hard to block, when to strike back, when to feint—for her to think about what else she could be doing.

Canthem occasionally stopped her to make small corrections, but for the most part they traded attacks back and forth, back and forth, repetition transforming intent into action into reaction.

The stars were a tapestry of light overhead, slowly being pulled across the world. They had shifted considerably by the time Canthem caught Illi by surprise and swept her off her feet. She hit the sand with a wide grin.

"Hah!" She started to get up. "Good one. I deserved that."

Canthem held out their hand and Illi took it and in one motion, Canthem pulled her to her feet, then to them. Suddenly
there was nothing between them but the fabric of their wraps
and Illi wanted to remove even that. The night was cold, but
Canthem radiated heat. She tilted her head back, met their eyes.
Canthem's hand went to their tagel.

Illi cleared her throat and abruptly stepped back. "Well, that
was a good lesson. Thank you."

Canthem's hand lingered for a heartbeat, then fell to their side,
as heavy as a rock. They started to reach for Illi, but she'd already
put another foot of distance between them.

"I should . . . sleep. We start before dawn and it's going to be a
long day." Each word felt even rougher than the last.

"I know that," said Canthem. "I've traveled with caravans many
times. Illi—what's wrong? Did I do something—?"

Illi smiled—too bright, too sharp—and shook her head. "It's
nothing you did. I'm just—I can't—"

Canthem held up a hand, stemming Illi's words. They smiled
at her, warm eyes full of understanding she didn't deserve. "It's
okay. You don't have to explain. I'll be here if you change your
mind. We can continue sparring. It doesn't have to be any more
than that."

Illi let out a breath. Canthem's understanding only made
her ache more for their arms, their hands, their smell. But she
could hold strong. She could just let it be the sparring between
them. She didn't have to feed that flutter in her chest, she
didn't have to care. She *wouldn't* care—as long as she cut this
short, now.

"Okay," said Illi, still too brightly. "Good. Well. I'll, uh, see
you tomorrow. Then."

Canthem gave her a curt nod, then disappeared into the yawning night, leaving Illi alone and colder than before.

The next day blossomed bright. The night's cold quickly faded to a chill, which in turn became warm, even hot. Illi rode and walked alongside Awalla at turns, taking her cue from the rest of the caravan. At midday, they rested again and a runner came by with tea.

As Illi accepted a scalding hot cup, she finally risked a glance backward. She gave the horizon a perfunctory scan, not allowing herself to analyze any of the bumps in the thin line where sand met sky. Ghadid was out of sight. Gone. The relief she felt was a surprise. As long as Ghadid had been there, still visible, she could have headed back on her own. But now there was only one path left to her: forward.

That way was easier.

She faced north again and finished her tea, then checked on Awalla. After confirming that her straps were still tight and her lead loose, Illi offered the camel a bundle of dried grass. The caravan hadn't found any grazing yet. There should have been more than ample grass around Ghadid, not enough for a herd, but enough for a passing caravan. Instead, there was only sahar, smooth sand without stones or rocks or even pebbles. Certainly no plant life. From the grumbling she overheard, she wasn't the only one who'd noticed.

Beyond the caravan was an endless nothing, but it was that same endless nothing that warned them of the attack.

A shout went up toward the front of the caravan, followed by a wave of heads turning and fingers pointing: south and west

Toward the Wastes. Illi swung onto Awalla for a better look. Dust smeared the horizon like smoke, billowing upward from a single dark point. Something was approaching, fast.

"Bandits!" called the caravan leader, her fist in the air commanding attention. "*Hel!* Warriors, to me! Guards, to me! The rest, form up!"

The caravan roiled like a kicked hive. Despite the chaos, there was trained order. Azal with swords and axes converged around the caravan leader, circling tight. Other iluk wearing the same reddish-brown tagel as Canthem joined them. With one gesture from the leader, the warriors and guards formed a wall between the rest of the caravan and the approaching threat. As the chaos turned to order, silence settled heavy in its place.

"Those aren't bandits." Heru had drawn up alongside Illi, his camel staring unblinking, its skin thin with sparse white fur and stretched over bones.

"Then what are they?"

"Guul," answered another, familiar voice.

Heru stiffened, but didn't turn. "I didn't solicit your input."

Merrabel had joined them, her camel a distinct contrast to Heru's with its healthy, thick beige coat and bright, alert eyes. Absently, she searched through her saddlebag with one hand. She pulled out a large leather satchel and set it in her lap. "Thank G-d I'm not asking for your help. Just stay out of my way and don't try to do anything and we'll all survive this."

The caravan leader approached them. "General Barca. What do you make of this?"

"Guul," said Merrabel. "Over a dozen of them, if that dust cloud is any indication."

The leader peered toward the dark point, which was quickly growing into a dark smudge. "How can you tell at this distance?"

"Trust me," said Merrabel. "And we're quickly losing time. Let me have my guards and I'll protect the caravan."

The leader nodded. "All right. I'll move my warriors back."

"What is your plan?" asked Heru. "That appears to be a significant number of incoming guul. I calculate you will need a great deal of blood to quiet and control that many, unless you know how to otherwise subdue them efficiently. Or—is that why you travel with such a large retinue? Introducing so many variables into the equation can only—"

"Shut up, Sametket," said Merrabel sweetly as she slid from her camel. "Try watching for once instead of using every moment to flaunt the little knowledge you have. Perhaps you'll learn something."

A guard broke off from the group and took her camel's lead. Merrabel brushed the dust off her dress and crossed to the western edge of the caravan, the leather satchel hanging from one hand. Illi couldn't shake Heru's question as easily as Merrabel had; a protective barrier was easy—there were at least three ways to draw one. But quieting the guul was another thing entirely, one that would require a lot of water they didn't have.

Perhaps the general had things under control after all, but *perhaps* was too thin a chance for Illi. She had years of experience with guul; she didn't need to leave anything to perhaps.

Illi drew her sword and kicked Awalla's flank. But even as her camel surged forward, Illi was held back. Someone had grabbed her wrap and it took all of her ingrained skill to keep from falling off. She twisted to find Heru uncomfortably close, his real eye glaring, his glass eye staring past her, as if fixated on the oncoming guul.

"You will not attempt to aide that woman."

Illi shook her head. "I'm not helping *her*. I'm going to help the caravan. I don't trust her with the guul, either."

"Absolutely not. I won't risk the guul harming the sajaami."

"You mean, harming me."

"Yes, that's what I said."

Illi started to say something, then stopped and shook her head. "Look—the guul can only harm the sajaami if they get to me, which they won't. I've got years of experience stopping those things, but they've never met one of *me* before. I'll be fine."

"While I respect your experience, if any harm comes to the sajaami's container, the wards may not be enough to restrain it."

"I'm glad you care so much about me," said Illi dryly.

"I don't think you comprehend the potential destructive force of an angry, uncontained sajaami."

"Maybe not, but I comprehend the destruction over a dozen guul can inflict, and that seems a lot more immediate right now. Besides, do you really trust that woman to not only quiet those guul, but let you collect them?"

Heru hissed through his teeth, his eye flicking toward Merrabel, then beyond to the approaching dust plume. For a moment Illi knew she had him, but then his eye settled again on her and narrowed.

"No," said Heru. "The risk is unacceptable. One sajaami can achieve damage several more orders of magnitude greater than a handful of guul. You'll stay far back and out of the way. If anything goes wrong, I'll handle it."

Illi gritted her teeth, but she couldn't find any fault in Heru's reasoning. As much as she objected to being considered little more than a container, Heru was right about the sajaami. A dozen guul might devastate their caravan, but one sajaami could destroy all that stood on the sands, including Ghadid.

With no small amount of regret, Illi re-sheathed her sword. She remained at Heru's side as Merrabel walked the edge of the caravan, pouring salt from her leather satchel onto the sand behind her. Rare, precious, and expensive salt that Merrabel was just pouring onto the sand as if it were, well, sand. Even in a thin line, Merrabel would quickly exhaust a year's worth of baats before she'd even halfway circled the caravan.

The kingdom of Hathage must be far richer than Illi had first assumed.

As Merrabel walked around the caravan, her guards took formation on the other side of the line. Although they all wore the same drab brown wrap and red-brown tagel, Illi easily picked Canthem out of the group. She knew their movements almost as well as her cousins', and remembering *how* she knew them brought warmth to her cheeks again—and her belly.

Worry gusted through her just behind the warmth. Only seven guards against almost twice as many guul. This was exactly why she couldn't let herself get too close to Canthem, to anyone. It physically hurt to stay back and watch, even though that was the safest thing she could do. She couldn't afford to care, couldn't afford to be weak, to make mistakes. After all, feelings were fleeting; death was forever.

So Illi waited. She watched. And the guul drew closer.

Talons and teeth flashed in the sun. Hyena limbs and vulture necks and gazelle bodies jumbled together in the mess of collected parts. But mostly, the guul wore human flesh: white bones and scraps of hair and skin turned to leather by the sun and the heat and the dryness. They ran on all fours with human arms and human legs and opened human jaws wide, even if they'd filled those jaws with cobra fangs and jackal teeth. After the Siege, the guul had had their pick of bodies.

The caravan shrank back, a worried murmur sweeping through them. Their warriors formed up on the inside of the line, while Merrabel's guards waited, patient, on the other side.

Merrabel, meanwhile, had just finished her circle of salt. As the guul galloped across the sands, she only gave them a quick glance before drawing a dagger and, without any hesitation, slashing her forearm. She held her arm over the salt, lips moving wordlessly. Blood welled and dripped onto the salt, staining the white red, and even though Illi had known the general must dabble in en-marabi magic, it was another thing entirely seeing Merrabel actually using it.

Then the guul were upon them. The guards moved as one, a wall of blades that cut down the guul, slicing off limbs and skin. Several guul still managed to get by, circling too far for the flashing blades to catch. These were rebuffed by the line of salt, sent stumbling back, heads shaking in confusion, only to try again a moment later.

But the guards quickly caught up with them. They cut down the guul with practiced efficiency, never panicked, never stumbling, while Merrabel—and the rest of the caravan—watched. Merrabel's guards were well-oiled gears grinding through the grit of the guul as if they were nothing.

Until one of the gears slipped.

One guuli toppled to the sand, its head falling several feet away. A darkness swarmed from its neck, curling tight upon itself before unfurling toward the sky. Illi's mouth went dry; the guuli had untethered, and now it was free to take any number of the bodies around it.

The guuli struck out one way, then the other, tasting the air like a snake. The guards backed away from it, but otherwise didn't try to contain it. Several glanced toward Merrabel, who had drawn her blade across her arm again. Blood dribbled down Merrabel's forearm and she raised her hand, fingers widening— then hesitated.

The guuli abruptly snapped toward Canthem, cracking across the air like a whip. Canthem had their back to it, busy driving another, embodied guuli away. They never saw it coming.

Merrabel's lips started to form words, but she wouldn't be fast enough. Illi felt the world slow, felt her heart pause, felt the wind stop. The air became as still as water. The guuli swarmed Canthem, its darkness winding around them. Warmth stirred inside Illi's chest.

I can help.

Illi didn't think. She reached out.

But not with her hands.

Her chest burned hot as coals and a *thrum* burst outward from her, rushing down her arms and legs and out her fingers and toes and the top of her head. Her heart started up again, and between beats, she could sense all of the guul, all fourteen of them, pinpoint their exact locations, and more. She knew their age, how many bodies they'd inhabited, the personalities they'd once had. She could see where they'd been, could feel their fear and desperation, their urgent will to *live*.

And at the center of each, she felt the bright fire that was them. She reached and held them all within her grasp, taking care to slide her will between Canthem and the guuli attacking them. Then she closed her fist and its fire dimmed, quieted. Went cold.

At the same time, warmth filled her body like a breath, stinking of burnt iron and laden with moisture. Her mind cleared and the exhaustion that had settled over her lifted. *Yes. Good.*

As if from a distance, she heard a collection of soft thumps, a sound she knew intimately—that of bodies hitting the sand. Illi's eyes snapped open. She didn't remember closing them. She was breathing in quick, shallow gasps. Her mouth was dry and her skin too hot and her wrists—her wrists were *burning*. She shook her hands and the bracelets shifted across raw, blistering skin.

An eerie stillness had fallen over the sands, replacing the chaos of the fight. The guards moved slowly, hesitantly, first examining each other, then the bodies littering the ground. Everyone held their breath, as if the guul's sudden disintegration was only a ruse.

But Illi didn't care for the guards—she sought out only one figure in the group. Canthem still stood tall, glancing around like the others. She'd stopped the guuli in time. She didn't need to ask Canthem if they were sane to know—she could feel it.

Inch by inch, the guards eased, relaxed. One prodded a guuli with their sword. When the guuli failed to react, they gave it a good kick. Then the guard laughed, an infectious gasp of relief that soon spread to the rest of the group. The laughter turned to cheers, which they poured on Merrabel.

Ignoring the praise, Merrabel crossed the salt and pushed through the guards. She dropped down to one knee next to one of the guul and pressed her thumb against its forehead. Then she looked up, her gaze falling on Illi like a hammer.

A wall of white stepped between them: Heru. He held out his arms, blood still dripping from his fingertips.

"Next time, I might not act so quickly."

"Fool." Merrabel flicked her gaze over Heru's arms, disdain smeared across her face. "I had everything under control. Or do you believe I'd leave my own guard defenseless?"

Illi shook her head, confused. Heru hadn't done anything.

Then understanding broke across her like a storm. He hadn't. She had. But he was taking the credit, the blame. He was protecting her from Merrabel. Which meant what she'd done—

Illi turned her hands over and the bracelets slipped across blistered, red skin. Not what *she'd* done.

What the sajaami had done.

12

That night, the caravan didn't stop. They'd lost too much time defending against the guul, and then again with the subsequent cleanup. The caravan pressed on despite exhaustion and darkness, because even a few hours lost on the sands could spell death if they ran out of water.

Illi's hands grew numb from the cold. When someone came around with tea near midnight, she gratefully accepted a cup. The heat from the glass was a welcome, if temporary, balm for her chilled and chapped skin. As the moon crept higher, she pulled herself onto Awalla's neck and let the monotony of the camel's motion draw her down into a dozing dream.

Illi became aware of a presence nearby during one of those dreams. Her eyes snapped open and snagged on a blur of white walking alongside her. Her hand went to her dagger before her brain caught up with her reactions: it was just Heru.

She didn't blame herself for not noticing Heru's approach. His camel, Anas, was unnaturally quiet. It was also dead. Illi recognized the simple binding that kept the camel going. Heru had performed a similar binding on the rodents and snakes he'd have her catch, animating their fresh corpses with guul from his collection.

For a creature seven years dead, it was holding up remarkably well. Some of its skin had thinned enough to reveal moving muscles beneath, and patches of hair were missing, but it wasn't in danger of falling apart anytime soon.

But it would eventually. Blood no longer pumped through Anas's veins, air no longer circulated through its lungs, and its tissues no longer repaired themselves. Heru could circumvent death by binding a jaani to a body, had even discovered a way to bind one's own jaani to one's body—a task previously thought impossible without serious loss of sanity—but he couldn't stop the body itself from falling apart.

The life Heru had given Anas was a false, impermanent one. Was that what Heru had done to her? But no, Anas had died and Illi had not. And the marks and scars Heru had given her were another development, one pioneered by the late Empress Zara ha Khatet. Illi could only hope Heru had perfected it.

"We're overdue for a discussion about what happened. For one, I precisely ordered you *not* to interfere. Do you have any idea what you did?"

"I stopped one of the guuli from possessing a guard."

"You did quite a bit more than that, girl. And, might I add, that guard would have been protected from the guuli by the charm they wore."

Illi's stomach twisted; of course Merrabel would have given her guards protective charms. Heru steered his camel closer, then looped the beast's lead over the pommel of his saddle. A pen and roll of vellum waited in his lap. He picked these up and looked at her expectantly.

"Well, go on. Describe how, exactly, you quieted the guul."

"*One* guuli," she corrected. "I didn't think. I didn't have time to—it had already untethered and it was about to get the guard." *Canthem,* she wanted to add, because it was important. But not to Heru; he didn't need to know about her weakness. "I just *reached*. I could feel each guuli. And I just . . . stopped them."

"You did much more than stop them," said Heru. "You quieted them. I retrieved the guul afterward." He patted his travel sack and Illi knew that if she could see through fabric, she'd find a dozen-plus glass spheres pulsing with an orange glow. Then his eye met hers and he added significantly, "Thirteen."

"But there were fourteen," she said, and knew it to be true, knew it down to her muscles and bones. She could still feel the individual thrum of each, knew their signatures if not their names. They'd had names once, but those had been sacrificed to the sands and the sun and the winds in exchange for an immortal half life.

Heru made a noise deep in his throat, somewhere between a grunt and a chuckle. His eye stayed fixed on Illi. "Strange, then, that I only retrieved thirteen."

"But I saved Canthem. I mean, they *seemed* sane."

"How're you feeling?"

"Fine." But the word tasted like dust. She turned her hands over, the metal sliding across her raw skin. "What did I do?"

"You didn't destroy the guuli, if that's what you're worried about," said Heru brightly. "No, this act of yours has confirmed a long-held hypothesis of mine. I've often wondered how the sajaam could maintain such strength and integrity despite not having bodies. A jaani will whither without a host. Even guul degrade given enough time. But the sajaam have withstood countless millennia, if the histories are to be believed. And they don't add to their numbers through errant jaan. Now I may have an answer to how they've withstood the entropic effects of the wind and the sun, as well as why we're not overrun by either guul or jaan. It appears they're cannibals, of a sort."

It took Illi a moment to understand what Heru meant. "I . . . ate the guuli?"

"Nothing so crude," said Heru. "I suspect the sajaami bound to you doesn't need as much energy as it would in its natural state. But even subdued, it still requires some amount of energy to sustain itself. On multiple occasions in my research, I've come across a theory that the sajaam created the guul—perhaps there's more to that than I initially suspected. They could have cultivated wild jaan for their own purposes, much as we have domesticated goats and camels."

Illi swallowed, then swallowed again as she tried not to be sick. Even though the guul were dangerous, deadly demons, they'd been jaan once—which meant they'd once had bodies, they'd once been people. Instead of crossing over, those jaan had gone wild. Whatever she'd done to the guuli, it would never cross over now. It would never know peace.

In saving Canthem, she'd committed blasphemy.

Heru was still talking, despite the ringing in her ears. ". . . would explain the sudden deficiency in my containment spheres. I first noticed that the number of contained guul didn't align with my records before we departed, but I'd assumed that had more to do with the unlawful destruction of my lab than the sajaami. The spheres, however, have been steadily losing guul every day. I've counted a total of four lost so far. While the number is not yet alarming, I suspect that it may be tied to your continued presence of mind."

Illi shook her head, as if that would help his words make sense. When it didn't, she pressed her palm against Awalla's neck, feeling the reassuring warmth of the beast, her steady pulse. "The guul you've captured—they've been disappearing? And you think it's because of me?"

Heru frowned. "That's what I just said, girl."

"Illi," she corrected, but she was too distracted by the implications of what Heru was saying to put any force behind it.

"I'd assumed that your relatively stable sanity and containment was due to my own expertise and precision, but even I must admit surprise at just how well such untested modifications have fared," continued Heru, scratching at the piece of vellum with his pen. "It's fascinating that even bound and contained and subdued, the sajaami can still exert its will. This doesn't bode well for its eventual release."

"Eventual?" echoed Illi.

"Nothing lasts forever, girl," chided Heru. "And considering how quickly the sajaami is burning through my significant guul collection, our time may be limited to a matter of weeks instead of the months I'd originally planned for."

"Then we need to *do* something."

Heru looked up from his writing and narrowed his eye. "We are. We're traveling to Hathage, where I'll set up a new lab and we can resume testing."

"But there must be something we can do *now*."

Heru gestured at the dark sands all around. "With what lab? With what equipment? We could, perhaps, conduct limited experiments on the guul we have at hand or, I suspect, you could summon your own guul from the Wastes. Even within a controlled environment, each of those options has its inherent dangers. And I suspect that continued use of the sajaami will necessitate expending more guul and will likely wear on the containment, so any direct experimentation will need to be exactly calculated to minimize risk."

"I don't want to experiment. I want to find answers." Illi shook her head; they were getting nowhere and she suddenly very much didn't want to discuss the sajaami with Heru as if it were some thought experiment. It was real. It was in her. And it was already finding ways to endanger the things she loved. "I've got to go."

"I thought you wanted answers," said Heru. "To find those answers, we'll need to understand what the sajaami is capable of, even through you. Fleeing from those questions will not make them disappear. I said, *fleeing* from them—girl—*Illi*—come back—"

But Illi had already yanked Awalla around and away. Heru's words chased her through the fledgling dawn, but she didn't have to listen to them if she kept moving. She didn't have to understand what they meant. She reached the edge of the caravan and dismounted, drawing her sword in the same motion.

As the caravan trudged on and away, she swung and parried and danced through the familiar movements of a fight, her only opponent the air—and the demon curled in her chest.

Because *she'd* done it, she'd reached and she'd crushed the guuli. The sajaami might have absorbed it or whatever it had actually done, but Illi was the one who had acted.

You didn't care about blasphemy when you worked alongside the en-marabi, said a voice that was her own, but whose words were not. *How is what he does to the guul he captures any different than what I did?*

It was different. Heru kept the guul, or he bound them in new bodies. He didn't destroy them.

But he doesn't help them cross over, either. He traps them.

He was learning about them, he had to understand them so that he could stop them. There was a *difference*.

I can help you understand the guul. I can give you so much. You can be so much more than him. He's hold back by fear, but you are propelled by it.

All you have to do is remove the bracelets.

She didn't need the sajaami's help. She didn't need *anyone*'s help. She was strong enough. She had to be strong enough.

Illi growled as she hacked at the air, driving away the sajaami's voice. For a few precious moments, she practiced in silence, the only sound the drumbeat of her own heart and the occasional *hel!* from the caravan. Illi wasn't concerned about being left behind; the burdened camels moved slow enough that she'd easily catch up.

You're the most dangerous thing in the Wastes. Just take off the bracelets.

Illi hissed. She held her sword two-handed, raised it overhead, and screamed. The sound came from deep within her chest and went on for as long as she had breath. She pushed with the scream, shoved hard against the sajaami, pressing it back down. At her edges, she felt other things topple and turn as well, as if her voice had the ability to break mountains.

Maybe it did.

Then she was out of breath and the scream broke off, leaving her gasping. She let the sword fall to her side and focused on breathing. There was a crack inside her, a fundamental flaw, and she wanted to keep screaming until that crack was filled. She knew it didn't work that way, knew she was being irrational, but at the moment she found it hard to care.

"Are you all right?"

Illi whirled. A rider pulled up nearby. As they slid from their camel, Illi recognized Canthem. Her heart thudded and the calm she'd briefly claimed for herself slid away like sand through grasping fingers.

"The screaming," continued Canthem, gesturing widely. "The caravan leader was worried it might be more guul."

"No guul here," said Illi, forcing herself to smile. "It's just me."

"Just Illi," said Canthem with a chuckle. "That's what I told them."

They came closer, the moon's light giving them an outline and little more. Illi couldn't see their eyes, couldn't gauge their expression, but she didn't need to. She could feel them, feel the pulse of them as they neared.

They were both already far from the caravan. No one would see. No one would hear. What was the harm in a little fun?

But she'd proven she couldn't handle even that when she'd used the sajaami to save Canthem. Worse—if Heru was right about the protective charms—to save Canthem when she hadn't needed to.

Illi drew in a shaking breath as she realized what she had to do. It wasn't supposed to be like this. If Canthem had just disappeared from her life like all the others, this could've been avoided. She'd thought she could walk the edge between disinterest and infatuation like a performer along a railing, balancing between toppling a few feet to the stones and several hundred feet to the sands. Only she was already falling, far and fast, and any moment she'd hit the sands and shatter.

But it wasn't too late to climb back up from the sands. She just had to be clear and she had to be firm and she had to end this.

"I can't."

Canthem frowned. "Can't what?"

"Can't *this*."

Canthem glanced around, as if there was something nearby that might explain her words. Then they lifted their hands helplessly. "I don't follow."

Illi growled her frustration and sheathed her sword. Her hands were shaking too much to hold it properly, anyway Why did it feel like she was gearing up for a fight?

She struggled to find the right words to make Canthem go away, but she kept tripping over her own tongue. Finally, she took a deep breath and decided on the truth.

"What we had in Ghadid—it was supposed to stay in Ghadid," said Illi, quick and clipped, her gaze not meeting Canthem's. "Now that we're away from the city, it has to end. All of it."

Canthem frowned, their warm eyes searching hers. They started toward Illi, hand reaching, then stopped. "I'll respect your wishes, but . . . why does it have to stop? What changed? Was it something that I did?"

"Nothing that you did," said Illi. "And everything that I've done."

Canthem nodded in understanding. "If it's your past as an assassin, then—"

"It's not that," cut in Illi. "I'm broken. I can't do *this*. I don't know *how* to do this."

Canthem's gaze softened. "Is that all? We can work through that, with time. For now, we can just keep practicing. I promise, you're definitely not broken." They reached out and this time their fingers connected, brushing Illi's knuckles. The touch was static, a shock. Illi gasped, felt her stomach roll as if she were falling. She jerked away.

"You don't understand," said Illi.

Canthem spread their hands. "Then help me understand. We had something, back in your city."

"No. We didn't. I was using you."

Canthem shrugged. "You were at first. But it was more than that."

"No," repeated Illi, stepping back. "It was only ever supposed to be a one-night thing. Maybe two. I used you and now we're done and that's—that's it."

"Illi—"

"Can't you *listen*?" snapped Illi, anger and hurt sharpening the edges of her words. "We didn't have anything, we *never* had anything."

"But you cared—"

"No," lied Illi. "You meant nothing to me."

The words filled the air between them, thick as smoke. Canthem looked stunned, as if she'd slapped them. After a heartbeat, their tagel fluttered with a sharp breath and they slumped in defeat.

"If that's how you feel . . ." They shook their head. "Maybe you should have made that clear the first night. I thought—well, it doesn't matter what I thought, does it?" They bowed in that same absurd fashion, fingers spreading like feathers. "It was a kindness working with you."

Canthem left Illi, striding across the dark sands for their camel. Illi watched them go, her throat tight, her mouth dry, her hands trembling. She felt sick; she should've been relieved. This was what she wanted, wasn't it? She'd expected to feel a weight lifted from her.

Instead she just wanted to scream again.

She calmed the need with several deep breaths. When the night had taken Canthem, she unhooked her water skin and sat cross-legged on the sand. She poured just enough water to coat one palm, then set the skin to one side and held the water close.

She didn't really know what she was doing. She hadn't been able to heal the last time she'd tried, but she'd been freshly scarred then, shaken and scared. Not that she thought healing would do anything to a sajaami, especially given how weak her own skills were.

But maybe—something—*anything*—

Illi closed her eyes, felt for the pulse of the water. Found nothing. She counted her breaths and tried again. Nothing. She stilled herself until her pulse thudded in the palms of her hands and the soles of her feet. But aside from that and a whispering breeze, she felt nothing.

Whispering. Once she'd been afraid of jaan, like any sane person. Now she realized she'd almost forgotten about them, even walking the sands where they could so easily slip into your mind and cloud your thoughts with madness. But she wore a charm and the sajaami was right: she *was* the most dangerous thing in the Wastes.

She ignored the whispers and tried again, this time forcing her will at the water. Yet the water remained resolutely still. Instead, her wrists warmed.

It wasn't working. It wouldn't work. She drank the small mouthful of water and then opened her hand to the air, letting the wind take the rest. When her palm was dry, she re-knotted her water skin and clipped it back to her belt. Her fingers brushed across one of her daggers.

Healing wouldn't work, but healing wasn't the only skill she'd learned. She'd worked at Heru's side for years and, while he'd never allowed her to involve herself beyond a fetched bowl or a held towel, she'd still picked up a few things. She knew the basics of en-marabi magic. Or "science," as Heru would correct her.

En-marab had bound the sajaam once. En-marab could bend jaan and guul to their will. Maybe, if she knew enough, she could bend the sajaami.

Illi freed her dagger. Hesitated. It'd been one thing to help Heru. It would be quite another to do what he did. She might no longer believe in G-d, but she still had a jaani, and she believed in that. Just as she believed in the jaan in the crypts and the wild jaan on the sands. They'd all been alive once, they'd all been people.

There was a very good reason why the en-marab had been driven out centuries ago and why her people distrusted Heru. While marab worked with G-d's will and quieted jaan, *en*-marab worked against the natural order of things. They stirred up what should have been at rest, took what wasn't theirs. They committed blasphemies without the slimmest shard of guilt. They risked their own jaan for a chance at immortality.

But Illi didn't want immortality. She wanted the sajaami gone. She wanted her city safe. She wanted to go home.

Maybe that would be enough to spare her jaani. And if it wasn't, well. Better she damn her own soul a hundred times than lose someone she loved again.

She drew the dagger across her palm. She squeezed her hand into a fist, felt the blood squish hot between her fingers. The sharp smell of warm metal drifted to her and Illi's stomach lurched. For a moment, she could smell smoke, too, hear distant screams, feel fingernails digging into her skin. Several deep breaths helped calm the ringing in her ears and remind her that she was far and away from that night and place.

The wind picked up. Unintelligible whispers swirled around her, no louder than the tumbling sand.

"Jaan are simple creatures," Heru had once said as he drew out a guuli from its bony confinement. *"You don't need the level of skill that is required to command a guuli. All you need is a connection. In most cases, blood will suffice."*

Blood dripped from her fist to the sand. The wind swirled tighter, and even in the darkness, Illi could almost see the jaani. It moved more like dye in water than smoke on the wind. As more blood fell from her fingers, a thrum filled the space between her and the jaani.

Illi spoke words she'd heard Heru mutter over his skulls. Their shape felt odd to her lips, and as she uttered them, they seemed to carry more weight than just her breath. The jaani responded and Illi could feel its attention focus entirely on her, waiting for a command. So she gave it one:

"Dance."

And the jaani began to turn and dive and swirl in the air. Illi watched, a fragile tendril of delight unfurling inside of her. The jaani spun and twirled like the gauzy fabric of a performer, snapping first one way, then the other. It danced until Illi's cut clotted and the blood dried. Then it faded to a whisper and the wind took it away.

And the entire time, her bracelets stayed cool.

13

At the end of the second week of their journey, dawn broke across a stretch of jagged peaks to the north that more resembled the bottom half of a jaw rammed into the sand than mountains. It was the first time that anything had broken the never-ending stretch of sand and stones and sand and scrub and sand. The waking dream that had been their journey was at an end.

The sudden spike of angry voices shattered any remaining panes of the dream. Illi lifted her too-heavy head, fighting off drowsiness. She squinted, just making out a splash of red in the cluster of camels and people ahead. The voices rose to a shout, then abruptly cut off. In the sudden silence, Merrabel's words were clear:

"Then keep the guards. No guul have troubled us for days and this close to Hathage, they won't dare. But I must go ahead."

The clump abruptly split. Merrabel steered her camel away and kicked it into a gallop. Two guards joined her, but at this distance, Illi couldn't tell which. Her throat closed up as she watched them go, heading toward the mountains.

Was Canthem among them? And if so, wasn't that for the best? Canthem had respected her wish and kept their distance. Illi had only occasionally caught sight of them among the other guards, laughing and playing and training as if nothing had happened.

Illi tightened her grip on the lead and was rewarded with stinging pain from the multitude of healing and half-healed cuts across her palms. At least *she'd* kept busy.

"Those are the Aer Caäs."

Illi whirled, her hand halfway to her dagger before she recognized the voice. Canthem walked a few feet away, gazing at the mountains as if they were a welcome sight. And, perhaps, they were. With a pang of guilt, Illi realized she knew very little about Canthem. Did they call Hathage home, or somewhere else?

It didn't matter. Illi kept her lips pressed tight and turned away again. The less she knew about Canthem, the better.

But Canthem didn't take the hint. "There's a pass only a half day's ride east. We'll be in the foothills by sunset. And after that, it'll take the caravan the whole night to cross. General Barca can make it in half that on her own and she's needed back in the city. The whole guard normally would take our leave here, since we should have left any threat of guul far behind, but the caravan leader is skittish. That many guul at once isn't normal, even so near the Wastes." They gestured at the front of the caravan, where the argument had been. "She wanted the general to stay through the mountains."

They paused as if waiting for Illi to comment, but they didn't turn her way. When she remained silent, they continued, "The rest of us will accompany the caravan up to the city and then we'll take our leave. But the most dangerous part of our journey is over. No guul have been seen this close to the Aer Caäs in centuries." They paused again and this time glanced at Illi. "What do you plan on doing once you reach Hathage? If you're in need of a place to stay, I know several. All you have to do is ask."

But Illi didn't ask. She continued to stare straight ahead, as if Canthem weren't there.

Canthem waited another heartbeat, then shook their head. "Hathage is a big city. I may not know much about you, Just Illi, but life outside the Wastes is very different than within it. If you need anything, don't hesitate to ask for me. I won't be difficult to find."

Still Illi didn't turn. Canthem hesitated for another moment before drawing their camel away and leaving Illi alone. She continued to stare at the mountains. The wind blew cold from the north, finding a way beneath her heavy wrap and stealing the warmth from her skin. Her vision blurred and she blinked to clear it.

It was better this way.

Canthem was right. The caravan reached the foothills by nightfall, the dying sunset casting the towering mountains with a red glow. Scrub popped up all around and the camels fought their handlers to grab mouthfuls. The caravan slowed to a crawl, then a standstill, as the handlers gave in. They all needed the respite. Tea was shared, as was laughter and talk. Illi took the tea but passed on the rest.

When they set out, the half moon's light cut through the dark, but the mountain's shadows ran even deeper. A general sense of unease wound tight and heavy in Illi's gut as they progressed up and up and up. Soon she was shivering from the cold even as sweat prickled her neck and her heart beat faster. Despite the slow pace, she was strangely short of breath and the others were taking quick gasps all around.

The stars shifted overhead and the moon appeared for a brief hour before disappearing again beyond the canyon they now found themselves in. It was not too unlike walking through a dune field, if the dunes extended upward forever and the only sound was the crunch of rocks and rustle of leaves instead of the slip of sand over sand. But it was just as eerie, and the caravan's desire to get through the canyon as fast as possible was all but palpable.

They climbed. Illi's legs burned like her arms did after a particularly strenuous training session. And they climbed. Her heart beat so hard she was sure it was going to burst. And they climbed. Each lungful of air was so cold it burned. And they climbed.

Patches of white grew more numerous along the side of the path. Illi paused to catch her breath and press some of the white stuff between her fingers. It was surprisingly light and melted like hot glass in her hand but it left her fingertips stinging with cold.

"Snow," offered a nearby Azali, who, Illi was heartened to notice, had also paused to catch their breath. "It's like rain, but it only falls when it's very cold. There will be more farther up."

The Azali was correct. As they ascended, the patches of white grew more frequent, spread. Several Azal paused long enough to wrap themselves in thicker blankets. Illi took every cup of tea that was offered, even though it meant relieving herself more often. She continued to shiver. The metal of her bracelets was cold against her raw skin.

The night felt longer than most. There was no hint of stopping. Illi dragged her feet, wondering how Awalla, who was weighed down by bags, could keep going. But the camel put one foot in front of the other, so Illi did as well.

Then the night fell away. Light spilled across the world, thin but bright. The darkness around them became rock and stone and brush. Illi looked back the way they'd come. She couldn't help it; she gasped.

They were so *high*. She could see for miles, a desert endless and gray with dusk. She scanned the horizon, but it was as flat as ever. No indication of platforms or soaring pylons. No sign of home.

Her chest tightened. She turned away. She put one foot in front of the other. She climbed. That was her only way home.

She didn't allow herself to feel any relief when the ground leveled out. It had done so a few times, only to climb again within a few minutes. But this time, it stayed level. Snow crunched under her sandals, her toes long since gone numb. Illi lifted her head. After the sun had broken free of the horizon, she'd taken to staring only a few feet ahead; seeing how much farther they still had to go was disheartening.

But now the trail snaked between rocks for some ways and then—disappeared. Down, Illi could only guess. A rustle of relief swept over the caravan as others felt the change and lifted their heads, but they were all too exhausted to speak. And they couldn't stop, not yet—up here, the air was thin and frozen and the wind chafed exposed skin. If they lingered too long, exhaustion would win out and they might never leave.

The trail delivered on its promise. Within minutes, the path began to slope down. At first, the downward slope was gentle and the caravan picked up speed. But soon it grew steep and slippery. Rocks that appeared to be sure footing gave out under her feet. After Illi almost fell the first time, she slowed down and picked her way more carefully.

Even then, the way down was much quicker than the way

up. A newfound energy buzzed through the caravan. The rocks ahead became sky and the world stretched away in front of them, much the same and yet entirely different from the world behind.

For one, the horizon was much closer than it should have been. Then the sun rose high enough to hit the faux horizon and it glittered like an expanse of salt, dazzlingly bright. Before the expanse was a city, little more than a smear at this distance, but clearly alive. Smoke curled up from its rooftops and while Illi couldn't actually see movement in its streets, she could imagine it.

The city spread toward them like spilled oil, dense at its center but then with thinner, searching fingers, and finally droplets. Between the mountains and the first of these droplets were stretches of green. Illi squinted, but couldn't figure out what the green was. Scrub? But scrub was rarely that vibrant, unless it had just rained.

The caravan slowed, then stopped. Confused whispers rose from the back, but the front had gone silent. Illi pressed forward, her hand on her hilt. But before she could get too far, she heard a familiar voice.

"Heru Sametket."

The caravan split, leaving Heru alone in an empty circle of dirt and dust atop his camel. The caravan leader plus a dozen armed guards approached him, their camels small and sleek, built for speed instead of crossing distances. The camels wore stiff leather armor across their necks and chests, dyed a dark blue. Gold thread traced sunbursts and similar, circular designs across the armor.

The guards themselves wore matte bronze helmets which covered their ears and foreheads. Dark cloth stretched across their mouths like tagels, but linked metal chains protected their necks. Each wore leather armor, a circle of dented metal across the chest. Most had a hand on their sword hilt, but a few had drawn their weapons.

Soldiers, Illi realized. Not guards. Canthem had mentioned that Merrabel was the general of an army, but she'd had trouble fully understanding what that meant until now. Stopping a guuli on the sands was one thing, killing a mark another. But if she had to go up against armored soldiers trained for combat? Illi mounted Awalla and kept her hand on her own hilt, but she didn't know how many she could take before going down.

I can help with that.

Illi pushed away the thought. She steered her camel between Heru and the approaching soldiers.

"Stand aside," said the soldier in front, voice high enough to be a woman's.

"Who are you?" challenged Illi.

"I'm Captain Amilcem." The soldier raised her voice so that it carried to the whole caravan. "And we are the Royal Guard. We're here on behalf of His Highness King Thamilcar to speak with Heru Sametket about matters pertaining to the security of the Hathage Kingdom. Step aside, unless you are he."

"You'll want to keep an eye on that one," said a familiar voice. The soldiers parted to allow Merrabel Barca through, followed close behind by the caravan's leader. She alone rode a horse instead of a camel. Her smile sharpened as her gaze fell on Illi. "She's his assistant."

Merrabel wore the same leather armor as her soldiers, but her helmet was under her arm, allowing her curls to flow free. She cast her gaze across the area before settling it once more on Illi.

"Thought you were rid of me, hmm?" Then she dropped her smile and any semblance of warmth and said to Amilcem,

"Search them both. I doubt Sametket would let anyone else carry it, but we should be thorough."

As the soldiers encircled them, Heru turned his anger on the caravan leader. "I kept you safe from wild guul and this is how you repay me? If it wasn't for my expertise, the general's foolish guards would have let untethered guul wreak havoc amongst your people."

The leader's tagel was pulled down, revealing her scowl. "The general says you're carrying something dangerous."

"The object in question may have drawn the guul to the caravan," said Merrabel. "If it wasn't for him, there wouldn't have been an attack in the first place."

Illi found herself reflexively waiting for the sajaami to correct Merrabel's claim, but for once it stayed quiet.

"If you endangered my people . . ." started the leader, her scowl darkening. She turned to Merrabel. "We cannot wait for you, you understand. We've already lost too much time and my people will revolt if we linger much longer."

Merrabel waved dismissively. "Then go. We can handle this from here."

The leader hesitated, as if she'd been expecting more resistance. Then she shrugged, gave a shrill whistle, and yelled, "*Hel!*" The caravan began to move again, but no one dared cross the threshold of soldiers.

Merrabel raised a fist and half her soldiers dismounted while the others circled tight, turning their camels so that their bodies formed a living wall. Captain Amilcem walked right past Illi and up to Heru, hand on her sword.

"Dismount."

Heru straightened and, for a heartbeat, Illi was certain he'd refuse. But then Heru glanced at her and relaxed a little. He slid from Anas somewhat inelegantly, his head held up the entire time.

"For the record, I do not assent to this search," announced Heru. "There is nothing to be found."

Ignoring him, Merrabel addressed the soldiers who'd begun to go through Heru's bags. "You're looking for a flask or jar. It'll be made out of glass or metal, and it'll be covered in symbols. Bring anything you find to me." She gestured at Illi. "Oh, and search the girl's bags, too. I wouldn't put it beneath Sametket to have his assistant carry such a dangerous object for him."

Illi flinched as one of the soldiers going through Heru's bags dropped an armful of parchment on the ground. Another soldier pulled out a leather bag and upended it, dumping fabric, ink, cloth, and other, small bags. Inside one, something shattered.

Heru twitched and held up a hand. "If you were truly looking for a glass container, you would be more careful."

Amilcem shrugged and finished pulling on leather gloves. She pointed at Heru. "Extend your arms."

Heru blew out a breath that rustled his tagel, but complied. Amilcem began systematically patting him down. She paused at Heru's waist and unclipped a small bag from his belt. She undid its knot and peered inside, the warm light from within bathing her face. She pulled out a single glass sphere, glowing red, and held it between two fingers. Illi held her breath: if the soldier shattered it, the guuli quieted within would be free.

"If you value your life, you'll put those back where you found them," said Heru.

Amilcem stiffened. Her gaze darted to Merrabel.

"That's not what we're looking for," said Merrabel. "But I'll take them."

Heru hissed, but didn't move as Amilcem returned the single

sphere to the bag, then handed the bag to Merrabel. She slipped it onto her belt and gestured for Amilcem to continue. The captain finished patting Heru down and turned to Merrabel, hands spread and palms up.

"Aside from that bag, he's carrying a few knives, some coins, and a water skin. Nothing like you described, mar."

Merrabel pursed her lips and turned to the rest of her soldiers. They'd just finished searching Illi's bag. They, too, spread their hands and turned up their palms. A hiss escaped from Merrabel's pressed lips. She narrowed her eyes at Heru.

"Where is it?" she demanded. "You took it with you when you left Ghadid. The caravan hasn't stopped anywhere along the way. There's been nothing but Wastes for days. So where did you hide it?"

"I don't know what you mean," said Heru, tone flat.

Merrabel glanced from Heru to Illi and back again, nostrils flaring. "I'll have it out of you, Sametket. The safety of my kingdom is at stake." Her gaze slid back to Illi. "Does the girl have it?" Then, to Amilcem, "Did you search her?"

"We searched her bags—"

"Search *her*."

Amilcem turned to Illi, expression rigid, and ordered, "Dismount."

Illi slid from Awalla and stood beside her. She held out her arms, compliant as a doll while Amilcem ran her hands down her front and sides. All the captain found was her sword and her assortment of small knives, which Amilcem turned out on the sand in front of her, a peace offering to Merrabel.

Merrabel wasn't pacified. "He won't have left it behind. It has to be here somewhere." She gave the camels a considering glance that Illi didn't like, then Merrabel let out a little gasp that was half laugh, half surprise. When she turned back around, her gaze fell on Illi.

Too late, Illi realized that during Amilcem's search, one of her sleeves had caught and hadn't slipped back over her wrist. Her burnt-metal bracelet now caught the light and Merrabel's attention. Illi shook her arm so that the fabric would fall back down, but Merrabel was already next to her, cool fingers tightening around her forearm.

"What's this?"

Merrabel jerked Illi's arm up to examine her wrist. Illi's free hand went to her belt, but her sword wasn't there: all of her weapons were splayed out on the sand before her, just out of reach.

"Don't manhandle my assistant," said Heru.

"Why *did* you bring your assistant along?" asked Merrabel, voice sweet. With her other hand, she turned Illi's bracelet, sliding it across the still-sore flesh.

"To assist," said Heru, as if it were obvious.

"Mmm." Merrabel dropped Illi's arm, but before Illi could move away, grabbed her other arm. Her fingers pulled up Illi's sleeve, revealing the silver bracelet. She traced a finger along the swirling inscription, her lips drawn back to show off her teeth in a terrifying grin. She dropped Illi's hand and turned that grin on Heru. "Do you typically bind your assistants?"

"It was a . . . precaution."

"You can't lie worth a damn, Sametket." Merrabel snapped her fingers. "Soldiers—seize the girl."

Illi stepped back and out of the way of grasping hands. Her weapons might have been out of reach, but she had what she'd learned from Canthem. As the first soldier lunged, trying to grab her arm, she blocked them and jabbed at their eyes. They jerked back and Illi slipped past two more soldiers to take her place next to Heru.

Even as she moved, she doubted. Why *not* go with Merrabel? She'd have a lab ready in Hathage. Illi could start finding ways to subdue the sajaami right away. Heru had admitted that it'd be weeks yet before he could be ready. Weeks during which Illi would be slowly draining his collection of guul, one by one by one. A collection Merrabel had already confiscated.

But Merrabel's actions had driven her and Heru from Ghadid and started this whole mess. If not for her, the sajaami would've still been contained, still hanging from the center of Heru's lab. *Still drawing guul.*

The thought festered in Illi and she wasn't sure if it was her own or the sajaami's. But it didn't matter whose—Heru had said as much himself days before, when she'd been preoccupied with so many other things: *you could summon your own guul from the Wastes.*

How long had he known?

"You will not take the girl," said Heru, his voice cold.

"You can find many assistants in Hathage," said Merrabel. "Or you can buy some. Either way, there's no shortage and I can refer several that are far more capable than this girl. Don't pretend you have a fondness for her; I've heard about how you treated your assistants in Na Tay Khet. They tended to die quite horribly."

"That was *once*," spat Heru. "And exactly the reason why I avoided assistants after. Humans are inconveniently fragile."

"Yet you have one now," said Merrabel. "One you insisted on bringing with you on a dangerous journey. Is there something special about her? Those bracelets must have been expensive, Sametket. If you tell me where the sajaami is, I'll leave her alone."

While Merrabel spoke, she lifted a hand and her soldiers

tightened their circle around them. As one, they drew their weapons.

"If humans are so 'inconveniently fragile,' she would be safer with us."

"She is safest with *me*." Heru stooped and picked up one of the discarded knives. "You will not take the girl."

"I have a name," said Illi.

They ignored her. Illi's bracelets thrummed, as if feeding off the rising energy of the moment. She all but burst for a fight after two straight weeks of monotonous travel, but she was increasingly uncertain who she'd be fighting. Heru was acting like she had no choice in the matter, like she wasn't even there, like she wasn't even a *person*. The itch to fight hardened into something else. Bitterness. Anger. Resentment.

Seven years. He'd had the sajaami for seven years and at any point during that time he could have destroyed it. He had chosen to do *nothing*.

Merrabel, however. Merrabel Barca was an en-marabi *and* a general. As soon as she'd learned of the disruption, she'd crossed vast distances to find it. She hadn't waited for the caravan. She had a lab. She had assistants. She had a plan.

"I have a name," repeated Illi, louder this time.

"I know, girl," snapped Heru.

And with that, Illi was decided.

"I'll go with you."

14

Silence greeted her words. Illi stepped away from Heru. He snatched for her arm, but she was already out of reach. A smile slowly lit up Merrabel's face, gradual as the dawn. She lifted a hand as her soldiers tried to grab for Illi and waved them away. Illi stopped in front of Merrabel and lifted her chin to meet the general's too-pale gaze.

"Do you have a plan for destroying the sajaami?" asked Illi.

"So you *do* have it." Merrabel clapped once with delight. "You'd turn on your master?"

"I'm not turning on Heru. I'm protecting my city."

Merrabel's gaze flicked to Illi's bracelets, then back to her face. "You are his creation."

Illi huffed. "I'm my own person. And you didn't answer my question: do you have a plan?"

Merrabel stared at her another long moment before answering. "I do. But is destroying it what you want?"

"If the sajaami is causing this disruption you've described, if it's bringing the guul out of the Wastes to Ghadid and drawing them to other places, then it has to be destroyed. Heru doesn't have the facilities to accomplish that." Illi didn't need to look to know Heru was glaring as only he could; she could feel the weight of it on her back.

"I *will*," said Heru. "And I know far more about the sajaami than this woman, Illi."

"*Now* you know my name," said Illi, rounding on him. "Did you know the sajaami was bringing the guul to Ghadid?"

"Well, I hypothesized—"

"How long have you known?" When Heru hesitated, Illi made a spitting noise in disgust. "That's what I thought."

"You don't understand, girl—"

"No, I think I do." Illi balled her hands into fists. "You weren't sure, so you had to run experiments, and you never once thought about how you were endangering Ghadid."

"That is inaccurate and misleading. If you would just give me a moment to explain—"

"You should listen to your assistant," said Merrabel. "With the proper training and without your interference, she'll go far."

Illi met Merrabel's gaze and held out her hand. "Illi Basbowen. If you can even begin to do what Heru hasn't, it'll be a pleasure to work with you."

Merrabel appraised her hand for a moment, then took it, a real smile warming her face. "The pleasure's all mine, Illi Basbowen."

"You can't take her," snapped Heru.

"In case you missed it, your assistant is going willingly," said Merrabel with no small amount of delight.

Heru growled, the sound disturbingly feral. He slipped a vial from his pocket and uncorked it with his thumb, all the while keeping his knife trained on Merrabel.

"No. No, I won't let you have her."

"I already decided," said Illi, exasperated. "This isn't up to you, Heru. Let me go."

Heru hesitated, his hand shaking a little as he considered Illi.

"You never could follow through, you know," said Merrabel,

her tone softer now, more conversational. "The sajaami's just another in your long line of failures. You were always leaving your half-begun messes for the rest of us. If you weren't completely certain of success, you just quit instead. How you made it as far as you did, and even took Samet's name, I'll never know. If you'd stayed Heru he Fet, perhaps we wouldn't have this sajaami problem. But then again, if you'd stayed he Fet, the Empire would never have fallen and I really *must* thank you for that. If one should even be thanked for their failures, he Fet."

"I do not *fail*."

Merrabel clicked her tongue. "Seems to me your entire life has been a failure, he Fet. What has all your trouble ever brought you?" She opened her arms as if to take in the rocks and dirt all around them. "Your Empire ground to dust. Exiled from a village in the Wastes. Your family—well, you never had one of those. And even your name, stolen from a man ten times what you could ever hope to be. Where's your immortality, he Fet? Where are your discoveries, your renown? You sacrificed everyone closest to you for glory and yet now even your colleagues barely remember you. Soon, you'll just be nothing—*again*."

"If you think I did it all for *glory*," sneered Heru, "you have been woefully misinformed."

He shook his head, disappointed, and then abruptly downed the contents of the vial. He tossed the empty glass over his shoulder. It shattered on the stones. He slashed his forearm then held the knife up, its bloodied tip pointed at Merrabel. A thrum rose in the air like the prelude to a storm. Warmth bubbled in Illi's chest, spreading long fingers outward. Her back itched and her bracelets grew hot.

Merrabel raised her hands as if in welcome. "Try it, he Fet. I survived your Empress. I can survive you."

Energy cracked like a whip between them. Illi felt a sensation not unlike a bone popping back into place and knew that one of the spheres containing the guul had cracked. But no guuli escaped. How could it when it had already been used? She knew that sensation intimately, because she'd been the cause of it herself last time.

Merrabel grunted and took a step back, as if she'd been pushed. The thrum snapped like a broken string and was gone. Heru dropped his arm, the knife pointing at the ground, but his shoulders stayed tense. Expectant.

Merrabel's laughter was as sharp as broken glass. She spat a mouthful of blood out onto the stones and grinned. "Is that all that the second advisory marabi to the late Empress Zara ha Khatet can manage?"

"*First* advisory marabi," snarled Heru.

He thrust his still-bleeding palm toward Merrabel and spat out a string of distorted syllables, the last a shout that ripped from his throat. Another *pop* and this time Illi felt queasy. One of the soldiers threw up.

Merrabel stiffened. Heat flared nearby and a moment later Merrabel's waist glowed. Charms. They held steady beneath Heru's attack.

The soldiers had backed away, but now they formed up around Merrabel, swords pointed at Heru, as if they could do anything. The caravan leader continued to stand as witness to the fight, even as the caravan slowly left them behind. At least that meant there would be fewer casualties.

"Is that all, he Fet?" taunted Merrabel through gritted teeth.

"What are you doing?" asked Illi. "Why are you taunting him?"

"*Sametket*," snapped Heru and he reached and *yanked*.

Illi stumbled forward, but caught herself. Merrabel was less lucky. Some of the spheres she'd taken from Heru flew from the pouch at her waist, spinning through the air and leaving glowing streaks in their wake. They hit Heru's waiting palm and he closed his fingers around them, eye glaring with anger—and determination.

In that moment, Illi knew exactly what Heru was going to do. "No!" she yelled, taking one step forward, then another. "Don't!"

Heru's eye flicked to her and for a heartbeat, some of that anger waned. Then Merrabel laughed and Heru squeezed his fist and the glass shattered, releasing the guul.

Their orange light smeared to red, then black, as the guul burst free. They were more jaan than guul now, free of their corpses. But these were far stronger and more dangerous than any jaan found on the sands or in the Wastes. These could plan and think and attack.

The three guul blurred through the air, rushing Merrabel and churning up dust and rocks. One rock grazed Illi's cheek and she winced. Nearby, Captain Amilcem cried out and grabbed at her arm, which had been grazed by a rock. When Amilcem lifted her hand to free her sword, her fingers were smeared red with blood.

But Merrabel remained unconcerned. With another laugh, she lifted a hand and swatted the rushing guul away like so many troublesome flies. Two swung around and rushed back to Heru. The third collided with Amilcem.

Her scream sliced through the air, sharp and abrupt and already gone. Her eyes widened and she sucked in a breath but when her lips moved, no sound came out. She fell to her knees, the cut on her arm pouring out smoke and widening with light. Part of Illi stared in horror while another part recited her lessons about jaan with calm precision. A wild jaani could possess, but the dissonance between it and the body's own jaani caused madness. A guuli was stronger. It could overpower the body's jaani. But it was too strong for its own good and inevitably destroyed the body as well.

Amilcem's eyes brightened. Blazed. The other soldiers backed away as she tried to stand. When she opened her mouth again, smoke poured out. Her mouth widened further, unhinging. Glowing cracks spread up her arm and across her face. Deepened. Spread.

It was too late to help the captain. Amilcem burst, dissolving into a mixture of fire and flesh and bone. Heru hardly seemed to notice even as the soldiers screamed, as Illi screamed. The other two guul had returned to his upraised, still-bleeding hand, and now he swept them back toward Merrabel. Back toward the defenseless soldiers.

I can help.

Illi didn't wait for the guul to take another victim. This time when she felt something reaching from her, she didn't fight it. Her chest hummed and her bracelets rattled against her skin, hot as breath, even as a sense of *rightness* filled her.

Illi saw the guul—both with her sight and this strange, extra sense. To her eyes, they were streaks of darkness, angry whorls that cut the air. To her other, newer sense, they were bright dots of heat. Of warmth. Of life. Illi wrapped her will around both as Merrabel raised a hand to deflect them once more. Illi braced herself. Then she clenched her fists and her will.

The heat sputtered and went cold as warmth slid up her arms, down her neck, and across her chest. Illi burned from the warmth, but it wasn't unpleasant. It felt like touching a warm kettle with frozen fingers, or the sun's kiss on an icy morning.

It was a wonderful, almost dizzying feeling and Illi wanted

more. Illi reached farther. She could feel so many more spots of warmth. She knew she could take them all if she wanted. Take them and make them hers and become stronger. She could be *so* strong. No one could stop her, no one could threaten her or those she loved. She could expand across the sky, break the horizons, become vast, endless. The world could be hers and hers alone if she just *reached*—

She brushed across the spots, felt them warm and close. All of them, except two. Those were cold and sharp. One sliced across her as she tried to wrap herself around it and Illi snapped back, opened her eyes—

Her teeth clattered in her jaw. She was shivering. Yet her wrists burned with heat, the bracelets searing her skin. She felt as if she'd just been cut off from something larger and cast away. It was a uniquely painful feeling. Worse, though, were the stares. Merrabel's expression was pure delight. Heru's was horror.

Merrabel started clapping. "Well. That was quite a show. Now, if you'll excuse me, he Fet—I have places I must be. Soldiers." She tilted her head toward them. "Seize him."

Heru didn't react as the soldiers closed in. He continued to stare at Illi, lips moving soundlessly, as they grabbed his arms and slipped the knife from his unresisting fingers. His eyebrows came together, considering, and Illi knew that look too well, knew that all Heru wanted at that moment was pen and paper. It was that look that sent a wind of disgust through Illi, hardening the foundation of her resolve.

"She won't help you," said Heru.

"Don't you have a shred of shame?" snapped Illi. "Somebody just *died*. Because of *you*."

"She was a captain," said Heru. "She knew the dangers of her position. Perhaps you failed to notice that your new friend did not attempt to protect her. Merrabel Barca will extend the same lack of courtesy to you."

"Merrabel Barca has so far not been stupid enough to attack somebody with guul. You're just proving all those ignorant idiots back in Ghadid right." Illi forced her fists to unclench and let out a sigh. "Seven years, Heru. I made my decision. For once, respect it."

Heru continued to stare at her with his single eye, but his lips stayed firmly pressed together. Merrabel's laughter rolled across the space like so many falling rocks.

"She's a strong one, he Fet," said Merrabel, approaching Heru. "You don't deserve her."

Without breaking stride, Merrabel freed a knife from her belt and drew its blade across her palm. As the blood welled, she grabbed Heru's cut forearm. Heru struggled, trying to wrestle free, but the soldiers held tight and Merrabel's grip was strong. Her lips moved and Illi felt something sharp and bright pass between them.

Heru let out a *whoosh* of breath, sagging between the soldiers. He shook his head back and forth and back and forth, but didn't try to slip free again.

"Take him to the nearest prison," ordered Merrabel. She pulled a length of cloth from a pocket and began wrapping her cut. "It doesn't matter how small. He won't try to leave."

Illi's throat tightened. "Why can't he come with us?"

"You saw what he's capable of," said Merrabel. "I won't risk that kind of behavior within my city."

The soldiers jerked Heru around. He moved slowly, as if not fully awake. Illi had seen Heru perform a similar action on simple creatures before, but never another human. Yet the outward signs were the same. Merrabel had bound Heru's jaani to her will. He would still function and act on his own—so long as his actions didn't contradict what Merrabel wanted. Merrabel had effectively put Heru on a lead.

Guilt rose in the back of Illi's throat, burning through her anger over Heru's reckless actions and fragile pride.

"Are you coming?"

Merrabel had already returned to her horse. She put a foot in the stirrup and swung up with ease. Illi went to Awalla. She didn't dare look back at Heru. He'd be fine. He could handle himself. He wouldn't do what was best for Ghadid.

So she would.

15

Two soldiers accompanied Merrabel and Illi from the Aer Caäs; the rest broke off and took Heru west as soon as the path leveled out. Their group of four quickly caught up with and then left the caravan far behind. Without dozens of burdened camels and caravanners on foot, the city rushed at them. Merrabel wasn't one for idle chat, so they rode in silence.

Illi hadn't realized how much sound the caravan had made until they'd left it. In place of the creak of leather bags and the rustle of wraps, the grunt of camels and the occasional hum of prayer, was the whistle of wind and the thudding of her own heart. The stench of so many camels was also gone, replaced by dust and a faint reek of salt.

One moment, they were riding hard between blurred fields of withered green, the next they were slowing to navigate dust-clogged streets. These first towns appeared like mirages. They'd pass a square and market and an empty, dusty basin and then they were out among the fields again. But the towns grew closer together and the fields farther apart until the towns themselves blurred into one and the beaten dirt path became stone, which in turn became foot-worn brick.

But even as the path became a street became a road and the traffic around them thickened, Merrabel refused to slow. Her horse galloped headlong through the city, Illi and the soldiers barely keeping up, the rapid clatter of hooves on brick somehow enough to cut a path through the crowd without injuring anyone. They received more than a few angry shouts and hurled insults, but only Illi seemed to notice.

Then the narrowing buildings abruptly opened, spilling them into a bright, round center filled with a crowd that refused to break for them. Merrabel pulled up short, her horse obediently slowing to a walk. She removed her helmet, spilling her mess of curls down her shoulders. A murmur started and spread through the crowd and heads turned. Merrabel straightened in her saddle and cleared her throat.

One of the soldiers announced, "Her Sun-Blessed Grace, General Merrabel Barca."

The murmuring wavered as those nearest moved away, bowing their heads and extending their arms backward in that same absurd, birdlike gesture that Canthem had used. Illi's gut tingled with the memory and for a moment all she could see was Canthem's lips, turned up at one corner in the beginning of a smile. They'd stayed with the caravan; who knew where they were now. Not here and that was all that mattered. As Merrabel rode through the crowd, it parted for her and the awe-tinged murmurs rose and fell like a winter's breeze. One man stumbled forward and touched the trailing edge of Merrabel's red cloak, his eyes wide and his mouth parted. More tried to follow his example, but the soldiers maneuvered their camels between Merrabel and the crowd.

Still, the reverence was palpable. Illi might not understand all the words that rose above the general murmur of the crowd, but she understood their gist. *Blessed. Mighty. Honored.*

Savior.

Rage, sudden and untethered, flared in Illi. What did this woman have that Heru didn't, that her people treated her with reverence instead of disgust? Heru had saved Ghadid just as Merrabel claimed she'd saved her people, and yet one was thrust to the outskirts and the other brought forward and outright celebrated.

Yes, and look at what you did to him, the only person who could stand him. You left him to rot in her prison, under her control. Perhaps it's not in your place to blame Ghadid.

The rage sputtered and died, cooling into a shame that was much heavier and harder to swallow. To distract herself, Illi looked around at the upturned faces, basking in Merrabel's presence. Thankfully, their attention slipped past Illi, rendering her almost invisible.

The buildings rose tall all around to three, four stories in height. Colorful curtains fluttered in open windows, and heads poked out here and there. Some buildings even had windows as big as doors, with metal railings all around, crowded with even more onlookers. Red and yellow ribbons had been tied to the railings, ruffling limply in an intermittent breeze.

The walls had been built from white sandstone and so the whole square glared with light. The buildings ran together in one long wall that extended the length of the open space, only ending when it met a road. At the opposite end of the square, another building soared, fronted by a vast arch that arced over half the square. Its surface was covered with geometric designs, inlaid with gold and turquoise and pale blue glass.

The building bubbled with domes and more arches, although these were less ornate. Beyond it all rose a wall, dark and metal and towering. The wall cut across the sky like a second horizon, extending east and west as far as Illi could see. She'd caught glimpses of its dark metal as they rode through Hathage, but only now did she see enough of it to understand its sheer breadth.

Why did they need such a wall? Guul roamed to the south and yet they'd passed no walls, no guards, no barriers at all on their way into the city. What was so much worse to the north?

Soldiers met them on the other side of the arch. Without a word, they let Merrabel and her company pass, then formed a line to block anyone from following. The crowd pressed against the soldiers, reaching but not struggling. Their murmurs turned to shouts as Merrabel slid from her horse. Illi dismounted as well and someone took Awalla's lead as soon as her feet hit the ground.

With the ease of routine, Merrabel left her horse and strode toward a large, wooden door. It opened before her on silent hinges, bringing them into a broad courtyard attended by waiting servants, heads bowed. When the door shut behind Illi, it dampened the rumble of the crowd. Illi took a deep breath, tasted citrus, jasmine, and salt.

The courtyard was awash in life. Not just the servants, now crowding Merrabel, but also flowers and trees and shrubs. It was so *green*. The fields they'd passed on their way in had seemed impossibly green, but now those were drab in comparison. Her mother would have loved to spend a year here, just getting to know each and every one of these foreign plants. The memory of dirt-stained fingernails stabbed through Illi, as unexpected as it was sharp, but nobody glanced at her when she stumbled. She pushed away the memory and looked past the plants.

Blue tiles peeked through the greenery, as vibrant as a winter sky. At the courtyard's center gurgled a fountain, a shimmering pool of clear water in a basin like the empty ones in the towns and villages they'd ridden through. Illi's mouth grew dry and she could all but taste the water.

Merrabel was unfazed. She kept walking, right past the fountain and the greenery, even as she stripped off her leather gloves, handed them to one servant, and accepted new gloves from another. She unclipped her cloak and let it fall, a servant there in time to scoop the fabric up before it touched the ground. Without looking, she held out her helmet, and again it was snatched up by waiting hands.

All of her attention was focused on the far end of the courtyard and a lone figure standing there, hunched under a fine silver cloak. The figure wore no tagel. As they drew closer, Illi picked out her hair, her features. The hair was short, but fine and soft like cat's fur. A light brown, it framed her angular face and just covered her ears. Eyes as blue as the tiles watched them approach, somehow brighter when set against skin as pale as sand. The top of her cheeks were stained pink, like the edges of white blossoms.

A darkness peppered her chin and neck: stubble. All at once, Illi realized the figure was a man, not a woman. She cast her gaze down out of habit, but could still see his face clear in her mind. His face—and the circlet of metal in his hair.

"Your Majesty," breathed Merrabel.

She stopped still a dozen feet away and knelt. Illi froze, unsure what to do before a king. She knew the title meant power, and a great deal of it, but what could a king do that a drum chief couldn't?

"*Kneel,*" hissed Merrabel. She grabbed the bottom of Illi's wrap and tugged.

But Illi remained standing. She'd never knelt for anyone and she wasn't going to start now. She bowed her head and placed her closed fist over her heart, the appropriate sign of respect for a drum chief, and even that felt like too much. After all, this man, this king, had no authority over her.

"Merrabel," said King Thamilcar, and his voice was much deeper than Illi had expected. More resonant. "Come, rise. You know you don't have to do that, not for me."

Merrabel rose. "Your Majesty, we've already had this conversation. I'll always kneel. It's your due, as our king and leader. Anything less would be disrespectful."

"From others yes," said the king, gesturing broadly. "But never from you. You are practically my equal."

"*Practically* is not the same as *legally*," pointed out Merrabel.

"There are ways to make it legal."

Merrabel stiffened. "Your Majesty. Please. Let's not get into this now. There are more pressing matters."

King Thamilcar glanced at Illi with disdain. "Of course there are. There always are." He sighed, spread his hands. "Who is it that you've brought home now? I thought you'd gone to find a disruption and, well, disrupt it. Not bring back strays."

"I located the disruption, Your Majesty," said Merrabel. "And this girl from the Wastes will help me find a way to rid us of it. The guul will come no farther than the Aer Caäs, I promise you."

"Good," said the king, but he didn't sound convinced. "I could use some promises. There've been multiple reports of guul attacking our traders to the west while you were gone and the court wants action, any action at all. I've held them off with assurances of your imminent return and—now you've returned. What shall I tell them?"

Merrabel made a small, aggrieved noise in the back of her throat. "The attacks will be seen to, but first I must have time and space to finish my exploration of this disruption. I'm close to a solution, but that still remains tenuous."

"Good. You can tell the court that."

"No." Merrabel held up a hand. "*You* can, *Your Majesty.*"

The king frowned his annoyance. "You would do a better job."

"*You're* the king."

The king sighed. "Perhaps that wasn't the wisest choice," he added quietly.

At that, Merrabel laughed and clapped the king on the back. "With every ounce of respect, you've never had the stomach to do what I do. And an army is an entirely different beast than a court. You're doing *fine*, Your Majesty."

"But the drought, the refugees, the guul—"

"Will all be solved soon," said Merrabel. "You can tell your court I've promised you myself. But I cannot appear before them, not yet. They'll make a hundred demands on me and I haven't the time or the patience. Give me a month, Your Majesty."

"You will have a week," said the king. "I'll reassign your duties in the meantime."

"And you won't send for me," added Merrabel.

"And I won't send for you. But I expect a report at the week's end."

"Fair. You'll have it, Your Majesty." Merrabel bowed deep, then gestured for Illi to follow.

The walls closed in around them as they left the courtyard behind. It wasn't until Merrabel had shut a thick door between her and the king and they stood in a wide, well-lit room swarming with servants that the tension left her and she let out a small sigh.

"That man," was all she said before crossing the room for another corridor, this one longer and taller and less confining. Her stride lengthened and Illi had to all but jog to keep up.

"He doesn't seem very . . . confident," said Illi carefully. She'd wanted to say *kingly*, but somehow she didn't think that'd go over well.

"He's still learning," said Merrabel tightly.

Illi frowned. "He's as old as you, at least. I don't know how kingdoms work, but our leaders go through years of training before taking up the drum."

"He's only been a king as long as Hathage has been a kingdom."

"And how long has that been?"

Merrabel cut a glance at Illi. "Since the Mehewret Empire fell."

"Only seven years. How did he become king?"

"Before the Empire decided to claim us as a province, we had kings and queens, a line of succession. But the Empire insisted on having their own governors in place and the royal line was executed. Nasty business, their bodies were left to rot in the public square for all to see. The Emperor at the time commissioned songs about it." Merrabel shuddered. "But somehow, they missed one and the royal line persisted, in hiding. When the Empire fell, we overthrew the governor. Then one of the royal blood revealed themselves and claimed the throne. He just so happened to be my fellow general, Hast Thamilcar."

Merrabel paused at a seemingly random door. It was wide and wooden like the others they'd passed and, like the others, indistinct. Merrabel reached for the handle, but let her hand rest on the metal without turning it.

"So no, he hasn't had the luxury of years of training," she continued, her gaze fixed on the door. "There's a lot to learn about leading a kingdom and he's still learning, yes. Sometimes he thinks he'd be better served if I were at his side, but he's wrong:

I'd be shackled like a dog and he needs me free. He's a good ruler. Fair when it's possible, decisive when it's necessary. He would do anything to keep his kingdom safe. But he can't." She lifted her gaze and settled it on Illi. "I can. And I will not fail him."

"Why aren't *you* king?" asked Illi. "Blood doesn't mean that much, not really."

"I'm better suited to a sword than a crown. And a king can't do what's necessary." Merrabel's lips twisted up in a sly smile, as if she and Illi shared a secret. "Besides, you studied under Heru, so you should know: blood means *everything*."

Still looking at Illi, Merrabel pushed open the door. She held it as Illi stepped through.

And into chaos.

That was the first word that sprang to mind as Illi took in the disorder and mess. Daylight spilled into the large room from skylights set in the high ceiling. The light picked across floating motes and the dust that was layered thick on various strange and familiar instruments.

Illi recognized the flasks and the beakers, the racks of vials, the burners, the clamps, the stands, the tongs, the scales. She didn't recognize the twisted metal contraption, which suspended five glass spheres in the air. Nor did she recognize the large wooden barrel in the center of the room, from whence several metal pipes poked out of the bottom and the top. Stains marred the floor, some of clear origin—oil, blood, fire—some not. Even the ceiling had a strange smear of charcoal red.

Merrabel headed for a wide wooden desk on the other side of the room. She leaned over the desk, her fingers drifting across several stacks of papers. Illi waited a heartbeat, but when Merrabel only continued to peruse her papers, she wandered around the room. Slowly, she picked apart the chaos and began to guess at each area's use. But she could only guess—Heru had ill-equipped her for anything beyond guul containment. He'd been obsessed with finding better ways to bind the guul. Whereas it appeared Merrabel was interested in more.

Illi tightened her fists and swallowed her guilt; she *had* made the right choice.

Merrabel finished writing something at her desk and straightened, the pen clenched between her fingers like a weapon. Her too-pale eyes cut across the room, pinning Illi to the spot.

"Now . . . what shall we do with you?"

16

"Not with." Illi met Merrabel's gaze. "Together. And *we* need to find a way to destroy the sajaami."

"Right to the heart of it, I see," said Merrabel. "No wonder Heru took to you."

"What's your plan?" pressed Illi.

Merrabel set the pen down and walked around her desk, her gaze running the length of Illi. "First, I have to know what we're working with, which means understanding exactly what Sametket did to you. Hold out your arms."

Illi lifted her arms, wincing as her sleeves first caught on, then revealed both of her bracelets: one a shining silver, the other a burnt gray. It felt deeply intimate, as if she were revealing more than just charmed jewelry. She took a breath and met Merrabel's gaze.

But Merrabel wasn't looking at her. The general had removed her gloves as she crossed the room and now ran her fingers across the silver bracelet, turning it as she traced the engraved script with her thumb. She pushed the bracelet up Illi's wrist, revealing the rough skin beneath, the blisters burst but long from fully healed. She made a noise in the back of her throat, then dropped Illi's arm and went to her other side, where she performed the same perfunctory examination.

But this time when Merrabel dropped her arm, she stepped behind Illi. A moment later, cold fingers touched her neck. Illi started to move, to turn around, but those fingers held her in place with an unexpected strength. A draft brushed across her back as her wrap was pulled away. Merrabel let out a soft gasp, halfway between awe and delight.

Then those cold fingers were tracing the marks Heru had carved into her flesh. Illi chewed her lower lip, breathing deep through her nose in an effort to remain as still as stone despite a desperate urge to pull away and cover herself. No one had seen those wounds since Heru had made them, not even Illi herself. She hadn't dared take a mirror to the mess he'd made of her back. But Merrabel had to understand. And to understand, she had to see.

Finally, Merrabel let go of Illi's wrap and stepped back into view, her lips pursed tight with thought. "I must admit, that's some clever work. I wouldn't have expected it from Sametket. He's made some impressive leaps."

"Now you're calling him Sametket again—why did you call him he Fet back on the mountain?" asked Illi.

Merrabel shrugged. "I was trying to rile him up and get him to reveal more about the sajaami. It worked."

"But it didn't. He attacked you. Your captain *died*."

"An unfortunate sacrifice," said Merrabel with a tight sigh.

"You could've avoided it. If you know him as well as you claim, you'd know he responds much better to praise."

"*Praise*." Merrabel rolled her eyes. "He's had more than enough of that. I won't be the one to further contribute to his ego." She brushed off her hands. "That man thinks he's suffered, like he's the only one who's ever been orphaned, when his Empress made orphans of us all. He doesn't have the faintest idea what it's like to really struggle. He's had nothing but opportunities handed to him, from being accepted into the Empress's school to his tutelage under Samet. He stood at the right hand of the most powerful woman in this land and learned secrets most of us would die for, demanding more as if it were his due. And then he runs off and hides in the desert when those who helped him needed his help the most." She spat on the floor. "Spineless traitor."

"The Empress turned against him," pointed out Illi.

Merrabel waved a hand. "Yes, but his city didn't."

"How do you know so much about him? You said you studied together, but that must've been years—decades—ago."

"As one of the Empress's own marab, he was known by every marabi throughout the Empire." Merrabel went to a bench and poured water into a bowl. "But you can learn a lot from a person during even a year or two of their youth. It's amazing how little people truly change."

"He's changed. He's not like that anymore."

"Is he not, now?" Merrabel pressed her lips together. "From what I've seen, he's still just as thoughtless, just as petulant, just as insufferably proud—and just as useless. What has he ever actually accomplished?"

Illi was ready with her answer. "The guul. He's kept Ghadid safe from the guul. He didn't have to stay after he cleared our water, but he did."

Merrabel considered, then gave a curt nod. "I'll give him that. Perhaps he has some loyalty in him yet. Or perhaps he decided your town is a conveniently quiet place to continue his experiments, a place where no one would understand what he was doing and be able to challenge him on it."

"What about this school you went to?" asked Illi, hoping to redirect. She didn't like the way Merrabel's words twisted in her like screws, skewing her own view of Heru. She knew Merra-bel was wrong about him, but her anger still bubbled, sour as old wine, and she couldn't remember the good parts. "Was there really an entire school for en-marab?"

"Technically, it was never for *en*-marab," said Merrabel. "The Empress wanted the very best of the best in her school. She took applicants from all over her Empire, including Hathage. At the time we thought it was odd that she'd open the gates to marab studies as wide as she did, but now, of course, we understand. She didn't just want marab, she'd wanted *en*-marab. Which meant she had to circumvent the traditional schools and create her own. She must have hoped that by encouraging the study of every aspect of jaan, and not just their quieting, she could scrape off the knowledge she needed and no one would realize what her true intentions were. Her plan worked beautifully."

"If you can call dying in the Wastes beautiful."

Merrabel laughed. "You're absolutely correct. The Empress was not as brilliant with the execution of *that* part of her plan."

She scrubbed her hands clean in the bowl, then wiped them dry on a towel before pulling her gloves back on. "If I'm reading them correctly, those marks Heru made form an intricate bind-ing, one that weaves the sajaami between your jaani and body, making it a part of you while also keeping it separate. The brace-lets, then, are dampeners. Without them, you could wield the full force of the sajaami's strength, perhaps even be stronger than the sajaami unbound. I would be tempted to test that theory—"

"Hypothesis," corrected Illi.

Merrabel finished pulling her gloves on and considered Illi. "You really are his assistant."

Illi felt a strange prickle of pride. Until Merrabel added, "And if you ever correct me like that again, I will have you turned out."

"You wouldn't."

"I don't have to work *with* you, Illi Basbowen," said Merrabel. "Eventually even such well-constructed ornaments as those bracelets will fail. The sajaami will be free again, and it might take some doing, but I could contain it. While I'd prefer to work together, as it would be faster and far less disastrous, I won't be disrespected in my own lab."

Illi crossed her arms. "And I don't have to work with *you*." As she said it, she realized she meant it. She was only here because she wanted what Merrabel had—both her knowledge and equipment. But she could get those without giving Merrabel anything in return.

Merrabel raised her eyebrows, then laughed. "Those marks on your palms—I'd assumed they were Heru's, but you've been practicing on your own, haven't you? You've been trying to learn how to bind . . . let me guess, wild jaan? You're playing with lightning, Illi. It's only a matter of time before you burn yourself. I won't have to wait long to collect the sajaami from the ashes."

Illi ground her teeth, but Merrabel wasn't finished. "Sametket clearly didn't bother training you, but I will. You'll have every resource Hathage has to offer available to you. You can even bring that knowledge back to your town in the Wastes, if that's your true desire. I ask only for your loyalty and your respect. Can we agree to that?"

Illi swallowed, then nodded. "I can. But I refuse to be treated as just an experiment, or just your assistant."

"I have decades of experience on you."

"I'm not saying you have to treat me as your equal," said Illi. "At least, not in this. But at least treat me like a student."

"I can agree to that." Merrabel cleared her throat. "As I was saying, I'd be tempted to test that *theory*—" She paused to glance at Illi, who kept her lips firmly pressed together. "—but in all likelihood, those bracelets are the only thing keeping the sajaami from tearing you apart. You've seen with your own eyes how quickly a guuli burns through its living host. A sajaami is a thousandfold stronger. Imagine, for a moment, what would happen."

Merrabel paused again, her gaze on Illi. After a few strained heartbeats, she loudly cleared her throat.

"I assume . . . I'd burn up as well," said Illi.

"Yes," said Merrabel, snapping her fingers as if Illi were a pet that had performed her trick well. "The sajaami's power would incinerate your body as well as your jaani. There would be nothing left of you."

Illi swallowed. She'd suspected as much and she'd wondered if that was part of Heru's hesitation. It was one thing to die, but another entirely to have her jaani destroyed. At least in death there was still hope for something else—heaven, if not another life. But not if her jaani were gone. "Is that what happened to Captain Amilcem?"

Merrabel's gaze slipped past Illi. "Unfortunately. But all of my soldiers are aware of the greater sacrifice they may have to make for the safety of our kingdom. That's the danger of living in these times, with the Wastes unstable and a sajaami loose."

"If I fall apart when I remove the bracelets, then how can we destroy the sajaami?"

"Now *that's* the question, isn't it?" said Merrabel. "But we're still getting ahead of ourselves. First, we must understand the sajaami itself. Only then can we decide on the right method to eradicate the threat."

We. Merrabel kept using that pronoun and every time it drew Illi in further, despite her better judgment. With Heru, it'd always been *I.* He'd never been interested in how Illi could help or what she could contribute, only how quickly she could bring him that knife or this bowl.

"I've been trying to understand it." Illi turned over her wrists, feeling the metal of the bracelets slide across them. "But Heru refused to. I still don't know why."

"Sametket was afraid of it."

Illi let her arms drop. "Heru? Afraid?" But hadn't the sajaami said the same thing? *He's held back by fear. . . .*

"Like any of us, he's spent his entire life devoted to untangling the mysteries of jaan and guul in order to understand, even achieve, immortality, but I doubt he expected the actual means to that end to wind up in his hands."

"Why not?" asked Illi. "If that's what he's always wanted?"

Merrabel tapped her fingers on the desk, her gloves muting the sound to a series of soft thumps. "You see, some people strive for things so far beyond their means because they can be content in the safety of never achieving those things. Their joy lies in the struggle of striving, not the goal itself. Achieving their goal would be the death of them. Sametket understands that he wouldn't know what to do with the power he seeks, which is why he's never done anything with the sajaami. Ask yourself, if you don't believe me—he saw the Empress achieve all of his goals, even if her execution was fundamentally flawed. Yet in all the time you've known him, has he once made any attempt to replicate what she did?"

Illi swallowed. She didn't need to think long to know that Merrabel was right, that Heru had never once tried to follow in his Empress's footsteps. He'd played with wild jaan and rats, with containing the guul and understanding their threat, but those were miles behind where he'd once been, what he'd once wanted. He'd made these bracelets, had them ready to use as soon as the orb shattered, and yet it had been clear he hadn't intended to use them himself, not then. Perhaps not ever.

But afraid?

Heru was supposed to be the one person who *wasn't* afraid.

Illi dug her fingernails into her palms. Merrabel was trying to distract her. In the end, this wasn't about Heru. This was all about the sajaami. "We should focus on what we know about it, first," she said. "We know where it came from and how it got there. We even know the method that was used to originally bind it, and the method used to release it."

"You just said it yourself," said Merrabel. "*Bind. Release.* While that's helpful information, neither will bring us closer to destroying it. We must understand how the sajaami works on a fundamental level. We have a unique opportunity; no one alive has ever seen a sajaami and very few of the surviving texts go beyond the mythological. Everything we know about sajaam is rumor and conjecture. Until now. Tell me." Merrabel picked up a pen and slid a piece of vellum to herself. "Those who've been possessed by jaan often have visions. Have you seen anything unusual since your possession?"

"I saw . . . a few things before Heru completed the binding. But they were jumbled nonsense."

They'd been more than jumbled nonsense. Illi could still see the expanse of water below her, taste the salt, hear the crackle of flames. But she'd found nothing helpful in those images, only a past long since buried. And while they might be the sajaami's memories, they felt like hers. She might be willing to trade a few things with Merrabel, but not those.

"A shame," said Merrabel. "I'd thought . . . well, never mind what I thought." She crossed the room to a large metal locker. "Let's see what else the sajaami might be capable of."

She drew a key from her pocket and inserted it into the lock, twisting it all the way around until it clicked. She opened the door, revealing a full-to-bursting cabinet. Every narrow shelf was stuffed with jars, utensils, vials, and fabrics with no discernible order or system. Merrabel plucked a small wooden box from the chaos, then shut the cabinet, pocketing the key.

Merrabel carried the box before her and carefully set it down on one of the less cluttered tables. She gestured Illi closer.

"What's in here?" she asked.

"Two guul," said Illi, and only after she'd answered did she feel them, twin spots of warmth that pulsed more strongly the closer she got.

Merrabel nodded and lifted the lid of the box, exposing two glowing spheres within. Their warm light illuminated Merrabel's face, giving her some much-needed color and softening her pale eyes.

"Take them."

Illi met Merrabel's gaze, focused and intent. The sajaami was already responding to the order, its heat spreading across her chest, down her arms to her fingertips. Carefully, gently, with all the precision and control she could muster, she let the sajaami *reach.*

The light went out of the orbs. Illi could still feel the guul. She held up one hand, her fingers trailing red and orange smears of light. She turned her hand this way and that, watching the way the light moved, slow and fat like fog. Like the way the light clung to her when she was healing.

Unlike the previous times she'd reached for guul, she felt no need or thirst. Only curiosity. After all, it'd only been that morning when she'd snatched three guul from Heru. How long would those last her? How long would they last the sajaami?

And what would it mean when she ran out of guul?

"Fascinating," murmured Merrabel. Her pale eyes reflected the glow as she examined Illi's hand without touching it. "The relationship between the sajaam and the guul has long been in the realm of myth, but this validates some of those claims. There is indeed an affinity between the two. Now"—she stepped back, folding her arms—"repeat what you did in the Aer Caäs."

Illi stopped turning her hand, but the red and orange continued to snake around her fingers. "What?"

"We must replicate what you did in the mountains in the relatively consistent environment of my lab. It's imperative that I understand what you did." Merrabel paused, then added, "It could be the key to finding the sajaami's weakness, Illi."

Illi swallowed, her throat dry. She felt the guul at her fingertips. She didn't need it, didn't need to do this. She was already thrumming with energy, despite having walked all night. Yet part of her craved *more*.

It's just an experiment, she told herself. She reached, felt the heat of the guul at her fingertips, and covered them with her will. They felt different from the guul on the sands. Docile. There was no fight to them, no kick, even as she squeezed.

They'd already been quieted. The realization hit her like a fist. Which meant what she was doing—

The guul were gone. Warmth spread up her arm and across her chest. She was hot all over, as if she'd swallowed coals. Heat prickled her skin uncomfortably and sweat beaded fresh on her brow. Worst, though, were her bracelets, their hot metal grating against raw skin. And the heat was intensifying, accompanied by an insistent urge to *act*.

In a reflex as involuntary as breathing, Illi reached out again.

But this time, her mind scraped across something cold and sharp. She pushed, but the sharp bit back, as painful as broken glass.

Illi's eyes flew open. She didn't remember closing them. Merrabel was no longer watching her with curiosity, but glaring with anger. Her cheeks were a bright pink, as if she'd been slapped. A soft glow faded around her neck.

Too late, Illi realized her error. She'd tried to take Merrabel's jaani, but whatever charms she wore had protected her.

"Well, that was illuminating," said Merrabel, tone clipped. "Don't ever do that again."

17

In the back of the lab, half hidden by a pile of dirty rags and broken instruments, was another door. Merrabel opened it to reveal a small room, choked with dust but fitted with a washbasin, a pitcher of water, a cot, a chamber pot, and a barred window set high in the wall. Cool evening light filtered in through the window and only then did Illi feel the first brush of real fatigue.

"These are your quarters," said Merrabel. "A servant will be by with food shortly."

Illi gave the room a cursory glance, then turned back to Merrabel. "Is this your room?"

Merrabel laughed, but the sound held no humor. "Of course not. But some of my experiments require attention day and night, and it has been helpful to have a room close by."

"And if I need to leave . . . ?"

Merrabel placed her hand on the door. "A servant will be by shortly," she repeated, then stepped back from the door. "Good night."

Before Illi could ask any more questions, Merrabel shut the door with a thud of finality. The lock clicked a moment later and Illi bristled. What would it take to earn Merrabel's trust? Illi had already willingly gone with her, willingly turned on Heru. Or did Merrabel suspect Illi was holding information back?

If she did, then she'd be right.

As Merrabel had promised, a servant appeared a few minutes later. Illi had pulled the cot over and was standing on it, examining the bars on the window, when she heard a polite knock. Before she could fully get down from the cot, a servant had opened the door, set a dish of food down, and closed and locked the door once more. Illi reached the dish just as she heard another door shut, this time on the other side of the lab.

The smell of stewed apricots and roasted almonds reminded her that she hadn't eaten since this morning. After cleaning the plate, she set it back on the floor where the servant had left it, then considered the door. Merrabel thought a locked door would keep her in. Well, Illi would just have to use that misunderstanding to her advantage.

Illi slid two picks from one of her braids and had the lock popped in a matter of seconds. With a gentle shove, the door opened onto Merrabel's darkened lab. The cheerful chaos of before now felt crushing in the gloom. Even if Illi had been tempted to use Merrabel's lab for her own experiments, she wouldn't know where to begin. No wonder Heru emphasized order so much.

Experiments weren't her goal tonight, anyway. She'd had enough of those to last her for days. No, she needed to learn more about Merrabel and Hathage, and the only way she could do that was if she left and explored the city.

So Illi slid her picks into the second lock and leaned her head against the warm wood as she felt her way around the lock's mechanisms. She closed her eyes, breathing in the door's faint, oily scent and wondering how much the wood must have cost as her pick cleared one tumbler, then another. This lock was more complicated than the first, but it still clicked under her hand.

Illi's smile grew. Merrabel thought she could contain a cousin, did she? Illi opened the door. Stepped into the hall. And froze.

A wall of soldiers greeted her. Their swords weren't drawn, but they didn't need to be to make their threat clear.

"You're not allowed to leave the lab, mar," said one. After a heartbeat he added, almost apologetically, "General's orders."

Illi's smile wavered. Her eyes flicked to the soldier's hand, settled on his sword, and in that instant, she could see the path to seizing that weapon for herself. But then she'd still be one cousin against a half dozen armed soldiers. It wasn't a fight she could reasonably win.

Not alone.

Heat thrummed in her chest in time with her pulse. It would be so *easy.* They were mere mortals; they'd have no chance against her.

One pair of eyes stood out from the rest, narrowed with suspicion instead of wariness. The rest of the soldier's face was hidden by a silver tagel; only two of the soldiers in the group wore tagels, the others choosing instead to leave their expressions open to all. But even without the tagel, the soldier's style of wrap and the kinds of knots they'd used reminded her of Ghadid.

That familiarity cut into Illi's awareness and she realized how close she was to letting the sajaami kill those soldiers. Her smile withered and bile burned her throat. She stumbled back inside and shut the door between them, harder than was necessary. She leaned against the wood and felt more than heard the lock click from the other side as she waited for her heart to slow, her hands to stop shaking.

That had been too close.

She still needed out; she cast around the lab for an alternative, but the windows were high and too narrow for her body to fit through. Illi turned and turned, but the lab offered no other way out. She was stuck, at least for now, at least for tonight. She took a deep breath, then another. She hadn't used the sajaami, that had to count for something. She was still in control.

If she was going to be stuck in here tonight, then she'd make the best of it.

She headed for Merrabel's desk. But when she reached the stacks of papers, she hesitated. *Not alone,* the sajaami had said. It had offered to help her multiple times, and although its offer was insincere at the least and most likely a trap, what harm was there in pretending to consider? Merrabel might have her years of study as an en-marabi, but Illi had something much better: the sajaami itself.

"Why?" She let the word out in a near-voiceless breath.

The warmth in her chest had cooled to skin temperature. Illi could feel her own pulse under the palms of her hands as she leaned against the desk. Her scalp was itchy, her hair stiff with dust, and she could still smell camel on her wrap. Maybe she should be cleaning herself up instead of whispering to spirits in the darkness. She was just about to push away from the desk and do just that when:

We both have little to lose and much to gain.

Illi's laugh came out as more of a cough. "What could I possibly gain from you? You're the one trapped, last time I checked. If I let you go, you'll destroy me and everything I love. I don't see the benefit here."

I have existed for countless millennia that your simple mortal mind cannot comprehend. The knowledge I possess would fill your libraries a thousandfold. My mere presence in your body is already a boon to your kind.

"Good, good," said Illi. "I'll be able to pass all that knowledge on when you burn through my body like that guuli did to Amil-cem."

It doesn't have to go that way.

Illi snorted. "Right. I'm sure you can control it. Just as I'm sure you can keep all the other promises you've made. If you're so all-knowing and powerful, how'd you get stuck in a vial hanging from a ceiling?" She paused, remembering that dusty afternoon surrounded by shattered glass, the memory now tinged with the smell of blood and fear. There'd been other memories then, memories not her own. Of a sea, of fire, and of darkness.

The sajaami *didn't* know everything. It couldn't, because it'd been trapped inside stone for so long. Maybe she had something to trade after all.

"If you were to go free now, what would you do? Where would you go?" asked Illi, quieter this time. "Do you even know how much the world has changed since you were bound?"

Mortals such as yourself still infest the world, so . . . not much.

"And the other sajaam?"

The others . . . started the sajaami, only to grow quiet.

"They're still bound to stone," said Illi. "You're the only one that's been released. And, considering how much planning and effort it took the Empress, you're probably the last."

No. Impossible. I am not the last. I will not be the last. There will be a way, once I am free of— The sajaami seemed to catch itself. The thrum of its heat cooled, hardened. *You will help me.*

"We'll see about that."

Illi closed her eyes and the room spun, the desk the only thing keeping her upright. Talking to the sajaami was surprisingly tax-ing. A part of her ached and stretched, seeking what she knew wasn't there. She'd need to find more guul eventually. Because if she didn't . . .

Illi didn't want to think about that. For now, all she could do was try to rest.

Illi was halfway out of the cot before she recognized a sound had woken her. She paused with her feet hanging over the side, just brushing the floor, and pulled the sheets around her tight, listening. But she couldn't hear anything over the thud of her own pulse and the occasional whistle of wind outside the window.

Let me help.

Before Illi could think of a reason to say no, she felt the sajaami *reach*. She didn't try to stop it; she didn't have time. In an instant, her awareness had extended beyond the door, brushing through the empty lab like a breeze. No, not empty. There: a spot of warmth.

The sajaami retreated without her willing it and Illi stayed still for a heartbeat longer, trying to understand as her wrists burned. Someone was in Merrabel's lab, but it hadn't felt like Merrabel. The room was dark, the window a rectangle of black, which meant dawn was still hours away. So who was here, and why were they approaching her room?

Illi stood and, on silent feet, crossed her small space. She pressed her ear against the door and listened. There: the scuff of shoe on stone. Close. Too close.

A hand thudded on the other side of the door, as loud as a hammer. Illi jumped.

"I know you're awake." A man's voice, as unfamiliar as it was unexpected. Illi cast around the room for a weapon, but there was only the ceramic chamber pot. That'd work.

"I've already picked one lock; this one won't take me long," continued the man outside her door. "But I haven't come here to threaten you." A pause, then, "You're from Ghadid."

"So are you," said Illi, knowing it was true, knowing now that he must be the soldier in the silver tagel from the hallway.

"Who hired you?"

"—what?"

"You're from Ghadid," repeated the soldier. "And here you are, sneaking about within the general's own chambers. Does she know what you are?"

Illi remained silent, too confused to answer. How could he possibly know about the sajaami? And even if he did, that was between her and Merrabel, not one of her soldiers.

"I would've thought you'd be better trained than this," continued the soldier.

"I have no idea what you're talking about."

"Then let me spell it out for you." The soldier shifted on the other side of the door, fabric rustling across wood. "You're an assassin. Someone hired you to kill the general. And I can't allow that."

Illi's throat tightened. She tried to laugh, but it came out as a wheeze. "*What?*"

"Who sent you? Was it the drum chiefs? The Serpent? Was it Amastan?" His voice wavered slightly on the last name.

Illi started at the names, warmth at their familiarity mixing with cold confusion. "Who are you?"

"So you don't dispute my accusations."

"Are you sane?" asked Illi, incredulous. But she didn't wait for an answer. "The drum chiefs have better things to worry about than some iluk they don't know in a kingdom they don't care about. And the Serpent is dead."

"She's dead?" The soldier let out a breathy laugh, somewhere between relief and bitterness. "At least there's some justice left in this world."

"I take it you weren't on good terms," said Illi. "But how do you know Drum Chief Amastan?"

A sharp intake of breath came from the other side of the door. "Drum Chief?"

Illi relaxed a little, letting the door take more of her weight. If he didn't know . . . "When was the last time you were in Ghadid?"

Silence for a heartbeat, two, then, "It's been a while."

"Who are you?" repeated Illi. When no answer came, Illi ground her teeth. "I'm not here to kill your general or anybody else, I can swear on that. I don't know how you know about my cousins, but things have changed since you were last in Ghadid. If you tell me who you are, maybe I'll be willing to tell you more." She paused a heartbeat, then added, "You miss it, don't you."

If she closed her eyes, she fancied she could hear the soldier breathing, quick and shallow. If he'd really thought she was here to kill Merrabel, he wouldn't be questioning her through a door. Which meant he was after something else. Maybe she could make a trade.

"Captain Yufit Uzbamen," said the soldier. "Of the King's Royal Border Guard. Colloquially known as the Guul Guard."

Any hope that she'd recognize the name was fleeting. Instead she flushed; would this captain know Canthem? Maybe she could ask him if they were okay. But no—Illi pushed the thought away as soon as she'd had it. Canthem was gone from her life, hopefully for good.

Still, a piece of her churned at the mere thought of them.

"Illi Basbowen," she said, a token in return for his name.

Another sharp breath. "You *are* a cousin."

"I never said I wasn't."

"But you said—"

"I said I wasn't here to kill anybody," cut in Illi. "And I didn't lie. But things have changed; we don't take contracts like we used to. Amastan saw to that."

"Has he," said the captain softly. "But I wonder if things have changed enough."

"You didn't know about the Serpent," continued Illi. "Which means you haven't been in the city since the Siege. How long have you been working with Merrabel?"

"Since the beginning," said the captain. "Since the Empire fell." A pause, a hesitation, as fingers scratched the wood of the door in thought, then, "It was easy enough to earn rank during all the chaos. The general needed any trustworthy bodies she could find; she didn't worry about where they came from. She proved herself to me and I proved myself to her in turn and together we kept this city—this kingdom—from falling apart."

"Is that why her city adores her so?" asked Illi, her tone snider than she intended.

"Of course," returned the captain immediately. "She found the king and kept him safe. She held the trial for the governor and made sure his execution was public and clean. She chased out the Empress's loyal followers, even purged the marab of the corrupt. She has dedicated her life to first establishing and now protecting this kingdom—you can't fault the people for praising her."

"I don't," said Illi. "But I wonder how far she'll go."

"As far as she needs to," said the captain firmly.

"And you?" asked Illi. "Will you follow her that far?"

"I came here to fight monsters. As long as there are monsters to fight, I'll follow her." The captain cleared his throat. "But what of Ghadid? I heard it weathered the Siege better than the other Crescent cities."

Illi's laugh was humorless. "We survived. Mostly through

luck, but also through skill. Those assassins you're so afraid of kept Ghadid from falling. But it was really Amastan who led us through."

"He . . . helped, did he?"

"You don't think they made him drum chief for fun, do you?"

"No." A low, long sigh. "*Drum chief.* Hah." Something clattered in the hallway and Illi felt more than heard the captain straighten and step away from the door. "I have to go."

"You're going to let me live for now, then?" teased Illi.

"The general doesn't appear to be in any immediate danger," returned the captain, cold as glass. "But I'll be keeping a close watch on you. You and your cousins aren't the only ones with your kind of training. If at any point I change my mind about you, you won't even know."

Before Illi could answer, his footsteps were clicking quietly away, soon swallowed by the night. Only by listening intently did she mark the far door opening and shutting, followed by the click of its lock.

18

Illi was shuffling through the papers on Merrabel's desk when she heard the lock click. Some of the papers fluttered in the breeze from the door opening, but Illi didn't look up. She'd been methodically searching Merrabel's lab since sunrise. An empty bowl that had once held porridge sat at her elbow. The servant hadn't seemed surprised that Illi was out of the back room.

Neither was Merrabel. "My captain informed me you attempted to leave once."

"I figured I might as well try."

"I appreciate your inquisitiveness." Merrabel crossed the room, carrying a box under one arm. "But it really is for your own good." She set the box on the desk and peered at what Illi had before her. "Can you even read that?"

Illi sighed and pushed the paper away. "No," she admitted. "I can pick out bits and pieces, but I don't know this language."

"I can teach you," said Merrabel. "That's a treatise on the various methods used today to quiet jaan and their efficacy. It's really quite fascinating. Here." She lifted the lid on the box, revealing several dozen tightly wound scrolls. "These are in your language, I believe. Or close enough."

Illi half stood to get a better look. "What are they?"

"A few introductory texts on jaan binding," said Merrabel. "I thought you could use something to fill your time outside of our ongoing experiments. I won't be able to be here every minute of the day. His Majesty may have absolved my court duties, but I still have an army to attend to and several delicate situations along our border to oversee. So we'd best be efficient, hmm?"

Merrabel left the box and walked back around the desk. "We've proved that you can contain and quiet guul, but the stories claim the sajaam are capable of much more, including calling storms and changing the land itself." At Illi's look of concern, she laughed. "Don't worry, I don't intend to look into those claims just yet. The more we know about how sajaam are similar to jaan and guul, and how they differ, the more we can refine our methods. For instance, guul and jaan are both susceptible to the elements, but releasing the sajaami just to observe what happens would be foolish. That means we're limited to poking and prodding and making deductions based on its reactions. For example, how many guards are outside the door?"

Illi felt the sajaami start to reach as it had last night, but quickly drew it back in. Feigning ignorance, she said, "How should I know that?"

"The sajaam were said to have controlled guul," said Merrabel. "Let's see if it has any affinity for jaan. Just—humor me."

Illi breathed deep, her gaze catching on the box of scrolls. Merrabel was holding up her end of the exchange. Illi could afford to give her a little in return. She let the sajaami *reach*. Immediately, her bracelets warmed. Like last night, the sajaami moved quickly, brushing past the door and across two spots of warmth just beyond.

"Two," said Illi.

Merrabel's smile sharpened. "What about in the whole palace?"

Illi hesitated; she hadn't even considered the possibility, but that would certainly be *useful* information to know. This time when she cast out, spreading the sajaami's awareness beyond brick and stone and metal and wood, her bracelets became uncomfortably hot and her wrists started to pulse with pain. She kept a silent count as she brushed across each warm spot. *Three . . . seven . . . twelve . . .* But as she found room after room, it became harder for her to keep track of the numbers.

The palace was *large*. Even though she couldn't really see it, she felt as if she'd walked it herself. And it bustled with jaan, some still, some moving from room to room, some almost as fast as her. Then the spots blurred together, her bracelets as hot as coals. She tried to focus on one more, but it was too much. Her awareness snapped like a severed rope.

The lab came back into focus. Illi blinked, her eyes scratchy and dry. The room spun lazily for a few heartbeats, her pulse too loud in her ears, before settling. Deep within her chest, the sajaami hummed.

Illi put a hand on the bench nearby to steady herself. "I couldn't get through the entire palace, but I stopped at one hundred and seventy-eight."

Merrabel made a noise of appreciation. She circled to the other side of her desk, leaned over it, and scribbled a few notes. When she straightened, she said, "With practice, I expect you can reach much further. For the record, there are currently two hundred and fourteen individuals in the palace, including guards, soldiers, servants, slaves, courtiers, healers, marab, and one king. You weren't far off. Now, hold out your hand."

Merrabel took Illi's hand between hers and examined it, turning it first one way, then the other. She pinched Illi's skin, prodded the bones of her wrist, and bent her fingers back one by one.

Then she drew a knife and slid the blade across Illi's palm. Illi yelped and snapped her hand to her chest.

"What in G-d's names—?"

"This has nothing to do with G-d," said Merrabel distractedly, trying to snatch Illi's hand back. "Hold still."

Illi hissed through her teeth, but let Merrabel have her bleeding hand. Merrabel held it, watching closely and counting under her breath as blood welled in the shallow cut and spilled free, rolling from Illi's palm to her wrist and down her arm. It tickled, warm and wet, but Illi stayed still.

Then, before the smell of blood could threaten to return her to the Siege, the cut began to heal, pulling itself back together in reverse. Merrabel took a sharp breath, her grip tightening until Illi thought Merrabel might crush her wrist. But there was no water nearby, no smear of blue, no evidence of healing magic. Just the plain fact of smooth skin where a cut had once been, and the blood that had leaked free, now crusted and dry. Her own mouth was as dry as dust and the room had begun to spin anew.

Still holding Illi's hand in her viselike grip, Merrabel steered Illi over to a table where a bowl of water waited. She wet a cloth and wiped Illi's hand clean, then set the pink-stained cloth in a bowl of its own. With the blood gone, there was only a thin line to indicate that there'd been any cut at all, and this was easily overlooked among Illi's other scars. Illi stared, turning her hand one way, then the other.

"But none of my cuts healed like this on the sands," she said, almost absently.

"You were dehydrated," said Merrabel.

Illi turned Merrabel's words over, trying to find meaning in them. Then horror filled her as she realized what Merrabel meant.

Water was a necessary component in healing, but water could be found in more than just a skin. "I used my own blood—?"

"Lacking another source of water, of course," said Merrabel. "It's inadvisable in most cases, since using blood to heal instead of water can create an unwanted link between healer and wounded, but if it's yourself . . ." Merrabel shrugged, then held the bowl of water out to Illi. "Here. You'll want to replace what you used."

Illi took the bowl but didn't drink from it. Instead she tried to feel for the pulse of the water, as she had on the sands and as she had in her room, covered in cuts and bleeding from the destruction of Heru's lab. But again, all she felt was her own pulse.

"Then why can't I heal when I want to?"

"That water is for drinking, girl." Merrabel glared at her until Illi took a long sip. Then she said, "To point out the obvious, you *are* wearing bracelets that were specifically made to restrain power, but they don't appear to stop you from healing yourself."

"But I've never been able to heal like *that* before," said Illi. "Never that fast." She finished the water and set the empty bowl on the table. "I'm not a natural healer, only trained to do the bare minimum: stop bleeding, speed up some healing."

"Hmm." Merrabel considered Illi for a moment, then went to her desk and riffled through her papers. She found a blank one and began writing. "That's exactly the kind of information I was hoping to observe. Sajaam have on occasion been linked to healing, but never in so direct a way."

"Essif was a healer," said Illi. "But she helped bind the sajaam."

Merrabel paused in her writing and looked up. "I'm sorry—what?"

"The story of the sajaam's binding. You know it, right?"

"Of course I do." Merrabel frowned in irritation. "But there was no mention of a healer."

Illi mirrored Merrabel's frown. "We must be talking about different stories, then. Everyone learns the story of the first healer. Essif's faith led her to bind the sajaam and she was rewarded by G-d with the ability to heal."

Merrabel snorted. "That's ridiculous. En-marab bound the sajaam."

"They helped. But it was Essif who knew what to do."

This time Merrabel actually scoffed. "A *healer* knew how to bind sajaam? The en-marab used blood and fire and thorns. Do those sound like healer tools to you?"

"No," admitted Illi. "But . . . there were signs from G-d. That's how she knew to use them."

"What makes more sense," said Merrabel carefully, leaning toward Illi, her too-bright eyes fixed on hers, "that a number of capable and well-trained en-marab bound the sajaam to stone in the Wastes, or that an untrained healer heard voices and knew exactly what to do?"

When Merrabel put it that way, it did sound absurd. "Essif was a real person," insisted Illi, but she didn't know if she was trying to convince Merrabel or herself.

"The names of real people get tied to unrelated events all the time." Merrabel shook her head and then picked up her pen, filling the lab with the sound of its tip *scritch-scritch*ing across paper.

Illi turned her freshly healed hand over, letting the light pick out her thin scar. *Is that true?* she asked the sajaami. But she only got smug silence in return.

She clenched her hand in frustration. "Why can't we just bind the sajaami to stone again?"

Merrabel sighed and set her pen down. "Rebinding the sajaami might help, but unfortunately it won't undo what its release disrupted. Besides, making such a long and arduous trek would be a needless waste of time and energy, especially considering the sajaami was already released once before. No, we'll need to destroy it to stop the Wastes from spreading and return balance to the sands and the sea. Destroy it, or find a way to harness its energy for our own use."

There it is. This time, Illi wasn't sure if it was her own thought or the sajaami's. Still, it didn't bother her that Merrabel wanted to do more than just destroy the sajaami. Illi had suspected as much since they entered the city. At least Merrabel wanted to *do* something.

"We'll destroy it," said Illi firmly.

Merrabel ignored her and stood, pulling on fresh gloves. "All right. I believe that's it for the day. I must attend to other urgent matters. You have your reading and a servant will bring food by again. Feel free to make use of my writing equipment if you must take notes."

Illi started. "You haven't been here hardly an hour," she protested. "Surely there are other experiments you could run. Or the story of the sajaam's binding—it could hold clues to how we might destroy it."

"That's what you can do, then," said Merrabel, already at the door. "Write down your people's myth and I'll add it to my collection in the morning. You can write as well as read, yes?"

Illi bristled. "Of course—"

"There you go. That should keep you busy while I continue to hold the entirety of Hathage together." Merrabel opened the door and stepped through, pausing long enough to offer Illi a thin-lipped smile. "Don't try to leave again."

The click of the lock echoed long after Merrabel had left. Illi stood for a while in the center of the lab, breathing in through her mouth and out through her nose to quench the anger that had flared. Then her gaze lit on the box of scrolls Merrabel had left her, and that anger turned to grudging gratitude. Heru had never once tried to teach her, yet Merrabel was willing to gift her a literal boxful of information.

Illi slid into Merrabel's chair and sifted through the bits of vellum and papyrus until she found one that had been neatly scraped clean. Merrabel might have dismissed the story of the healer Essif and the sajaam as a mere myth, but it was true. It had to be true. Maybe once Merrabel read her version, she'd know it, too.

Centuries ago, when the sajaam had been terrorizing the world of men, a single healer named Essif had gathered all the marab of all the tribes together to stop them. G-d had given Essif the tools she'd needed to subdue the sajaam: thorns to protect her from the sajaam, fire to keep back their guul, and blood to bind them to stone. The marab had helped her, writing the names of G-d and forming a seal to keep the sajaam in.

Illi reread what she'd written; the story looked so simple when shaped into letters and words, instead of spoken aloud. But there had to be something here, had to be—

You are wrong.

Illi set her pen down. "Yeah? Then why don't you tell me what happened?"

And potentially hand you the keys to my own destruction? The sajaami sounded affronted, yet somehow still smug.

"I don't know if that's in here," admitted Illi. "But if a healer could figure this out, then surely I can."

Essif was no healer.

"Of course she was, she was the first healer. I mean, I guess according to this she wasn't a healer until *after*, but still." G-d had supposedly given Essif the ability in return for her devotion and sealing the sajaam, but that part had always felt a little off to Illi. That part required she still believe in G-d.

Essif was no healer, repeated the sajaami. *She took that from us.*

Illi's breath caught. She opened her fist and stared at the scar on her palm, or what was left of it. "Sajaam can heal?"

We can do a great many things. Essif was greedy and broke off just a piece of us for herself. But even a piece is powerful enough to cross generations.

Illi was only half listening as she pulled open the drawers of Merrabel's desk, searching for a knife. Finally she found a small one for sharpening the point of a pen. She didn't hesitate before pressing it deep into her palm and splitting the skin. She sucked in a breath as she watched the flesh come together before her eyes again. The dizziness that followed was like a gentle breeze, easy to ignore.

The thirst was harder to ignore. Thankfully, Merrabel had left her an entire pitcher of water. Illi broke her skin again, deeper now, and this time blood welled free from the cut before it could heal. The room spun and she thought she smelled smoke, but she tightened her grip on the edge of the desk and remained there. Under her breath, she muttered words she'd heard Heru say while binding guul and jaan, but nothing happened.

Of course not; the sajaami was already bound to her.

What are you trying to accomplish? The sajaami sounded amused.

Illi cleaned off the blade and put it back in the drawer. She took a long drink of water, but it didn't ease the swirling in her head. When she stood, the room pitched momentarily into darkness before settling once more. She sat back down.

"Let's practice something else for now," she said to the empty room.

And she began to count the guards in the palace again.

19

The days in the lab blurred together. Illi marked the time by the click of the lock that signaled Merrabel's arrival in the morning and the click of the lock as she left.

Some days, Merrabel arrived with breakfast and left well after the servant had brought dinner for them both.

Some days, Illi had enough hours of daylight to go through all of the scrolls in the box as well as the notes Merrabel had left out on her desk. She was even beginning to understand some of them.

Merrabel had been right about the scrolls being in Illi's language, but even though Illi recognized the individual words, together they made little sense. The text reminded her of the few times Heru had spoken at length about his work: dry, rambling, and convoluted. Now, at least, she knew where he'd learned how to speak like that.

To think that he and Merrabel had actually *studied* together. It was difficult enough to picture Heru as an advisory marabi to the Empress, with all the power and facilities that must have entailed. Imagining his life before that, before he'd become an expert on jaan, a student who hadn't known much more than Illi—that was all but impossible.

Some days, Illi only had the evening to practice her burgeoning understanding of en-marabi science. Letting the sajaami *reach* one night, she'd quickly discovered that Merrabel had doubled the guard in the hall. The guards were only the thickness of a door away, yet that distance made many of the bindings she wanted to test ineffective. According to the scrolls, her own blood was only half of the connection; she needed theirs as well. But there were other ways to affect the guards' jaan than just binding them.

So she slid the knife across her palm and squeezed her hand until the blood rolled between her fingers and each time the scent of smoke and the distant punch of screams was a little weaker. She muttered the words she'd read in Merrabel's scrolls—half that she recognized from Heru, half that were completely new to her—and pointed at where the guard's heart would be if the door weren't in the way. The first few times, she felt nothing. She almost slipped and used the sajaami instead, to its delight, but the heat of her bracelets warned her in time.

Then one night, after Merrabel had taxed her control longer and harder than usual, Illi muttered and bled and pointed and something shifted. Illi could almost see the line between her and the guard, frail as a spider's web and taut as a loaded bridge wire. She tugged. On the other side of the door, someone cursed.

Illi's smile was triumphant. And then her wrists flared with white-hot heat, and dizziness crashed over her, sending her to the floor. By the time the bracelets had cooled and her ears had stopped singing, whatever tenuous connection she'd created was long gone.

But this cut on her palm didn't heal like the others. A silver scar ran through the lines of her palm, cutting them all short. The sight was strangely reassuring. She'd wondered at the hundreds of silver scars lacing Heru's arms and hands, why someone as vain as he hadn't asked a healer for help with those, why he hadn't used a sharper knife. But now, at last, she had an answer: the scars were tied to each connection, even the failed ones.

Too bad it wasn't the answer she was looking for.

The next time Merrabel visited, she noticed the new scar immediately. Illi had just enough time to add a mark to her tally on one of the sheets of paper—the eighth of its kind—before the general took Illi's hand between her own gloved ones. She prodded the line of flesh, then tightened her grip and met Illi's gaze.

"Why do you insist on meddling with this when you can do so much more?"

Illi stared back. "I'll do whatever it takes to destroy the sajaami. Will you?"

Merrabel sighed and looked away. "Of course."

Then she'd drilled Illi on different types of bindings before testing and retesting her ability to feel the presence of jaan. By the time daylight thickened with evening, Illi was more than just physically exhausted. Her head was stuffed with cobwebs and her ears whined with a persistent ringing. For the first time since she'd arrived in Hathage, Illi was glad when Merrabel declared her day done early and left.

Illi was done, too. Done with staying in this lab. She'd made the decision the night before, but she hadn't been willing to act just then. She'd read and reread every scroll, had picked over every cabinet, every drawer, every bench in Merrabel's lab. She'd pried the sajaami for more information, but it had stayed smug and silent. And Merrabel's captain hadn't bothered to threaten her again.

It was as good a time as any for her to explore the city.

Some things were better done in the darkness of night, so

Illi passed the time by rereading the scrolls and the notes she'd written. Exhaustion clung to her and more than once she stared longingly toward the bed in the other room, but she'd made her decision. Getting out would help her feel better. Of course she felt so thin and frail—she'd been stuck in this small room for over a week.

As she read, she periodically let the sajaami *reach* past the door. There were only two guards now, which was both a compliment and an insult: that Merrabel didn't trust her not to try again, and that only two would suffice. If she'd wanted to leave and never return, Illi could have thrown open the door and been through the two guards in moments.

But she just wanted some air; she didn't want Merrabel to throw her out. Even though it'd become painfully clear that the general was dragging her feet instead of finding a way to destroy the sajaami, Illi was learning too much to burn through the trust they had, however tenuous it might be. Besides, it was refreshing to be treated like a pupil for once, instead of another piece of lab equipment.

Illi checked the time; the sand had almost fully run through the hourglass, which she'd already turned several times. It had to be closing in on midnight; there'd be no better time for her attempt.

The blade slid easily across her palm and blood welled in the wound like a welcome friend. She crossed to the door on bare and silent feet, muttering the few words of binding she knew under her breath. She pointed at where she'd last felt the guard and as blood rolled down her wrist and arm, she felt the thread grow taut.

She *pushed*, sending a sensation of urgency through the connection. The guard grunted and then she heard a low murmur of words just on the other side of the door. A clank of metal. Then a thud of boots retreating.

Illi allowed herself a small smile. From Merrabel's scrolls she'd learned that the balance between jaani and body was so intertwined that the needs of one were indistinguishable from the needs of the other. Just a little push had been enough to convince the guard he desperately needed relief.

Now she wiped the already drying blood from her arm, steadying herself against the door as another wave of dizziness washed over her. She was just tired. Fresh air would fix that.

But to get that fresh air, she had to do something she'd been avoiding. She could make one guard leave through a weaker connection, but she'd need to physically be in contact with the remaining guard to bind him to her will. While influencing another living person was one thing, controlling them was a step too far. That left her only one other way she could safely take the guard out of commission: use the sajaami.

She'd just have to take the risk.

The sajaami eagerly *reached* when she brushed her hands across the door and this time she didn't draw it back when she felt the warmth of the guard's jaani. Illi let the sajaami slide like a knife between the guard and their jaani.

Her wrists flared with fresh pain as the bracelets turned hot, but she steadied her breathing and kept her focus. If she lost control for even a heartbeat, the sajaami would snatch up the jaani for itself. It pushed against her, its yearning for just that leaching into her until her jaw ached from clenching against the need.

One, just one, and you could be so much more powerful—

Illi hummed a half-forgotten prayer deep in her throat and pushed away the sajaami's wants. Quiet. That was all she needed: to quiet the jaani. She wasn't even sure she could, but the scrolls had gone on at length about the role of the jaani and its body, and how one animated the other. Which meant that, if she was right, then—

Thump.

Illi let out the breath she'd been holding, warm relief stirring inside her. But as her focus relaxed, so did her control, and instead of letting go of the guard's jaani, the sajaami tightened around it. She was so tired, so drained, so hungry—

Illi snapped back, stumbling away from the door as horror replaced the relief. Frustration lodged in her chest like a foreign object. Her bracelets were as hot as midsummer glass and she felt something warm trickle down her wrist and across her palm. A growl clambered up her throat and she wasn't sure if it was hers or the sajaami's.

She was tempted to wait and regain her composure, but she knew she'd only have a minute or two before the other guard returned. Still shaking from having almost lost control and killed the guard, Illi picked the lock and opened the door.

The guard was slumped on the ground, head nearly touching their boots. But their back moved with breath, so Illi allowed herself a small amount of pride. She'd quieted a jaani. Not only that, she'd quieted a jaani still tied to its living body. She doubted even Heru had ever done something like that. She pictured his look of skeptical incredulity when she told him, and smiled.

When. Her smile faded as she searched the guard for a key and relocked the door. She'd turned on Heru, abandoned him, and all but forgotten him. If that wasn't the most thorough way to burn a relationship, she didn't know what was. And for good reason, too—he'd used her, he'd lied to her, and he'd refused to see her as a person.

Yet returning to Ghadid without him felt *wrong.* She might

never fully forgive him, and he forgive her, but he was still Heru, the only person who'd known how to clear the plague from Ghadid's water, who'd found a way to quiet wild guul, the one person she never had to pretend to be okay around—she could just *be*. *When* this was all over, *when* she'd learned all she could from Merrabel, *when* the sajaami had been destroyed, she'd return to Ghadid with Heru.

Assuming he would even want to go. Assuming she could find him. Assuming he was all right.

Intermittently letting the sajaami *reach*, Illi found the courtyard without running into anyone. She'd had to stop and hide a few times, but no guards came thundering through the hallways. As she'd hoped, the guard must have woken up and, feeling ashamed at falling asleep on duty, said nothing. A twist of the doorknob would prove that it was still locked, and no one could have escaped if that were the case.

Each time she let the sajaami *reach*, though, dizziness blew through her and her wrists ached even more. When she stepped into the night-blanketed courtyard, she stopped reaching. No one would be looking for her out here.

The courtyard reeked of jasmine, the scent weighed down by the water in the air. Small, lit torches lined the path to the towering doors, and Illi welcomed their brush of warmth as she passed. Then it was a simple matter of pushing open one of the doors and walking through the arch—and she was free.

The moon's light flattened the warm, vibrant colors of the doors and windows along the street. While the streets were certainly quieter now, there were still more people out and about than Illi had expected. That was for the best; this way she wouldn't stick out so much.

Illi breathed deep. Merrabel's lab had a window, but nothing compared to the movement and sensation of open, fresh air. She caught whiffs of jasmine, of other flowers she didn't recognize, of roasting meat and hot almonds and spiced apricots, of sharp salt and something else, something too sweet like decay.

She picked a direction and started walking. She didn't have a destination in mind, or a plan—it was enough to be out. It was enough to be free. Maybe it was small of her to need to commit this act of defiance, but could she be blamed when Merrabel had insisted on locking her up?

Besides, she'd never been in another city before. And Hathage was unlike anything she'd ever imagined.

The buildings were all several stories high with neither beginning nor end, blending seamlessly together for blocks at a time. Ahead both they and the road curved out of sight. Most of the walls were white, with the occasional gray or beige thrown in. But the doors were splashes of blue, red, and yellow, and equally colorful braids of cloth hung from windows and balconies. Bells jangled in the constant breeze.

And the *trees*—

Before the Siege, a few drum chiefs had cultivated date palms. But those seemed small, mean things compared to these trees, which stretched over her head farther than she could reach. And there were so *many* trees. One grew every other door.

Her gaze followed the line of buildings curving away until they abruptly stopped at the solid gray wall that had cut behind the palace. The wall drew Illi down the street, its implications gnawing at her. What did it keep out? What did it contain?

She wanted to know. And those towers spaced along the wall would offer a perfect view of the city, of everything she'd been denied.

The wall loomed higher over her head, blocking out more and

more of the stars and the moon's light until, from one step to the next, she walked through shadow. Then the street diverged sharply east and west and the buildings ended suddenly, as if cut by a knife. The only thing ahead was the wall, so expansive and monochrome that Illi could believe the world ended right here.

The sharp reek of salt was stronger now and cut with something pungent, bright, and only a little off-putting. Like vinegar, if mixed with winter and sunlight. But overwhelming it all was the familiar and alluring taste of water lingering in the air, as if there'd just been a storm. But no clouds blocked the stars, and even deep within the palace, Illi would have heard thunder.

Merrabel had mentioned a drought; if this was a drought, what was it like normally?

West now, she followed the base of the wall until she came to one of those towers. It was a simple construction, metal that bulged from the wall itself with no decoration or fanfare. The whole thing was very utilitarian. There should've been carved images or geometric designs or *something*, but the wall was just flat metal, occasionally interrupted by a rivet. Whoever had built this wall hadn't cared about aesthetics or beauty; they were solving a problem.

The entrance was an open arch that led into a confined space with the only options either back out or up the steep, narrow steps that twirled upward and away. Illi began to climb.

As her foot came down on each step, she imagined what must be on the other side. Another city, cut off from this one after they'd betrayed some ancient rite. The desert, dropping away and away to an endless horizon and filled with nastier monsters than the Wastes. Or the detritus of a terrible plague, the wall their only solution.

She heard it first: the distinct slap of water against metal. But even as she recognized the sound, so much like water sloshing inside of a flask, she couldn't comprehend it—it was too *vast*.

Then the stairs ended and Illi stood in another open doorway, the breeze slapping her with that same sharp, salty reek that had thickened on her way up. Her eyes teared up and she pulled her wrap tight; it was much colder up here.

The top of the wall cut through the night sky. To the left, the city, startlingly white even in the darkness. To the right—

It looked like metal, glittering under the stars and the quarter moon. Metal that stretched to the horizon. Metal that moved. Metal that rippled and undulated like a bowl of water, sloshing quietly. But magnified a hundred times, a thousand times. It wasn't metal *like* water, though.

It *was* water.

The water was mesmerizing, glittering as it slammed into the wall over and over and over again, throwing up spatter and spray that flickered like diamonds in the moonlight. So much water, endless water. It was unreal. Impossible. And yet.

Shoc scuffed against stone. Illi snapped back to herself, her hand going to her empty belt before she remembered she still had no knives. Her thumb brushed across her rings and she remembered Thana's gift: she had something far deadlier, if it came to it.

Someone stood in the doorway, in clothing so colorful even the moonlight couldn't dull it. Swaths of green fabric swirled with blue mingled with red and the whole ensemble was held together by a beaded belt that useful for anything but decoration. But the same dusty red tagel covered their face, if lower than Illi had last seen it, and Illi would have known those eyes, warm as sand, anywhere.

Illi sucked in a breath. "Canthem?"

Those eyes smiled. "Just Illi."

Illi felt suddenly very fragile, as if someone had replaced all of her bones with sand and the slightest breeze might send her toppling. Her heart thudded too loud in her ears, masking the sound of wind and waves, and her stomach might as well have been filled with shattered glass. She was torn between grabbing Canthem to find out whether or not they were real and putting as much distance between her and them as she could.

She did neither. Her feet could've been glued to the spot. She opened her mouth to speak, but all the words she might have said stuck in her throat.

Canthem's smile wavered, crashed. "Are you all right?"

Illi looked down at the water on one side, the city on the other. At any moment, she could topple either way. "Yes."

Canthem sighed. "You don't have to lie to me. I'm just concerned. You look . . . unwell. And down below, you walked right by me, like you weren't fully there." They paused, cleared their throat. "You went with the general, didn't you."

It wasn't a question, so Illi didn't answer.

"Are you sane?"

That startled Illi into answering. "Of course. Why . . . ? Does your beloved general usually rattle the brains of those she's around?"

"I would never speak ill of my general," said Canthem carefully. "But she doesn't limit herself when it comes to her country. There are rumors about what she's willing to do. What she's done. And she's taken an interest in you."

"I'm fine," said Illi, lifting a hand to brush a braid back over her shoulder. "I can take care of myself."

Canthem stared. "Your hands . . ." They cleared their throat again, a tick that was beginning to irritate Illi. "You didn't have those scars when we first met. I would've remembered."

Illi dropped her hand and curled it into a fist so her palm wasn't visible. "You're observant."

"Illi . . ." started Canthem, then they stopped, shook their head. Tried again. "I'm sorry. I can't pretend I don't care about you. And I can't pretend I'm not worried. When the general returned and you disappeared from the caravan, I assumed the worst." They laughed, but the sound was humorless and dry as dust. "I thought you were dead."

"Clearly I'm not."

"No. Not yet. But those marks—I know what those mean. You're binding jaan. Don't, Illi. It'll ruin you."

"But you're fine with Merrabel—"

"General Barca has already sold her soul," said Canthem earnestly. "She accepted the price, and she would accept it again in a heartbeat. But you don't need to do that."

"You don't know what I need," snapped Illi. "Nor what I've already sacrificed. What's a little blood?"

"You do know the cost, right?" asked Canthem, their eyes searching hers.

"It's blasphemy." Illi shrugged. "But so what? G-d's back has been turned on me for a long time."

"*No,*" said Canthem, sounding almost angry. "Binding jaan—it's the blood, Illi. The connection. There's a cost, there's always a cost, and the cost of binding is your own jaani."

A chill wound through Illi along with a thought not her own, *They're not wrong.*

Then why didn't you say anything? she bit back.

What need do I have for your jaani?

"That doesn't make sense," she said, trying to buy herself time to think. Then, "How do *you* know all this?"

"My mother was an en-marabi," said Canthem, sounding bitter. "She was reckless."

"And it killed her?"

"No, the general did."

Illi stared. "But you serve Merrabel."

Canthem looked away, fingers curling into fists. "Yes. Because it was the right thing to do."

"Oh . . . I . . ."

"Your mother didn't dabble in en-marabi magic, I hope."

"No," said Illi. "She only dabbled in dirt. She was a glasshouse gardener."

The words came out as easily as if she talked about her mother every day. What would her mother think of her now? Alone in a foreign city, collaborating with the very person who'd threatened Ghadid? Illi had slipped away from her home and her cousins in the cold stillness of morning, had betrayed the one person she'd ·felt safe around, had extinguished the warmth of guul and jaan alike. She'd committed multiple blasphemies without a single hesitation.

And she was prepared to commit more.

Illi balled her hands into fists, felt the scars on her palms pull and itch. It didn't matter what her mother would think. Her mother was dead, her jaani one of hundreds lost to the Wastes. And yet, a small piece of her flushed with shame.

Illi turned to the vast and impossible water, pushing those thoughts away. "What is this?"

Canthem followed her gaze. "The sea?"

"The sea," echoed Illi, turning the sound of it over in her mouth.

She took a step, then another, until she stood at the edge of the wall. There was no railing, no ridge to keep her from falling. She'd stood on the very edge of a platform once, her toes overhanging nothing, a drop of over a hundred feet between her and the sands below. Even though this water was much closer, Illi felt the same rush of adrenaline, the same inexplicable, self-destructive urge to *jump*.

Yet now there was something else, a chill of fear deep in her chest that seemed to be pulling her back even as she wanted to step forward. The sands would have been an instant death, clean. This sea, however . . .

"What is it?" she asked. "How much water does it contain? And why? Is this where Hathage keeps its reserve, out in the open air where anyone can steal it?"

Canthem laughed. Illi took a step back from the edge, clasped her hands behind her back, and waited. Their laughter faded awkwardly into silence.

"You're serious."

"I am. This isn't possible. The water should seep through the sand or evaporate or . . . was there a storm recently? Maybe I didn't hear the thunder."

"I—it doesn't. The sea is just the sea. It's always there. I don't know how much water it has, but the ships that dock at our port sail for weeks along the coast. The sea hasn't always been this high." Canthem prodded the wall with the toe of their boot. "A few centuries ago, the people who lived here built this wall in a desperate attempt to keep the sea from flooding the city. They'd built walls farther out, even ditches and levees, but none of those could stop the sea."

Illi didn't know what *sailing* meant, but she could picture weeks of travel. She tried to imagine that much water, but her imagination quickly came up short. She looked down at the sea only a dozen feet away, then at the city several dozen more. They'd built the wall before the sea had reached them. And then it had kept coming.

"It's actually gone down a bit in the last few decades," said Canthem.

"Like the sands," said Illi quietly.

Whoever had built Ghadid had set the city on platforms above the sands to escape the creep of dunes. The dunes had risen, but they'd also subsided. The city had started out barely a camel's height from the sands, within reach. Now the sands were hundreds of feet away. The world had shifted and changed everywhere.

And they blamed us.

"We were one of the lucky ones, believe it or not," said Canthem. "A lot of cities had been built along the coast once, but the sea took its tithe. It seems satisfied for now, and we'll be fine so long as the wall stands."

Illi considered the sea for a long moment. All that water, just out in the open for the taking. What Mo wouldn't give for such a blessing. But Ghadid was hundreds of miles away; this water was useless to her. And useless to Illi, as long as she kept these bracelets on. Hathage didn't have healers like Ghadid did. It seemed unfair that they'd have so much water instead.

Canthem moved closer and Illi stiffened. She'd let herself get too comfortable. It was so easy to just *be* around Canthem. Their very presence was reassuring, solid. Safe. A familiar pylon in these foreign sands.

Her hand found theirs. Squeezed. She'd escaped Merrabel's lab to breathe, to relax. Canthem was safe here, in the city, where there were no guul for days. She knew; she'd've felt them. At the thought she *reached* just in case, feeling along the length of the wall even as she leaned into Canthem.

She wasn't expecting to find anything. But she felt someone. In the tower. No, not in.

On.

Illi spun around just as the assassin threw their knife.

20

Illi yanked Canthem down. They let out a breath of surprise as a knife pinged off the nearby stone. Illi grabbed the knife, then put herself in front of Canthem, throwing out her arms to keep them back. The assassin leapt down from the tower's roof, landing on the wall in a crouch. They wore a black tunic, belted tight, their muscular arms left exposed. A hood buried their features in shadows.

Illi was on them before they could straighten. The assassin stumbled back, moonlight flashing off a blade in each hand as they countered her assault. Illi pressed them back step by step, her attacks relentless. But even though the assassin gave ground, they kept up with her, even managed to slip in a few counterattacks. And Illi was tiring, fast.

Too fast. She was used to sparring with her cousins for hours, just as all-out. But after only a minute, her breathing was ragged, her pulse out of control. What was wrong with her?

Pain flared across her shoulder. The assassin had scored their first hit. Emboldened, they pushed her back. Illi was now the one giving ground. Blood trickled from the wound. Despite all the water in the air and below, Illi's mouth had gone dry.

She couldn't afford to be distracted. The assassin turned away her every blow, their own blades coming dangerously close. Illi's arms ached. With every heartbeat, her chances of making a deadly mistake rose.

Let me help.

As the assassin turned Illi's blade away and swept around with their own, Illi let the sajaami *reach*. She felt their jaani, bright as a hearth fire, strong and hot. She wrapped the sajaami's will around it. Her bracelets flared with heat, burned. All she had to do was relax and let go. She'd feel so much better after she took that heat for her own.

But she hesitated.

The assassin's blade caught her forearm. Sliced deep. The pain wrenched her back. Her weakened fingers let go of the knife. The assassin seized their opportunity and sliced toward her throat.

Canthem shoved her aside, caught the assassin's arm, yanked. They twisted the knife from the assassin's hand and drove a knee into their stomach. The assassin stumbled back, but already had a second knife out and ready. Their hood had fallen back, revealing a pale face, darting, dark eyes, and a closely cropped beard. Illi recognized this man; he'd been part of the general's guard that had accompanied the caravan.

So why was he trying to kill Canthem?

"Usaf?" said Canthem, equally surprised.

Illi growled. She had no weapons at hand, at least no knives. But she still had the rings on her fingers and Thana's gift. "You can't have them."

The assassin had the audacity to look confused. Then Canthem distracted them with a punch to the jaw. Despite the exhaustion dragging at her, Illi lunged. Her fist clipped the man's chin, her rings breaking skin. The assassin tried to give ground, but Canthem was there, blocking his way.

The assassin's knives flashed, but the wound on Illi's forearm was already closing; she could afford to be a little reckless. The assassin didn't expect her to press forward and he wasn't ready in time; his knife only grazed her side. Then her hand slid around to the back of his neck, grabbing tight to his hair so he couldn't get away. She brought her other hand to his mouth, but not in a punch. Just as her rings grazed his lips, she popped the top off one and white powder spilled out, sucked into the assassin's mouth as he gasped for breath.

She let go and pushed him away. The assassin stumbled. Illi carefully put the cap back on the now empty ring. The assassin drew another knife. Illi waited, fists up. The assassin began to cough. The knife dropped. The assassin choked.

Thana had been right. It didn't take long for the assassin to die. He gasped breathlessly for a few moments, mouth opening and closing on nothing, then his eyes rolled up into his head and his legs gave out and he crumpled to the ground. Illi waited another moment before prodding the body with her foot; the assassin didn't respond. She was briefly tempted to roll the body over the side of the wall and into the sea; if anyone deserved to have their jaani go wild, it was someone who'd just tried to kill Canthem. But she resisted the urge. There were still lines she wouldn't cross.

Canthem grabbed her arm. "Are you all right?" Their fingers rubbed across the dried blood on her arm, found the freshly healed skin. "What—?"

Illi yanked her arm away. "I'm fine. What about you? Did he get you at all?"

"No. But he wasn't after me." Canthem's gaze lingered on Illi's arm for another heartbeat before they lifted their gaze to hers. "That knife was aimed at you, Illi. When I tried to distract

Usaf, he was still fighting *through* me, to get to you." They turned to the corpse, made a strange circular gesture over their chest, and bowed their head. "May your jaani pass swiftly, but what in G-d's infinite names were you doing, Usaf?"

"He was one of the Guul Guard."

Canthem nodded. "It's not unheard of. Our particular skill set is well-suited for such precise work. Someone hired him. The captain must have known. That's why . . ." Their gaze sharpened. "What enemies have you made?"

"None," said Illi, baffled. "I never had a chance; I never left the lab."

"Well, someone's been waiting for you."

Illi crouched and began running her hands along the body.

"What're you doing?" asked Canthem.

"Just . . . checking . . ." Illi turned out a pocket, but all it held were a few loose coins and lint. She found another knife strapped to the assassin's thigh, which she slid through her own belt before beginning to undo Usaf's.

"Okay, *no.*" Canthem put a hand on hers. "If it's an incriminating note you're looking for, he wouldn't be so stupid as to carry it around with him."

Illi huffed her annoyance, but left the belt alone. "I'm not convinced the target was me." But even as she said it, she remembered Merrabel's warning if Illi left. *You're playing with lightning. . . . I won't have to wait long.* Would she have been so reckless as to risk releasing a sajaami in her city?

But Merrabel had said as much already. Illi just hadn't believed her. And now her thoughts were whirling away from her, too thin to grasp. As she straightened, the world narrowed, the night closing in. She didn't fall, but only because Canthem was

244   //   K. A. DOORE

so close, their body as solid as a wall. She leaned against them, waiting for the dizziness to pass. But this time it didn't. This time it grew and it grew and it grew until it was a roar in her ears.

Illi? she thought she heard Canthem ask, but she couldn't be certain.

Just reach.

I'm right here. Arms lifted her up, a body pressed close.

All you need to do is reach.

Put your arms around my neck. Illi tried to comply, but all of her muscles felt as if they'd fallen asleep. A tingling spread through her entire body and she knew what was happening. She'd fainted before. There was no point in fighting it.

She let it take her.

The darkness closed over her like a shroud. But unlike the handful of other times she'd fainted, she was still present. She was aware. The darkness churned like the flames in a furnace. Red smeared the air before her and it didn't need to grow a face for her to name it.

Nejm.

That is a name I have carried with me for ages.

Is it your *name?*

The red tightened until it became almost tangible. *Does it matter?*

Names have power.

Behind the red, the darkness was thinning, clearing. Blue showed through, and beneath, endless beige.

It is a name given to me, ages and ages ago. Unlike yours, Illi Bas-bowen. You wear yours like a child.

I'm not a child.

To me you are.

The beige blurred, undulating like a piece of flowing fabric.

Blue pulsed in the beige, haloed by green and gray. Above, clouds flitted like dreams across the sky. They darkened and threatened and dissipated in the same heartbeat, gone as quickly as they formed.

Centuries, child. Millennia. I have seen your kind come and go and come again.

The beige shifted. Darkness scattered across it as if blown by the wind. Cities, rising and falling and rising again. They overtook the blue, covered it. The clouds thinned. Stopped altogether.

We were not always at odds, your kind and ours. But in the end, that didn't matter. You wanted what wasn't yours. We tried to stop you.

The cities spread. New clouds appeared, but these were strange, off somehow. They sprouted as long, thin trails that dissolved almost as quickly as they'd appeared. Lights glinted in the blue sky, even in the middle of the day. The air itself seemed to thicken.

You didn't want to be stopped.

The spots of blue thinned and disappeared altogether. The cities began to recede, but slowly. They thickened, turned dark. Smoke curdled the sky.

Then the world shrank and shrank and shrank until each grain of sand was nearly a mountain. The sky *crack*ed and stone covered it, sealed everything in. The air was sucked away and then there was nothing.

Ages of nothing. Eons.

Why are you showing me this?

I want you to understand. The darkness thickened, then the smear of red returned. *We are more alike than you think. Unique. Alone. With the world against both of us. Together, we are stronger than the world. But apart, I will always be stronger than you.*

The red seethed, twin pits of darkness opening in its center.

You are fragile and falling apart. You cannot destroy me and I have nothing to lose. All I have to do is wait, and I have already waited so long. But all you have to do is take off those bracelets, and you could work with me. Together we could crush all of your enemies and grind them into the dust they came from. Nobody would dare threaten you.

Why?

The red seemed to hesitate, even pause. . . . *Why?*

Yeah. Why wait? If you're so powerful, you could overcome me at any moment.

Why waste the effort? A hint of smugness tinged Nejm's words. *Your mortal life is little more than a whisper of wind, here and gone in the same instant.*

Illi couldn't feel anything in this cold, dark space, but she mentally squared her shoulders and matched the pits of darkness with her own stare. *No—that's not how this is going to work. For one, you're wrong. I'm not alone. I have a family, a city, that I need to protect. They are free and alive while your kind are all bound to stone. The world has moved on. No one truly fears you anymore. For another: why are you even still here? This world isn't yours. You don't belong here.*

Now the red swirled tighter, angrier. *How dare you—*

There's no point in sticking around anymore, pressed Illi. *I'm not going to take off my bracelets and I'm not going to let you win. Maybe, instead of threats and coercion, you should try something new, like passing on.*

The red whirled violently, blazing and brightening, overwhelming the darkness, overwhelming her. She felt Nejm's anger like the heat of summer, oppressive and paralyzing. Yet at the same time, she felt herself reaching, stretching beyond the heat to something cold and small and dark. Then: a pop. The cold gone, but the heat lessening, receding.

You will fail. You have always failed. And when you do, I will be here.

And you'll *be alone,* said Illi.

Nejm hissed, a sound that started low but quickly filled the space like the tumble of a million grains of sand—beating, beating, beating like a drum that was calling Illi elsewhen, elsewhere—

Illi gasped, opened her eyes to complete disorientation. Her body was being jostled with each step, as if she and whoever was carrying her were falling down and down and down. She stared into a bundle of bright orange fabric and she breathed in salt and cinnamon. Arms held her close. Her own arms had been looped around a neck. Her fingers tightened on damp fabric.

Nothing made sense, but already the memories were returning. She'd left the lab. Climbed the wall. Met Canthem. Been attacked. Felt dizzy. Weak—

The pieces fell together. She was in the tower and headed down the stairs. Canthem was carrying her. She could feel their pulse in their hands, in their shoulder pressed against her cheek. It was reassuring. At least they were all right.

Nejm's anger lingered, haunting her. Illi hadn't thought it would be possible to insult such a creature, but she'd clearly struck a chord. All she'd done was suggest it cross over, of all things.

Of all things . . .

Illi gasped, the sound knocked from her by Canthem's movement. The answer was there, right *there.* The sajaami didn't need to be destroyed. It needed to cross over.

The knowledge burned in her. Merrabel. She needed to tell Merrabel. The scrolls she'd read had touched on the crossing ceremony and how it might be used for wild jaan, even guul. It'd never been considered for sajaam, but why not?

It was thin, it was tenuous, but now she had a *plan*.

Illi started to squirm out of Canthem's hold when they reached the street. "I can walk."

"Can? Sure. Should? No," said Canthem firmly. "I don't know what Usaf did to you, but I'm not going to risk it."

"He didn't—" started Illi, before stopping. Canthem didn't know about the sajaami. If they'd reacted that poorly to her doing a little en-marabi magic, what would they think about her eating a few souls?

Cold stole over her. She'd tried to take Usaf's jaani, but she hadn't. Right? Yet she felt warmer now, more steady. Her mind still fuzzed at the corners, but she was thinking. And there'd been that sensation toward the end of their conversation, when she'd angered Nejm. That had just been the sajaami proving a point. Right?

But Illi couldn't lie to herself. And she couldn't lie to Canthem. So she let the sentence hang unfinished and she let Canthem tighten their grip and carry her all the way back to the palace. She was thankful for the small mercies of the moment: that it was dark; that she could hide her face in Canthem's shoulder; and that none of her cousins were in the city to see this.

It didn't hurt that Canthem smelled so nice.

Merrabel was waiting for them in the courtyard. She stood in almost the same spot as the king had when they'd first arrived, with almost the exact, rigid posture. But her expression was far more furious.

"I ordered you not to leave." Merrabel's voice was even and clear and all the more terrifying for it.

"We were attacked by an assassin, mar," announced Canthem. Then, to Illi, "Do you think you can stand?"

Of course I can stand, she wanted to say. But they'd just saved her and carried her halfway across the city and even though she knew she should drive that wedge between them again, she couldn't find the energy. "Yes."

As Canthem set Illi on her feet, Merrabel crossed the space between them and grabbed Illi's arm and yanked back the sleeve. Her fingers found and examined the silver bracelet, then pushed and prodded up her forearm. Illi started to pull away, but Merrabel's grip tightened. Her thumb brushed across the recently healed flesh of the assassin's cut and she hissed.

"How are you still alive?"

Illi had expected a dozen and more questions, but not that one. Thankfully, Canthem answered, "She's fast, mar. And well-trained."

But that hadn't been what Merrabel meant. Illi pressed her lips tight, unsure how to answer. Merrabel grabbed her chin and yanked her head up, forcing Illi to stare into those glass-pale eyes.

"Are you sane?"

"Yes," said Illi.

Merrabel let go but didn't step back. This close, her musty breath made Illi gag.

Without taking her gaze off Illi, she said, "Your assistance in locating my charge is appreciated, Guard Canthem. Go, tell the rest of the guard to ready to leave within the hour. I've received some disturbing reports of guul in the foothills. Captain Yufit is already on his way with his own force. You'll join him. You're dismissed."

Canthem bowed, their fingers spreading in that ridiculous birdlike way. Illi didn't laugh. Instead, her chest tightened as she watched them go. It hadn't been her choice to send them away this time and a part of her wanted to defy Merrabel and leave with them. What if they were wrong, and the assassin had been contracted for them?

Yet the other part of her knew Canthem was right, and knew they could handle themself. Besides, Illi was more of a danger to them than anything else in this city. Hadn't she just proven that when she'd taken the assassin's jaani?

As soon as Canthem was gone, Merrabel asked, "What did you do?"

"I was attacked by an assassin."

Merrabel shut her eyes and let out a tightly held breath. When she reopened them, she seemed no less furious. "We've been over this before. If you lie to me or evade the question again, I *will* turn you out. And now you've seen the danger you're in, the danger that's outside of these walls and my control."

Did you send the assassin? Illi wanted to ask, but the words stuck to her tongue.

"Someone must have seen you arrive," continued Merrabel. "They noted my absence in court and put the two together. All they had to do was wait for you to leave." Her tone sharpened. "Which you should never have done. So I ask again: that wound—what did you do?"

"I healed it," said Illi. "And then I killed the assassin."

"With the sajaami?"

"No. With poison." It wasn't a lie, so Illi was able to meet Merrabel's gaze straight on. "But . . . healing that cut made me weak. I passed out. That's why Canthem had to carry me."

Merrabel pressed her lips tight together, eyes searching Illi's face. Then she said, "Yes. I'm surprised that's all it did. Just because the sajaami is healing your body doesn't make you invincible, Illi. Every crack is a weakness the sajaami can use against you. The markings and the bracelets are keeping the sajaami in check, but only just barely. If your body is damaged too much, the sajaami *will* break free. It will destroy you. That's all it wants."

"It wants to destroy much more than just me," said Illi, remembering Nejm's hatred and anger. Then, with a sudden urgency, she added, "But we don't have to destroy it. I know what we need to do now, what we *can* do. We don't destroy the sajaami—we make it cross over. If there are ways to help guul make the crossing, then we can find a way to adapt the seven-year rite to a sajaami."

The seven-year rite. As the words left her lips, panic unrelated to the attack, unrelated to Merrabel, unrelated, even, to the sajaami, began to rise within her.

"What day is it?" she asked just as Merrabel opened her mouth to speak. Illi turned, checked the sky, tried to remember what phase the moon had been when they'd left Ghadid. "How long until the shortest day?"

"That's a superstition," said Merrabel dismissively. "The rite can be performed on any day of the year. But I was going to say—"

Illi counted and counted again. Two weeks with the caravan. Eight with Merrabel. No, no, it couldn't be too late. "*How long?*"

Merrabel sighed. "Nine days."

"It's not too late." Illi felt as if someone had tossed a glass vial her way and she'd somehow caught it. She hadn't missed the rite. She could still make it back to Ghadid in time if she left today. If she rode hard, she would have a day or two to find an answer. And she knew the answer was close, knew it in the sajaami's evasions and sudden anger.

"It doesn't matter," said Merrabel. "We don't have time to prepare for a rite. We're needed in the foothills."

Illi blinked. For the first time, she took in Merrabel's attire; it *was* a little strange that the general was wearing a full wrap, as well as her red cloak, gloves, and boots, in the middle of the night.

"But that's what your guard are for."

"Yes, I will need them, too," said Merrabel. "But I'd come to fetch you because, seeing as this is the first possible incursion of guul on this side of the Aer Caäs, I wish to be personally involved. And seeing as how there are already assassins after you, it couldn't come at a better time. Don't worry; we can continue our ongoing experiments in the field."

But that wasn't what Illi was worried about.

21

The camp looked as if it'd been thrown together in under an hour. Maybe it had. The shallow valley stirred with movement and noise, most of which was coming from a makeshift, circular pen at its center. Soldiers and guards alike moved with purpose around the pen, some adding heavy wooden boards to an already thick wall, some holding torches for light, and some standing watch along the perimeter of the camp.

Illi shivered under her wrap, which was inadequate for this kind of cold. Her nose had gone numb and she kept her fingers under her armpits to keep them from sharing the same fate, only bringing them out to wipe her trickling nose.

The cold blue of dawn cracked the horizon, but day's warmth was still hours away. They'd ridden hard and fast through the dead of night and now the jagged peaks of the Aer Caäs split the sky in half: one side full of stars, the other full of stone.

At the edge of the camp, Merrabel slid from her horse and handed the reins off to a waiting soldier. She approached the pen without fear or hesitation, even as the walls shuddered beneath a heavy blow from within. Illi took her time dismounting, not ready to let the sajaami close to the guul. It was humming again, excited.

"Captain," called Merrabel. "What's your report?"

A man broke away from the soldiers and approached, hands loose at his sides. He wore a silver tagel, knotted high enough that his eyes barely showed. But the torchlight caught on his eyes all the same as they flicked across Illi and widened with recognition. His hand twitched toward his sword, but he caught himself and looked at Merrabel. "All contained, mar."

If Illi hadn't already recognized Captain Yufit by his tagel, she would have by his voice: as cold and smooth as his eyes. "Three guul total," he continued, ignoring Illi. "They attacked a farm nearby, killed two of the farmhands and a goat. We drew the guul away and trapped them, as ordered."

"Any surviving witnesses?"

"Another farmhand, who was smart enough to run instead of trying to fight," answered the captain. After a heartbeat, he added, "And several goats."

"We'll have someone compensate the farm for their loss," said Merrabel. "Now, show me these guul."

"Yes, mar."

The captain gave Illi another glance before turning and leading them toward the pen. Inside, a guuli snarled and launched itself at the wooden stakes that made up the pen's walls. A soldier shouted back at the guuli and shoved their sword into a gap between the stakes and boards. Then the soldier shouted again, this time with surprise as their sword was yanked out of their hands and into the pen.

"*Back away,*" snapped Merrabel.

The soldiers turned at her voice and, upon seeing her, immediately fell into a line, one hand over their chest, the other at their side. A clacking noise came from within the pen and, as they drew closer, Illi realized one of the guul was running its talon along the wooden stakes. Testing for weakness.

Merrabel slid her gaze along the row of soldiers, then pointed at a guard just beyond them. Even though they wore the same dull brown wrap and rusty red tagel as the other guards, Illi immediately recognized Canthem.

"You," said Merrabel, drawing Canthem toward her with a hooked finger. "We'll need bowls and clean water. Bring those. The rest of you," she said to the soldiers, "will fall back. Keep any civilians from getting near and otherwise stay out of my way."

Canthem's gaze flicked to Illi, but they didn't dare hesitate. They nodded once before turning with the other soldiers and giving Merrabel space. The general breathed deep as she paused in front of the pen, one gloved hand raised, as if in greeting. Then she dropped her hand and began rummaging through her belt pouches. She moved with an energy Illi hadn't seen since she'd first met Merrabel.

This close to the pen, Illi didn't need the sajaami to feel the three bright spots of heat. They were strong, stronger than any guul she'd encountered before. Illi's chest hummed and it took her a moment to realize that the charms around her neck were vibrating.

"Why haven't your guards quieted them yet?" asked Illi. "Why did they only capture them?"

"Because I ordered them to." One of the guul clattered past, its talon briefly piercing through the space between the slates, inches from Merrabel, but the general remained as still as stone. "We have a unique and profound opportunity in these guul, Illi, an opportunity no one has ever had before. We might finally be able to understand the relationship between the sajaam and the guul. These are the first guul ever caught on this side of the Aer Caäs, the first guul I've captured. Bringing them back from the Wastes has always proven too dangerous. But now we'll finally be able to test the full extent of the sajaami's capabilities."

Illi peered through a gap in the slates at the guul trapped within. These looked far more human than any of the guul she'd fought before. In lieu of their usual collection of body parts from various species, these wore almost entire human bodies, with scavenged vulture talons and jackal jaws. One had jammed jagged stones into its shoulders and down its back, but it still looked remarkably human. Which made these guul far more horrible, because Illi knew exactly where those bodies had come from.

"But . . . why?"

Merrabel turned her gaze on Illi, lips pursed in a frown. "We've been over this, Illi. I'm beginning to question my initial evaluation of your intelligence."

"No, I mean—we have an answer now," said Illi. "We need to help the sajaami cross over. How is any of this going to help with that?" Illi gestured widely, taking in the pen as well as the soldiers and hills. She could feel time slipping through her fingers, precious and fleeting.

"It's not," said Merrabel. "Because that's not our goal. I already told you that I disagree with your assessment. We must continue to understand the sajaami before we can find a way to destroy it." Merrabel unlatched a pouch from her belt and turned away. "Come."

Merrabel walked around the pen until she reached a place where a board was secured to the next by a lock and a length of thick chain instead of nails: a gate. She stopped and spilled salt from her pouch on the ground in front of the gate. She slipped a knife across her forearm and stained the salt red with her blood. Then she pressed her other hand against the wound until Canthem returned with a bowl of water and a clean cloth. After she cleaned and bound her wound, she unlocked the chain and opened the gate.

The guuli that had been testing the slates was already there, talons reaching for their faces. Illi jerked back but there was no need; the guuli hit an invisible wall. It spit and hissed its irritation, but didn't try again. The other two tested their way forward, but Merrabel held up her hand, still stained with her own blood, and spat words at them. They edged back.

"Take them," ordered Merrabel. "Make them obey you."

Illi gritted her teeth. "I don't see what this has to do with destroying the sajaami."

Merrabel ignored Illi and gestured at Canthem. "Guard, stand behind us. We can't risk these guul escaping."

"But the salt—" started Illi.

"Salt can be smudged," said Merrabel. "Everything will be fine as long as you control the guul."

"This is a waste of time."

"Then you'd better be quick."

Merrabel shoved Illi over the line of salt and into the pen. Illi cried out but caught herself before she could stumble and fall. Behind her, Canthem shouted a warning. But Illi was already dodging the first guuli, its talons slicing her wrap but only grazing her side. The second and third wakened from their daze and rushed her. Illi grabbed for the knife she'd taken off the dead assassin, but her hand found only belt and cloth. She glanced at Merrabel for help, but the general was waving a knife. *Her* knife.

Illi gritted her teeth, but she didn't have time for anger. She dodged one guuli, blocked another, and then her back hit the pen wall. She was trapped.

"Illi!" warned Canthem.

The third guuli's claws came for her face. Illi closed her eyes and let the sajaami *reach*. She waited for the bite of those claws across her cheek, but it never came. All three guul had stopped. She could feel each of them like a pulse in her palm. Hot and alive and straining against her will and so very, very tempting. But they stayed still.

"Good." Merrabel's voice drifted to her from across the pen. "Now make them obey."

Illi opened her eyes. She was trembling, her wrists burning from the bracelets, the blisters reopening. She could barely hold these three guul as it were. "No."

"You seem to be under the impression that my orders are optional."

Merrabel slashed her arm again with Illi's knife, opening a long, narrow wound that soon brimmed with bright red blood. Canthem shifted uneasily on the other side of the salt, their hand on their sword. Merrabel's lips moved wordlessly and her hand swept the pen, taking in the three guul. Illi felt her control slip just before the guul were wrenched from her grasp.

She stumbled, her back hitting the stakes. Dizziness washed over her as fresh blood trickled down her wrists and between her fingers. The guul were moving away, if jerkily.

"We're going to try this again," said Merrabel, her breathing strained. She stepped back and her foot smudged the line of salt. She glanced down, saw the damage, then said, "Well. Shit."

The guul broke free of her control. They rushed Merrabel. She threw her arms up, as if that would be enough to stop them. But they never had a chance to try. Movement blurred and then Canthem was standing between Merrabel and the guul, their sword deflecting one and catching the arm of another. But the third seized their opening and claws came for Canthem's neck.

"No!"

This time when Illi *reached,* she swatted the guuli back. It whimpered, ducking its head as if it were a submitting dog. But the other two pushed around the suddenly docile one and continued at Canthem. Illi knew she didn't have the strength or finesse to stop all three, so she wrapped her will around the first and *pushed.*

Protect.

The guuli snarled and raised its claws, but instead of striking Canthem, it hit one of the other guul. Canthem took the second, their sword separating its human head from its human body. Illi pushed the other guuli on, encouraging its relentless attack on its brethren. Her wrists burned, but the pain was less than she'd expected; directing the guuli's rage was far easier than trying to stop it.

Canthem's gaze flicked between Illi and the remaining, uncontrolled guuli. Illi nodded. They moved behind it and beheaded the guuli in one easy motion. It was too simple a reaction to pluck the guul from their bodies before they untethered, to take their warmth for her own.

The last guuli swiped the air where the other had been, then spun and locked gazes with Illi. In that heartbeat, Illi was back in Heru's lab, trying to step out of the way of thirteen angry glares.

These blazing eyes held no anger, not anymore. They blazed with something else. Awe. Fear. Worship.

Illi felt the guuli in her skin and bones, energy and will bound together in its purest form. A spark of life, a piece of G-d, if the myths were to be believed. If it truly was a piece of G-d, then what did that make her, bending it to her will?

The sajaam decided they would rather be G-d. Mo's voice came to her across all those miles, reciting the story of the first healer.

Who wouldn't want to be G-d? said a different voice, much closer.

Bile rose in Illi's throat. Not her, never her. All she wanted was to protect her home, her family. She didn't need to be G-d to do that. She just needed to be herself. She just needed to go home.

A slap rang out through the sudden silence, followed by a second and a third. It took Illi another moment before she realized it was Merrabel. Clapping.

"Excellent." Merrabel approached the last guuli, her fingers still dripping blood. "That was most illuminating. I wasn't quite certain you'd be able to take control in time, but it seemed that sufficient motivation helped you focus. Do you realize what you've done? You're controlling a guuli with no formal training. A task that would take decades of study took you mere seconds. Just imagine what we can—Illi? What are you doing?"

Illi had crossed the space between her and Merrabel. She drew Merrabel's sword, then turned back to the guuli as Merrabel sputtered her surprise, ignoring her words.

Words. The sword didn't have the proper words engraved into it to trap the guuli. Illi tightened her grip. No matter. The sword had her.

Illi swung. At the same time, she guided the guuli with her will, forcing it up, into the skull. The blade connected with its neck, separating its head from its body. The head hit the soft dirt with a wet thwack. The body thudded to the ground a moment later.

Illi reached, felt the guuli still contained within the head. Trapped, for now. Then she let go. Her arm fell, the weight of the sword dragging it down. Illi stared at the corpse, dry flecks of red the only blood it had left. Exhaustion swept through her like a breeze.

"What a waste," said Merrabel, surveying the damage. "We could have learned so much from that guuli. Well, no matter. Now that guul have crossed the Aer Caäs once, they'll certainly do so again. We can set up camp here and continue our experiments. Guard Canthem, go fetch the captain. We'll need to begin preparations immediately."

As Canthem departed, Illi dropped the sword next to the body. Without looking up, she said, "No."

"I suspect with some additional training, you'll be able to control more guul," continued Merrabel. "You could draw them safely from the Wastes. Imagine: an entire army of guul at your command. No one would dare attack Hathage, let alone our caravans. The court would finally give me room to breathe."

"An army of bound," said Illi faintly. Merrabel would have her become the very thing Illi had vowed to defend her city against.

"Yes," said Merrabel.

"No."

"No?"

"No. I'm done here." Illi turned, took her dagger from Merrabel's unresisting fingers, and slid it back into her belt. "The seven-year rite is in a week. I can still make it back in time if I leave now. I have to be there, I have to understand how we can make the sajaami cross over. And if I don't, I'll take it back to the Wastes, where it will do far less harm."

"You're not leaving."

Illi barked a *hah*. "Try to stop me."

She started to walk past Merrabel and through the gate, but the general blocked her way.

"You're being willfully dense," chided Merrabel. "You can't take the sajaami to the Wastes. Think of the harm it would cause, the harm it's already caused since its release."

"I have," said Illi. "But I don't think *you* have."

Merrabel held out her arms. "We've been given a gift. You can't just throw that away. We'll find a way to use the sajaami to solve the problems it has caused. We will turn its disruption to our advantage. We can become unconquerable. Listen to reason, child."

She's not wrong.

Illi clenched her fists, pain spiking up her arms from her blistered and bleeding wrists. "Step aside."

"Don't make this harder than it has to be."

Illi continued toward Merrabel. When the en-marabi refused to move, Illi *reached* and swatted Merrabel to the side like a fly. Or, at least, she tried to. Illi might as well have swatted at a wall. Her will slid across something slippery-sharp, and too late Illi remembered the charm Merrabel wore.

Merrabel's expression tightened and any remaining warmth left her. "I warned you before not to try that."

In one motion, Merrabel slipped a dagger from her belt and slashed her palm. She squeezed her fist until blood dripped from between her fingers. Illi stepped back, but not far enough. Merrabel lunged, slapping her palm, now slick with blood, against Illi's forehead.

Words dropped from Merrabel's lips, more breath than form, each syllable as strange and foreign as when Heru spat commands at the guul. Illi stiffened as a fuzzy sensation spread across her, thin as gauze but strong as glass. Her wrists burned and her back itched. The words continued and the energy grew taut, like a bridge taking the weight of a first step.

Illi didn't notice when the words stopped. Her ears were still ringing with them, even though Merrabel's lips no longer moved. She stood as still as stone, her limbs stiff and her senses dulled as if she'd been wrapped in a thick woolen blanket.

Merrabel removed her palm from Illi's forehead, her skin sticking for a moment with the drying blood. She stepped back through the gate and laid one hand on it, ready to slam it shut. She watched Illi. When Illi didn't move, a smile turned up her lips.

Merrabel drew a stained cloth from her pocket and began wrapping it around her palm. "You were warned. You will stay here. Someday you'll understand. Until then, you will remain bound to my will. Hathage requires your service. You're not going home, not until I say so."

22

Illi stood helplessly in the center of the room, far from any escape or weapons. All of her senses were smothered, as if she'd been plunged into a bowl of oil, but Merrabel's words still whispered in her ears. Merrabel had escorted her to the nearby farmstead and the survivors had all but fallen over themselves to accommodate her in their gratitude. They'd offered her food and water and glass; she'd asked for a room.

The room was a simple one, with a bed and a table and a window. No bars, no steel, no reinforced walls. Illi doubted the window was even locked. Merrabel had taken no precautions because she'd already taken the biggest precaution: Illi was bound to her will. Merrabel had told her to *stay*, and so Illi was trapped in this room as surely as in a jail cell.

Or so Merrabel thought.

It took her a moment, fighting the blurry sensation blanketing her all the while, but Illi only had to *stretch*. Merrabel's binding broke with a snap and Illi could smell and see and hear crisply again. Her wrists burned like hot irons and Illi tried not to think about how her blisters were continually reopening each time she used the sajaami's power. Something warm trickled down her palm. Illi brushed her hand across her wrap, smearing red across dirty gray.

So Merrabel thought she could keep Illi here. Like a servant. Like a pet. Like an experiment.

Well. Illi stretched her arms overhead, feeling a satisfying *pop*. She'd see about *that*.

Merrabel had relieved Illi of her weapons, but while searching the small room Illi found a pen and its knife. She pocketed the ink, too, just in case. Then she checked the window: unlocked, as she'd suspected. Illi couldn't help feeling a flush of annoyance. After all their time together, did Merrabel really think so little of her?

But Illi wasn't going out through the window.

She rested her head against the wood of the door and closed her eyes. Then she *reached*. She felt the tethered jaan that meant living people scattered throughout the house and was surprised when she found none immediately outside her door. Merrabel wouldn't be *that* reckless, would she?

Then—ah. Someone approached. Perhaps they'd only stepped away for a moment. Illi tightened her grip on the sajaami and waited, listening to the *thud* of nearing footsteps. Her wrists throbbed with pain and her hands were stiff with dried blood and her body pulsed with exhaustion but she wasn't going to rest until she was well away from here.

The rite was only a week out and she still had to gather supplies, a camel, and Heru. What had started as a question only a few hours ago had quickly hardened to a certainty: Heru would be coming with her, whether he wanted to or not. Heru might have lied to her, might have used her, but those crimes paled next to Merrabel's blatant manipulation, to throwing Canthem in harm's way to make Illi obey.

And even if Heru couldn't help her, for all the time Illi had spent in his lab, he might as well be family. She might as well care about him.

The person had reached her door. Illi had just begun to slide her will between the cracks when the handle rattled. She jerked back and away, her fist tightening around the penknife. A key turned in the lock. Illi pressed her back against the wall next to the door. She'd been able to feel their jaani, which meant it wasn't Merrabel on the other side. Just a guard. And she could handle a guard.

The door opened. Illi held her breath. A guard stepped through. Illi raised her hand to strike—eyes first, throat second, then she'd sweep out their legs and choke them unconscious.

Then the guard turned, eyes finding Illi.

"Canthem?"

Their gaze flicked to her upraised hand and she dropped it. Without thinking, she fell into them, curling her arms before her and knowing they'd catch her. And they did. Canthem held her close, grip tight and strong. She breathed in the sweet cinnamon of their scent for one heartbeat, two heartbeats, then pushed away. She didn't have time.

"You're all right," said Canthem, marveling. Then their gaze took her all in and their expression clouded. "Maybe not in the best shape. What did she do to you?"

"She bound me," said Illi. "What are you doing here?"

"Checking on you," said Canthem. They glanced away, gaze roaming over the small room instead. "And, maybe, rescuing you if the need arose." Then they stiffened and stared at Illi, eyes wide. "The general *bound* you?"

"Yes. But it didn't stick."

"That doesn't—"

"Aren't you disobeying direct orders by being here?" asked Illi.

"No," said Canthem, and their eyes glittered with mischief. "She never ordered me not to rescue you."

"Even if she did, you'd be clear. I don't need to be rescued."

To prove her point, Illi stepped out the door. She'd half expected to meet a wall of resistance, but there was only air. She started down the narrow hallway, *reaching* just far enough ahead to be sure she wasn't about to run into anyone.

Canthem caught up to her at the end of the hallway and put a hand on her arm. "I can still help."

"Right now, being quiet until we get out of here would be a *great* help," whispered Illi.

Pans clattered and water hissed and voices murmured just out of sight. The scents of fresh herbs and sharp cheese were denser here. She *reached*, but even as she counted the jaan in the room beyond, Canthem brushed past and out into the open. Too late, Illi grabbed for them, but the fabric of their wrap slipped from her fingers.

"Hey, that smells delicious, sa," said Canthem loudly. "Do you need any help?"

The clattering paused. "Oh no, sa. This meal is the least we can do for your soldiers saving us."

"Please—I insist. The general's got me cooped up in here and I'm going stir-crazy."

"If you insist, sa. There *are* onions that need chopping."

"Can you show me how?"

"You don't know how to chop onions, sa?"

Canthem chuckled. "I suspect my way of chopping might be different from yours. Just—real quick, sa."

"All right . . ."

Illi peeked around the corner just as Canthem joined one of the farmers at the counter. They nudged the farmer so that their back was to Illi as she crossed the room. A few more guards sat around the hearth, but they were too busy watching Canthem with amusement to notice her slip outside.

The warmth of the house fell away like a glove removed and she welcomed the cold bite of early morning. The sun was only just climbing into the sky, but its heat was still little more than a distant candle's flame. Illi hesitated for only a moment as she took in her surroundings. The hills rolled away to either side but here the ground was relatively flat. A field full of withered stalks and desiccated vines, long without water, spread to her left, and another building sat short and long to her right.

A horse huffed inside. Illi headed right, hoping the farmers had more than just horses. She was disappointed. The long building held several mounds of hay and a number of stalls, half of which were stuffed with goats, the other half with horses. There wasn't a camel in sight. Illi eyed the horses with distrust.

"At least they don't bite."

Illi turned to find Canthem leaning against a wall. "Did you at least finish with the onion?"

Canthem's eyes lit up with a grin. "The onion stung my eyes, so they sent me out into the fresh air."

"Good." Illi walked along the stalls, examining each horse, hoping one of them might be less frail, less skittish. "You can distract them again when I leave."

Canthem cleared their throat. "That'll be hard, since I'm coming with you."

Illi stiffened. "You can't leave your general. She ordered you to come here and fight the guul."

"Yeah, but she didn't order me to *stay*."

"Canthem—"

Illi turned and they were so much closer than she'd expected.

Her breath caught and her fingers lifted, drawn to the knots on their tagel. Canthem took her hand between their own.

"Illi," they said, quieter this time. "I think the general ordered Usaf to kill you."

Illi stiffened. *She* knew that, but if Canthem suspected . . . "Why?"

"I don't know. But the captain said he'd seen a messenger with the royal insignia arrive before Usaf left."

"But that doesn't prove it was her. It could've been the king. Or someone else on his court. They seem to always be after her about something, maybe they were trying to get her attention."

"General Barca handpicked the king's court herself," said Canthem. "They're all loyal to her—perhaps too loyal. If any of them did send the assassin after you, it would have been under her orders. She doesn't tolerate disobedience." Their gaze slipped past her to the horses. "That's why I came to find you and help you escape. What makes her an excellent general doesn't always make her an excellent person. I respect her drive to keep Hathage safe, but unlike her, I believe you can go too far."

Illi shook her sleeves back and held up her arms, revealing her bracelets, raw red skin peeking out beneath. "It's too late for that."

Canthem had the decency to gasp. "What did she do?"

Illi dropped her arms. "Nothing. Yet."

"But what are those?" Canthem reached for her, but their fingers only brushed her arm.

"What she wants," said Illi. "Well, what she thinks she wants."

"And what does she want?"

Illi hesitated. Instead of answering, she pulled at her sleeves, worrying at the ends. If anything would permanently drive

Canthem away, it would be knowing what Illi had done, what had been done to her. But now driving them away was the last thing Illi wanted. She was tired of being alone. Yet she also needed their help, and if they helped, they'd need to know.

She had to risk it. "Do you know why Merrabel came to Ghadid?"

"To find Heru Sametket."

"But why?"

Canthem gave a half shrug. "She thought he could show her how to get the guul under control."

Control. That's all it had ever come down to. Merrabel had feigned interest in the disruption, in the changes to the Wastes and the climate, but she'd been planning to use the sajaami for control all along. What had happened in the pen with the guul and Canthem hadn't been an accident; it'd been a culmination.

Illi found she wasn't at all surprised.

"Did she ever tell you why she thought that?"

"No," said Canthem. "But then, it wasn't our right to know."

"Heru had a sajaami." Canthem's sudden sharp breath cut through Illi's resolve like a claw, but she forged on. "Merrabel wanted it."

"Did she get the sajaami?"

"For a little while," admitted Illi. She forced herself to meet Canthem's gaze as she held up her wrists. "But now I'm leaving." When Canthem's brows furrowed in confusion, she continued, "These bracelets keep the sajaami in check. Heru bound it to me. If your mother was an en-marabi, you know what that means."

Canthem took a step back, tagel fluttering with shallow breaths, eyes wide. "I do."

Illi's hope collapsed. She could practically watch Canthem's remaining trust in her drain away. It was for the best. Canthem would be safer if they stayed away from her. They could live out their life in Hathage, fighting guul. She wouldn't have to worry about them, or be distracted by them.

"That's why you could control the guul in the pen," said Canthem faintly.

Illi nodded, not trusting herself with words, waiting for Canthem to call for help, to draw away, to abandon her. She waited for the inevitable.

But instead of doing any of those, Canthem asked, "What do you need?"

"I—you—but your general—"

Canthem stepped forward and took her hands. Theirs were warm and that warmth spread up her icy fingers and through her arms. "If trying to break you out from my own general didn't make it clear enough, I care about you, Illi. So: how can I help?"

"Thank you." Illi fought the urge to lean into Canthem and let them hold her up; she didn't have time for that. "We have to get rid of the sajaami before Merrabel can get it. We can't destroy it, but we might be able to find a way for the sajaami to cross over. The seven-year rite is our best bet, but it was created for quieted jaan, not sajaam. I don't know how to modify the rite so it'll work, but I do know my city will be performing the rite in a week's time, and this one will be much bigger than any before. They've already had to modify the rite to account for wild jaan. If I talk to the marab, I can learn what and how and find a way to create a ritual that will force the sajaami to cross."

She gestured at the horses. "Which is why I need to make it to Ghadid in seven days. And before I leave, I need to find my old master. But I don't know where he is."

"Just south of here," said Canthem immediately. "I saw where they took him. The soldiers kept pace with the caravan until they reached the jail."

"For once some good news." Illi puffed her relief and began to unlatch the stall door in front of her. "Great, lead the way."

But Canthem held up a hand. "I just want to be clear you know what you're doing. Breaking a prisoner out of jail is a capital offense."

Illi raised an eyebrow. "*Now* you're concerned about laws? Don't worry, we won't be caught."

"You sound so certain."

"I know what I'm doing."

Illi slid into the stall. The horse huffed at her, ears flattening against its skull. Illi started to reach for its neck, but then realized she didn't know how to guide the animal out of the stall without a lead. The horse wore no halter and there hadn't been one hanging nearby. Illi considered the beast; it considered her right back.

Behind her, Canthem laughed. "Need help?"

"Aren't there any camels?"

"Not for miles." Canthem edged around her, holding a rope halter in one hand. "There'll be some in the town your friend is jailed in. We can trade this horse for a camel or two there."

"Oh thank G-d." Illi couldn't imagine trying to cross the sands on a horse. The poor thing would collapse from dehydration after only a day at the pace she intended to ride.

Canthem slid the halter over the horse's head and tightened the knots. Then they led the horse out of the stall and into the center of the barn. They gave it a few whispered words and soothing pats before settling a blanket on its back.

"What I don't understand is why the general would send Usaf

after you." Canthem lifted a saddle from a pile against the wall. "She of all people must understand how dangerous the sajaami is."

"She understands," said Illi. "That's why she wants it. I can only guess that she was getting impatient."

But Canthem shook their head. "Usaf left the barracks shortly after the general returned." They finished tightening the strap that went beneath the horse's belly, then straightened and met Illi's gaze. "Usaf was in the city the entire time you were."

Illi sucked in a breath. "He was just waiting. Merrabel had no intention of ever letting me leave."

"And yet, here we are." Canthem gave the horse an appreciative pat. "I will do my best to keep you safe, Just Illi."

Illi smiled. "I can keep myself safe. Just . . . keep me company."

Canthem raised both eyebrows at that, but before they could comment, a shadow shifted outside. Illi stepped back into the darkness of the stall, the penknife in hand, just as Captain Yufit entered the barn. Canthem bowed, spreading their fingers wide behind them, then straightened and coughed.

"Sa."

But the captain wasn't looking at Canthem. He was looking into the stall, directly at Illi. Even in the wan light, Illi could see that his eyes were a liquid gray. "Will you kill her?"

Illi lowered the penknife. "Sa?"

"The general," said the captain, annoyed. "Do you plan on killing her?"

"No," said Illi.

Captain Yufit considered her for a long moment, then drummed his fingers against his thigh and narrowed his eyes. "But she has no such reluctance about you. I was there when the messenger arrived for Usaf. I overheard what he'd been instructed to do, if not to whom. That's why I sent Canthem into the city, to keep an eye on Usaf and stop him if needed. I can't allow my guards to commit murder."

"If your general ordered it, does it count as murder?" asked Illi.

"Yes," said the captain. "I've kept a close watch on you since you arrived and as far as I'm aware, you've committed no crimes and shattered no oaths. Yet. But if you and Canthem walk out that door and break a man out of jail, you will have. And then I won't be able to defy the general's orders. So I ask again: will you kill her?"

"With respect, sa, I already said no," said Illi. "Merrabel can attempt to kill me again if she wants, and if she tries herself I can guarantee I'll shove a knife through her throat, but I see no reason to preempt her. She just wants to protect her home, by whatever means possible." Illi spread her hands. "I can respect that."

The captain tilted his head, watching her as if she might still change her mind. Then his eyes brightened with a smile.

"Things truly have changed since I left Ghadid."

Illi's stomach twisted and she smelled smoke and fire, heard screams. She tightened her fists until her nails cut into her palms and she breathed. "You'd be surprised by how much Ghadid has changed." Then, struck by sudden inspiration, she added, "Why don't you come see for yourself?"

The captain stepped back as if Illi had physically pushed him. His eyes flicked left and right, before settling on a point not far above Illi's head.

"No, I—that wouldn't be wise."

"Why not?" pressed Illi. "Merrabel's down to one guuli bound to a skull, and she's got more than enough soldiers for that. If you stay, you'll only be complicit in whatever she's planning next.

And I'm sure it's going to include more than just a little murder." When the captain remained stubbornly silent, Illi added, "Drum Chief Amastan could find a place for you."

She dropped Amastan's name as casually as a rock, and the captain's reaction told her more than any words. He stammered incoherently, then looked away and shook his head. But he didn't say no again.

"We could use the extra sword, sa," said Canthem from beside the horse. "Four will be safer than three. It's a long road and we'll be riding fast, so we could use someone with as much experience as you. And you're not disobeying any orders, not directly. We're to see travelers safely through the Wastes, any who ask. Illi is asking, sa."

"To see it again," said the captain slowly, softly, as if savoring the words. "I've camped below, with other caravans, but I've never been back up on the platforms."

"There'd be no hiding this time, sa," said Illi. "I can introduce you to Amastan myself."

"Asaf," said the captain.

"What?"

"Nothing." The captain took a deep breath, then nodded. "Perhaps it's time I stopped hiding. I overheard everything you said about the sajaami. I've dedicated my life to stopping monsters and if the general refuses to do so herself, then I will have to step in. You will have my sword."

"Glad to have you with us, sa," said Illi, stepping around the captain and out of the stall. "Looks like we'll need another horse. And where do you keep your weapons?"

23

Heru Sametket looked for all the world as if he were in his own lab back in Ghadid instead of locked inside a tiny jail cell. He'd found a pebble and was busy scribbling across the solid rock wall at the rear of his cell, his back to the door. The wall was crammed with tiny, precise marks—letters and numbers and symbols from ceiling to floor.

He didn't turn as the jailer led Illi and Canthem down the short hall to his cell. Captain Yufit had gone to trade their horses for camels and acquire supplies while they addressed the problem of removing Heru. Illi took in the drab and simple surroundings: dirt floor, rock walls, metal bars. No windows. A smoking torch was the only source of light. Illi tested the bars of one cell as she passed, giving them a firm yank. Strong enough. But strong enough shouldn't have been able to keep someone like Heru.

And yet here he still was, the edges of his white wrap blackened with dirt and dust. Sweat stains spread out from his armpits, around the base of his neck, and down the center of his back. Had he ever been so filthy in his life?

As they approached, Illi heard humming—a thin, strained sound, but a hum nonetheless. The rock continued to scratch.

"How long has he been like this?" she asked the jailer.

The short, balding man spread his hands. "He just sat and stared at me from the floor for my entire shift the first day—all seven hours of it, mar. Then he found that rock and started marking up the wall. I figured there was no harm in him writing, so I let him keep at it."

Heru had paused at the sound of Illi's voice and now his hand hovered in midair. Finally he turned, pivoting as if on a pedestal, until he faced them fully. Illi drew in a sudden breath at the shock of his exposed face, his tagel drawn down to his chin. A shadow spilled across his cheeks and down his neck, the beginning of a beard. His features were drawn and tight with exhaustion and dehydration, but for the span of a heartbeat, those features cracked with something else, something raw like surprise, like relief. Then that was gone, his expression smoothed over with his usual haughtiness.

"Has Barca sent you to fetch me?" he asked. "Did she finally give up on trying to solve this riddle on her own? I knew she would eventually realize how very far out of her depth she is, but I had sorely underestimated her ignorance."

The jailer crossed his arms. "Visiting only, prisoner. I've received no orders to let you out."

"You're going to need to tell me everything she's already tried so we don't duplicate her efforts," continued Heru as if the jailer hadn't spoken. He pursed his lips. "On second thought, it would behoove us to duplicate her efforts. We can't be too careful in these circumstances and I certainly don't trust that she's adhered to strict protocols. I don't suppose she sent any detailed notes along, did she?"

"Merrabel didn't send me," said Illi.

Heru frowned. "Then why are you here?"

"I'm here to get you out."

"If you have orders, you should have said earlier," said the jailer, raising his voice.

"Nope, no orders."

Illi's elbow hit the jailer in the side of the head. He stumbled back and into the bars of Heru's cell, one arm already up to block her next attack and the other going for his sword. Illi freed a knife, one of a half dozen the captain had found for her. The guard's gaze fixed on the blade, which, while not his first mistake with them, was his last.

Heru stepped up to the bars. The jailer's eyes rolled up into his head and he crumpled to the floor as if he were little more than a bag full of water. Heru pulled his bloody palm back between the bars. He dropped a jagged rock to the floor and withdrew a piece of thin white fabric from one of his pouches. This he used to wipe his palm clean, then wrap around the cut on his arm, blood staining the fabric a bright red.

Canthem stared. "What did you do to him?"

Illi dropped next to the jailer and unhooked the ring of keys from his belt.

"I utilized a simple quieting method on a still-living man, which had the intended result of bringing him under my control." Heru finished bandaging his hand and glanced down at the unmoving body with disgust. "Although it appears it overwhelmed his system and led to a temporary state of unconsciousness. Seeing as how this accomplished the same purpose as I'd originally intended—"

The lock clicked and Illi swung the door open. "*Later.* We've got to go before anyone notices something's wrong."

But Heru didn't move. He stayed just that side of the door, his lips pressed into a thin line.

"Come on." Illi started to grab his arm, but then thought better of it.

"I . . . cannot."

"What?" asked Canthem. "It's too late to worry about the legality of it; we've already knocked out a guard."

Illi's gaze roved over the scratches on the walls. She'd assumed it was just Heru being, well, Heru, but what if they meant something? Then she remembered: Merrabel pressing her bloody palm against Heru's, binding him to her will. No wonder he hadn't left this pale excuse for a prison. No wonder she'd felt comfortable tossing him in here, so far from her reach. He'd never been beyond her reach.

"Yes," said Heru gravely. "Barca bound my jaani to her will. I've spent my time here building a charm to break that binding. I was able to construct one despite the binding, but, given the meager materials at hand, it's limited to the inside of this cell. If I step beyond its protection, I'll once more be under her control. It was difficult enough the first time; I could at least circumvent her will by convincing myself I was merely doodling. But I highly doubt that will suffice a second time."

"If we can get what you need, how long will it take for you to break the binding permanently?" asked Illi.

"Twelve to fourteen minutes, at most," said Heru.

"All right. What should we get?"

Canthem gestured at the body slumped against the bars. "We don't *have* ten minutes. Someone will notice that this guard is missing before then, and they'll notice even sooner if we try to leave here without him."

Illi had already assessed the length of the hall and the cells they'd passed. There hadn't been any windows, no other way but the way they'd come in. Another guard was waiting outside that door. She could take him, it wouldn't even be hard, but what if he called more guards? The captain had made it clear that he was only willing to break so many laws; his help was contingent upon them not making a scene.

"No chance of just using what we have at hand, is there?" asked Illi.

Heru looked down at the unconscious jailer. "Somehow I doubt either of you is carrying enough water, nor would you be pleased if I took it from this man. Either way, I would prefer not to use blood in this instance—the sympathetic link that would engender between myself and Barca would be messy. So: no. But if your concern is tied to the conscious state of this man, that can be rectified."

A ghost of a smile tugged at the corner of his lips, and before Illi could stop him, Heru flexed his fingers, blood still drying beneath his nails, and muttered a few choice syllables. For the first time, Illi recognized and understood the words he used: words for binding, for movement, for control.

The jailer twitched. Canthem jumped back. The jailer's head rolled around and then his eyes opened. But they were unfocused, unseeing. The jailer stood, the movement erratic and awkward, as if he were being pulled up by strings. It took another moment for him to assemble his limbs, and then he started walking jerkily back toward the front of the jail.

"Shards and dust, Heru," said Illi. "That's only going to make things worse."

Heru shrugged. "Then you'd better hurry."

Illi sighed. "All right. What do you need?"

"Do you have any paper?" When Illi shook her head, it was Heru's turn to sigh. "We'll have to rely on memory, as imperfect as it is. For one, I require a roll of vellum. I'll also need fresh black ink—emphasis on the *fresh*—five glass charms, a thin length of leather, a bowl, a sponge, a bar of soap—preferably scented, preferably with mint or lime—two full water skins, and a sheep-cheese brik."

Illi had been repeating each item in his list and frowned as she came to the last one. "What?"

"I passed a cart that sells them on my way to this jail," said Heru. "They smelled delicious."

"What does that have to do with making a charm?"

"Despite my best efforts otherwise, I still require sustenance," said Heru. "The slop they gave me here was completely inedible."

"All right," said Illi, moving away. "I'll be right back."

But Canthem stopped her. "You stay. I can go. It'll be less conspicuous if only one of us leaves."

Illi hesitated, but only for a moment. "Be quick."

Canthem touched her shoulder and looked briefly as if they wanted to do more, then they shook themself and left, giving the shambling jailer a wide berth. Illi kept her gaze on the door and her hand at her waist and counted to ten. At the count of nine, the door cracked open and the other guard glanced in. Illi tensed, but the guard only nodded at the jailer, asked, "All right, then?" and, without waiting for an answer, closed the door again.

Illi dropped her hand and turned to the cell. Heru stood just shy of the cell's door, arms crossed over his chest, considering her. She met his gaze and they watched each other in silence. Heru was the first to break the silence.

"What did she do to you?" he asked conversationally.

"Enough," said Illi. "But if you're concerned that I'm under her control, don't be. I escaped once I realized what she was doing."

"Escaped?" Heru blinked. "Was Barca holding you against your will?"

"What do you think, Heru?" snapped Illi.

She took a breath, twisted one of her braids. They were so dusty. She'd redone them a few times as she leaned over the washbasin in Merrabel's room, but they needed to be combed and cleaned and oiled, and the trip to the foothills hadn't done them any good. She brushed her braids back over her shoulder; she couldn't worry about hair right now.

"She never intended to help me; she only wants the sajaami. I guess I knew that from the beginning, but I'd hoped we both wanted the same thing. But no, she was just using me to control it, and to control guul."

"I could have told you that."

Illi sighed. "Yeah. But it wasn't like you were going to help, either."

"I most certainly *was*," huffed Heru. "I told you it would take time and materials. Instead of being patient, you betrayed me the first chance you got."

"I had no reason to trust you!" Illi curled her hands into fists. "You were purposefully keeping the sajaami so you could draw more guul from the Wastes and use them for your experiments. You were never going to *do* anything with the sajaami."

"I don't know where you are getting these baseless accusations," said Heru, his tone clipped and angry. "I most certainly was not drawing the guul on purpose."

"Yet you admitted to knowing that the sajaami was the cause."

"I did not *know*. I had begun to suspect and I was developing an experiment to test my suspicions, but I did not *know*. It was not until you were able to exert such control over the guul that my suspicions even turned to theory."

Illi crossed her arms. "Then why did you keep the sajaami for so long? Merrabel claimed you were afraid, but I didn't believe it. Not at first."

"I wasn't afraid," said Heru. "Fear is a useless emotion. I simply didn't have the resources."

"What else could you have possibly needed?"

"More glass, more water, more capable assistants. All the knowledge that had been lost when the Empress murdered the bulk of my colleagues."

Illi shook her head. "You didn't even try. Merrabel didn't have any of that, either. But that didn't stop her."

"Because she had the sajaami in a convenient and easily accessible package," snarled Heru. "One which she clearly didn't care about breaking through experimentation."

"That's real rich, coming from you."

"I never *broke* you."

In response, Illi held up an arm and shook the bracelet at him. They glared at each other through the open doorway. Illi forced herself to take a breath and unclenched her fists.

"I didn't come here to argue with you," said Illi. "I came here because I want to find a way to make the sajaami cross over. Merrabel won't consider it because she wants the sajaami for herself, but I'd hoped you—"

Heru actually sucked in a breath, interrupting her. "Wait. Cross over? That is—that couldn't be—yet I see no reason why it wouldn't be possible—" He trailed off, fingers twitching as if he could scratch notes into the air.

"Does that mean you'll help?" pressed Illi. "Even if you don't have all the resources?"

"At the time we were considering a different method of dealing with the sajaami," said Heru. "For the record, I still maintain that destroying it is impossible. But this brief incarceration has given me sufficient time to cogitate and I've developed a few hypotheses which are in line with your conclusion. The sooner we can test them, the better, for I can't say how long the containment I made will hold."

"You mean my body."

"Yes," said Heru. "Living flesh may be stronger than glass, but the sajaam were bound within stone for a reason. The sajaami can still flex its will, so to speak, through you. As long as it's in you, it's not truly contained. It's a threat."

Illi turned over her hands, the bracelets sliding across her blistered skin. A wave of dizziness washed over her, but a few steadying breaths made the ground solid again. "Yes. I've realized that. We need to work quickly."

"Quickly *and* safely," said Heru. "We'll only have one opportunity to perform this rite, and it must be perfect. I suspect the most difficult part will not be in designing the rite itself, but in removing the sajaami from containment first."

Illi stiffened, her fingers pressed against the whorls on the silver bracelet. "Please don't tell me you never considered how the sajaami would be removed before creating these."

"Oh, *removing* is simple enough." Heru made a *hmm* noise deep in his throat. "If you removed the bracelets, then the sajaami would burn through the marks binding it to you and destroy your body. It could take anywhere from several seconds to several hours, and there may be ways to lengthen the process to give us more time, but I imagine that would turn an otherwise briefly painful process into a much longer and more excruciating one."

Illi's throat tightened. "Oh."

"But then, of course, we would have a fully corporeal and uncontained sajaami, and that would be less than ideal," continued Heru. "So we must minimize the time that the sajaami is without a host *or* we must discover a way to perform the rite while it is contained within the body. I have a few hypotheses based on the foundational theories of en-marab study and my own understanding of this rite you speak of, but of course, being able to see the rite in person and interview those who regularly perform it would elucidate many problems."

Heru began pacing his cell as he talked, turning sharp at each corner so his wrap swished against stone and air, his words as precise as his steps. "The biggest assumption of this seven-year rite, as I understand it, is that the jaani will have been weakened by its time spent outside of, if still close to, its body. After seven years, the tether between the body and its jaani that the marab have been attending to will have become so thin as to be nonexistent, at which point the danger of the jaani becoming wild increases exponentially. Thus, during the seventh year post death the conditions are at their most advantageous for successfully guiding the jaani from this world to the next—the jaani is at its weakest point before the tether is gone entirely. But how do we translate such baseline assumptions to something as strong as a sajaami? How much do jaan and sajaam have in common? What properties do they share? A jaani's energy can be siphoned away until there is nothing measurable left, but can the same be done with a sajaami? Can a sajaami even cross over? These are the questions we seek answers for. Ideally, I would have an entire lab devoted to this question, with sufficient, experienced assistants and a wide sampling of sajaam. Instead, I have one bound sajaami, no lab, and two untrained assistants." Heru stopped abruptly, his single eye staring up at the ceiling. "You expect no less than a miracle from me. Thank G-d I am a genius."

"I'm so glad jail didn't affect your ego," said Illi. "But we need to focus on one question only: *how* to get the sajaami to cross over. Everything else is unimportant. Merrabel's going to notice I've slipped her soon, if she hasn't already, and I don't think she's going to let me go that easily."

"*Everything* else?" asked Heru. "Your own life is at risk here, girl."

"It's mine to risk," said Illi.

"Be that as it may," continued Heru. "*I* will not have this done sloppily and risk loosing an enraged sajaami on the world or losing another assistant. We must progress with care. This could take weeks—"

"We don't *have* weeks," snapped Illi.

"I am aware that Barca is searching for you, but she is one person and—"

"*I* don't have weeks." Illi stepped closer, heart beating like a drum in her chest. "Heru, these bracelets, this containment you designed—you said it yourself, it's not perfect. I can't stay this way indefinitely. They *will* fail and the sajaami *will* be free if we don't act soon." She swallowed. "I already have to take jaan to keep from slipping. And every time I use the sajaami, it gets worse."

"Then don't use the sajaami."

Illi twisted the burnt bracelet. "It's not that simple."

Heru coughed a laugh. "It *is* that simple, girl. You didn't even have a sajaami nineteen days ago."

Illi sighed and dropped her hand. The world had moved and irrevocably changed outside this jail, yet Heru continued to treat her like a naïve child. Merrabel's intentions might have been bad, but at least she'd treated Illi like an adult, if not quite an equal. Heru refused to change.

"Maybe I don't need your help after all."

"You are foolish, yes, but not *that* foolish."

Illi held up her hands, displaying the silver scars that crossed her palms. "I've learned enough about—"

Heru interrupted her with a barked, "*Idiot!*"

He reached for her through the open doorway, but Illi re-flexively stepped back and his hand slammed into an invisible barrier. Heru snarled, briefly the mad, untethered en-marabi everyone had always claimed he was, and then he calmed his features. The sudden juxtaposition made him look older again by half. He wrapped his fingers around one of the bars, gripping it so tight his knuckles turned as white as bone.

"You *fool*," he said, still irate but more controlled. "What have you been doing? Have I not repeatedly warned you to care for the sajaami's vessel? Every crack is another weakness the sajaami can exploit. Every break is another week you lose before the con-tainment fails and when it does, *you will die*. And you have been wounding yourself so *willingly*?"

Illi felt guilt tightening her throat, but she pushed it away. "How convenient that you suddenly care about my well-being *now*," she shot back. "I needed to understand the sajaami, and to do that I needed to understand jaan. If you'd taken a few mo-ments out of your day and actually treated me like a person in-stead of—of a—an *ambulatory bowl holder*, then I wouldn't have needed to do this."

"Perhaps we would have all been better off if you had *remained* an ambulatory bowl holder," snapped Heru. "Perhaps then you would not have willingly gone with Barca. Perhaps then you would still be safe."

This time, anger curled in her, burning away the lingering

traces of guilt. "I can leave you here," she said quietly. Not a warn-ing; only the truth.

Heru barked a humorless laugh. "You'll do nothing of the sort. You need me, girl."

"Do I?" Illi took a step back, then another. "You've never treated me as anything more than an object; I'm not even an interesting experiment to you. I thought you were safe because you didn't care, but that was then. Now it matters. Even though you've never formally taught me anything, I've watched you for years, Heru. I know your methods and I can reproduce . . . most of them. Merrabel taught me more in a few days than you did in all those years. The marab in Ghadid will fill in the rest. Your as-sistance would be helpful, but if you refuse to see me as a person, then why should I trust you with the sajaami?"

"You can't keep me here."

"Can't I?" Illi opened her arms. "Then step through those bars."

Heru's frown turned to a glare. He didn't move.

"Right," said Illi. "That's what I thought."

As she basked in his glare, Illi's anger unfurled. Her wrists itched from all the healing blisters and her back was a mess of scars and her home was hundreds of miles away and she was harboring a demon more powerful than the Wastes themselves, than every guul it contained, and she might see home again but she couldn't return, not until the sajaami was gone, and she missed her family, her cousins, even those stupid celebratory eve-nings in the inn, Zarrat's laughter and Yaluz's jokes and Dihya's quiet strength—

Merrabel had pulled the levers that smashed Heru's lab, but Heru had held the sajaami together long enough to ask:

Do you trust me?

Tears prickled at her eyes and her anger collapsed in on itself, exhaustion filling the space it had carved with the weight of sand. She wanted more than to go home. She wanted to go back. She wanted Ghadid as it was before the Siege. She wanted her parents, her old room, the stringwork she'd tied herself hanging from her window, all of it before it was burned to ash and scattered to dust.

More than that, she wanted herself back. The Illi who had been excited about her lessons with the Serpent of Ghadid, who had kept up with her cousins and practiced her fighting in the darkness of her room, window open and the sounds of a city deep asleep wrapping around her like a tight blanket. She wanted to love someone without constantly knowing they would die.

She wanted to feel safe. She would never feel safe.

But she could at least make certain the city that had survived centuries of raids and centuries of peace, only to fall at the hands of its own people would survive. Would thrive. Would remain unconquered.

With or without Heru.

She started down the hallway, Heru's heavy stare on her back. She counted her steps. One. Two. Three—

"You *can't* leave me here."

Four. Five. Six.

"After all I've done for you."

Seven. Eight. Nine. Illi stepped around the jailer, now staring blankly at the wall, and reached for the door.

"Fine!" Fabric rustled as Heru threw up his arms. "You are more than an ambulatory bowl holder, girl. I will grant you and your suggestions the respect that they would deserve from an assistant. Does that suffice?"

Illi grabbed the handle. Turned.

"Illi Basbowen," said Heru, his voice cracking. "I will treat you like an equal, even though you are mortal and extremely fragile. It is the least I can do, since you are, in fact, bearing the physical burden of the sajaami. I will assist you in researching and constructing the rite. I am no good at begging. Do *not* leave me here." He paused. Swallowed. "Please. It's quite filthy."

24

Illi set the pace of their journey, pushing all four of them to long hours and short nights. They rested while riding and hurried while walking, so they stayed warm through the long, cold darkness. What started as a quiet journey soon became completely silent from exhaustion. But no one complained, not even Heru.

That wasn't the only way Heru acted differently. He was already prone to bouts of silence, but now he volunteered to brew the tea and was predictably precise and perfunctory in his duty. Every few hours, the toasted warmth of tea wafted in Illi's direction and Heru would step out of the darkness, proffering a cup. At first, Illi had been careful, rolling a sip of it around her mouth to test for poison or other doctoring attempts. But by the end of the second day, she accepted every cup without hesitation.

He'd also left a strange present in her travel bag. Or at least, Illi could only assume it'd been him, even though she couldn't figure out how he'd come by its contents. She'd become aware of the small sack of glass orbs during one afternoon rest. They pulsed with a familiar life and, as her exhaustion had stretched and unfurled, she's found herself *reaching*, if only out of habit. She'd started when she'd brushed across the six spots of warmth, as unexpected as they were welcome. Upon closer inspection, she'd found the small bag tucked on top of her things, the glass orbs glowing faintly orange.

Illi didn't ask about the orbs and Heru never brought them up. Not acknowledging them somehow made it easier to *reach* and take and keep the dizziness and frailty away a little longer.

Besides, asking about them would bring up another question: *why*. The obvious answer was that Heru was making absolutely certain that the sajaami container wasn't damaged or otherwise compromised. But he was taking more care than was strictly necessary and giving her space as he never had before, which made her wonder if he truly did see her as more than just a container, if he finally recognized her as a person.

If Illi asked, she might get an answer. But she wasn't sure which answer she wanted. So she took the tea and she took the orbs and she left the question unasked.

They ran into guul only once. After that, Illi checked for nearby guul throughout the day. Any she found, she urged north and toward the Aer Caäs and Merrabel's very capable Guul Guard. Illi suffered no guilt from those actions; if Merrabel wanted the guul so badly, she could have them.

Even though there were only the four of them, Illi found plenty of ways to avoid being alone with Canthem. There was always a pack to sort or a wrap to mend or an idea to exchange with the captain. Captain Yufit had turned out to be an invaluable resource when it came to guul; as head of the guard, he'd spent much of his time studying them. Unlike Merrabel or Heru, he'd come to understand the guul on a much more practical level.

As dawn cracked the sky on their eighth morning of travel, Illi walked alongside the captain. Even though all around them was featureless sand and gravel, Illi felt home looming closer with each step. The feeling was a weight on her chest, a hope tangled in fear at what she might find. It'd been weeks, after all, since she'd last seen her city, and she knew from experience that so much could happen in just one night. But today, today she would see it. Today she would know.

Illi wasn't sure she was ready.

To distract herself from her growing anxiety, she prodded the captain. "Why?"

"Why what?" he returned, lifting an eyebrow at her.

"Why do you hunt guul? What brought you to it?"

"Why do you?"

"They attack Ghadid."

"You could have left them to the watchmen."

Illi snorted. "The watchmen are for crowds and riots. They wouldn't know what to do in an actual fight. It's *our* job to protect the city."

The captain folded his arms. "I see some things haven't changed. But, better guul than people. Still—why *you*? If Amastan's still around, I take it some of your other cousins are, too. It's not on you alone to stop the guul."

But it is, Illi almost said. She bit her tongue; the captain wouldn't understand. "I promised it'd never happen again."

"That what would never happen?"

Illi swallowed and looked to the horizon, the black of night only now fading to blue as dawn broke behind them. "The Siege."

And then she saw it—barely a speck on the horizon, a smudge only as tall as her nail, but Illi knew the speck for what it was: home.

She was reaching for the seeing glass before she realized what she was doing. Putting the thick lens to her eye only made the city a fraction bigger, but it was enough. Platforms and buildings smeared together at this distance into a lump that seemed to float above the horizon. Ghadid. The impossible city. The city in the sky. It was only a trick of distance and light, of course; the pylons would materialize as they approached.

But at that moment, it didn't matter. The sight, as imperfect as it was, took Illi's breath away. She didn't realize she was crying until the streaks the tears left behind grew cold. She still didn't know if everything was okay, if Thana or Mo or Dihya or Yaluz would be waiting for her up there, but in that moment it was enough that Ghadid still stood. There was hope.

"You mentioned this Siege before," said Canthem, and Illi started; she hadn't realized how close they'd come. "What happened?"

The captain was watching her with keen expectation. Perhaps it was that and not the sudden, aching relief of seeing Ghadid again that let her talk for the first time in any true detail about what had happened that night. But as Illi began to speak, she found the words coming faster and easier, until it was almost impossible to stop.

"It was the night our dead wouldn't die," she began.

Illi told them how the first slave had been pronounced dead, only to rise moments later and attack the marab in attendance. She told them how Drum Chief Amastan—just Amastan, then—had pieced together what was happening before anyone else, how he'd anticipated the dead rising from the crypts and stopped them from destroying the city from the inside.

How even that hadn't been enough.

She told them how the dead from other Crescent cities climbed the carriage wires and attacked at night, how every person they lost was another soldier for this blasphemous army. She told them about her cousins' strategy to first defend, then burn the city, how even beheading the bound dead only worked for so long. She told them how she'd volunteered to help spread oil and fire, because she was fast and she was small.

How she'd really just wanted to find her parents.

How she'd been too late.

She told them about their last stand, when so many of her cousins had sacrificed themselves so more citizens could escape. She told them about descending to the sands in shocked silence. How the survivors had watched from afar as Ghadid burned.

Illi stopped suddenly, unsure how to end her story, because it hadn't ended, it had never ended. She was still living that night, every night. She was still watching Ghadid burn.

A hand touched hers. Canthem looked at her with wonder, not a trace of pity in their eyes. Illi unclenched her fist and slid her fingers between theirs. She became aware of a pen scratching across paper and turned to find Heru nearby, perched cross-legged atop his camel and scribbling furiously. After a moment, he looked up and noticed them all staring.

"I thought you knew what happened," said Illi.

"Of course I do," said Heru promptly. Then he cleared his throat and added, "But some of the details you provided are new. Much of what I understand about the night I've gleaned from casual conversation. No one has been so willing to discuss what occurred during the Siege."

Not with you, I'd suspect, thought Illi, but she kept the sentiment to herself. Instead, she allowed herself a small amount of surprise that in the seven years since the Siege, no one had simply told Heru what had happened. Thana would have known. Or would she? After all, Illi and her cousins who had survived the Siege never spoke about it beyond vague mentions here and there.

Perhaps she wasn't the only one still reliving that night.

"It's your turn now," she said to the captain. "Why did you leave Ghadid? Why do you fight guul?"

"I came to Hathage ready to fight monsters," said the captain carefully. "I'd spent some time in the Crescent cities as a watchman, but after the Siege there was nowhere left for me to go but north."

"You were here during the Siege?" asked Illi, surprised.

"I was in Sofide. Not many people from that city survived. But I helped fight for as long as I could, and then I fled north with other refugees. The general was very interested in what had happened, and offered some of us the opportunity to train under her, so we would be ready if something similar happened again. She wasn't too far off. The guul started attacking her caravans only a few years later."

"We have a lot in common," said Illi.

Captain Yufit considered her for a long moment, his gray eyes unreadable. "Yes. I suppose we do."

They lapsed back into silence, the only sound the *shh-shh-shh* of their feet through the sand, but this time the silence felt easy, reciprocal. The weight that had sat on Illi's chest had eased, if only by a little. But it was enough.

Ghadid grew as they approached, from a smudge on the horizon to a fully formed city still an easy hour away. Illi looked and looked again through the seeing glass, although every time she chanced a glance her throat closed up with worry. She expected to see smoke, to see fire, to see some evidence of destruction, but instead all she saw was a city, gently drifting upon an endless expanse of sand. Sooner than she'd expected, she could pick out the individual pylons and the platforms that capped them. Sooner than she'd hoped, she was able to count each pylon and map the city as she remembered it, the city as it always would be.

Atop the platforms, buildings blurred together in the glare of light. Atop the buildings, glass sparked and glinted and occasionally revealed flashes of green: the glasshouses. Illi could almost see the movement within the glasshouses as their attendants chased the short growing season. Her mother would have been one of them, once. She could hear the clatter in the streets as the city moved and breathed and made the most of the cool weather.

She had started to bring the seeing glass down when she caught a flutter of real movement on the sands below. She frowned, refocused. Squinted. Found the platforms again, followed the cables down to the sand where the carriages sat. People swarmed around the carriages, between them. As she watched, another carriage hit the sand and figures began unloading the jars and barrels that had been lashed down, uncovering a thick stone slab.

Several people carried the slab to the center of the bustle, where they added it to a long, rectangular shape. They'd already built one side of the pyre and now they were building the other. When the pyre was done, it would run the length of a platform, built off the sands for optimal airflow. Illi had seen the plans, had listened as Menna explained the construction to Thana and Mo, but it was so very different seeing it built.

"What are they doing?" asked Canthem, lowering their own seeing glass.

"They're building the funeral pyre," said Illi. "They keep the pieces in the crypts and bring them all down for the rite. Otherwise they'd get lost in the sands."

"But there's . . . so many."

Illi nodded. "This is the rite for those who died during the Siege. So it will be much bigger than usual."

"Oh." Canthem was silent a moment, then they added. "I'm so sorry."

Sorry. The word was the spoken equivalent of an awkward pat. But Illi wasn't sorry. She could never be sorry. She could only be. After all, those days of chaos, that night when her whole world had gone up in flames, had defined her as surely as her training as a cousin.

Who would she be if the Siege had never happened? Who would she be with her family intact? Who would she be if she hadn't seen the people she'd entrusted with her safety and life without answers, if she hadn't watched her strongest cousins broken and killed by the dead?

Maybe she'd be happier. Maybe she'd be able to look at Canthem without feeling such a mixture of pain and need and fear. Maybe she could laugh with her cousins. Maybe she'd never have gotten tangled up with Heru and the sajaami, with Merrabel and Hathage. Maybe she could have clung to innocence a little longer.

But what good did innocence do anyone? Someday, those who were supposed to be strongest would fail. Someday, those who were supposed to protect her, wouldn't. At least this way she was ready. She could be strong, she could protect. And she wouldn't fail.

Illi pulled herself onto her camel before Canthem could say anything else. She didn't want to meander through what-ifs. This was the only what-if she got. And she was going to meet it head-on.

She kicked her camel into a loping run, then a full gallop. She leaned forward, gripping hard with her knees as she rode the camel's rolling gait, glad for the tagel that kept the wind's chill from her face. Behind, she heard the thudding of feet as the others followed. Ahead, the movement shifted, changed. A cry went out. A group separated from the crowd and came to meet them.

When she was still over a dozen feet away, Illi slowed her camel to a walk, then slid from its back and dropped its lead in the sand. She took a deep breath and held her hands out, empty and unthreatening, as she approached. She knew how her group must look, coming across the sands all by themselves with no caravan for support: only bandits and madmen traveled in small packs. Which were they?

Drum Chief Amastan walked at the head of the small group, the long chain and its collection of rings the only sign of his station today; he'd traded his embroidered wrap for a simpler, dusty gray one. Behind him, Dihya loomed, a hand on the grip of her machete. Zarrat kept pace with her, his wide eyes betraying his nerves. Then Dihya squeezed his upper arm and he seemed to straighten, if only by a hair's breadth.

Amastan stopped a dozen feet away and raised his own hands, empty and palms out. "Peace."

Illi swallowed, her throat suddenly tight. "Peace."

"Are you sane?"

"I am, praise be to G-d."

Dihya sucked in a breath, recognizing her voice. "Illi!"

Illi bit the inside of her cheek, letting the pain center her even as other emotions tried to smother her. She undid the knot of her tagel and pulled down the cloth.

Before the cloth had even settled, Dihya was there, arms wrapped tight around her. "You're back," she said into Illi's braids, her breath as warm as sunshine, as familiar as stone. "You're *back*."

And then she released Illi and crossed her arms. "Where in the seven hells did you *go*?"

"Illi can answer that question soon," said Amastan calmly, his voice cutting through their reunion. "But first we have a more pressing one: why is Heru Sametket with her?"

Dihya turned, brows furrowed. Heru stood slightly away from the group, hands open and empty at his sides, as if he were trying to look as nonthreatening as possible. Some of that effort was undone by the camel beside him, its glazed, staring eyes fixed on Amastan and its patchy sides unmoving. Dihya's hand went to her machete again.

Illi stepped in front of Heru, her arms out. "He won't go into Ghadid. He'll stay down on the sands, with me. We're not going to be here long."

"What happened to the sajaami?" pressed Amastan.

"We have a plan," said Illi. "But our path brought us near, so I thought—so I hoped—" Illi took a breath and tried again. "Please. Let us stay for the rite."

Drum Chief Amastan considered her, his dark brown eyes as unreadable as the captain's. Then he sighed. "He was exiled from Ghadid, not the sands. I see no reason why he can't observe the rite with us." Then his eyes crinkled in a fraction of a smile and he added, "As luck would have it, he's already appropriately dressed."

"Thank you, sa," said Illi.

Amastan's gaze caught on her and narrowed at the *sa,* then he looked past her, at Canthem and the captain. She was only a foot from the drum chief, so she heard his sudden intake of breath.

"And who are your companions?" This time, Amastan's voice was strained.

Illi watched Amastan closely as she said, "Guard Canthem and Captain Yufit."

There: despite the bright light, Amastan's pupils widened at the captain's name, while the rest of him stayed as still as stone. The captain stared back across the dozen or so feet between them and for a heartbeat, two, they saw nothing else. Then Drum Chief Amastan let out a breath, breaking the tension.

"Are you sane?"

"I am," said the captain immediately, Canthem echoing him only a moment behind. Then, more softly, "G-d preserve you, Asaf."

Dihya hissed through her teeth, her machete free from its harness and in her hands. But before she could take a step, Amastan was in front of her, hands raised.

"No," he said. "He's come in peace." He glanced back at Yufit. "Haven't you?"

"I have," said the captain, louder now. "I'm even helping your young cousin with her task. Turns out there are more monsters in this world than one man alone can handle. I'm only here to help."

Dihya's grip tightened on her machete. "How can you believe anything he says, Amastan, he—"

"—is a man of his word," said Amastan. "He's never lied to me. Trust me, Dihya."

Dihya growled deep in her throat, then she shoved her machete back into its harness and crossed her arms, her glare intent on the captain. For his part, Captain Yufit ignored her.

"Come, rest," said Amastan. "Our beds are your beds, our food your food, our water your water. May you find peace here."

"Come now, Asaf," said the captain, approaching with one hand held out. "Those are words for a stranger."

"It's been sixteen and a half years, Yufit."

"Yes, and somehow in only that time they made you into a *drum chief*?" The captain reached Amastan, his hand still waiting. "You have to tell me everything."

Drum Chief Amastan hesitated for only a moment before taking Captain Yufit's hand, his gaze never leaving the captain's. Amastan led him away from the group without another word, as if the rest of them had ceased to exist entirely. Illi met Canthem's glance and shrugged. Then Dihya was beside her, linking her arm through Illi's and pulling her toward the bustle. She heard more than saw Canthem and Zarrat following behind, exchanging awkward conversation as they let Dihya have Illi.

"You can stay, you know," said Dihya. "The Circle didn't exile you, only the en-marabi."

Illi glanced longingly up at the platforms, so close and yet somehow still so far. "He's my responsibility."

"Where are you even going after this?" Dihya gestured broadly at the sands all around. "Only one other Crescent city has been reclaimed."

"The Wastes."

Dihya looked at her as if she'd been possessed. "Why in all the sands would you go there?"

Illi's cheeks warmed, and as she shifted, her bracelets rubbed against her raw skin, sending a flicker of pain up her arms. But Dihya didn't know, *couldn't* know, about the sajaami.

Dihya sighed. "You and your secrets." Then she patted Illi's shoulder. "I'm glad you made it. This rite is something we have to face together. Seven years, but it feels like only a week ago. There are parts of that night that are still fresh to me, as vivid as if I were living them again and again."

Illi started, stared. "You've never said anything about that before."

"I'd hoped that if I didn't talk about it, those memories would fade," said Dihya. Her eyes flicked back and forth as she watched the pyre being assembled. "And yet the memories I tried to hold on to, those are the ones that faded. Like trying to grapple sand. I can still feel the crunch of his neck beneath my ax, but I can't remember Azulay's laugh. I can't remember his hands, his favorite food, what he sounded like when he was annoyed." Dihya's voice cracked and she blinked rapidly, as if she'd gotten something in her eye.

Illi reached out, grabbed Dihya's hand. "I don't remember my father's voice. I can barely remember his face; every time I try, I keep seeing what I found of him instead."

Dihya nodded along to Illi's words. "I bet we all have similar stories." Then she laughed, a broken, cracked sound. "Az' would've put money down on it."

Illi leaned into Dihya, feeling her strength and her warmth, and wondering how she'd never noticed Dihya's pain.

"It's going to be a long night," said Illi softly. "But we'll do this together."

25

Building the pyre took the rest of the day. As the sun hit the eastern edge of the world, shattering cold light into warmer reds and oranges and purples, Illi helped slide the last stone block into place. Her muscles ached, but the pain was welcome. She'd re-knotted her tagel so that she could sink into the crowd, unnoticed and unobtrusive. She'd asked Dihya not to mention to the others that she'd returned, not yet. She wasn't worried about Amastan telling; he hadn't left the captain's side.

But now as the carriages began to descend in earnest and the first mourners came from the city, bearing their carefully wrapped dead, Illi removed her tagel and tied it to her belt. It was time to stop hiding and fully be a part of this rite.

The bodies were borne one by one to the pyre, sometimes carried between two people, sometimes accompanied by an entire group of ten, more. There weren't many whole bodies; most had been burned during the Siege and immediately after. The few intact corpses belonged to those who'd died after Heru had figured out how to reverse the curse that jerked the dead back to life.

They were laid out across the pyre, their once-white shrouds now gray with ink and dust and time. Next came smaller bundles, wrapped in white cloth: the remains of those who had already been through fire once. Their broken pieces contained no

jaan, but there was still hope—however frail, however vague—
that these pieces were enough to build a connection. Somewhere
in the Wastes, their jaan ran wild. If the marab had figured
things out, tonight those jaan would know peace.

The cold brightened and sharpened as soon as the sun sank
out of sight. One by one, small fires were lit around the area,
casting warmth and flickering light across the sands. As each
group deposited their burden on the pyre, they joined the growing crowd. Aside from a few soft murmurs here and there, the
crowd was respectfully silent. The rustle of flames and the whistle of wind were louder.

The faint, musical clink of glass on glass drifted on the breeze.
All around the perimeter, marab had pounded metal poles into
the sand and hung chains of charms. Usually, charms were used
to keep jaan away, but these had been specially made for the rite:
their jangle was a call, saying *here—come, and know peace.*

Illi had heard the sound of those charms once already; she'd
attended a seven-year rite only the year before the Siege. The
jangle of glass had been reassuring then, a reminder that the jaan
knew and obeyed certain rules, that they could be controlled.
That they were safe. But now a soothing calm wrapped around
Illi and she felt as if the charms were tugging at her. It wasn't
until her bracelets grew warm that she realized they *were.* They
were tugging at the sajaami.

That last rite had been much smaller, the pyre barely wider
than her spread arms. Only the close family of the deceased
typically attended, and even then not everyone was willing to
brave the sands. But that time, the deceased had included two
cousins, murdered under unfortunate circumstances. All of the
family had turned out, family by blood and family through
blood and others besides, some knowing what had actually

happened and some believing the official story. That had felt like a lot then.

Now it seemed as if the whole city had come down to the sands. After all, what was there to be afraid of when they'd been forced down once before? When their streets had teemed with the dead? After the Siege, the sands had become familiar, if not welcoming.

The last burden was placed on the pyre, little more than a sack of dust and bones. The last murmurs quieted as the marab stepped forward, taking the space between the crowd and the pyre. Illi felt a presence at her side; she didn't need to turn to know Canthem was there. They stood within reach, but they left the choice of bridging that gap to Illi. She nodded at them, appreciating that choice. She had to do this alone.

The marab called a prayer that was imperfectly echoed back and swallowed by the night. Each marabi took their turn explaining the rite, the process of passing over. Then they called for individual prayers.

As they spoke, a novice marabi had drifted through the crowd, handing out pieces of vellum to anyone who hadn't brought their own. A young girl with long braids like Illi's, hardly twelve seasons old, trailed behind the marabi carrying a basket.

Illi took a piece of vellum and twisted it in her hands as she waited for the ink. Such a small space for all the dead she could name, all the family she had loved, all the words she could say, all the prayers she could offer. If she'd stayed in Ghadid, she would have spent a week writing her own prayers, as Thana had been doing when Illi left. But now when the ink came to her, all she could do was write their names.

First her cousins, her family through blood. *Azulay, Ziri,*

Usaten, Tamella. Then her whole family by blood. *Talal.* Her mother. *Garrem.* Her father. Her aunt, her uncles. Her grandmother.

The names filled the vellum, smothering it in ink. Illi passed on the pen, her fingers stained black. She held the vellum by one unmarked corner, her gaze fixed on the names, reading and rereading a list she had long since burned onto her soul. So many gone, so many lost. Only her grandmother had been spared that night, having died some months before. Illi had never run into her corpse, one small mercy among so many horrors.

When the novice marabi and her assistant returned to the front, the marab began calling out the names of the deceased. One by one the names were echoed through the crowd. Individually and in clumps, people approached the pyre, their prayers and the names of their dead clutched tight to their chests. The marab guided them in wiping the vellum clean with a wet cloth, then squeezing that cloth into a large glass bowl. Ink-stained water slowly filled the bowl.

"Azulay Saäfen," called a marabi.

Illi stayed, watching as Azulay's family walked forward. Dihya stood with them, even though they were only distantly related. When Dihya turned back around, her face was as still as stone, but firelight picked out the wet trails on her cheeks.

Illi remained still for each of her cousins' names. She watched as her living cousins went up, one by one by one, to hand the marab their prayers. The names were in no particular order and kept coming, the reading itself a litany.

"Tamella Basbowen."

Thana walked to the front, hand in hand with an older man, bending like a palm with age. Thana handed off her ink-blackened strip of vellum, and when she turned back, seemed to walk a little taller, as if the vellum had weighed hundreds of pounds.

Illi didn't hear the next few names, but "Talal Zirbemen" broke through her distraction, followed by "Garrem Zirbemen."

And then Illi was approaching the pyre and the waiting marab. More names blew around her as she walked, but Illi felt strangely detached, as if someone else were moving her feet, as if someone else were using her ears. She held the vellum out to the marab, but they gently pushed it back toward her. *Oh yes,* she remembered. This was her act.

A hand guided her to the bowl of water, now as murky as smoke. Another hand held out the cloth, likewise stained with ink. Illi wiped the names clean from her vellum, watching the dribbles of black-stained water run down her hands, fall into the bowl. Names mingling with other names, prayers and hopes and love and grief. All of it become water, become smoke, become ash.

As one day she would. As one day everyone here would.

The marabi took the vellum and the cloth back. Illi resisted, but only for a moment. The names continued to roll, relentless and unending, and behind her more mourners were waiting their turn.

Illi walked slowly back. She'd been hoping to feel lighter, as Thana had seemed to. She'd thought she could shed her grief as easily as the water washed the ink away. But instead, it clung to her just as heavy, just as tight. She headed for a space in the crowd where she could stand alone and watch.

But someone stepped in front of her. Thana.

"You're back," said Thana.

And then she did the kindest thing: she didn't ask why. Thana only opened her arms and Illi fell into them, tears cracking through the stony façade she'd built up over the long, grueling afternoon. Salt from her tears mingled with the salt from her dried sweat and she thought dimly about how bad she must smell.

Thana didn't seem to mind, or at least she didn't try to get away. Illi breathed deep, letting Thana's familiar, sharp scents center her. Thana didn't move, didn't say a word.

They stood that way for hours, seconds. When Illi was ready, she pulled back and slipped her hand into Thana's, as she had when she'd gone with her mother to the market a hundred times before. The memory brushed over her as fleeting as a shadow, but as vivid as a flower. The feel of her small hand in her mother's larger, rougher one; the whirl of the market; the promise of one, *just one*, spiced almond cake; the cool weight of a baat in her other hand.

Thana guided Illi through the crowd to a cluster of cousins. Dihya and Zarrat, Azhar and Menna, Yaluz and Hamma. Mo was there, too, along with Thana's father, Barag. Even Drum Chief Amastan stood with them, his necklace, the sign of his office, tucked away and out of sight for now. Tonight, he was just Amastan.

Her cousins didn't smile, but there was a welcoming warmth nonetheless. Illi held out her other hand and Mo took it, her own smaller, softer. In silence, they watched as the last of the mourners brought their prayers to the marab.

A few more words were said, their cadence mattering more than their meaning. As the marab spoke, two more walked the length of the pyre, drenching the bodies and the cloth in oil. Then the marab took up their unlit torches and spread out around the pyre. As one, they dipped their torches into the waiting fires. As one, they turned and lit the pyre. It caught. It flickered. The wind caressed it, encouraged it. Fire flared and blossomed.

The heat took its time growing. The flames crackled and spat, and within the conflagration oils and fat hissed and old bones cracked.

Illi watched the fire and for once she didn't think about the Siege and who had died. Instead she thought about her parents and how they had lived. Her mother's hands, rough from glass-house maintenance and fingernails perpetually blackened with soil. The times her mother had shown Illi how to secure all the vents before season, to avoid losing any moisture during the driest time of the year. How to roll out the shade cloth to keep the more delicate plants from being burned. How to feel the soil between her fingers, how to taste it, how to smell it, how to know what it needed, when it was ready. Her mother's arms around her, steadying the knife as Illi pruned a vine.

And her father, Drum Chief Basil's cook. His voice, warm like the liquor he used to drizzle over fig cakes. His amused sigh as Illi failed again to remember the right ingredients or combine them in the proper order, and his inevitable exaggerated grimace when he tried whatever had resulted. His gentle corrections, always careful to tell her what she had done right along with what she could improve.

She thought about both her parents' glowing pride as Illi became stronger, faster, and more confident. They didn't know about her secret lessons with Tamella, that she'd been chosen to continue the line of assassins, that someday she was expected to kill. But Tamella's training had transferred to other, unexpected aspects of Illi's life. Tamella had taught her patience, had taught her focus, had taught her that the details mattered. Illi could still see her father's pure delight when he bit into her first perfectly cooked goat pie.

Illi would never see that delight again, or feel that intense, burning pride. But it would always be there, that memory, as well as all those moments—a part of her. Her parents had shaped her and even the Siege couldn't undo that.

She knew they'd be proud of her, even now.

When the fire was burning solid and bright, the marab took up the bowls of inky water and began pouring them out along the length of the pyre. White gouts of steam were coughed into the sky, roiling like clouds. So much water, all for this—an attempt to quiet the unquieted. They'd saved for a year to collect just these few bowls of water. Enough for a family for a couple of months. Enough to heal several terminal diseases.

Hopefully enough to bring the jaan and lay them, finally, to rest.

The steam curled into the sky, where it met the wind and was blown west, toward the Wastes. The marab finished pouring the water, and the last cloud of steam lifted away like a final exhalation. The fire continued to burn, lower but brighter. More efficiently.

All around, the mourners settled in for a long night. The seven-year rite was only performed once a year, on the shortest day and through the longest night. While it wasn't mandatory that the mourners hold vigil on the sands, and the weak and the old were encouraged to return above as soon as the steam had abated, it was tradition.

Illi tightened her wrap against the cold. Her face was warm from the fire, but a shiver of goose bumps ran up her back. Her cousins clustered in close, rolling out bedrolls in their shared silence. Canthem slipped into that silence as easy as a knife, and this time Illi didn't feel the need to push them away.

As the night deepened and the stars shifted, the silence started to break. First with a few moans and rustles as other mourners celebrated life and tried to stay warm—then with whispers and murmurs.

It was traditional to mourn. But it was also traditional to celebrate. To exchange stories. To remember the lives lived and not just their deaths. So as Illi wound her arms tight around Canthem and drew in their warmth, she wasn't surprised to hear her cousins start to speak.

Dihya was the first. "Azulay would've been betting on just how long we could sit here quiet, freezing our butts."

"Remember that time he won two goats off an iluk?" asked Amastan.

Dihya laughed and the silence shattered. "Shards and dust— he was so proud of himself. And so panicked because he didn't know the first thing about goats."

A murmur of amusement wove through them, bringing them closer, tying them together. They shared memories and talked and talked and talked until the tears had come and gone and the fire was no longer the only source of warmth.

26

Illi hadn't realized she was dozing until she opened her eyes and stared at the moon, hardly a sliver in the sky. Dawn was near but the camp of mourners was now truly silent. Beside her, Canthem shifted and turned, their arm falling away. The pyre was hardly more than a bed of embers, the occasional crack within the only sound.

No—not the only sound. Something else had caught Illi's attention, brought her back to wakefulness. The glass charms were singing and the air was stirring, but not with a breeze. It was too warm to be the wind and it came from the west, not the east.

Warm. But the air *wasn't* warm, not really. Illi was shivering despite multiple thick blankets and the press of bodies. She sat up. Her bracelets shifted, fell down her wrists. They were warm, too.

Illi reached. She swallowed a gasp. The air was *full* of warmth, smeared with it all around. She squinted, tried to see, but nothing moved. At least, not to her eyes. So she closed her eyes.

Then she could see. The sky seethed with streaks of warmth. Not bright spots like the jaan and the guul she'd encountered previously. These were much weaker, spread thin: wild jaan. Jaan that hadn't been quieted, hadn't been kept tethered to their bodies. Jaan that had roamed the Wastes and the sands and lost their form and strength until there was little of anything left.

Even as weak as they were now, they were still dangerous. In a way, wild jaan were even more dangerous than the guul, which could at least be seen and fought. A wild jaani was unseen, unfelt, unheard. It could easily slip inside the mind of a traveler and drive them mad. Unless the traveler wore a charm.

Illi's charm now warmed, but not unpleasantly. She touched the pouch, snug between her collarbones beneath her wrap, as she watched the jaan dance.

They swirled and spun on invisible eddies. More and more joined them, streaming in from the Wastes. Yet the number above never seemed to increase. Illi teased one out, followed its movements as it danced in the sky. And then it was gone, slipping through her grasp as easily as water.

Illi stood and carefully stepped her way through the tangle of sleeping bodies. She needed the space and the cold, and she couldn't risk drawing any jaan to her cousins. When she was a good distance away—not quite out of sight—she tried again. Found one, followed it as it whirled in and among the others. Then, just as suddenly, it, too, was gone. This time she focused on where it had disappeared. Steadied her breathing. Reached.

The cold was like a slap. She reeled back, gasping, nerves tingling with pain. Her skin felt as if a razor had been dragged across it, rough and stinging. She didn't dare try again. She knew—or at least she suspected—what that was.

"You can feel them, too."

Illi started, turned. A shadow shifted in the nearby darkness, their wrap colorless, an inky black. Illi couldn't see their face, but she knew Mo's voice. The healer's head was tilted back, taking in the full breadth of the sky.

"How—?" asked Illi.

"Part of training to be a healer includes learning to feel jaan," said Mo. "It's an important skill. We heal the body, not the jaani, but if the connection between jaani and body is too frayed, we can do little. Plus, it's always helpful to know when you've got a madman along with the broken leg on your hands."

She turned toward Illi, the dim firelight glinting off her eyes as they moved. "But we hadn't gotten that far in your training."

Illi swallowed. "I learned from someone else."

"While you were gone?" asked Mo, her voice carefully neutral. "Thana said you'd be all right, but you left without even saying good-bye. Where did you go? Didn't you think we'd be worried about you? Didn't you think about anyone you might hurt?" Her tone sharpened with each question until her last words tore into Illi like a knife. "The sands don't just cover you."

"If I'd told you, you would've tried to stop me," said Illi. "Then you *would've* been hurt."

Mo snorted. "Or maybe I could have helped you."

"You don't even know what I was doing."

"Then tell me."

Illi looked at her hands, at the silver scars. At the glowing embers. At the sky. She couldn't. No one could know. This was her task and hers alone. And it was time to work on it again. The period for mourning was past; she had a future to protect.

As Mo waited for her response, Illi looked again at the pyre, seeing it with fresh eyes. She picked it apart piece by piece: the pyre itself, made from stones; the bodies; the prayers; the ink; the fire; and the water. All pieces of marabi magic, but she could see the en-marabi, too. The only difference, really, was in the blood.

"Do you think the rite drew any guul?" asked Illi.

Mo's eyes glittered as she blinked. "Guul? No . . . but . . ." She tilted her head, considering the pyre along with Illi. "If they were weak enough, it could be possible."

"But you think a similar rite could do the same to guul?"

Mo took in a breath, let it out slowly. "I'm not a marabi, Illi."

"No," agreed Illi. "But neither was Essif."

Now Illi could hear the smile in Mo's voice as she responded, "I'm no Essif."

"Did she actually exist?"

Mo turned and considered her. "Of course."

"I heard another version of the story while I was gone," said Illi carefully. "The storyteller had never even heard of Essif; this story claimed that the marab acted alone, without any healers. But the rest of the details were the same."

Mo snorted. "I'm not surprised. The marab have never liked the idea that a healer outdid them."

"But they used blood," said Illi slowly. "Were they really marab?"

"There was a time when the distinction between en-marab and marab hadn't been made yet," said Mo. "Besides, the blood they used was provided by G-d."

"It ran in the wadi, like water," said Illi distantly, the familiar cadence of the story underlying her words. "But they also used their own blood." She rubbed her forehead; all the pieces felt as if they had something drawing them together, but she couldn't yet see the whole. "So marab can use blood. Can healers?"

Mo didn't answer for some time. When she finally did, her voice was almost a whisper. "In theory."

"You sound like Heru."

Mo winced. "He only ever thinks about what he *can* do, never about whether he should. Blood is personal, it creates a link which can be manipulated and abused by the wrong person. A healer doesn't want or need that kind of control. But yes—blood is mostly water. If there's no other water around, it can be used to heal."

"If you don't want control, though . . ." Illi felt as if she almost had something, an understanding, an idea, but it was as thin and precarious as a cobweb. She closed her eyes and let the sensation of the swirling jaan wash over her as she felt along that web, trying not to break it.

Fire and thorns and blood for binding. Fire and ink and water for quieting. The thorns Essif had torn free had stained her hands blue. The first ink the marab had ever used had been concentrated from the broken branches of a bush. If the thorns and the ink were the same, then the only difference between binding and quieting was in the blood—in the control. She didn't need to control the sajaami.

And there was her answer, clear as glass. Above, the weakest of jaan swirled and disappeared, crossing over to whatever lay next. The marab had scavenged and saved water for years just for this rite. It was the largest rite the city had ever known, but these jaan had been spread thin by the wind and the years. Nejm was much stronger, and much more powerful. Unless she found a way to weaken it, she'd need a lot of ink, a lot of fire, and a lot of water.

She knew how she could make the former two, but where would she find enough water? She'd need barrels of it, an entire aquifer, an incredible amount, enough to sustain the entire city for a year.

Incredible.

Illi *had* seen that much water before.

"The sea," she breathed.

"What?" asked Mo.

But Illi only shook her head. All that water, just on the other side of the wall. And she'd just *been* there, staring at it. Like it was a wonder, an impossibility—but nothing more. She was so *stupid.* How hadn't she seen it sooner?

She didn't need to go to the Wastes. She needed to return to Hathage.

Illi breathed in the cold air, laced with sand and sweat and cinnamon, and resisted the urge to gather her supplies and camel and leave right then. Instead she smiled at Mo in the dark, a real smile lightened by relief. She couldn't leave just yet; if she didn't time it right, her cousins would try to stop her.

"The things I saw while I was gone," said Illi. "Water as far as the eye can see. A wall as tall as Ghadid. Mountains like teeth."

Mo came closer, drawn by the promise of story. As the wan light caught her face, Illi saw a real hunger there.

"Tell me," ordered Mo.

And Illi did.

When the cold had numbed her lips along with her fingers, they returned to the wedge of warm bodies and thick blankets and Illi slid back beneath Canthem's arm. But she didn't fall asleep. She stared at the stars, picking out their familiar shapes as the jaan whirled overhead. Slowly, the jaan abated, became little more than a breath of breeze. Mo's breathing slowed as well, grew even.

Illi waited a little longer, until she felt sleep creeping up on her as it had before. All around—and above—the camp was still. She inhaled Canthem's scent one last time, then brushed her lips across their forehead. Slowly, she peeled away the blankets and slid out from under Canthem's arm. Sat up. Got to her feet.

Step by aching step, she crept across the sands toward the camels. One stood out in the darkness, its white fur a beacon: Anas, Heru's dead camel. Illi had been surprised at first to find Anas alongside other, living camels in the stable near the inn.

But then, Merrabel had probably kept the camel around to study, later. The stable hands had all but forced them to take the beast. Anas turned its head toward Illi as she approached, but didn't so much as grunt. The other camels slept around it, legs folded beneath them and long necks strung out on the ground like snakes.

Their packs had been left in one big heap. Illi had just begun to pick hers out of the pile when someone cleared their throat. Illi spun, her hand on her sword. A shape peeled off from the darkness, their wrap almost the same olive black as the shadows: a cousin. They'd been waiting for her.

"Where do you think you're going?"

Illi dropped her hand from the hilt of her sword. It was only Thana; she'd understand. "I told Dihya already—I can't stay. I was here for the rite, but now it's time for me to go."

Thana put herself between Illi and the camels and crossed her arms. "Where?"

Illi was briefly tempted to lie in case anyone tried to follow her, but this was Thana. She could hold her tongue. "Hathage."

"And you're going to cross the desert alone?"

"Not alone. I'll have Heru." Illi cast around. "Once I find him."

"By all that's holy and whole," swore Thana. "Have you been touched?"

Illi's fingers went to the charms at her neck, but she knew they'd be cool; the last of the jaan had disappeared before she reached the camels. "I'm fine. You just need to pretend you didn't see me, okay?"

"Yeah, no. That's not going to work."

"You let me last time."

"With a *caravan*," snapped Thana. "A well-guarded one, at that."

"You're one to talk. *You* went off into the Wastes with just Heru and Mo."

"Because I had no choice," said Thana. "Ghadid had been emptied. We had no idea there were any survivors, let alone where they were."

"If there had been anyone in Ghadid, would you really have taken them with you?" pressed Illi. "Even now, knowing how dangerous your journey was? You would've been signing their contract. No—you would've slipped out in the middle of the night just the same."

Thana's voice softened. "What are you facing that's so dangerous, Illi?"

"The same thing you faced: the sajaami."

Thana looked away. "You didn't destroy it."

"No."

"But you think you can now."

Illi moved around Thana to grab her bag; this time Thana let her. "I know how to help it cross over. It's simple. With enough water, anyway."

She picked up her bag and approached her camel. She gently nudged the beast, but it only let out a long sigh, eyes shut.

"You're right," admitted Thana. "I wouldn't have asked for help. I was too proud. And we *barely* survived. But—if I'd had help, if another cousin had been there, they might've seen the things I wasn't able to, and maybe we could've stopped the Empress from releasing the sajaami at all. If I'd had help, maybe we could've avoided all of this. Hard things don't have to be borne alone, Illi."

"I can do this one alone," said Illi, dropping her bag to pat the camel's neck, more firmly this time. Its eyelids flickered but stayed firmly closed. "I have to. If anyone helps me, they'll only be at risk."

"And you won't be?"

"One of us has to."

"And why does it have to be you?"

Illi didn't meet Thana's gaze, keenly aware of the bracelet's cold metal bite against her wrists.

When Illi didn't respond, Thana let out a long, annoyed sigh. "Illi. We've all been through the same training. We've all learned how to kill, how to fight, how to survive. We've all experienced the same loss and none of us want it to happen again. *None* of us want to lose another cousin or another family member. So why should I let you sacrifice yourself? We can help you. Two cousins to a mark, remember? We've always worked together. Together we're stronger. Together, we're a family. We—"

"Because it *has* to be me." Before she could change her mind, Illi lifted her arms, shaking them just enough so that her sleeves fell away. Revealing her bracelets.

Thana's eyes darted across the bracelets, taking them in. Her expression didn't change. "You had those when you left." Then her nostrils widened. "Oh, in all of G d's names. *Heru*. The sajaami."

Illi only nodded. She dropped her hands, letting the sleeves cover them again. She turned back to her preparations. Finally, the camel was beginning to stir. It let out a long, low groan and blinked sleepily.

"No."

Illi froze, her fingers having just slipped the knot of the lead over the camel's neck.

"No," repeated Thana. "You're not doing this alone."

Illi clenched her teeth and whirled on Thana. "You saw! I have no choice—the sajaami is bound to me. It *has* to be me. I'm a danger to everyone until it's gone. I've come this far alone—I can make it the rest of the way."

"You're right," said Thana, and Illi relaxed, just a little. "I can't undo what Heru did. And even if I could, I don't know if I could take that burden. But you don't have to go alone. I'm coming with you."

"You don't understand—"

"Then help me understand." Thana's hands shot out, caught Illi's. "Tell me exactly why what you're doing is so dangerous even a cousin can't help you."

Illi resisted the urge to yank her hands back. Instead, she glanced east. The horizon was still dark, dawn still distant. If she was fast, she could convince Thana to leave her alone and be far away before the camp began to stir. Before Canthem woke up. Because she knew this time, she wouldn't be able to leave if they did.

"Fine." Illi met Thana's gaze. "You've seen the sajaami before. You know how dangerous it is." She swallowed the words *and yet you let Heru keep it like a pet for seven years*. Being combative wouldn't help, not now. "These bracelets weaken it, keep it controlled, but I've still hurt people—jaan—unintentionally. And sometimes intentionally. The thing is, if I'm threatened, I don't know exactly what I'll do. And if someone I care about is threatened . . ." She stopped, shook her head, remembering the guul she'd plucked out and smothered the moment Canthem had been in danger.

"The less people I have to worry about, the less danger we're all in," continued Illi. "And that's not even touching on how the sajaami draws guul like flies. I can control the guul, but every time I do, these bracelets burn through more skin and the sajaami gets stronger."

She held an arm out to Thana, sliding the bracelet back just enough to expose the blistered, red flesh beneath. Thana brushed the ruined skin with her thumb, her expression as still as stone.

Finally, she asked, "So what do you plan to do with the sajaami?"

"I'm taking it back to Hathage," said Illi, folding her arms so that the bracelets were tucked away. "There's water—lots of it. More than you can imagine. And I'm going to use all that water to usher the sajaami across. But I don't know if it'll work and if it doesn't, there will be an angry and fully corporeal sajaami loose. I don't want to risk anyone else being hurt."

"And that's exactly why you need us," said Thana.

Illi's stomach twisted. "No." She'd been so *close*. "Aren't you listening? Anyone near me will be in danger."

Thana stabbed her finger at Illi. "You keep forgetting—you don't get to hoard all the danger for yourself. And what do you even know about sajaam, aside from what you've learned from Heru? Have you talked to Mo? Have you talked to a marabi? Menna has changed the way we deal with wild jaan. Her work was vital in creating the rite that let us quiet all those lost jaan tonight. You say guul have been a problem, but you know Dihya and Yaluz and Azhar can handle those. And me—well, I've crossed some sand in my time. Look, I know you think you're keeping us all safe by doing this alone, but have you considered that maybe, just maybe, we'd be safer if you let us help?"

Thana put her hand on Illi's arm. "You said yourself you don't know if you can do this. You said we've only got one shot. Why not throw everything we've got at it? And if we still fail, then by G-d, we'll be there by your side to take on the sajaami again."

"You'll be hurt," said Illi. "You'll die."

Thana dropped her hand and raised an eyebrow. "You sure have a high opinion of your cousins."

Illi looked at her hands, twisting them together. "You failed before."

"Did we?" Thana glanced back at Ghadid, at the pylons even now glowing ever so faintly with torchlight. "I thought so, too. At first. But what we were up against—I don't know if we could have done better. You know what happened to the other cities. No, we came together and we survived. We chose to protect our city, even if it meant our lives. And after we mourned the dead, we rebuilt. Let us have that choice now. Let us protect Ghadid, together."

Illi's gaze slid past Thana to the city. Her stomach twisted and her throat closed up. Tears stung at the corners of her eyes. Hadn't she had enough grief? But this wasn't grief; this was relief, spreading through her like a crack in glass. And once glass shattered, there was no putting it back.

"Okay." The one word was small and empty in the darkness. Illi swallowed, met Thana's gaze, and tried again. "You can help."

27

Thana gave Illi some time alone with the camels as she woke and gathered their cousins. Illi recognized the gesture as one of trust, and it meant more to her than anything else Thana had said.

Especially since even after all that, Illi still fought the urge to slip away alone.

But she sifted through her bags instead, taking stock of supplies and what she should replenish if they were going to be retracing their steps instead of hurtling headlong into the Wastes. As she worked, she heard the distant groan of waking bodies, the clatter and rustle and crackle as blankets were shifted and fires stoked. Dawn arrived as suddenly as a season's storm; the sky was already suffused with it, but the moment light cracked the horizon was still as unexpected as lightning.

The sun caught the edges of the platforms first, their metal blushing red then glaring white. Within seconds, the light had rolled down to Ghadid's feet, cutting its pylons out of the haze and casting them in stark relief before spreading its warmth across the sands, illuminating what was left of the rite: stones and ashes and blackened bones. Already the marab were sifting through the remains, collecting the ash and the bones and the dust in thickly woven baskets for use in the glasshouses. Nothing went to waste in Ghadid.

A memory flashed of her mother, turning the ashes from a rite over in the soil, the gray mixing and blending and disappearing into the black. Soil darkened her mother's hands, lined her fingernails, and found every crease in her palms. Later her mother would try to scrub off the dirt, but a little always remained. Illi let the memory come and go, its pain no more than poking a fading bruise.

One of the marab broke away from the others and approached the camels—and Illi. All the marab had traded their white funeral wraps for an unassuming gray, but this one still wore a white belt. A reminder. The rite might be over, but grief had no set end.

The marabi pulled down their tagel as they approached, revealing a pale face and bright eyes: Menna. She opened her arms and Illi allowed an embrace, if briefly. Then she pulled back, but Menna held her by the forearm.

"Thana told us everything," said Menna, her gaze darting to Illi's wrist then back up to her eyes. "I've got a few ideas, but first—can I see?"

Illi rolled back her sleeves and held out her arms. Menna whistled low and touched the burnt bracelet with her thumb. She traced the marks, lips moving soundlessly. Then she looked up and met Illi's gaze.

"These don't bind the sajaami."

Illi swallowed. Nodded.

"Then what does?"

Illi turned around before she could hesitate, undoing the knot of her wrap at her shoulder. She let the fabric fall, just enough to expose one shoulder. She heard Menna's sharp intake of breath. Then Illi was busy re-knotting her wrap, shivering from the brush of cold despite dawn's promise of warmth. Across the sands, more of her cousins approached; at least they hadn't been around to see her scars.

"Shards," breathed Menna. "Did Heru do that to you?" But she answered her own question before Illi could. "Of course he did—you couldn't reach your own back. And that's his handwriting, no doubt. Did he—did he force you—?"

"He asked."

Menna met her gaze, held it. "Did you know what he was asking?"

Illi shifted uncomfortably, then looked away. "I had to protect Ghadid."

"What's passed is past. We work with what we have. Which is a very dangerous sajaami, apparently. But also all the expertise of your cousins. And one marabi."

"You're a cousin."

This time Menna looked away. "Cousins don't mess up contracts. Kaseem was always very explicit about that. But here I am, talking about the past." She smiled, but it didn't quite reach her eyes. "I'm the best sands-scoured marabi, is what. And we're going to do what no one else has ever done before—we're gonna usher a sajaami across the worlds. And here I thought the Empress was mad for wanting to *bind* a sajaami." She let out a *hah*, then clapped her hands together. "Well. We'd better not follow her example. She's dead, after all."

"Yeah, I'd rather avoid that."

"So. You have a plan, eh?" asked Menna. "Thana said that's why you're ready to go. You know what you're doing."

Illi stared at her hands. "Of a sort. I still have some details to figure out."

Menna breathed out in exaggerated relief. "Oh good. Here I was worried you'd become an expert marabi *on top* of being a healer and a cousin and whatever else you've decided to excel in next."

Illi blinked. Lifted her gaze. "But I'm not good at any of those."

"Uh-huh," said Menna. "You save your mastery of deceit for the others. I can see right through it."

That made Illi smile. "You always could."

"Right." Menna yanked a blanket from the pile, spread it out, and settled down. "If you want to conduct a rite for a sajaami, we'll need its name. You didn't happen across that in any dusty old scrolls, did you?"

"It told me," said Illi. "Nejm."

"Nejm," echoed Menna, rolling the sound in her mouth. Satisfied, she nodded. "Well, that's one thing I thought was gonna be a bit harder to get. Now the other, impossible thing: we're gonna need a lot of water. Like, a *lot*. I'm talking shatteringly unfathomable quantities."

"I saw something in Hathage. It's called a sea. It's—"

But Menna cut her off with a wave. "I've heard about those. That should work. You, plus the water, plus the right words, the right kind of ink, and a bit of applied heat . . ." She trailed off, frowned. "Not *directly* applied. I don't think. Well, I hope not. That would be counterproductive. But words, steam—yes. We can do that."

"Excuse me."

Both women turned at once, hands on their weapons. But it was only Heru, a pale shadow approaching in the morning light.

"Before you go and reinvent the whole of en-marab understanding, you may wish to speak to an actual en-marabi," he said curtly. "If you wish to open a path for the sajaami as you would the jaan, then you will have to destroy the girl's—" He paused, shook his head as if trying to disturb flies, then corrected, "—Illi's body. The burning of flesh linked to the jaani is a core component of the procedure. This has plagued me this past week as a central problem that I have been unable to untangle."

"We can work around that, though," said Illi. "All I have to do is keep the bracelets on, right?"

Heru's eye settled on her, but the glass one continued staring straight ahead. "No. You're conflating the issues at hand. The removal of the bracelets is a separate difficulty entirely, although a potential, if inadvisable, solution for the issue of a carnal component. The rite, however, requires a component of sacrifice from the associated body. The sajaami doesn't have a body itself, ergo Illi's is the closest we can get. Since we're all agreed that we want to avoid Illi's untimely death, we need to devise a better method of securing the rite than setting fire to her flesh and hoping for the best."

Illi swallowed. "How much flesh?"

Heru turned his whole head toward Illi and now she felt the sightless weight of that glass eye on her as well. "I would have to make some calculations, but you bring up a valid point. Perhaps only a limb or two will suffice."

"You're not going to lose *any* limbs," said Menna. "We'll figure out another way."

"First we need to establish that there *are* any other ways," said Heru. "You have not been working on this problem as long as I have, child."

Menna crossed her arms. "Oh? And how long has that been? I recall your recent exile being in part because you *weren't* working on this problem."

Before Heru could reply and turn their disagreement into an argument, Illi said, "I'll do whatever's necessary."

"You won't die," said Heru suddenly, earnestly. "I refuse to allow that eventuality. But an arm or an eye—that shouldn't be ruled out."

"*No,*" said Menna. "There will be another way. We've got the whole journey to Hathage to work it out."

"You're coming with us?" asked Illi, surprised.

Another voice answered. "We all are."

Mo stood nearby, a full water skin over one shoulder, a bundle of blankets under the other. Behind her gathered more cousins: Thana and Azhar, Dihya and Yaluz, Drum Chief Amastan and Zarrat, along with Canthem and Captain Yufit. Amastan argued with Thana about logistics, Azhar helped Dihya and Yaluz pack the bags and load the camels, while Zarrat brought full water skins from the carriages. Even Hamma joined them, if only briefly, leading more camels to join their slowly growing herd. For the first time, Illi recognized her reticence to join them on guul hunts as a symptom of the Siege, not a weakness.

Illi had expected Thana to come, and Mo with her. But the others . . .

She tried to swallow past the sudden knot in her throat.

"Well," said Menna, "'Stan's gonna stay behind to keep the other drum chiefs in line and Zarrat promised to help Hamma with any guul that attack while we're gone, but the *rest* of all of us are coming with you."

"But first we should prepare," said Heru. "I will need appropriate supplies."

"Oh yeah, we've got those." Menna gestured at the bags.

Heru pushed past Menna, heading for the bustle. "I'll need to personally inspect them. Only the highest-quality materials will suffice."

"Hey—don't you touch my things. I've got them packed the way I want them," said Menna, abandoning Illi to hurry after him.

Illi cast around, at a loss for what to do with herself. Her cousins were handling all the preparations and from the way the camels were clustering, packs tied against their humps, they were almost ready. They'd be leaving soon. So soon. Illi glanced at Ghadid. Now that she'd had a few more minutes, she wanted a few more.

"There you are."

Illi turned just as Canthem pulled her into a hug. She stiffened, remembering how she'd been so close to leaving them behind. Again.

Canthem pressed their face into her braids and muttered, "How're you doing?"

"I . . . I don't know," admitted Illi. "You?"

"Like I just spent the night trying to sleep on the sands surrounded by whispering jaan," said Canthem. "Honestly, I didn't expect us to return to Hathage so soon. Why the sudden change of heart? Aren't we fleeing Merrabel?"

"I tried to leave you." The words slipped from Illi like drawn water. She'd meant to say something else, but she'd also expected Canthem to chastise her. "Again."

"Yeah, you're making a habit of it." Canthem pulled back and considered her. They wore their tagel low, just over their nose so that the tops of their apple-round cheeks were visible. "Will you try it again?"

Illi stared at the sand, unable to meet Canthem's gaze. "Probably."

Canthem laughed and when Illi looked up, their cheeks were crinkled in a smile. "At least you're honest."

"I just—I don't want you to get hurt," said Illi quickly, needing Canthem to understand. "And if there's a moment or a chance where I can protect you, I will. I can't promise anything less than that. You would be safer staying in Ghadid than coming with me. You said it yourself—we'll be running right back to Merrabel. And I honestly have no idea what she'll do. She's not going to be happy with me—*or* with you. Won't she treat you like a deserter?"

"Probably. Even though I'd claim that I was only doing my duty by protecting you from guul, there were enough witnesses on that farmstead to blame me for your freedom. If she catches me, she'll have me executed." Canthem shrugged, as if that possibility were little worse than losing a bet. "But first she has to catch me. And I've got your friends here to watch my back. The captain trusts them and that's good enough for me." Then Canthem turned to her fully, their eyes on hers, their hands on hers. "Instead of thinking about the worst—what if everything works out all right?"

Illi looked into those eyes and lost her breath. "What do you mean?"

"Exactly that." Canthem squeezed her hands. "You're so focused on all the ways this could fail or go wrong—but what if we succeed? Have you planned for that?"

Illi's stomach twisted. "Of course I have."

Canthem waited a beat before pushing, gently, "And?"

"Then we succeed. The sajaami will be gone."

"But what about after? What will you do?"

"I . . ." Illi dropped her gaze to her hands, comfortably enclosed within Canthem's larger, paler ones. "I don't know. Go back to Ghadid."

"How will you feel?"

Illi shot Canthem a glare, but their smile was still earnest. Real. She sighed, letting her shoulders drop. "I don't know."

"That's okay," said Canthem gently. "But you should think about it. Think about after. Because we're going to succeed and I don't want you to be disappointed."

"What makes you think I'd be disappointed?"

Canthem searched her gaze. "You've been fighting a long time. When the sajaami is gone, when you have nothing left to fight—who will you be?"

"There'll still be guul," pointed out Illi.

Canthem laughed, a soft, small sound. "And there you've just proved my point. Let's pretend for a moment that the guul are gone, too. What then?"

"The guul aren't going anywhere," scoffed Illi, but even as she did, she felt a chill of fear. The sajaami and the guul coming from the Wastes were linked, after all. Before the Siege, before the Empress had cracked the sajaami free, guul had been little more than a story told by the passing caravans. They'd never come close to Ghadid.

What if they never did again?

Who will you be?

"You don't have to answer now," said Canthem, quieter. "But you should think about it. There's more to life than fighting."

"You're one to talk," said Illi, sharper than she'd intended. "You fight guul, too. What will you do?"

"I've always wanted to garden."

Illi dropped Canthem's hands and all but pushed them away. They might as well have slapped her. Canthem's eyes widened as they realized what they'd said.

"Oh G-d—I'm sorry. I didn't mean—I'd forgotten about your mother."

Illi took several deep breaths, but the pain that had come on so suddenly now faded just as quickly. What would her mother have thought of Canthem? So earnest, so persistent, so full of heat and life. She would have insisted on Canthem joining them for a meal, and her father would have pulled out all the stops with date cakes and marinated goat and oven-baked cheese. Her parents would have asked them pointed questions and Canthem would have answered them all, honestly and passionately. Her parents would have loved Canthem.

Why can't you?

"I do," she said softly.

"I'm sorry," continued Canthem, not hearing her. "I just wanted to remind you that you're not alone. And there's joy in this world yet, if you're brave enough to take it."

"I'm brave."

"Are you? Then why did you push me away?"

"You were distracting me."

"You were afraid," corrected Canthem.

"Well—yes, okay," said Illi. "Of course I was afraid. You almost died. And because of that, I made rash decisions. I was weak."

"Love isn't a weakness."

Illi breathed deep through her nose. "It is when the person you love dies."

"Is that weakness? Or is that living? People die. All of us, even your en-marabi. We'll all die. Is it worth avoiding love to avoid grief? Imagine this, as far-fetched as it might seem to you: We succeed. We all live. And you're *happy*. What does that look like?"

Happy. The word echoed like a drum in Illi's skull. Being happy was being safe. But that wasn't completely true. There were plenty of times she'd been happy before. She'd been happiest running down guul on the sands. She'd been happiest with her cousins at her side, her heart beating as hard as a drum, her breathing one with the wind. She'd been happiest with a blade in her hand and her task simple and clear before her.

She'd also been happiest at home, helping Mo grind grain,

helping Thana patch leather. Their silence a warmth and a balm. Happiest catching Thana giving Mo a kiss when they both thought she wasn't looking. Happiest staying up late by the hearth, Mo guiding her through the motions of healing, telling her—again—the stories of the healers.

And she'd been happiest walking the markets, picking out new faces and challenging them to spar. She'd been happiest learning from them, new styles and methods of fighting along with other things. And those three days with Canthem in the beginning—

They'd been so dangerous because she'd been so happy.

Is that what life could be, after? Not a constant fight, but a dance? She couldn't imagine ever truly letting go of her fear, because the next disaster was always just around the corner, but maybe that's what Canthem meant. Knowing you could lose it all in an instant and yet living—and loving—despite the fear.

"It's not easy," said Canthem after a few moments of Illi's silence. "But nothing that's worth doing is ever easy. It'll take work, but just as much work as you've put into surviving. Please . . . consider it."

Illi stared across the desert to the north, to the horizon, imagined the Aer Caäs and what lay past them, imagined bringing the sajaami to the sea and ushering it across to the other side. Imagined returning without it, alive and whole, her cousins at her side and Canthem—

"What will you do, after?" asked Illi.

"I've heard a lot of nice things about Ghadid."

"You're joking."

Canthem met her gaze and smiled. "No." Then they tilted their head back toward the sky and added, "Of course, I'll still want to travel . . ."

"What if we can't make it work?"

"What if we can?"

"You don't even know that much about Ghadid," pressed Illi. "What if you tire of it? What if it's not what you expected? What if you get bored? What if—"

"Shh," said Canthem gently, placing a finger on Illi's lips. "One day at a time, Illi. We'll take it one day at a time."

28

When they were finally ready to depart, the sun was high overhead and the funeral pyre had been dismantled, its many pieces already settled back in the crypts. Amastan stood with his arms out, palms up, the chains of his office glinting as he shifted from foot to foot in the sand. He was no longer Amastan their cousin, but Drum Chief Amastan.

And the drum chief spoke.

"You leave today to perform a great service to Ghadid," he said. "I know you will succeed, because this is what we do. The family has always protected Ghadid and always will, in whatever form that takes." His gaze flicked to the captain, but Yufit had his head bowed as if in prayer. "When you return, you'll be welcomed with open arms and celebrations." Now he turned to look directly at Heru. "On behalf of the Circle, any sentence of exile will be rescinded for those who aid in this task."

Heru nodded, as if it were his due. But the captain's head jerked up.

"*Any?*"

Drum Chief Amastan met the captain's gaze. "Any."

Captain Yufit let out a small noise. Thana glanced between them, but it was Menna who whooped. She patted the captain on the back, who took it as readily as a wall might, then swooped in and wrapped a startled Amastan in a hug. When she let him go, she wiped at her eyes, then turned and fell into Azhar's embrace.

"But first you must be rid of the sajaami," said Amastan shakily, as if trying to regain control of the situation. "And then— if you want to, because I know you have made your home in Hathage—"

Captain Yufit crossed the space between them. Took Amastan's hands. Held them in his. "My home is Ghadid."

"Things have changed," continued Amastan. "So much has changed. People don't remain the same."

"You're not the only one who changed," said the captain. Then he leaned forward and brushed his fingers across Amastan's forehead, as gentle as a kiss. "I'm coming back. Thank you, Asaf."

The captain let go then, turning abruptly and striding toward his camel. He mounted and lifted his hand in a two-fingered salute, then pressed his closed fist over his heart. The others—Menna, Thana, Mo, Azhar, Dihya, Yaluz, and Canthem—all echoed the gesture. Drum Chief Amastan returned it, bowing slightly as he did. Beside him, Zarrat waved and Hamma inclined her head.

They mounted their beasts and then, as one, they all turned to Illi. She sat frozen under their stares, weighed down by their expectations. Of course they would look to her. This was her burden and she had asked for their help. Even though they would assist her in the journey and the rite, the sajaami was still her responsibility—and they were her responsibility if they got hurt.

She swallowed. She, too, put her fist over her heart. Nodded to Amastan. Then she let out a loud "*Hel!*" and kneed her camel into motion. Dust and sand was kicked up as they set off and began putting distance between them and Ghadid for what she hoped was the last time.

Illi could have closed her eyes and walked this path in her sleep. She'd always thought the desert looked particularly *same* but now she recognized even the meanest shrubs and trees. The group had strung out into a long line within the first day, Illi leading while Dihya kept guard at the back. They'd sighted guul only twice during the ten-day journey and Illi had sent both groups north with little trouble. Her wrists were even beginning to heal, the flesh no longer so raw. She'd felt more normal during this journey than at any time since the sajaami had been bound to her. It was as if Nejm had curled up inside her, content to wait for now.

Then one dawn, the Aer Caäs jutted from the night to snap at the sky like the jaws of a jackal, and the general feeling of unease that had been gnawing at her since they left flared as if it'd been doused in oil.

Despite Canthem's reassurances that there would be an *after*, all she could think about was the sea and the rite. Menna and Heru had hammered out more of the necessary details while assembling tinder for the rite each night they rested, but they still hadn't found a way around sacrificing Illi's body. If Illi were to do the rite as they currently understood it, she'd die. And Illi very much did not want to die.

Captain Yufit broke the monotony that had fallen over them like a thick drape when he turned from the path. Illi stared blankly at his retreating back, not quite comprehending what he was doing. Before he could get too far, Illi kicked her camel forward and cut him off.

"Where are you going?"

"I know a better way over the mountains," said Captain Yufit. "It's much faster than the caravan route, but it's also a lot steeper and narrower. We'll have to leave our camels behind. But don't worry—there's plenty of forage for them in the foothills. They'll be safe. And I know where we can pick up horses on the other side."

"You've done this before."

"We've had reason to catch up to caravans and guul on other occasions."

"Why not just take the caravan route? It can't be that much slower."

"We'll cut off hours of travel time." Yufit hesitated, then added, "And she'll be watching the main route. Best to avoid it if you want to reach the capital unimpeded."

"How do you know she'll be watching the road?" pressed Illi.

"Truthfully, I don't know for sure," admitted Yufit. "But I know the general. She doesn't let go of things easily, and it would only take a few spare soldiers to keep watch."

Illi nodded. "All right. I'll tell the others."

They followed Yufit's lead, winding through the foothills until the path abruptly began to climb. It was narrow and steep, just as Yufit had promised. They unburdened their camels and took only what was absolutely necessary after Yufit had assured them once more that they'd find an outpost and resupply on the other side of the Aer Caäs. They took their time, drinking extra and resting on the scattered rocks, heads tilted back toward the sun. This late in winter there was no reason to set up tents.

Illi sat cross-legged on a blanket at the front of the group, trying not to think about what would happen on the other side of the mountains—and failing miserably. As usual, Heru arrived with a steaming glass of tea cupped between his hands like an offering. Throughout their journey, Heru had persisted with his new habit of bringing Illi tea on a regular basis. He'd even started brewing enough tea for the whole group, but only Illi received a cup from him personally.

Usually, Illi let him come and go without a word, but this time when Heru started to set the tea down beside her, silent as a breeze, Illi stopped him with a finger across the back of his hand. His skin was smooth, if cold. When she turned, he had one eye on her, his glass eye on the mountains, the gold iris glowing with the sunlight.

"Why?" she asked, the word a puff of cloud in the cold air.

Heru drew back and into himself, leaving the tea but hiding his scarred arms in the folds of his wrap. "You must be more specific. There are a literal infinity of answers I could give to such an open question, but we don't have the time for that."

Illi's smile was almost as light as her breath. "I'm not going to let you get out of this one so easily. You know what I'm asking."

Heru's real eye slipped past her, unfocused. "You ask why I'm bringing you tea."

Illi nodded, once.

"That should be clear enough," said Heru. "You need to remain healthy and strong to survive the rite. I cannot risk anything less."

"If that were the only reason, you'd bring tea to Menna, too. Or any of the others. They're all important if we're going to pull this off."

"I don't worry about them." His eye flicked back to her and then he realized what he'd said and he looked away again. "They've proven on multiple occasions that they can take care of them-selves. You, however, have an unfortunate tendency toward recklessness and self-martyrdom."

Illi picked up the tea and sipped it; perfectly brewed as always. "There's still more to it than that," she pressed. "Back in Merrabel's jail, when you first saw me—you'd thought I was dead, didn't you?"

Heru tensed. "It was the most logical conclusion."

"But you were relieved to see me."

"Of course. It meant that Barca hadn't acquired the sajaami, which would have been disastrous."

Illi sighed. "Of course." She closed her eyes. Why did she bother? But she tried a different tactic. "Merrabel said your other assistants never lasted long. Was she right?"

"Barca is full of lies and misunderstanding." But Heru's words were clipped, short.

"What happened to them? She mentioned some died—" Illi cut herself off before she could add, *horribly.*

Heru was silent for a long time. But Illi could clearly see the muscles around Heru's eyes tense and relax as he struggled for words. So she waited. Finally he drew a deep breath and let out his answer.

"One."

Illi continued to wait, but Heru didn't offer up anything else. Yet he didn't stir to leave, either. He stared at the western horizon, but his eye was unfocused, his gaze distant. Illi sipped her tea, its heat warming her throat and chest.

When he finally spoke, his voice was low as if he were talking only to himself. "It was an accident. The wrong reagent at the wrong time. That chemical shouldn't have even been in my lab. And she shouldn't have—" He stopped, shook his head. "It doesn't matter. I learned what I could from the incident and moved on. It's not my fault if others believed me a monster for it. I've been more careful since with the assistants I take on, if I take on any."

"You're afraid it'll happen again."

Heru snorted. "I'm not *afraid*. No, I am . . . careful."

"And yet, here we are." Illi gestured, turning her bracelets so that they caught and reflected the sunlight.

"Here we are," echoed Heru.

Illi let his words roll off into silence, seeing him as she never truly had before. She'd watched his actions closely, yes, but not *him*. She hadn't dared. There'd been safety in not knowing him, but what had that safety ultimately brought her?

Here they were.

Seven years, and he'd never done anything with the sajaami. But almost as many, and she'd never bothered to learn who Heru Samctkct really was.

"Why?" askcd Illi, and when Heru looked at her, she added, "Why do you do it? Why do you study guul and jaan? Why did you stay in Ghadid? Why—"

"Did you want me to actually answer onc of those questions or do you prefer to listen to the sound of your own voice?" interrupted Heru.

"It's just—Merrabel knew a lot about you," said Illi more carefully. "But I don't know how much of what she said is true."

Heru *hmph*ed. "It's difficult to refute accusations I haven't heard."

"They weren't accusations. She said she'd studied with you. That you were an orphan and I was wondering—"

"—whether the state of my parentage had any bearing on my motivation to become an en-marabi?"

Illi blinked. "Well. Yes."

Heru drew himself up, like a vulture craning its long neck. "Of course it did. There were frequent outbreaks of plague in the less wealthy crevices of Na Tay Khet and those of my blood succumbed one way or another. It was pointless, as death often is. Watching the marab attend so many bodies only to quiet their jaan, I knew there had to be another way. Everybody takes death for granted, but I alone recognized it could be treated and eventually overcome. Guul are a testament to that, in their own particular way. And sajaam the ultimate proof of all, for they have existed for ages beyond our own understanding."

Illi couldn't help herself. "And yet when you finally had a sajaami, you did nothing."

"I wasn't *ready*," snapped Heru. "I couldn't risk it. Ideally, I would have gone myself into the Wastes after decades of study and preparation and bound the sajaami to my will. But the Empress was impatient and now instead, I've been forced to use untested and incomplete measures in an attempt to simply keep the sajaami from wreaking greater havoc and destroying another one of my assistants. But I deal in reality, not the ideal, and I will see this experiment to its conclusion."

"And you'll give up the sajaami?" pressed Illi.

Heru's smile was genuine, if alarming. "I know where to find the other sajaam in the Wastes when I'm ready. The knowledge we'll gain from this rite will be integral to my work. You'll survive this because I'll need your assistance when I return to the Wastes and unravel the last remaining theories about immortality for good. Your recklessness may be less than ideal, but you're the only one capable." He paused for a heartbeat before adding, "But only if you are willing, of course."

For the first time in a long while, Illi felt reassured. If Heru could believe in an after, so could she.

"Of course."

29

It was midday when they began to climb.

Even with regular breaks, Illi's breath soon burned in her chest and her legs ached with each step. The patches of snow had grown, meeting them even earlier this time. The air itself tasted like ice, despite the prickle of the sun on her shoulders. Their climb was slow and laborious, but it went over boulders and unwaveringly straight up where the main path had meandered. When dusk fell around them like a shroud, their tricky climb turned treacherous. Twice Illi slipped on rocks before Thana had the sense to light a torch.

But flickering torchlight stole Illi's depth perception, flattening the rocks and forcing her to concentrate twice as hard on the climb. The others had similar difficulty, except for Heru, who had long since grown used to a lack of depth perception. Any lingering chatter soon fell away as they focused on the next step, and the next.

With the night came the cold, worse than any Illi had ever experienced. Despite the exertion and the extra layers of cloth, it crept through to her skin, to her blood and her bones. Her breath came out in thick clouds that drifted away, already frozen. Her nose ran, first clear, then streaked with blood. The cold bit at her exposed skin and even burned her throat. But they kept climbing and kept moving forward despite the darkness.

It was fully dark when they crested the mountain and fully dark when they started to descend. So perhaps they could be forgiven for not noticing the army sooner.

Azhar picked out the campfires first. At this distance, they shimmered and glinted like stars, a disorienting inversion of the sky above spread across the foothills below. Their small group came to a stop. Thana peered ahead as if she could cut the gloom with her glare. Menna pulled a seeing glass from her bag and panned it across the fires.

"They're soldiers," reported Menna. "Or at least, they're dressed as such. But I doubt that many people would show up at the base of a mountain just to put on a show."

Captain Yufit put down his own seeing glass. "It's General Barca."

"No," said Menna. "I'm pretty sure that's an army, not a single person."

Yufit shot her a long-suffering look. "The general has assembled her forces below. I don't know what she intends, but this doesn't appear to be a warm welcome."

"Why's she even there?" pressed Menna. "You said she'd just have a soldier or two watching the main road. Well, sa, we didn't take the main road and this ain't exactly a soldier or two."

"She must have anticipated we'd come this way instead." Yufit's jaw tightened. "She must have realized I'd be with you."

"I wouldn't give yourself so much credit," said Heru. "Merrabel also knows that I'm in attendance and it's not such a stretch that we'd return so soon. After all, to do anything remotely successful with the sajaami, we would need a large amount of water. Aside from the Great River, our sea is the nearest body of water that would suffice, and Hathage's wall the easiest way to approach said sea. She would have realized that I'd advise you against going anywhere near Na Tay Khet, so that leaves us Hathage and its wall."

Illi stared out across the prickles of campfires, her stomach plummeting. "How are we going to get past *that*?"

"It's not too late to head for this great river you mentioned, is it?" asked Menna.

But it was Thana who answered. "It'd take us another week, if not longer. We don't have the supplies."

"And again," piped up Heru, "I would, in fact, advise against it. The sajaami's containment will not last long enough for us to find another access point to sufficient water."

"Then the only way out is through," said Dihya. She scanned the valley below, lips pressed tight. "There's nine of us. Several hundred of them. But perhaps we can use that to our advantage."

"Each of the general's soldiers is hand-selected and highly trained," cautioned Captain Yufit. "She works under the philosophy that it's better to have a hundred completely loyal and deadly efficient soldiers than thrice that. They'll have orders to look out for a girl from the Wastes. An honor guard will only draw attention to Illi."

Glances were exchanged. Her cousins shifted uncomfortably, weighing the implications, but Illi knew what Yufit meant. She knew what she'd have to do, what she'd always had to do. It could never have been as easy as Thana claimed it would be. Illi wouldn't be able to keep them safe any longer. At least, not by staying with them.

"Wait," said Menna, turning to Yufit. "How do we know you didn't lead us into this ambush on purpose? You still answer to your general, don't you?"

"For one, it's not exactly an ambush." Yufit gestured broadly at the campfires. "For another, it would've been much easier to lead you straight up the caravan route instead of climbing all these rocks with you. The other route would have also led you into this army."

Menna narrowed her eyes. "She's still your general, though."

"How can we be certain you won't turn us in?" asked Dihya, one hand on the hilt of her machete. She nodded at Canthem. "Or this one, too, for that matter."

"I pledged my sword to the general to protect civilians from the guul," said Yufit. "Nothing I've done and nothing I plan to do has been counter to that pledge."

Dihya narrowed her eyes. "That's real rich, coming from you. If you'd turn on your leader, how can we believe you won't turn on us?"

The captain huffed a breath that fluttered his tagel. "The general made her intentions for the sajaami quite clear. She'd rather risk her city and her people by harnessing its power for herself than by safely being rid of it. She may truly believe that what she's doing will benefit Hathage, but I don't. She's going too far and I don't want to see her undo all the good she's done. Hathage is my home as much as Ghadid, and I worked alongside the general to make it a safe one. The sajaami needs to go. So no, I won't betray you. You have my word."

"Amastan trusts you," said Menna, as if that decided it.

But Dihya was still looking at Canthem, fingering her hilt. Canthem blindly reached out a hand to Illi, who grabbed it and squeezed.

"The captain is right, ma," said Canthem. "General Barca has performed miracles for Hathage. She steered us away from ruin when that seemed our only choice, kept our caravans safe, and trained us to fight guul. Normally, I would go to the ends of the world for her. But this isn't about the guul or even Hathage anymore. She crossed a line when she sent an assassin after Illi—"

"Wait *what*?" interrupted Menna. She turned to glare at Illi. "You didn't mention *that*."

"It isn't relevant," said Illi.

"That is *highly* relevant," said Thana. "It tells us what sort of woman this general is. What she's capable of."

"She's highly capable of being reckless," said Heru. "But then, that isn't novel information." He glanced over Illi, his glass eye boring into her as if he could see past her skin and through her bones. "However, the information is relevant in another way: if you'd been injured in any way, the consequences would've been dire."

Illi swallowed; she hadn't mentioned the incident at all. In fact, between the rite and the guul in the foothills and the journey to Ghadid and back again, Usaf had completely slipped from her mind. The first time she'd killed a person, and she'd almost *forgotten* about it.

"Canthem saved me," said Illi, tightening her fingers around theirs. "I trust them completely."

Canthem took a deep breath. "That alone would have been enough, but the general tried again with some guul later. I know what General Barca would do to Illi if she catches her, what she's already *done* to Illi. No—you have my word as well. I'll protect Illi with my life."

Dihya considered Canthem for a long moment, then her hand dropped from her weapon and she nodded. The group eased, the tension going out of them all as if a cord had been cut.

"Well," said Menna brightly. "We've come this far with two potential spies and traitors. What's to stop us from going a little farther? Right, guys?"

Nods were exchanged like so many handshakes, but Illi set her back to the army's campfires and steeled herself. "We have to change our plan."

Thana narrowed her eyes. "What do you mean? There's only one plan, and that's getting us all through an army and to this wall of yours."

"We can't all go," said Illi. "It's gotta be just me and Heru."

Canthem let go of her hand. Stared. Thana started to protest, but Illi pressed on. "You heard the captain—if you all come with us, you'll guarantee we're caught. We need a distraction, not an honor guard. If you stay up here and draw their attention, I might be able to slip past." Illi swallowed. "But it means putting yourselves in a lot of danger."

Thana cracked her knuckles. "We can handle danger."

"Everyone who was at that farmstead will know what you look like," said Yufit. "And the general will have briefed the rest of her soldiers. A girl with dust in her hair and a wrap like that will draw them immediately. As it did me."

Illi met Yufit's gaze. "Which is why I'll need your clothes."

Yufit snorted, but when Illi crossed her arms and didn't look away, he shook his head. "You think you can pass as a captain?"

"If you show me a few things, yes," said Illi. "We're the same height, close to the same build. I can carry and wield a sword just as well as you. And in the chaos we're hoping for, they won't look twice."

"They will at a captain going the opposite way." Yufit frowned. "Why not take Canthem's clothes?"

"They're just a guard," said Illi. "Someone might actually question why they're headed for the city. But you—you're high enough rank that nobody should question you. I saw the way the other soldiers treated you, sa."

Heru crossed his arms. "I refuse to wear another's clothes."

"You won't have to," said Illi. "You'll be my prisoner."

"Barca will be expecting me," said Heru cautiously.

"Perhaps," said Illi. "But you're not he Fet anymore, Heru. Whatever you started from, you're Sametket now. And she's afraid of you."

Heru puffed up a little. "Is she now."

Illi wasn't even sure if Merrabel had thought about Heru once since leaving him imprisoned on the edge of Hathage, but she wasn't going to tell Heru that. If nothing else, Merrabel had no reason to suspect that Heru had slipped her binding and was free to work against her.

"We'll draw them up and out of the hills," said Thana, addressing the others. "We'll split into pairs and scatter among these rocks and boulders. Our strengths lie in speed and surprise, and this landscape will give us both. Dihya and—"

As her cousins planned, Canthem put a hand on Illi's arm. "You've already thought this through." Their tone was only mildly accusatory.

Illi swallowed, but nodded. "I thought we might need a distraction to get past Merrabel and up the wall. I just didn't think it'd be so soon."

"You're not going alone," said Canthem. "A captain on their own would be suspicious. But if you have a guard at your side, they won't question you."

Illi met Canthem's warm gaze. She'd steeled herself to the possibility of having to do this on her own, but now that she was offered a way out, she found her resolve evaporating like water spilled on hot stone. She was tired of being alone.

You're not alone, said Nejm, for the first time in almost a week.

Illi hid her startle by grabbing Canthem's hand, but even as she did so, she could see Amilcem's eyes burning, her jaw widening with cracks of light and heat. Illi's stomach churned and bile rose in her throat.

It doesn't have to happen that way, continued Nejm. *I can protect everything you love. But if you try to go through with this, I will destroy it instead.*

"Are you okay?" asked Canthem, voice and body close.

Illi took a deep, shuddering breath and pushed away the images that Nejm was putting in her mind. "The sajaami—"

That was all Illi needed to say. Canthem squeezed her hand, their eyes intent. "It's trying to scare you, isn't it? It's only doing that because we're so close. It must be afraid."

Afraid. The word echoed in Illi, both accusation and threat. She felt Nejm withdraw at the word. *I'm* not *alone.* She held Canthem's gaze.

"You and me and Heru—we'll do this together."

She felt Canthem relax an instant before their eyes lit with a smile. She didn't let go of their hand as she sought out Heru in the growing bustle. While her cousins checked weapons and reorganized supplies, he stood off to one side with his back to the mountain and his face toward the campfires below. His expression, normally inscrutable even when his tagel was low, was impenetrable in the darkness.

Illi stood beside him and stared at the encamped army for a few moments, trying to see what he saw. But all she could make out were the flickers of orange light. She cleared her throat. "I need to know one thing before we do this."

"That is inaccurate: you need to know many things."

"When I take off the bracelets, how much time will I have?"

Heru shifted his weight but didn't look at her. "It's difficult to know precisely. There are many variables that must be taken into account, such as your weight, your hydration levels, the current state of your body, the pH of your blood, the salinity of the air around you—"

"I don't need the seconds," cut in Illi. "Just a guess. Will I have an hour? Minutes?"

"As long as nothing impinges on the integrity of the container—and by that I mean your body remains unharmed, Illi—you'll definitely have minutes. Twenty-three to twenty-four of them, if I've calculated the variables correctly. But I'd advise against treating my calculations as anything more than mere conjecture. The only other instance of sajaami possession that I'm aware of was the Empress and while she didn't fall apart at the time, I've since come to the conclusion that she must have prepared herself in other ways to strengthen her flesh against the sajaami's power. We can't know for certain whether or not the sajaami would've destroyed her in the fullness of time without any dampeners." Heru finally turned and fixed Illi with his one-eyed stare. "You will, of course, only take the bracelets off when you're ready to perform the rite."

"Of course," Illi said immediately. "I just wanted to know how long I'd have to do the rite."

"The rite itself should only require two, maybe three minutes of setup and take all of one and a half minutes to execute. You'll have more than sufficient time as long as you wait to remove the bracelets. Did the marabi give you the directions? You'll have me to walk you through each step once we begin, but it's best to be prepared for any eventuality, including one where, for some reason, I'm unable to be at your side."

Illi patted the pouch where she'd put the tightly rolled scroll, which was filled with Heru's neat, precise script. "Don't worry, you'll be there. Besides, Menna explained what I need to do on the way up. The hardest part will be slipping through the army."

Illi stared out over the glittering campfires, trying not to think about her cousins up against *that*. They'd be fine. She couldn't worry about them.

"The hardest part will be surviving the rite," corrected Heru. "But we'll come to that when we must."

Illi drew in a deep breath. Behind her, quiet had settled on her cousins. When she turned, she found them watching her, waiting. They were ready. She had to be ready.

She smiled, the gesture more teeth than humor. "All right—now if the captain would just give me his clothes?"

30

They parted ways. The Circle broke and the other drum chiefs swept through the door one by one, leaving Amastan alone in the room. He breathed in the smell of his small victory: the sharp scent of stress, of sweat, of salt, of too many people arguing for what felt like the sake of arguing. But they'd come around to his view. They always did, if he was just patient and gave them time to arrive at his conclusions on their own.

After all, he'd already made the decision, so they had no choice. Thana and the others *would* return, and when they did, Yufit would need a home. Ghadid would be that home again.

"I've heard a few things from your cousin," Yufit had said before the rite. *"Are they all true?"*

Amastan had carefully dodged the question. *"People say a lot of things about me."*

"I never found anyone like you." Yufit had met his eyes, held his hands. *"I tried. I lived, like you'd told me to. I found a lot of things, but I never found you."*

Amastan hadn't had the courage to tell Yufit that he'd never looked. *"You seem to have had a change of heart."*

"Not a change. More like a growth."

"G-d was kind."

Yufit had only laughed at that.

Now Amastan opened a window. Cool air brushed across his face like a light hand. He breathed again, winter sharp in his throat.

Then the drums began.

Amastan's first instinct was denial. A servant had misunderstood a command. A watchman had seen a sand twister and jumped to conclusions. Another drum chief had decided to have a calling, unrelated to the matter they'd just been discussing. Or related—in any case, he needed to quell the panic before it could catch and spread.

But when he stepped into the pale afternoon light, the drums persisted in a rhythm he knew too well. This was a calling, but of a different sort. This was a calling for swords and camels, a calling for defense, a calling for cousins. As always when he heard this particular beat, he hooked a finger beneath the chain of his office, felt the weight of the metal rings that gave him so much sway, lifted the chain until the weight was off his chest. As always, he let the chain fall again; he'd given up any claim to being a cousin when he'd become a drum chief.

Once a cousin, always a cousin. His words, his phrase, his promise given to Menna all those years ago. But she was out there somewhere on the sands, not here to defend the city.

"Amastan!"

Zarrat skidded to a stop just feet away, his breathing ragged from running. He'd already strapped on his sword—or maybe he'd been wearing it when the call came in. That kid had always been a little overeager.

Zarrat straightened and added, "*Sa.* They've spotted guul. Twenty and counting and more still coming. What do we do?"

Fear unfurled in Amastan like a vulture spreading its wings. It was happening again. And this time there was no strong defense, there was only him and this former slave and his cousin Hamma with her bow. The three of them couldn't stand against this many guul.

"Sa? Where are you going?"

Amastan had started walking without realizing it. He had no time for fear. Ghadid had to be here when Thana and his cousins returned. When Yufit returned. Already a plan was forming, as clear as glass. There weren't enough cousins and the guul couldn't be allowed to enter the city. They'd have to cut the cables. All of them.

"Find Hamma," ordered Amastan. "Meet me at the lookout."

He didn't wait for Zarrat to acknowledge his order. The lookout wasn't far; only a few platforms away. But it felt like he'd crossed half the city by the time he started climbing the ladder. A new one had been forged just for this building, just to make the climb a little easier for the watchmen who hadn't been trained as cousins. He appreciated the ladder when his old wounds started acting up.

The two-story glasshouse took up most of the roof. A watchman waved over the side at Amastan.

"Guul spotted, sa," she called. "Coming fast. There's a whole horde of them this time. I've never seen anything like it."

"I'm coming up."

Amastan entered the glasshouse, his focus so narrow that he barely took in the riot of growth all around him. He climbed another ladder to the second floor, then opened the door to the ladder that would take him to the roof. The watchman held out the seeing glass as he approached. She pointed toward the dust plume on the horizon, then stepped out of his way.

Amastan counted twenty-seven guul, but beyond them was more movement and therefore probably more guul. It didn't matter; there were already more guul than they'd ever faced before, even with a full militia of cousins. No, they wouldn't be fighting these guul, not this time. They wouldn't survive it.

"Cut the cables," said Amastan.

He felt more than heard the watchman hesitate. "Sa?"

"All of them," added Amastan. When the watchman still didn't move, he snapped, "*Go.*"

"With respect, sa," said the watchman quickly. "Isn't that a decision for the Circle—?"

"With respect, ma," said Amastan. "The last time we waited for the Circle on such an important decision, over half of our people died. We don't have time to waste."

The watchman swallowed, but then she was scrambling down the glasshouse ladder. Amastan kept the seeing glass trained on the guul. Watching. Waiting. Counting.

At least this time he didn't have a broken ankle and, if it came to it, he could fight. As a drum chief he wasn't supposed to, of course. He also wasn't supposed to keep up his training, but he had anyway. His free hand tugged on the chain around his neck, lifted it, let it drop again. As heavy as it hung at times, the burden was his and his alone to bear. The people had plenty of cousins to keep them safe. What they needed was a leader.

You've fought enough. You're needed here, to lead.

Tamella's words echoed across the years to him from that night, the night she and countless other cousins had died, and they were as heavy now as they'd been then. Tamella had slipped the chain around his neck, her last order for him to find Thana, protect her, and *live.* Then she'd distracted the bound while he'd led the survivors to safety.

Some days he still wished she'd kept the chain and lived instead.

Amastan tracked the guul. He counted. He rubbed his eyes. He tracked them again. That was odd. They didn't seem to be getting any closer. He counted the time since the guul had first been spotted, the distance they would've been spotted at, the speed they usually traveled. They should be closer by now. Much closer.

Yet somehow, those distant dots hadn't grown at all. They still remained distant. But they *were* moving. The dust streaking the sky attested to that. Just not toward Ghadid.

No.

They were heading north.

"Watchman!" Amastan dropped the seeing glass, found the watchman just below in the street. She'd stopped. "Abandon that order! Leave the cables and bring me ink and paper!"

The watchman looked confused, but she hit her chest with her fist to confirm, then went back inside the building. There'd be scribe supplies below. And while Amastan knew already what he'd seen, he had to confirm. He had to know for *certain*.

Because if he was right, then that meant the guul were heading for Hathage. For Thana and Illi and Yufit. For his family.

They parted ways. Illi picked her path through the rocks and gnarled shrubs, the gloom of dawn quickly obscuring her and her guard and Heru. Thana lingered, watching, for only a moment, two. Long enough to worry for the girl—no, not a girl any longer, not for years now. Long enough to wish she were walking that path instead, but not just because she wished she could take Illi's burden. Illi could handle it, she was a cousin through and through.

But if—no, *when*—Illi got rid of the sajaami, it would be the first time anyone had done so. Her name would be remembered when Thana's wouldn't.

Thana tucked her jealousy away and turned to her other cousins. Illi would only make it if they distracted the soldiers. And besides, there was room enough in the songs and scrolls for all of them. No one would forget the family and their role in protecting Ghadid for a long, long time. Amastan would make certain of that.

Thana gave Illi a few minutes before lighting the torch, which flickered and hissed and threatened not to catch at all before finally giving in with a flare. She passed the torch to Yaluz, who started down the path alone. The others melted into the darkness around Yaluz to keep him safe. Thana picked her way across the rocky terrain, as silent as a snake, one knife at the ready, her garrote lightly tapping her thigh.

It didn't take long to draw the soldiers' attention.

Shouts struck like falling stones in the camp, and motion whirled around the campfires, spinning lazy flames to dance. The torch slowed. Hesitated. As soldiers spilled up the path, some on horses, most on foot, the torch turned and fled.

And then the torch abruptly went out.

Thana counted under her breath to ten, then struck a spark on her waiting torch. The dry dung caught immediately, flames flaring bright and hot. She held it above her head and ran, barely suppressing a giggle as the soldiers cried out in confusion. Excitement beat in her chest like the way it used to when she was younger and training with her cousins. The light stole her night vision, smearing the rocks under her feet, but she ran anyway. And when she stumbled and fell into a thorny bush, she rolled to the side and got back to her feet and kept going.

Behind her, the huff of a horse closed in, its hard feet

clattering across stones and rocks. Thana climbed, judging the distance and the time that had fallen by how hard her lungs were burning. The rider on the horse shouted at her, but Thana didn't catch the words. She threw herself behind a boulder and smothered the torch in the dirt.

Another torch lit. Dihya's turn. Thana watched it flare and begin moving away from Thana but still up. The horse was close enough that Thana heard the rider cursing in confusion. This time, Thana *did* giggle.

Then the horse was around her boulder, its rider staring right at her. Thana straightened, waved, then grabbed the rider's leg as they freed their sword. She yanked. The rider fell, the horse sidestepping away at the same time. Thana briefly considered the horse, then slapped it hard on the rump. It took off down the hill, back toward the camp.

The soldier sprang to their feet, sword in hand. But Thana was already off and running, heading back the way she'd come. The soldier swore and followed. That was all right. They'd agreed at the onset that there was no point trying to fight an entire army, but if she had to, she could take this one. But Thana was an assassin, not a killer. If she was going to take lives, she wanted to be paid for it.

She bounded over rocks and shrubs. In the distance, another torch went out, and farther away another was lit. Menna this time. Thana ran, relishing the sensation of pumping blood warming her fingers and skin. She was tired of being cold. This was what it was about, this was what she'd missed. And she still had it, even if Mo insisted she keep from fighting the guul. It was so good to feel *alive*.

The *wshk* of an arrow caught her off guard. A second *wshk* stopped her short. A third sent her diving for cover behind a nearby rock. It was barely two feet high, but it'd have to do. Thana held her breath, so surprised by the arrows that she was still searching for another explanation. Illi had assured them that this general wanted her alive. After all, it would be madness to release the sajaami without any seal or containment in place.

Yet the arrows kept coming.

Thana thought she heard a distant cry of pain. Had that been Mo? Fear pinged through her, solidified into anger. How *dare* they shoot at her. Maybe they'd figured out that Illi wasn't actually among them, that they'd been tricked. Thana loosed one of her smaller knives. Well. Just because she wasn't being paid didn't mean she couldn't defend herself.

She closed her eyes, waiting for the next arrow. But it never came. Instead, a clatter of what sounded like too many knives across stone sounded to her left. And beneath that came a familiar growl that turned her fear to dread.

She'd know that sound anywhere. She'd felt it in her bones once, felt the shape of its scream in her chest.

Guul.

The screams followed. Soldiers, but she thought she recognized one of those screams. Then Thana stopped thinking and she was on her feet, darting around the boulder, the knife resheathed and her sword free. The sun hadn't peaked yet, but dawn was far enough along that Thana could see the shapes of soldiers rushing to meet the strange, loping creatures that were spilling down the mountainside. There were so many of them; dozens upon dozens, more than Thana had ever seen in one place. The guul moved like shadows, smooth and hunched and all wrong.

An arrow sliced through the air, uncomfortably close. But it didn't *thunk* into the ground nearby. Instead, Thana heard the unmistakable sound of arrow hitting flesh. She whirled just as the guuli crashed into her. And then everything else was forgotten as she fought for her life.

They parted ways. Behind Illi, rocks scraped and clattered as her cousins continued down the path. In another moment, they'd light a torch and pretend to be her, hopefully drawing enough of the soldiers away so that she and Canthem and Heru could slip among them unnoticed.

Yufit's uniform was tight around her shoulders and a little long around her ankles, but the darkness should cover the mismatch. The uniform was similar to Canthem's simple outfit, the fabric a little finer and the belt a bit wider. Yufit had shown her the three metal pins just above her heart that indicated her status. In the spirit of authenticity, Yufit had insisted on trading swords as well. Her fingers kept playing across the too-smooth hilt of his sword again and again as she wove down the side of the mountain, farther and farther from her cousins.

The soldiers' fires drew closer until Illi could smell their smoke and hear the crackle of their hunger. Softer still were the sounds of so many people. Most waited in silence, mere shadows with their backs to the fires. But the wind caught and tossed snatches of whispered conversations, mutters and mumblings, and once a loud burp followed by a harsh laugh and a silencing hiss.

Illi grabbed Canthem's arm and they both stopped, not more than a dozen feet from the nearest group. Heru nearly ran into them; he let out a soft curse instead. The three of them crouched in the darkness near a scraggle of bent trees and waited.

Without the warmth from moving, the cold quickly crept through Illi's layers. She flexed her fingers, trying to keep them from growing stiff with cold. She envied the soldiers their fires, even knowing it must make them all but blind to anyone approaching. It also made them easy targets. Illi frowned, shoving her hands under her armpits. Why have the fires at all? Sure, it was bitterly cold, but if it hadn't been for the fires, she and her cousins would have walked right into Merrabel's waiting hands.

No, Merrabel had wanted them to know her army was there. But why? Was it a show of her might, an attempt to intimidate Illi into giving up and turning herself in? Or was it a trap? Illi's stomach turned. Should she warn her cousins? But then the torch caught and flared on the mountainside. It was too late.

The army grumbled alive. Soldiers shouted to each other and metal clanked and horses snorted and then they were spilling up the path, toward the approaching torch. As soon as the soldiers in front of her had moved from their campfire, Illi jerked on the edge of Canthem's wrap and they dashed across the empty space and past the cast-aside camp rolls and blankets and cards.

Then they were in the camp proper, surrounded on all sides by a roiling disorder that cloaked their movements. Some soldiers scurried toward her cousins' distraction, some yelled orders, some went the opposite way. Only a handful even seemed to notice Illi, and all it took was one look at the pins on Illi's chest before their gaze and feet continued on.

A horse snorted. Illi jerked to a stop just as a soldier barred their way with a broad gray beast. They wore a tagel and a uniform much like Yufit's, but instead of the three pins she had, they only had one. A subordinate.

"We'll need that horse, sa," Illi said with as much authority as she could muster.

The soldier's eyes narrowed. Canthem coughed loudly and said, "Come on! Follow the captain's order, sar, and give over your reins. And your friend there, too." Canthem gestured behind at another mounted soldier who had paused to watch. "Both of you. I wouldn't keep the captain waiting—the general herself ordered us to bring this captive back to Hathage."

That finally did it. Both soldiers dismounted, putting their reins in Canthem's waiting hands. The second soldier strode off toward the fight, but the first lingered, watching to see how Illi would treat their mount. Illi eyed the beast, nervously prancing in place like a child commanded to *stay still*. How could anyone sit on something so flighty?

No use waiting. Illi sucked in a breath, put her boot in the metal ring as she'd seen Merrabel do, then grabbed the top of the saddle and *pulled*.

It wasn't the most graceful thing she'd ever done, but Illi managed to haul herself up onto the horse's back. Canthem handed her the reins, then gestured for Heru to mount the other horse. Heru did so clumsily, and Illi wondered how much of that was for show. Then Canthem swung up in front of him.

Illi kneed her mount and leaned forward, ready for its loping stride. But a horse was not a camel and its sudden, springy gait caught her off guard. She slipped before she grabbed the edge of the saddle, grateful for its bulk. She righted herself and found the horse's rhythm and together they cut a path through the dark camp.

But not dark for much longer. Dawn was filling the sky, turning it from black to dark blue. The campfires still flickered but Illi could see beyond them, could make out the hills and the shrubs and the fields. At her back, the Aer Caäs loomed, a solid darkness not unlike the pylons themselves at sunrise.

They were almost out of the camp when something tugged at Illi. She circled her horse around and peered back the way they'd come. But she didn't need to see to feel them. She *reached,* her wrists first prickling, then burning with pain as she sought what had tugged at her. There: a bright spot of warmth, then another, and another, and ten more, a dozen more, no—*dozens* more, a hundred, *more*—

Illi gasped.

"What is it? What's wrong?" Canthem had pulled up alongside her.

But Heru answered for her: "Guul."

Illi nodded.

"They've been following us for a few days," continued Heru. "Just . . . following. I decided it wasn't worth mentioning until they came closer or attempted to threaten us. I'd assumed Illi knew about them and that, perhaps, she was the reason they were following us."

"No," breathed Illi. "I'd sensed some along the journey, but I sent them all . . . north . . ."

"North," echoed Heru, somehow infusing that single word with heavy disdain.

"Dust." Illi started to *reach* again, to count, but she decided she didn't need to know the exact number. It was more than they could handle, than *she* could handle.

No. Not more than us.

Illi started. A new fear prickled in her, one she shoved away for later. Now, she had more pressing concerns. Such as the fate of her cousins.

"The army," said Canthem suddenly. They slapped their thigh. "*That's* why General Barca sent them, why they were waiting for us. They *weren't* waiting for us. She would've only needed a dozen guard at most. She knew about the guul."

"Merrabel brought the guul here," said Illi slowly. She didn't know why, she didn't know how, but the knowledge settled like truth in her mouth. Merrabel must have learned something from Illi during all that testing. Learned a new way to control the guul. To call them. It eased some of her own guilt at guiding the guul north; she had sent some, certainly, but she was not responsible for the sheer magnitude of guul that had arrived.

And now all those hundreds of guul were loose in the foothills, where her cousins thought they were only fighting soldiers. They'd been trained to kill and they knew how to fight guul, but not that many. Not like this.

Illi sucked in a breath and felt the quieted guul in Heru's pouch. She plucked out one, two, and when she felt a bit less dizzy and a bit more whole, she *reached*. The guul were like a barely controlled fire burning up the mountainside. Between them she felt the warmth of her cousins and the soldiers. Distantly, Illi heard the clank of bones, the rustle of feathers, the thunder of a thousand feet. If she lingered, she could tease them apart, but already her wrists were throbbing and fresh blood dripped from her fingers.

She didn't have time to tease. She could only do one thing.

Quiet. The command rolled out from her as gentle and unstoppable as a shifting dune. It caught the soldiers and the guul alike. Silence fell like a thunderclap and in the sudden stillness, Illi could hear the rustle of grass, the sigh of the wind, the creak of her saddle, and the whir of insects. Distantly, a bird screeched.

"What did you do?" whispered Canthem.

The world tilted. Illi caught the edge of her saddle before she could tilt with it. She dug her fingers into the soft leather and willed her head to stop spinning.

"She alerted the fine general to our presence, is what she did," said Heru.

"I stopped the guul," said Illi. "Come on—I don't know how long it will last."

Canthem didn't question her further, for which she was grateful. Illi was still reeling from the ease of the command, the power of it. Fingers dripping blood, she tightened her grip on the reins and kneed her horse into a gallop, putting more distance between her and her cousins. They'd be fine.

They had to be fine.

31

The night whipped by, cold as glass, cold as metal. The force of the horse's canter thudded up through Illi's body, making her jaw ache. The silence went on and on and on. Lights twinkled in the distance, a promise of civilization and warmth. Illi's hands grew numb from the wind and she had to check more than once to make sure she was still holding the reins.

Now that she knew what to look for, Illi recognized the edge of the city this time. The shacks that turned into houses that became buildings, the way that condensed to a path that widened to a street. The cracked, empty fountains and dust-choked gardens. Sand turned to dirt turned to rocks turned to smooth stone and then they were racing through the city, the clatter of hooves echoing off the walls and back at them.

Torches lined the road in thicker and more regular clumps until their light burned away most of the lingering shadows. The road curved ahead, toward the center, toward the palace, toward the wall. Now that Illi knew where to look, she could pick out its dark gray metal peeking between the buildings here and there.

The city seemed almost exactly as she'd left it over three weeks ago. Exactly—save for the emptiness. The roads were empty, the city silent but for the occasional creak of an unlatched window shade and the rustle of the trees in the wind. Illi had first noticed the quiet in the outer part of the city, but even then she'd spied people dashing inside or twitching their curtains closed. She'd spied life. Here, Hathage felt hollow.

Reflexively, she reached out, feeling for the people she knew had to be there. When she found them, tucked away deep within the buildings, huddled together for fear or for warmth, she let out a sigh of relief. She might not care for Hathage as she did Ghadid, but that didn't mean she wanted them to be hurt.

"Curfew," said Canthem.

They pointed at a freshly drawn sign hanging over an empty basin, its black ink still glossy. Words stood out in bold letters, but the script was utterly incomprehensible to Illi. She slowed the horse down for a better look, but it was different from what Merrabel had used.

"It doesn't say much," admitted Canthem. "Just that, by order of His Royal Highness, all citizens are to be indoors by sundown and stay until first bell. First bell is right after dawn, which isn't much further away. We'd better finish this before then."

"The guul," said Illi. "She's protecting them from the guul. But she's the one who's controlling them. Why would she need to protect her own people?"

Canthem met her gaze. "Maybe she knew *you* were coming."

"I suspect the guard is correct," said Heru. "Merrabel did not call the guul, but she knew they would come. The sajaami has proven multiple times that it has an affinity for guul and draws them to it. It would be logical for her to conclude that when you did return—and that you would—you might bring guul with you. She's a general, above all else. She prepared for war."

"I wouldn't—I would never—" Illi started, then stopped. She'd never what? Control an army of guul? North, she'd sent them all north. If that hadn't been her intent, what had? She rubbed her forehead. She'd promised herself she'd never become what she most hated, and yet here she was, sending monsters to a foreign city. Forcing its people to defend themselves, to hide. To fear.

"She thinks we're an invading army," she said.

"Correct."

Illi's neck prickled, but not with heat or fear. Someone was watching. Of course they were. In Ghadid, bandits had once been allowed to enter the city, only to become disoriented by the pylons and bridges. That's when the family would pick them off, one by one.

One by—

"Go!" shouted Illi.

She kicked her horse into motion. It surged ahead faster than she'd expected and she slipped. She grabbed on to the saddle with both hands, heart hammering, and barely heard the sound of something sharp and thin cutting the air behind her. But she felt it across the back of her neck.

Canthem grunted. Illi didn't glance back; she was too intent on staying on her mount, and its hooves were greedily eating up the street. Canthem was a better rider than her. They'd keep up.

The wall loomed and grew and obscured the sky. After what felt like mere seconds, they reached its base. Illi pulled her horse to a stop within feet of a tower. Now that she knew what was on the other side, she thought she could hear the interminable crash of waves and the gurgle of water. She could certainly smell the sea, its ripe, salty scent saturating the air.

"Girl," said Heru. Then, "*Illi.*"

Illi turned in her saddle. Canthem stared up at the wall, Heru still behind them. For some reason, Heru had wrapped his arms around the guard. Had they been going that fast? What was

Canthem staring at? Their eyes were glassy, unfocused. Part of their wrap was darker than before.

Then Illi saw the arrow.

The dark green fletching stuck out only inches from their chest. Canthem fumbled with the reins as they slid precariously to one side. Heru gripped tighter, clearly the only reason Canthem was still upright.

Illi didn't remember dismounting. She didn't remember crossing the space between her and Canthem. She only knew the paleness of Canthem's skin, their sharp, staccato breaths, the smell of blood. She only knew the color of the arrow's fletching, a green like olive flesh. She only knew Heru's pale arms shaking with the strain of holding Canthem up.

The darkness on their wrap was spreading.

Illi opened her arms and Heru let go with a sigh. Canthem half slid, half fell, grabbing the saddle on their way down. Illi caught them, eased them to the ground, her fingers already finding their neck, their pulse, her eyes assessing the damage. But she knew it was bad without having to draw on water. It wasn't a matter of *if* the arrow had hit anything vital, but *what*. Lungs? Aorta? Heart?

She ripped open Canthem's wrap and her fingers ran across their chest as if she might be able to see the damage through the skin, through the muscle. She brushed the fletching but she didn't grab it; the arrow had to be removed, but it also might be the only thing keeping Canthem from bleeding out faster. Where was Mo? Why was she so far away? Why hadn't Illi insisted that she come with them?

"Breathe," said Canthem and there was a gurgle in their voice that told Illi: *pierced lung.*

Illi realized she'd matched Canthem's short, shallow breaths with her own. She took several deeper, steadying ones, and the tightness at the edge of her vision loosened. Still, she was numb all over. Numb and lost. She couldn't help Canthem. She couldn't heal. Not with the bracelets on.

Not with the bracelets on.

Oh.

Oh.

A cold clarity smothered all her doubt and fear. She looked up, met Heru's eye. "Twenty minutes, right?"

Heru's brow tightened and she felt the weight of both his real eye and his glass one. "Do not remove those bracelets. We still have a wall to climb and a rite to perform. Every second you lose increases the likelihood that your body will deteriorate beyond any chance of repair. Do *not*—Illi, I said *no*—"

Illi found the clasp on the burnt-silver bracelet. It popped open with ease. Then she unclasped the polished bracelet. They hung loose on her wrists for a moment, her choice not yet fully made, still able to change her mind. She met Canthem's eyes, already clouding with pain.

She dropped her hands and the bracelets fell off.

The change was as sudden and irrevocable as oil catching light. One moment, she was numb, the thud of her heart the only reminder that she could still feel things. The next, she burned. She *ached*. She was alive, she was vast, she was infinite. She could feel the guul miles away, still frozen, still quiet. She could feel the soldiers around them, knew their names. She found her cousins—Thana, Dihya, Mo, Azhar, Menna, Yaluz—and she released them, an act as simple as breathing.

She felt the lives in the city, thousands of them, sleeping and waiting and watching, living and living and *living*. She grew dizzy in their numbers.

And before her she felt Canthem, their jaani still strong but their body growing weak. It took effort to focus on what was right there, in front of her, but as she reined in the sajaami she felt its focus shift.

Heal, she thought, or maybe the sajaami did.

She didn't need to unknot her water skin. The very air was suffused with moisture. It clung to her like dew, first a sheen, then a mist, then droplets that rolled like sweat down her forehead, her arms, her back. Blue pulsed beneath her skin in time with her heart, brighter and thicker than she'd ever seen it before. The blue spread across Canthem like billowing gauze, but where it touched it stuck.

Illi didn't need to close her eyes. She could see the wound just as well with them open. Canthem's forehead eased as she took away their pain. Then she spread her fingers across their chest and traced the edges of the wound. She'd been right; the arrow had pierced a lung. It'd also nicked an artery. Canthem was losing blood with every heartbeat. They didn't have long.

Illi didn't need long. Blue filled the wound and pulsed beneath her hands, accelerating the body's own ability to heal. First the artery: clot then scar tissue then smooth the arterial wall. Next the lung, filling the hole and pushing out the arrow. She siphoned blood and other fluids from Canthem's lung while luring the arrow out bit by bit. Normally, she would have shoved the arrow all the way through Canthem's chest to avoid causing any further damage, but now she healed the lacerations as the arrow head retreated.

Finally, the arrow fell out and clattered to the stones. Canthem's eyes were closed, but they were breathing normally. No hint of the gurgle remained. Illi lifted her hands and the blue began to fade, filtering away like so much water in soil. Despite the power thrumming through her, she felt calm. Peace. Was this what Mo felt when she healed? What every healer felt? This absolute power, this knowledge that she'd thwarted G-d?

Thwarted G-d . . .

The understanding dropped into her like a glass beaker, shattering as it hit. Illi had never been able to heal like this before, not even close. This wasn't G-d's power: it was the sajaami's. Laughter bubbled in her chest like overfermented wine, but it wasn't her own. Just as the healing wasn't.

Essif. The first healer. Every subsequent healer.

Yes, said Nejm. *They stole that from us.*

Canthem sighed, pulling Illi back. She could ask Heru about the implications later. He'd be more than happy to oblige, probably with diagrams and charts. For now, Illi reached out and brushed a strand of dark hair from Canthem's eyes. They fluttered open, at first glazed and unfocused, and then they found Illi.

"What—?"

"Shh." Illi stayed kneeling next to them, her other hand on their chest. Through her palm, she could feel their heartbeat. Strong. Steady. Reassuring. Her hands felt unbearably light after wearing the bracelets for so long, as if they could just float up and free.

"You are wasting time," said Heru, words clipped. "Your friend is stable. We must go."

"Canthem needs another minute."

"You do not *have* another minute," snapped Heru. "And they will die as surely as you will and the rest of this city if the sajaami is freed. Leave them. They can handle themself."

"Go," said Canthem, pushing at Illi with as much strength as a fly. "I'll find an alleyway to hide in, in case anybody else comes."

"But—"

"*Go.*"

Illi went. The stairs wound up and up and up. They seemed narrower than before, or maybe that was just the sajaami, pushing against the confines of her skin and bones. She hadn't slept since the other side of the Aer Caäs, yet she felt as fresh as she had during her very first ride on the sands to meet the guul.

It was Heru who slowed her down. Every full turn of the stairs, he stopped, gasping for breath as he leaned against the metal wall. The fourth time this happened, he gestured wordlessly for her to continue. As loath as she was to leave him, she knew he was right. The sajaami was giving her energy he didn't have. She could start the rite on her own.

As she climbed, her back began to itch, then burn. Each individual scar ached as if it were being cut again, line by line and yet all at once. The sajaami thrummed in her chest, a sensation both painful and comforting, not too unlike a cat kneading her with sharp claws. Aside from that and the energy pulsing through her, she didn't feel any different. She definitely didn't feel as if she were falling apart. Twenty minutes, Heru had said. How long had it been?

The stairs ended and the smell of salt and water and murky, living things struck her across the face. The wall stretched ahead, matte gray in the burgeoning dawn. On one side, the pale white of the city. On the other, the metallic glint of so much water, too much water. Any moment the sun would finally crest and light would spill and scatter across the sea. She needed to be done before then. Jaan were weakest during the liminal phases of the day, so it followed that the sajaami would cross over most easily now.

Illi got to work. She set down the pack she was carrying and pulled out the balls of tinder. She placed them in a circle on the wall, then sat cross-legged in its center. She lit the first tinder, then smoothed the piece of vellum across her knee and painstakingly transcribed the words and symbols on the scroll Menna had given her. She could read some of it, recognized half, but the remaining symbols might as well have been the illegible scribbles of a child.

She lit another tinder. She finished writing and undid the knot of her water skin. She rolled the vellum into a funnel, then carefully poured the water from the skin across the vellum. The water mixed with the fresh ink, absorbing the prayer. Before it could spill, she directed the flow of ink-stained water onto her wrap. As the water seeped through fabric to skin, even the sajaami's heat couldn't keep Illi from shivering. She realized then that she wasn't wearing white; just a dull traveler's beige. It shouldn't matter—color wasn't a part of the rite—but she wasn't sure what *should* matter.

She hesitated, the striker over the third tinder. What if she'd missed something—a stroke, a word, a movement? She didn't know enough. Any little piece of this rite could be wrong, out of place. Where was Heru? He should have made it up the stairs by now. Was he really that weak?

Focus. She had a task to complete and her time continued to fall, each second another few grains gone forever. She couldn't wait for Heru.

She struck a spark. It fell. The tinder flared and caught, another spot of warmth in this too-cold place. And as its light bathed the metal wall, footsteps echoed up from within the tower. Finally.

But the sound was wrong. There were too many steps, too loud, too fast. Metal clanked against metal: armor. Heru hadn't been wearing armor.

Illi stood, her hand on the hilt of Yufit's sword even as Nejm gently admonished her. *You don't need that anymore.*

A figure appeared in the darkness of the tower's doorway. She wore the thick leather armor of her soldiers, with metal chain around her neck and polished plate across her chest, but her helmet was under one arm, her tangled brown curls trailing free, her glass-bright eyes fixed on Illi.

Merrabel had arrived at last.

32

Kill her.

The words were more impulse than thought. Illi was already *reaching* before she even realized what she was doing. Then Merrabel stepped to the side and two soldiers yanked a pale and flustered Heru Sametket through the doorway, hands bound behind his back.

"Let him go," said Illi, her breath burning her lips. When had she become so warm?

Merrabel cast Heru a dismissive glance. "Him? Oh, so now you care about your old master? Perhaps something really did change after you turned on me." She shrugged, a casual gesture that was betrayed by the tightness in her shoulders and around her lips.

Illi's gaze slid past Heru, searching for Canthem. Had they gotten away? Had they been able to hide? Or was Merrabel keeping a worse surprise within the tower?

But when Merrabel lifted her hand, no one else appeared. Instead, one of the soldiers holding Heru shifted her grip and stance so that she could press a knife to Heru's throat.

"These are the terms," said Merrabel, careful and clear. "Your obedience in exchange for Sametket's life. I'd rather not extract the sajaami at this time, but I will if I'm forced to. I'd prefer to have it fully under my control, since you've already broken my trust once, but you've forced my hand."

Without warning, Merrabel took three steps forward and struck Illi across the face. The general was back where she'd been standing before Illi could process what had happened, the sting on her cheek the only reminder.

"You could have stayed," continued Merrabel. "You could have spared the lives of many soldiers and more, perhaps, by the time this is all over. Together, we could have protected the kingdom of Hathage and all of the Wastes, including your small town. You need never have feared guul or invasion again. But instead you chose selfishness. You wanted the sajaami only for yourself."

"I don't want the sajaami," said Illi. "I *never* wanted the sajaami."

Merrabel spread her arms. "Wonderful! Then give it here and let's all go down from this dreary place."

The breeze curled around them, biting against Illi's wet skin. Time spun with the breeze, there and gone, gone, gone. If the rite wasn't completed soon, it never would be. Illi looked past Merrabel to Heru for any hint as to what to do, but he was dazed, disoriented. He kept closing his eye, as if the faint light were too much for him. The glass eye stared, fixed ahead on nothing.

When he opened his eye again, his pupil was wide. *Concussion*, said Mo's voice, thinned by distance and time.

Cold anger whirled in Illi, fighting back the rising heat. "What makes you think I'll keep my word?"

Merrabel shrugged again. "Honestly, I don't trust you to. But as we speak, my other soldiers are rounding up your friends. I'll have plenty of hostages to make certain you obey me. And you *will* obey me. But you have served beneath me. You know I'm not needlessly cruel. I'm honest and I'm fair. I'm just doing what I must to keep my people safe."

Merrabel reached inside her cloak and drew out two pieces of curved metal, one burned to a matte gray, the other a polished silver. The bracelets. Merrabel tossed them to Illi, who didn't bother trying to catch them. They landed, clanking, at her feet.

"Put those back on."

Illi stared at the bracelets. She couldn't imagine a future where she was forced to obey Merrabel's every whim. But she also couldn't let Merrabel kill Heru. Shards and dust, Heru was supposed to have been the one safe thing in her life, the one person she *didn't* care about. He wasn't supposed to die. He couldn't die. She curled her hands into fists as rage pumped through, not entirely her own.

He wouldn't die.

"How did you evade the sajaami's power?" asked Illi, stalling for time. "I quieted the guul and I quieted your army."

Merrabel smirked. "Seems even a sajaami can't get through the charms I've personally made. I have you to thank for that, and all the experiments we ran together in my lab."

Illi's skin prickled with heat. The water she'd drenched herself in was beginning to evaporate, despite the humidity. Even with the power thrumming through her, she felt thin. She could feel the sajaami's impatience growing.

This must end soon.

Illi agreed.

She picked up the bracelets. Merrabel smiled, thin and humorless. Illi stared at the bracelets in her hands. *Do you trust me?* Heru had asked, before releasing the sajaami. She lifted her gaze. Heru was little more than a crumpled old man on the wall, pale as bone and as fragile as a bird, far from the en-marabi that had terrified her the first time she'd found his lab and dared step inside. His fingers were stained black with ink from all the

writing he'd done during their journey, all the theories he'd exchanged with Menna while hunched over the fire every night.
He'd worked so hard for this, harder than he had on even the
guul. And for what—to destroy something powerful, something
he'd lusted after himself.

Heru's eye met hers. His lips moved, but no sound came out.
But Illi could read the shape on those lips and knew exactly what
he was saying.

"Finish it."

There was resolve in that single eye and Illi knew, deep in her
bones, that Heru had a plan. He was going to outmaneuver Merrabel. He had something up his sleeve. Illi just had to act, and
he'd take care of the rest.

Illi met Merrabel's smiling gaze and smiled back. Then Illi
tossed the bracelets into the sea.

"*No!*"

Merrabel started forward, hand outstretched, as if she could
pluck the bracelets out of the air. Then they were gone, swallowed up by the fathomless water with hardly a ripple. Illi didn't
know how much longer she had, but now it would have to be
enough. Her skin was as thin as paper, her lips brittle and raw.

Merrabel snarled and drew her sword. She shoved the soldier
with the knife out of her way. Heru grunted as she slammed her
hand against his shoulder, driving him down to his knees. Then
Merrabel drove her sword through his back and out his front.

Heru gurgled. Merrabel yanked her sword free, its metal dripping crimson. Heru toppled forward, eye wide. He coughed and
coughed again. Red foam spilled from his lips and onto the tagel
around his neck, red blood pulsed from his back, quickly staining his white wrap, pooling on the wall around him. It reeked
of copper and decay, and Illi was simultaneously on the wall

and back in Ghadid, smoke swirling around her, bodies nearby. Everyone she'd loved, gone.

"No," said Illi.

Heru had a plan. He had to. Yet he didn't move, he didn't stir. Red spread across his white wrap and Heru just lay there. Not. Moving.

Merrabel cleaned the blood from her sword with a cloth. "That was unfortunate. As annoying as he was, Sametket did have a few decent ideas. No matter; his blood will be of some use yet."

The smell of blood filled Illi's nostrils, metallic and hot. She pushed back panic. She wouldn't let Heru die. But first—

"If you still haven't changed your mind," continued Merrabel, "your friends are below—"

All it took was a brush of her fingers. Merrabel's eyes stayed wide as she toppled backward, her last words still stuck in her throat. Illi flung her jaani away like a piece of dreck. Then she swelled, her power vast and growing vaster. Nejm unfurled.

She could feel them all, every soldier of Merrabel's that had gotten away from her before. They wore charms—simple things around their necks and waists, only enough to keep her from noticing them, but nothing more. They wouldn't stand against Nejm.

With a flick, the charms broke. With a flick, she tore away their jaan. She swelled further. She was unstoppable.

Then the memories crashed into her, their sights and sounds and smells as real as now. The spread of sand below, endless and unquestionable. The sweep of storms that had regularly rolled across the land, bigger then and more frequent. Clusters of green life that she'd once nurtured, guiding the storms to carve these gardens out of the emptiness. The people who had found them, sullied them, destroyed them. The people who had crept into her lands. The people she had snapped like twigs beneath her power.

But they'd kept coming. They'd forced her and her brethren back with their persistence. They'd braved the storms and survived them, survived everything she and her people could throw at them. And then they'd changed the world itself with their machines, with their metal birds, with their drilling and burning and digging. The gardens died, but they kept coming.

In the end, they'd come with fire and words. They'd used up all their water and were left only blood. But they had no qualms with blood, especially if it wasn't their own.

She remembered the screams of the dying.

She remembered the feeling of stone, all around.

She remembered the sensation of centuries passing. Of time wearing at her shell.

She remembered how her fury had dulled to rage had faded to anger had hardened into resentment.

She would kill them all.

Then: pain. It was such a small thing, so cold and precise. It struck her arm and snapped her back to herself. She was amazed that she could still feel pain, that she still had a body. Which meant she wasn't Nejm; she was Illi. She was human. She was here and she was now and so was the pain.

Illi touched her arm and stared at her fingers, red with blood. Her gaze met the soldier's, standing so close with a bloody knife in hand. Illi wondered, distantly: how had she missed this one? But even in her fury, she'd cast wide, hoping to miss those closest to her, to miss Canthem.

The soldier quailed, stumbled back, whatever courage she'd gathered vanished in that moment. She turned and ran, the other soldier right behind. Leaving Illi alone with two corpses.

No.

Illi could feel the pulse of Heru's life, but it was weakening.

He clung on. The sea sloshed to one side. So much water. So close. She could heal him, but—

But the *pain.*

It spread like a crack in glass. Illi stared at the blood on her hands, then the light that poured from her wound. The light spread, crackling up and down her arm. Her skin puckered outward, broke.

Dimly, she remembered Captain Amilcem. The light pouring from her eyes, the smoke from her mouth. Heat built up inside of Illi, pushing and pulsing against her skin, which could no longer contain her. Contain Nejm. She was going to fall apart. Was this how Amilcem had felt in those seconds before she'd shattered and broke, torn to pieces by the guuli?

Help me, she said to Nejm. *You don't know what will happen if I fall apart while you're bound to me. You still need me.*

A rich smugness filled her, completely at odds with her own numbness. *I don't need you.*

Illi didn't have the strength left for fear. Heru, she needed Heru. She fell to her knees next to his body, slipping a little in the blood. So much blood. Yet for once, she wasn't drawn back to the night of the Siege. Instead, the present grew sharper, more real.

She could still feel Heru, a swirl of warmth. Alive, if dimming with each betraying pulse that left him a little less blood. His eye fixed on hers.

"Go," he said with one breath.

Illi shook her head. She grabbed his hand even as cracks spidered across hers. Nejm was roaring in her head like a fire gone wild, but if she focused just on Heru, she could still hear. Still see.

"Fool." Heru coughed and blood dribbled from between his lips. "Do . . . the rite."

"I can't. It's too late. But you—"

The cracks widened and Illi felt as if she were burning up, as if someone had placed the sun within her and now her organs were withering, cracking with the heat. But she could feel something else. The water so near. She could still heal Heru, still save him.

Heru snarled and tried to sit up. Instead he crumpled and fell. But he caught himself and kept his gaze fixed on Illi. "Basbowen," he growled. "If I've learned one thing . . . about you . . . cousins, it's how fucking obstinate you are. You're afraid, but you're not a coward. Illi Basbowen—*perform the rite.*"

And he shoved her. Just a little, not enough to off-balance her, not enough to hurt, but just enough to make his point. She wouldn't have time to heal him and do the rite. She only had time for one.

Illi swallowed, or at least tried to; her throat was too dry. She pulled the striker from her pouch with shaking, breaking fingers and struck a spark on the last tinder. The sajaami screamed. Illi's head felt like it was going to burst. Perhaps it was. Every nerve was on fire, literally. As her fingers fell apart, Illi picked up the burning tinder and breathed in its oily smoke.

I can save him, promised Nejm.

She took a step backward, toward the wall.

I can save you.

Another step.

I can save everyone you love.

Any barrier that had existed between her and Nejm had been wiped away, and although she and Nejm blurred, she could see the truth as plain as if it were her own. Illi had seen the destruction Nejm had caused and now she could see the fear and the loneliness and the doubt, as well as its resolve to live despite, in spite. Humankind had wiped out its people and it would return the favor.

So she held tight to Nejm, and as the pain overcame every fiber of her, she thought of her parents. She thought of the Siege. The pain and terror she felt now was nothing compared to that night. She had lost everything once. She wasn't about to lose it all again.

Another step.

Nejm fought and Illi watched her hand dissolve. She clutched the burning tinder to her chest with her remaining hand.

Let me go, pleaded Nejm.

I will, she promised.

Then she closed her eyes, held the tinder tight, hummed a prayer, and stepped back and off the wall.

She fell.

She hit the water.

Steam slapped her face.

And the world ended.

33

Illi was pulled in all directions.

Illi was whole.

Illi was broken.

Illi was the world.

Illi was the water.

Illi was dead. Illi was alive.

Illi was.

Impressions: boiling water; calm surface; a scream; a pull; light; tearing; rending, ripping, roaring; darkness; pain, pain, *pain*. And through it all Illi held and held and held and then—

She sucked in a breath, got only water. She screamed. The scream was swallowed up whole.

Slowly, over the course of only seconds, she began to realize she wasn't dead. Her body still existed. It had stopped falling apart. It was knitting back together. She had shattered only to be melted down and recast. All around her was water, but something else swirled with her.

She tried to *reach*, but felt nothing. Nejm was gone. Still, she could hear the whispers of jaan, unintelligible as they were intangible.

Then something grabbed her and she gasped water and then she was being dragged up, up, *up*.

Her head broke the surface. She tried to breathe, but her lungs were full of water. She choked instead. Hands tightened around her shoulders, arms. The world spun and spun and spun—

Hands pulled her up and more hands tugged at her and the water let her go, let her and whoever was holding her spin, dangling, in the air until finally she was pulled over and onto cold metal. Voices spilled around her, just as dizzying as the sky. Even though she felt the solid surface against her back, she was sinking. The water was closing over her head again, buzzing in her ears. She was still choking, still suffocating.

Hands compressed her chest. Again. Again. Water spilled from her throat and then she was on her knees—*how'd she get there?*—throwing up water, so much water. *What a waste.*

When the water stopped coming, she sucked down breath after deep breath. She stayed on her hands and knees, shaking too badly to move. Voices stirred the air, trading back and forth. Illi slowly teased out words, sentences, and finally meaning.

"—she do it? Is the sajaami gone?"

"—see her wrists. She had bracelets—"

"Heru? *Heru?* No—"

"Shh," said a voice near her ear. Illi looked up into Canthem's familiar, warm eyes. Their tagel and hair were wet, both stuck to their face. "Just focus on breathing. You're all right. It's over."

But it wasn't over. Not quite. Not yet. Illi could feel that as she returned to herself, felt her body again, cold now, so cold.

"He's dead," said another voice. Thana. "He can't be dead. That's just . . . that's not possible."

Illi sat up slowly, so slowly. Thana hunched over a bundle of red and white. Heru. Illi reached reflexively before remembering the sajaami was gone. Everything felt so dull, so numb. More approaching footsteps vibrated through the ground, up her arms and shoulders.

Her wrap was sodden and growing colder by the moment. Water still streamed down her back, off her braids, trickled down her face. She was shivering. Shaking. A warm arm wrapped around her shoulders. A body pressed close. Illi leaned into it, hungry for heat.

She wanted to move, to help, to say something. But she was too tired. She could only watch as more people clumped around Heru, who was still unmoving. She stared at him, waiting for his chest to rise, to fall, to breathe, to live. Thana was right. He couldn't be dead. Illi was going to travel with him to the Wastes. He was going to finish his life's work.

And yet.

And yet he didn't move. The stars did, shifting overhead, but Heru remained still. Illi felt the air churning over the sea, heard the whispers of nearby jaan, but Heru

did

not

move.

A body cannot lose such a volume of blood and remain viable, Heru would have said. He would have clucked his tongue at her for wasting time on something as inefficient as emotion. *Accept the truth and move on. There is much to do.*

Much to do . . .

Something wet splashed against her cheek. Then her wrist. Then it was drizzling, rain mixing with blood, turning red, then pink. Washing away. The rain came down harder, began to pour. The people around Illi broke into motion, hurrying back under the cover of the stairs

Canthem pulled her up. Illi didn't trust her legs to hold, but they did, and she stumbled to safety. The sound of the rain was muted in here, muffled by the rasp of breath all around. Beyond the stairs, the rain came down even harder, obscuring the world, the wall, the rising sun. But not the body, left behind and washed clean. As he would have wanted.

And through it all, above it all, swirled the jaan. Illi didn't need to *reach* to feel them; there were so many. They swirled over the sea as they had over the pyre, faint streaks of red against the low white clouds.

A hand took hers. A familiar voice spoke. Mo.

"I don't know what you did, but the jaan are crossing over. All of them. They were pulled from the guul. I don't think there are any guul left. At least, not on this side of the mountains. You've brought peace to them all." Mo squeezed her shoulder, but the gesture lacked warmth and her words were distant and hollow. "You should be proud."

Illi didn't feel proud. Just numb and cold, so cold. But then Canthem wrapped their arms around her and she let out a sigh.

Then a shudder.

Then a sob.

Then, all across the city, the dawn bells began to ring.

EPILOGUE

It rained.

The small clouds built to bigger ones, turned gray then black, and the rain came down.

It was raining the day they interred Heru Sametket, first advisory marabi to the late Empress. It didn't take much to bribe a few marab to perform the rite—and to care for his jaani, after. Illi would always remember the smell of wet funeral whites, a faint aroma of ammonia cutting through the air. In Hathage, the crypts were aboveground and the funeral was held outside. Rain plastered the gray shroud to his body, so thin and empty that it was easy to believe that it wasn't him, that he had a head start on her toward the Wastes, or that he'd found Merrabel's lab and taken over.

After all, it wasn't like Illi could check. The king had reacted swiftly to the death of his best general and there were notices posted on every corner calling for the heads of the traitors. King Thamilcar might not know exactly who had killed Merrabel, but Illi wasn't about to risk traipsing through his palace.

They hadn't risked staying in the city, either. Captain Yufit had put them up in a training ground on its outskirts, far enough from anyone who had seen them that they could stay a few days. At least until the rain let up. At least until they buried Heru.

The rain hadn't let up, but the marab carried Heru into the crypt. Their prayers echoed around the small courtyard and Illi wondered what he would have thought of all the proceedings. So obsessed with immortality, he'd never once acknowledged that he could die.

And Illi had believed him.

It was still raining when they left Hathage and crossed the Aer Caäs. The path had turned to mud and the rocks slipped out from underfoot, human and camel alike. It was treacherous uphill and it was treacherous downhill and the rain followed them.

It took them twelve days to return to Ghadid. It rained the entire time. Sometimes a shower, sometimes a drizzle, but the precipitation was persistent. When they reached the pylons of home, the wash that cut beneath them but only ran once a year was now twice as wide and twice as strong.

Illi tried to heal a few times on their way back, but even her meager ability to heal had vanished with the sajaami. She wasn't as bothered by the loss as she would've expected. In a way, it was another burden off her shoulders. Another relief.

It was three weeks before the rain stopped. By then the marab were already talking about a gift from G-d. The drum chiefs debated baat allocation with the sudden rise in the aquifer. The healers found themselves attempting to heal things they'd never dared before, from chronic pain to old injuries.

But only Illi understood the real consequences of what had happened. That a balance had shifted somewhere in the Wastes, enough to bring the world a little bit closer to what it had been, once. What it might have been. What it could still be.

On the roof, the city smelled strange. The wind stirred intermittently, bringing with it flashes of roasting meat, of burnt cloth, of wet dust. Illi had kicked off her shoes to climb up here and now she stepped into a puddle and froze. A shudder went up her spine but she didn't move. She'd have to get used to that feeling; the stormsayers predicted more rain in the coming weeks.

A second season, they were calling it.

The Circle wanted Ghadid to be ready.

Which is why Illi was up here, surveying this roof as a possible spot for a new glasshouse. It had potential. After all, the old metal frame still stood. They just needed to replace the panes—and get past the superstition that the place was cursed because of all the glass that had been shattered there.

Illi had believed in that curse, once. She didn't anymore. Glass was glass: nothing happened just because you broke it. Things happened because of the choices people made after the glass was broken, how they acted, how they reacted—how they didn't act.

This had been her mother's glasshouse, once. The memories lay broken at her feet, mixed in with the glass. Although they were still sharp enough to cut, Illi wasn't afraid of them.

Illi picked her way around the puddles and the broken glass. She rested her hand on the cold metal of the frame. Then she leaned on it, testing it. The frame held. Despite everything—despite the Siege, despite the fire, despite the years it'd been left alone, neglected in this abandoned part of the city—it didn't give beneath her hand.

And it'd be stronger once the glass was in.

Metal clattered on the roof a few feet away from her. A broom, tossed from below. Just beyond the broom, a hand cleared the edge of the roof. A moment later, a body followed.

"Can't you people put in ladders?" asked Canthem, rolling to their feet and brushing themself off.

"That would take the fun out of it," said Illi.

Canthem picked up the broom, then glanced around, their gaze taking in the glass, the dust, the puddles, and the frame. Finally they looked at Illi and they smiled. They held out the broom.

"Well, when we're done here, I'm going to put in an official complaint with your Circle."

Illi took the broom. "That's not how it works."

"All right: I'll forge a ladder from metal myself."

"There you go."

Illi began to sweep. Canthem pulled on leather gloves and picked up the larger pieces of glass, dropping them one by one into a sack. None of this would go to waste. Even old, shattered glass could be melted down and recast, reused. Illi swept and breathed in the dust and the memories.

The world had ended.

But then it'd kept going.

They'd clean up this roof and they'd cast new panes and in a few weeks, there'd be shoots of bright growth in the glasshouse. Illi would tend that growth, turning in the ashes from the rite to feed the soil. Canthem would help. Hopefully, they'd stay.

But that was something she could worry about later. For now, Illi was content to sweep away the broken glass, the dust, and the memories.

ACKNOWLEDGMENTS

As with all things in life, a seemingly solitary effort is quite the opposite. None of this would exist without the love and support—and occasional hand-holding—of friends and family, beta readers and editor, publishing house and agent.

I would like to thank the publishing team at Tor—the copy editors and page proofers and marketers and publicists—who together took a large chunk of words and made them into a *book*.

Thank you to Diana Pho, my editor, who gave me the space to turn a book into a world, whose energy and excitement helped me believe I could actually do this, and understood all along what I was doing.

Thank you to Kurestin Armada, my agent, who likewise trusted me to see this through and who still loves these characters and these books after so many years.

Thank you to my beta readers—Kim Callan, Eldridge Wisely, Sarah Doore—who helped me sort through several messy drafts to get at the heart of this book and see the forest through all the trees.

Thank you to my agent-siblings, who've been there at five a.m. and five p.m. and every time in between to cheer me on and calm me down and otherwise provide wonderfully arbortastic distractions.

Thank you to my parents, who have become my own personal hype squad in this crazy endeavor. And, you know, did all that raising and rearing stuff, too.

Thank you to my readers, who have helped turn this world into something more than just in my head, who have loved it as much as I do, who have turned what was merely imagined into something a bit more *real*.

And thank you—especially, specifically, thoroughly—to my wife, who has taught me again and again that I don't need to do this alone, that asking for help is a strength, not a weakness, and that together we are always, always stronger.

ABOUT THE AUTHOR

K. A. Doore was born in Florida but has since lived in Washington, Arizona, Germany, and now Michigan. She has a BA in Classics and Foreign Languages and an enduring fascination with linguistics. She is the author of the Chronicles of Ghadid, starting with *The Perfect Assassin*.

kadoore.com
Twitter: @KA_Doore